They All Needed Her

MICHAEL—Mary's charming, feckless husband, who wanted her as a combination wife-mother, to puff his
ego and take charge of his life

JAYNE—Mary's lovely twenty-one-year-old
niece, who sought Mary as a model of how a liberated woman
should pursue a career and not be
ruled by a mate

CHRISTOPHER—The first man ever to penetrate
Mary's defenses to claim all of
her, leaving her torn between
new-found fulfillment and fear of
the unknown

*For each of them, Mary Morgan was a
necessary woman—but now she had to
discover who she really was and what
she herself truly needed. . . .*

*"HELEN VAN SLYKE
is a superstar!"*
—*Jennifer Wilde*

A NECESSARY WOMAN

Helen Van Slyke

FAWCETT POPULAR LIBRARY • NEW YORK

A NECESSARY WOMAN

Published by Fawcett Popular Library, a unit of CBS
Publications, the Consumer Publishing Division of CBS Inc.,
by arrangement with Doubleday & Company, Inc.

ISBN: 0-445-04544-2

Printed in the United States of America

First Fawcett Popular Library printing: April 1980

10 9 8 7 6 5 4 3 2 1

Introduction

Without realizing what she was doing, Mary put her hand to her lips, as though to retrace the kiss. She'd kissed Michael thousands of times these past fifteen years, in dozens of different ways. Shyly, at first. Passionately later. And, later still, comfortingly, compassionately, reassuringly, almost maternally. As though he were her child rather than her husband.

The kiss she'd given him less than an hour ago at the gangway was all of those and none of them. It was a lying "I'll miss you too" motion. A Judas kiss. Perhaps the kiss of death for the marriage that suited him well and was, for her, a kind of love-hate union filled with disappointment and a sense of failure. Not only his failure but her own.

She leaned against the polished mahogany railing of the big white ship, watching San Francisco recede into the fog. Sixty-nine days from now when she sailed back into this harbor, she would have made THE DECISION. That was how she thought of it. Two words. Capitalized. At the end of this South Pacific cruise she would have decided whether or not to stay married to Michael Morgan.

"She would have decided." The realization of her own thought processes brought a mirthless smile to her lips. As though it were all up to her. But that's how it was and always had been in her marriage. Not only in her marriage; in almost the whole thirty-eight years of her life. From girlhood, she'd made her own decisions, not selfishly but as though she felt from her earliest days she was expected to be self-sufficient. She learned to seem calm and self-assured, and people admired her control, her capacity for dealing with the difficult business of living. "Disciplined," they called her. "Efficient and organized," they said.

How little they knew her, any of them. Beneath the unflappable surface, the serene exterior, was another Mary Farr Morgan. That one was the eternal, unquenchable female longing to be protected and to admire the protector. That hidden Mary did what she hated to do, like millions of other women who accepted a leading role that had somehow been thrust upon them. There were so many like her. Women forced into a dominant position. The eternal earth-mothers. Her sisters-under-the-skin. Some, like Mary, climbed their way to modest success in business, literally supporting their husbands with their earnings. Others stayed at home, but their influence was equally great. They took charge of the husband's paycheck, set rules for the couple's social life, planned the vacations and spoke as the voice of authority to the children. They did what was required, whatever their station in life, some willingly, others with resigned awareness of the strength that held the family together: their strength.

Did they chafe under their ties to men who couldn't measure up to their dreams? Wish, as she did, to respect a husband as well as love him? She didn't know about all those others. She knew only that she'd pledged her life to an engaging, adoring, undemanding man-child who accepted her as lover and provider, and who had come to expect her to chart the course of their life together. She wasn't sure she could go on with it. She wanted something more than a charming little boy who'd never grow up.

Respect. In the end, it always came back to that. Though they lived in apparent harmony, her love had slowly diminished in proportion to her respect for Michael. Why was it so important to her that he be the stronger one in their relationship? Why did she care so much for the surface things, allowing them to overshadow what should matter more: his ungrudging pride in her success, his unconcern about the lack of his own, his unfailing gentleness and eternal optimism? He was a good man in so many ways and yet she saw him as a failure.

Standing alone on the deck, she played devil's advocate. By whose standards was Michael a failure? The world's, because he'd never had a good job, never kept even a mediocre one? Society's, because her generation expected the man to be the wage earner and decision-maker? Her own inbred belief that her husband should be the leader in their marriage?

I'm the result of early conditioning, Mary thought sadly. If I'd been born twenty years later, perhaps none of those things would matter to me. I could handle my lovable loser because I wouldn't see him as one. I'd consider him a partner, contributing the things of which he's capable. Doing his own thing, as the kids say. I wouldn't want him to be my master. I wouldn't wish him to be smarter and stronger than I. I wouldn't look down on him because he's vulnerable and spoiled and weak.

But I can't handle that kind of rational, 1977 approach. I'm a product of another time. Like so many other wives, I want to be the secondary partner. It's the way I think things were meant to be. I pretend to be modern and "liberated," but I'm hopelessly old-fashioned. The eternal, starry-eyed, woman's-magazine-type romantic, eager to give herself fully to a man's demands, secretly fascinated by the male ego.

I must be crazy. Other women would kill for a husband so handsome, so gentle, so amenable to my every wish. Michael is an expert lover, though it's been years since I've been able to respond as I want. Even in bed, my mind won't rest. I accept him. I even want him. But this creeping resentment takes the joy out of love-making. He must notice, but he doesn't comment. He simply accepts, as he accepts everything I do, unquestioningly, loyally, almost deferentially.

On the surface, we're the prototype of the perfect couple, she thought wearily: well-suited and happy, living

7

proof that fidelity and compatibility are alive and well within the confines of matrimony. And one of us is tortured with doubts.

She stared into the cold, gray February waters of the Pacific. Why do I blame Michael for what he is? How much of this is my fault? Much of it. Most of it, probably. What compels me to take charge? Why do I have this unwilling thirst for power, this drive that translates itself into domination? Ego. God knows I don't feel egotistical, but I must be. Inside, I must believe that I, and only I, can keep myself safe. Maybe, unwittingly, I never gave Michael a chance to be what I want him to be. I was always too quick with answers, too impatient to let him solve his own problems, too frightened to put my trust in him. Maybe I really like it this way. Perhaps I couldn't put myself in a minor role in any marriage, no matter how strong or dependable my partner.

Some women are born like that. They want to be helpless and it's impossible for them. They know what's right and do what's wrong. And they end up hurting others and themselves through the misguided belief that they know best.

Am I one of those? What do I want? A different kind of marriage with the same man? That's impossible. Neither of us is going to change. It's too late for that.

But, God, how I wish we could.

PART I

Chapter 1

Thirty-eight years and a thousand decisions preceded that bleak winter morning when Mary Farr Morgan sailed toward the South Pacific. And through them all she had always felt alone. Her earliest memories were those of existing apart, even from her parents and her sister and brother. In later years, she would feel some closeness to Patricia, who was nearly seven when Mary was born. And she would make an uneasy truce with the aging parents who still lived in the old Riverside Drive apartment in New York. A continent between them made for a less tense relationship than she'd had in her girlhood. And maturity helped her to realize that in their own way they loved her and her sister, even though they mourned the only son, who died so young and whom they loved most of all, in death as they had in life.

But through the early years, the youngest of the Farr children wore a protective cloak of independence, a defense against the instinctive knowledge that Camille and John Farr thought Patricia more beautiful and John Jr. more promising than their last-born. She yearned for her parents' admiration and determined to earn it. In school her marks were higher, her awards more plentiful, her recognition greater than her pretty sister's. But her mother and father accepted her accomplishments as something to be expected of her. "The child *should* have brains," she once overheard Camille say. "Poor thing, she'll never get through life on her looks, the way Patricia will."

The words hurt, but they also strengthened Mary's determination to be the star of the family. There was no longer a drive to outshine John Jr. as there'd been in the first eight years of her life, for the boy was no longer there. It was so senseless. One minute he was a lively ten-year-old and the next he was dead under the wheels of a car that couldn't stop when John ran in front of it. In that moment and forever after, her parents made no secret of their feelings. Overwhelmed by grief, they spoke what was in their hearts, not caring what their words did to their surviving children. To the people who came to pay sympathy calls, Camille said the same thing over and over. "We've lost the best one," she told them, her voice full of anguish and self-pity. "We've lost the best one."

John Farr Sr. said little, but the tragedy turned him into a remote and bitter man. After Mary's birth, Camille had had a hysterectomy. There'd be no son to replace the one he lost, and he seemed consumed by sorrow. Young as she was, Mary sensed that if—unspeakable thought— he'd had to give up one of his children he'd have sacrificed one of the girls. He never said that, of course, but the child knew it at the time and became more convinced of it as she grew older. She came to feel sorry for him, remembering how much he loved John, but she was angry, too. Angry at both her parents for loving her brother more. Angry at them for not appreciating how hard she tried to make them happy. She realized what "partial" meant, and resented it. People weren't supposed to favor one child, she thought. When she grew up and had children she'd love them equally.

And yet, despite the anger, she wanted to please them, to bask in their praise, at least to have them say she never gave them a moment's worry.

Not so Patricia. Patricia didn't seem to know that the favorite was dead. She was sorry her brother had been killed but not sensitive enough to realize that his death had left an unfillable void in her parents' lives. Thick-

11

skinned, self-centered, boy-crazy at fifteen, Patricia gave no thought to the terrible impact the tragedy had on all their lives. Once, years later, when they were grown, Mary tried to explain that John had been more important to their parents than either of them. Patricia had just stared at her. "You're crazy. They loved us all the same. I don't know what gets into you, Mary. They were good to us, weren't they?"

"Good, yes. But they never loved us blindly, the way they did him."

Patricia, already married and with a baby of her own, had shrugged. "Love. At eighteen I don't know what you think it is. Some kind of magic potion, I expect. They aren't very affectionate, I suppose. At least not by your standards. But you always want people falling down in worship at your feet. Don't expect it. It's not all that important anyway."

Mary didn't argue the point, but she knew Patricia was wrong. Love was important and John Jr. had had it. He wasn't considerate of his parents. He disobeyed them and they adored him all the more. He worried them with his boyish escapades and they never punished him. He got more hugs and kisses than she and Patricia, more praise for every halfway important thing he did. Yes, they loved him more. He could do no wrong. He was idolized. And someday she'd find someone who'd give her that same kind of blind devotion. Meanwhile, she'd make her mother and father proud of her. Not as proud as they'd have been of John if he'd lived, but impressed enough to feel she was worthy of their love.

As far as her parents were concerned, it never quite worked out that way. They thought it was a good idea when she got a secretarial job at a local radio station after she graduated high school. They seemed to be quite pleased that she'd focused her intelligence on the business world, but they were hardly impressed.

"You should meet some nice young men there," Camille said.

"Is that all you want for me, Mother? A nice young man?" Mary had been disappointed that they weren't

12

more excited about her job. "What about a career? Don't you think I might be on the way to becoming a success?"

John Farr had looked up from his newspaper. "Success is marriage and a family, Mary. If you accomplish that, we'll be satisfied."

She'd wanted to scream. "You still think I'm the ugly duckling, don't you? You probably think nobody will ever love me, but I might be lucky enough to trap somebody, the way Patricia did!"

"Mary Louise Farr!" When her mother used her full name, Mary knew she was angry. "How dare you speak that way about your sister!"

"Well, it's true, isn't it? If Stan Richton hadn't had to marry her, your precious beauty might still be single and on your hands!"

"Go to your room!" John Farr's eyes blazed. "And never say such things again while you're living under this roof!"

Mary's defiance totally collapsed. It was terrible of her to remind them that Patricia had been pregnant when she married. They'd been so ashamed, so fearful "people would know." John Jr. would never have found himself in the predicament Stanley Richton did. He'd have had more respect for women. He'd never have taken advantage of a young girl as Patricia's boy friend did. They'd said that to her when she told them she "had to get married." Patricia hadn't seemed bothered by the oblique comparison, but Mary found herself thinking, even now. Even after all these years everything is measured against my brother. Stan Richton is a nice fellow. He's no more to blame than Patricia is. He loves her. She's lucky to be marrying someone who loves her. I wonder what John would have been like if he'd lived. Would he ever have disappointed them the way Patricia has, or the way I do?

She'd apologized that evening and a month later found herself a one-room apartment on West End Avenue. Camille and John made only a feeble protest when she moved out. Mary felt they were actually relieved that they no longer had to pretend. With Patricia married and Mary on her own, they could rid themselves of the last responsi-

13

bilities of parenthood and concentrate on the memory of the boy who never became a man. But when she said this to her sister, Patricia frowned. "You're really obsessive. I don't think they spend as much time dwelling on that memory as you do. You know, you're not easy to understand, Mary. You're a good-looking girl, you've gotten yourself a good job and now a place of your own. Will you ever start to relax and believe you don't have to prove something every minute?"

Mary bounced her one-year-old niece on her knee and seriously considered her sister's remarks. It was true, she supposed. She had turned into a reasonably pretty young woman. At least people said so, though privately she thought her looks were no more than passable. On her driver's license they read like a remarkably average description: hair, brown; eyes, brown; height, 5' 5"; weight, 110; birth date, April 10, 1938. The motor-vehicle statistics did not detail her flawless skin, the slim, perfect figure or the alert, interested expression that was so appealing. But Mary could never think of herself as attractive. In her mind, she'd always compare her looks with Patricia's almost theatrical blondness, with her sister's melting blue eyes and striking, five-foot-eight figure.

It was also true, though, that she had a better mind that Patricia, who'd drifted from one stupid little job to the next until she married. Mary's job was exciting, unimportant as it was. She loved the super-charged atmosphere of the radio station's newsroom, the vitality of the men who worked there, the daily challenge of making herself more and more indispensable so that one day she might really get into communications herself. That was her dream. A strange dream for an introverted loner, but one she cherished. Someday she'd like to have her own radio show. She'd be famous and admired and loved. She supposed, deep down, she did believe in herself, but Patricia didn't understand that she had to prove it.

"I'm relaxed," she said. "I really am, Pat. I like having my own place. I've even begun to do a little entertaining."

"Really? Intimate candlelit dinners for two?"

"Not exactly. More like sit-on-the-floor suppers for five

14

or six. Chili and red wine and candles stuck in Chianti bottles."

"How Bohemian!"

Mary smiled. "At least it proves I'm relaxed."

"How's your love life?"

The question made her uncomfortable. At her sister's age, Patricia had had more "invitations" than she could accept and Mary was secretly ashamed that she knew why Pat had been so sought after. She had, to put it mildly, a free-wheeling reputation. Damn it, call it what it was: Patricia was always a pushover, an easy lay. I can't be like that. In 1957 my morals are left over from *Little Women*. And my date book reflects it.

As though she read Mary's mind, Patricia laughed. "Relaxed, are you? Come on. You're about as Bohemian as Elsie Dinsmore! I'll bet you're still a virgin!"

"None of your damned business!" But a blush confirmed it. "Anyway, what if I am? Does that make me some kind of a freak?"

"Not a freak. But possibly an oddity." Patricia picked up little Jayne and held the baby close. "Look at your Aunt Mary, sweetheart. She may be the only chaste woman of nineteen you'll ever see."

Walking home from the Richton apartment, Mary was furious. What was so terrible about not falling into bed with every man who asked you? Why did she feel embarrassed about having no "love life" as Patricia called it? Pat should be glad her sister had a sense of discrimination, an unwillingness to experiment until she felt love. She had no right to criticize Mary for decent behavior. Particularly when that behavior was the result of watching her sister's flagrant sexuality. And where had Pat's behavior gotten her? Into marriage to a man she didn't care any more for than a dozen others. Into unplanned motherhood. Into a dull little apartment and a stagnant life. She's dumb, Mary thought. No matter how beautiful she is, she's stupid and out of control of her destiny.

It was then she decided she'd never be out of control of hers.

15

* * *

A light touch on her shoulder brought her back to the present. Jayne, a twenty-one-year-old reproduction of her mother, was standing beside her on the deck, smiling quizzically.

"What are you doing up here, Aunt Mary? It's freezing!"

"I was just about to come to the cabin. Thought I'd let you get settled before I unpacked. There's hardly room enough for both of us to be flinging things around at the same time."

"It is a little small for two, but when you consider that it's free . . ."

". . . it's practically palatial," Mary finished for her. "You're right, darling. I shouldn't complain. I still can't believe people really win things like this as door prizes at charity balls. Especially me. I've never won anything before in my life!"

"Well, you sure got off to a good start. Sixty-nine days in the South Pacific. Tahiti, Tonga, Australia, New Zealand, Hong Kong, Japan, even Red China! I can't believe it myself! And I do feel a little guilty. You should have taken Uncle Mike instead of me. A second honeymoon. I'm surprised he isn't furious."

"He couldn't make it, Jaynie. I told you. He's on the verge of a big deal." One more little lie. What did it matter? Anyway, it was only a half lie. Michael really believed he was going to get the great job he always said was just around the corner. There'd been so many of those corners in the past fifteen years. Mary no longer believed in them, but he still did. At least he said he did. The truth was, she hadn't asked him to come along. She had to get away from him, to put the perspective of time and distance between them and their marriage. It had been Fate, that insane business of winning a trip for two. It was her chance to think things through, as calmly and dispassionately as possible, without the silent reproach of his presence.

He had no idea what was in her mind. He'd been

16

happy about her good fortune, delighted that she'd sent for her only niece from New York to share the trip with her. If he was hurt, or surprised that she didn't invite him, he covered those emotions with the quick response that he "couldn't leave just now because something big is on the fire."

"Have a good time, baby," he'd said as he left the ship. "I'll be counting the days until you come home."

"Are you sure you'll be all right?" The question was involuntary, an automatic reaction, as though he couldn't get along without her. Long-standing habits are hard to break.

"Don't worry. I'll be fine. Lonesome but fine. And I'll cable you the minute the new job's sewed up."

"Yes. Do that."

Damn him, Mary thought now. Why was he always so generous, so infuriatingly unselfish? Another man would have insisted on coming along, or demanded she stay home if he couldn't go. But not Michael. Never Michael. If just once he'd put his foot down, "put her in her place" as her father would have said. If only he would assert himself.

"Coming, Aunt Mary? They've sounded the first call for lunch."

She nodded. "I'm on my way."

The phrase struck her as bitterly ironic. She really was on her way, in quite a different sense.

Chapter 2

Cabin 320 on the port side of Adriatic Deck was far from the plushest of accommodations on H.M.S. *Prince of Wales* but, small though it was, it was compactly designed and scrupulously clean. Still, one bed under the portholes and another near the bath, a small dressing table, plus two chairs and a coffee table left very little "walking-around space," and Mary looked with dismay at the three small closets and six less than capacious drawers in the dresser.

"Good Lord! How are the two of us going to manage in here for two months? There's hardly enough room for one person's clothes!"

Jayne had the flexibility of the young. "Not to worry. I'll take one of the bigger closets and you can have the other, plus that teeny one in the corner. And I only need a couple of dresser drawers. I've already met our steward-ess and found out the suitcases go under the beds and our life jackets are in that counter thing over there and there's an ice bucket and glasses hidden in . . ."

"Whoa!" Mary clapped her hands over her ears. "I can't stand such efficiency! You've probably already learned your way around the whole ship."

"Far from it. It's enormous. But I have been studying the floor plan—or is it deck plan?—in this brochure. Look." Jayne thrust a small pamphlet under her aunt's nose. "We're here, on Adriatic. The hospital and theater are on this same deck."

"Nice." Mary's tone was ironic. "We can be entertained and seasick without having to take the elevator."

Her niece grinned. " 'Lift,' please. Not 'elevator.' And is that any kind of attitude for a woman on a pleasure cruise?"

"Sorry. I guess I'm just a little apprehensive. I've never been on a ship before, and my maiden voyage is ambitious, to say the least."

"It's okay." Jayne sounded like the older of the two. "I know how you must feel, particularly leaving Uncle Mike for so long. You miss him already, don't you?"

Mary was evasive. "It's our longest separation in fifteen years."

"You're not sorry?"

"No. Honestly. Married people should get away from each other now and then." She stopped before she revealed too much. "Show me more about the ship."

"Okay. The deck above us is Caribbean. Then comes Indian Deck where the reception desk is, plus the shops and beauty salon. Moving right alone, we ascend to Dominion Deck where we find the Westminster Dining Room and the London Lounge with bingo in the afternoon and entertainment in the evening. Behind that is the swimming pool and sun deck."

Mary was suddenly absorbed in the ship's layout. "I see. And one flight up is the Promenade Deck with the British Bar and the Soho Club—whatever they are—plus the library and writing room. Above that is the Bridge Deck where the captain hangs out."

"Right. And on the very top is the sports deck and the Trafalgar Room, a kind of observation bar where they serve midnight supper."

"It'll take us sixty-nine days to find our way around." Mary studied the plan again. "Also looks like a very liquid cruise. Let's see. I count three bars plus whatever drinking one does in the dining room and the London Lounge."

19

"Well, there are nearly five hundred passengers on this little twenty-two-thousand-ton dinghy."

Mary frowned. "And I'm afraid ninety per cent of them will be over sixty-five. Anyone with enough time and money for a cruise like this has to be rich and retired. I hope you won't be bored, Jaynie. It'll be terrible if there aren't any young people. It doesn't matter to me. I'm just here for the sight-seeing and the chance to unwind, but you might get terribly restless with no one your own age around."

"Come on. You're my age. I mean, what's seventeen years difference, especially with somebody like you?"

"Almost eighteen," Mary said. But she felt ridiculously pleased. She adored this child. No, not child; young woman. Jayne was an adult, even though she could be her daughter. At such moments, Mary regretted not having children of her own. Perhaps if I'd had babies, she thought, things might be different with Michael and me. But I didn't dare. I was afraid to put such responsibilities in his hands. I never really had enough faith in him to think he could provide for a family if I stopped working. Even in the beginning I knew I'd have to take on the job of seeing that we had a good life. Wait. Did I *have* to? Or did I *want* to?

She was aware that Jayne was rattling on. "Anyway, I'm sure the ship's officers are bound to be attractive. And there's a whole group of entertainers—singers, dancers, impressionists. I won't be bored, Aunt Mary. It's the most exciting experience of my life and I have you to thank for it."

"Me and that lovely old dowager who drew my number out of the lottery box."

Jayne bowed her head in mock solemnity. "Bless her ample bosom, wherever she is."

They began to giggle like schoolgirls.

"And bless your mother for letting you come with me."

"And Daddy for ponying up for a bunch of new clothes!"

"And Charlie Burke for giving me a leave of absence

from the station as long as I promise to tape one interview a week while I'm gone."

Mary stopped laughing. Charlie Burke was not only her boss, he was also in love with her. There'd been nothing between them, nothing physical, not even a declaration on his part, but they both knew how he felt about her. Charlie was the only one who knew she wasn't happy with Michael. They had a drink sometimes after work and Charlie had a way of getting her to say things she could say to no one else. Perhaps she felt a closeness to him because he, too, was trapped in a marriage from which his conscience would not let him escape. Tracey Burke was an alcoholic. Had been for years. His friends urged him to divorce her, but Charlie couldn't. "What would happen to her, Mary? I'm all she has. If I left her, it would be like abandoning a child. Tracey needs me. God knows I'd like to be free, but I can't be that inhumane."

"You have your life to consider, too, Charlie. Years of it."

He'd looked at her knowingly. "So have you. How much does an individual owe himself, at the expense of someone else?"

She hadn't answered. It was a question she asked herself over and over again, never finding an answer she could live with. Sometimes she thought that if she ever left Michael there could be a future with Charlie. He was her kind of man: strong, successful, secure enough to handle a wife with a career of her own and still be "head of the house." He was all the things she thought she wanted in a husband, and perhaps if she made the first move . . . No. Charlie wouldn't leave his wife. She wasn't sure she could live with his guilt if he did. Nor with her own. He'd have an affair with her, gladly. Maybe one that would be as firm and long lasting as a marriage. But that wasn't what she wanted. What she wanted was impossible. What she wanted was a strong Michael. And those two words were contradictory. She pulled away from her thoughts. Plenty of time for them in the days and nights ahead.

"Hey, I'm sorry," she said. "I got lost there for a

21

minute, trying to figure out a dozen interviews! Come on, Jaynie love, let's go to lunch and see whom we drew for tablemates."

* * *

Mary felt a momentary letdown when she and Jayne entered the Westminster Dining Room. It was big but surprisingly severe despite its beautifully set tables with fresh flowers, its wide windows with a view of the sea and its seemingly endless array of captains and waiters hovering solicitously around the diners. She'd expected something like the pictures she'd seen of the dining salon of the old *Queen Mary* or the *France* with its curving staircase down which elaborately gowned women made their entrances. She'd imagined great opulence and, again, as in their cabin, she'd found tasteful simplicity but no lush elegance.

She introduced herself to the maître d', who responded enthusiastically.

"Mrs. Morgan! Delighted to have you and your niece aboard. We have you at the purser's table. Mr. Telling's. I'm sure you'll be quite happy there."

Jayne whispered to her aunt as they followed the man. "Purser's table. That's a good sign. All the snappiest people are put at officers' tables and the purser's is super. He gives a lot of parties."

"How do you know?" Mary hissed back.

"I read it in the New York *Times*."

They were the last to arrive. Five other people already were halfway through their lunch. The maître d' made the introductions. "Mrs. Morgan, Miss Richton, this is Mrs. DeVries and Mrs. Lawrence, Colonel Stanford, Mr. Spalding and Mr. Andrews. I'm sorry Mr. Telling will not join you for luncheon. He's very busy at sailing time but he'll be down for dinner. Enjoy your meal."

They took their places, murmuring acknowledgments of the introductions and apologies for their tardiness. Mary found a vacant chair on her right. Obviously she was on the left of the absent Mr. Telling. On his right was Mrs.

22

Lawrence, an attractive woman in her fifties who leaned over and struck up a conversation.

"You'll like George Telling," she said. "Charming young man. This is the third voyage I've made with him."

"Oh?" Mary did not conceal her surprise. "You've made this trip three times, Mrs. Lawrence?"

"Please call me Peggy. My dear, I've made this trip *five* times. In all, I've done twenty-five cruises on this ship. I'm aboard eight months of the year, and have been for the past three years. So if there's anything you want to know, don't hesitate to ask me."

"Thank you, I shall. It's my first cruise and I feel literally at sea." Mary tried to hide her curiosity. Eight months of the year on this ship? Incredible! She wondered who Mrs. Lawrence was. Rich, obviously. Idle, undoubtedly. Probably bored with some empty life at home. "Where are you from, Mrs. . . . uh, Peggy?"

"Chicago. Lovely city but lonely for a widow. My husband died three and a half years ago. And you?"

"I live in San Francisco now. I was raised in New York."

Gail DeVries, a plump, white-haired, smiling woman in her seventies, spoke up. "I know who you are, Mrs. Morgan. You're Mary Farr Morgan. The lady who has that marvelous radio show. I never miss it. I'm really delighted to meet you." She turned to the man between her and Mary. "Maybe you don't know that Mrs. Morgan is a celebrity, Mr. Andrews, but in our town she is. Why, she's as famous in San Francisco as Barbara Walters is across the country!"

Mary smiled. "Hardly, I'm afraid. I just do a local half-hour interview program."

Christopher Andrews had a clipped, public school English accent. "I'm sure you do it very well, Mrs. Morgan. I admire successful women. They have to work so much harder for recognition, even in your country."

Across the table, Colonel Stanford snorted. "No offense, ma'am, but I can't agree. This woman's thing is getting out of hand. Not because I'm a Southerner, but I like a woman to be soft and dependent. Appears to me they're mighty aggressive these days."

Jayne, sitting next to him, turned on her most brilliant smile. "Why, Colonel, I can't believe you're a male chauvinist! You're much too attractive."

The elderly man smiled. "You a southern girl?"

"No. I live in New York."

"Well, you got the winning ways of a southern girl. Bet you'll have that young man next to you wound around your finger before we get to Tahiti."

All eyes went to Terry Spalding on Jayne's right and a little ripple of indulgent laughter for the colonel's tactlessness spread around the table. Only Terry looked uncomfortable, fiddling with the heavy gold bracelet on his wrist.

"Don't worry, Mr. Spalding," Jayne said lightly, "I promise not to pursue you."

"I'm not worried, Miss Richton. It would be a pleasure."

Like hell it would, Mary thought. Just our luck. A young, handsome man at the table and even a blind woman could tell he's gay. Really, the colonel was too much! He probably had no contact with men like Terry Spalding, but everyone else must realize. She caught Jayne's eye and the girl gave her a half smile as though to say, I know. Ain't it a shame?

"Don't let it trouble you," the voice beside her said quietly. "Your niece will find plenty of company on the trip."

Her smile thanked him. "I do want her to have a good time. Young people should find every day exciting."

"Only young people?"

She turned and looked squarely at him for the first time. Andrews was an attractive man. About fifty, she guessed. Not handsome, as Michael was, nor intense in the way of Charlie Burke. His features were irregular, the nose a little too short and the jaw a bit too square. It was hard to tell while he was seated, but Mary thought he was probably no more than medium height, almost stocky, though one could see he was more muscular than fat.

24

Funny, his rugged looks were somehow at odds with his cultured voice. It was an intriguing combination.

"You're English, I gather, Mr. Andrews."

"Australian, actually. And the name is Christopher."

"Australian? I thought they spoke with a different accent. I mean . . ." She stopped, feeling gauche.

"You thought Australians spoke a crude language all their own. Well, many of them do, in a way. The workingman's lingo is practically undecipherable to Americans. I was born in Sydney, but I went to school in England and I spend half the year traveling on business."

"What do you do?"

"I'm in antiques." The expression on her face amused him. He lowered his voice. "Don't worry. Terry Spalding and I are cut from different cloth. I've never worn a gold bracelet in my life."

They exchanged understanding smiles.

"You're aboard for the whole trip?" Christopher asked.

"Yes. You?"

"No. I leave the ship in Sydney. I was in the States on a project and decided to go home the easy way. A little vacation from February tenth to March sixth. Quite a few of us do that. You'll find that about half the ship changes in Australia, people boarding and debarking there. But that's almost a month away. We'll see a great deal of each other before then, I hope."

"That would be very nice," Mary said almost primly. Christopher smiled again and turned to chat with Gail DeVries. Instantly, Peggy Lawrence began to talk with Mary across the purser's vacant chair.

"I hope you and your niece will join us after dinner tonight. The captain and I and a few people always sit at a table in the rear of the London Lounge. Tomorrow he'll have a 'welcome aboard' cocktail party for all the passengers before dinner, but I'd like you to meet him in advance."

"That would be lovely. I suppose you know him very well by now."

Mrs. Lawrence gave a smug little smile. "Yes. Very well. In fact, I always have the suite next to his on Prom-

25

enade Deck. You must come to some of our cocktail parties. Just a few of the officers and some select people." She lowered her voice even more. "Not all of them at this table, I might add. But Tony . . . I mean Captain Robin . . . will like you, as I do. In fact, Mary, I do hope we'll spend a lot of time together."

It took a minute for Mary to realize what was going on. Peggy Lawrence obviously was more than a friend of the captain's. Of course. That explained her constant presence on the ship, her proprietary air about the vessel and its master. Good Lord, what a life, following a sea captain around the world! Mary wondered whether Captain Robin was married. Could be. Poor Peggy. What a wasted existence. She seemed nice enough, but Mary had a sudden, uneasy feeling that Mrs. Lawrence would swallow her up if she wasn't careful. It could turn out to be difficult if she were trapped with this woman day and night for more than two months. She's the kind who'll confide all her troubles, Mary thought. I don't need that. I have enough of my own.

Unexpectedly, she realized she'd much prefer to spend the next few weeks in the company of Christopher Andrews. There was something about him that she found enormously attractive. In the next breath she was appalled by her thoughts. She hadn't come on this cruise looking for romance. Anything but. What on earth was she thinking of? Besides, for all she knew, Christopher Andrews had a wife and six children in Australia. And, she reminded herself, I have a husband at home. It might be a good, safe thing if she allowed Peggy Lawrence to take over her life. At least it would keep her from some foolish, reckless act. Come on, Mary, she said silently, get yourself together. You've been aboard two hours and you're imagining all kinds of crazy things including a shipboard flirtation with an Australian! What on earth was the matter with her? She'd done one rash, unthinking thing in her life: falling in love with Michael. And it had led her to this state of desperate confusion. She wasn't about to clutter up her life again with an infatuation. Even though they'd exchanged only a few brief sentences,

26

she had a sinking feeling that in her present state of mind she could fall all too easily into the arms of Christopher Andrews.

Deliberately, she turned her attention to the portly old gentleman across the table.

"Tell me, Colonel Stanford, what part of the South are you from?"

"Atlanta, Miz Morgan. Gateway to the South. Beautiful city. You ever been there?"

"No. I've always wanted to go. I hear it's charming. Have you lived there all your life?"

"Yes, ma'am. All seventy-nine years of it." He launched into an account of the city and the life there. A good life. A gracious life. Mary listened with genuine interest to his amusing anecdotes, told with old-fashioned charm. He'll be my first taped interview, she decided: a man who's lived long and well and is still actively enjoying life. My listeners will enjoy and identify with that. And it's the kind of thing Charlie likes.

"You travel a great deal, I take it," Mary said when she could get a word in.

"One cruise a year for the last eight years. My children and grandchildren think I'm crazy. Think I'm going to die aboard someday. I told 'em, fine if I do. I'm enjoying my money now, so they needn't count on inheriting from me. And it would save a lot of fuss and nonsense if I was buried at sea. Gail would take care of it."

"Gail?"

"Miz DeVries there, talking to young Andrews. She and I are friends. Met on a North Cape cruise eight years ago. Decided we'd get together once a year and go on a trip somewhere." The colonel's eyes twinkled. "No hanky-panky, you understand. We just enjoy each other's company."

Mary laughed with delight as did Jayne, who'd been listening intently. Peggy Lawrence raised her eyebrows to indicate she thought the colonel was a silly old fool. Mary found him warm and funny, a character made to order.

"Colonel, would you tape a radio interview with me? It was a condition of my leave of absence that I bring back tapes of fascinating people I meet on the trip, and I think you're completely captivating." She smiled and added, "Even if you don't have much use for working women."

"Me on the radio? Well, now, Miz Morgan, I'd consider that an honor. I surely would. Your place or mine?"

The whole table, which had suddenly stopped talking, burst into affectionate laughter. All except Peggy Lawrence, who smiled stiffly and excused herself.

"Seems like Miz Lawrence isn't too happy with me," the old man said.

"Pay her no mind, Beau," Gail DeVries said. "We've sailed with her often enough to know how she is."

"Beau?" Jayne repeated. "Is that your first name, Colonel?"

"Sure is. Beauregarde Calhoun Stanford. Retired Colonel, U.S.A. Ain't that a mouthful?"

"I love it," Jayne said. "In fact, I think I'm in love with you."

The colonel patted her hand. "You know what, little lady? You wouldn't be the first."

"Nor, I daresay, the last," Mary said. She felt relaxed and happy. Contemplating an interview always did that for her. When everything else seemed complex and confusing, the professional in her took over. She couldn't wait to do her first tape of the trip. And she'd find eleven more personalities just as delightful. It was a relief to know she could justify her long absence from the station by bringing back some top-notch material. For a moment she forgot about the real purpose of the cruise. For the first time in days, her thoughts were not with Michael.

Chapter 3

Michael seated himself at the typewriter in Mary's "office" and rolled a thin sheet of airmail paper into the machine. It was strange to be sitting at her desk in the small room of the high-rise apartment on Taylor Street. He was used to seeing his wife in this chair, absorbed in preparing the weekly interviews for her radio show. Gently, almost reverently, he touched the things she dealt with: the silver stamp box, the letter opener with her initials, the old china cup he'd found in a junk shop, a cup that said "Love the Giver." It was crammed full of pens and pencils and Michael absently fingered them, thinking how often he'd watched her automatically reach into that container. She probably no longer saw the words inscribed on it. He forced himself to consider that perhaps they were no longer true for her. Not that anything had been said. Not that either of them was willing to admit the strain between them. But Michael knew. He sensed her discontent in the overly considerate way she treated him, as though her restlessness made her guilty. And he knew she was only a dutiful wife in bed, not an eager one. It was the kind of thing men knew, even when women tried to fool them. He'd failed her. He'd lied to her from the start and he lied every day, pretending it was just a matter of time before he became the success she wanted him to be.

He swiveled around in the desk chair and looked out of the window. From this vantage point he could see much of San Francisco. It was an exciting view, but it reproached him. He had no right to be enjoying such comfortable living when he contributed virtually nothing to it. So what else is new? he asked himself. You never have contributed to any of the women who've taken care of you. Not to your mother, the widow who struggled to put you through school. Not to your first wife, who gave up on you when you were twenty-eight and still "trying to find yourself." And not to Mary, who married you two years later, believing you were what you were not.

Fifteen years of marriage to Mary. Fifteen years of unimportant jobs easily obtained and quickly lost or more quickly left because they didn't offer enough of a future. Who the hell was he kidding? He'd always had enough looks and charm to get himself into an organization, but not enough guts to stay with anything for the long, slow climb upward. Damn you and your stupid vanity, Michael Morgan. Nothing's ever good enough for you. Nothing is "worthy of your talents." What talents, for God's sake? Why don't you admit that at forty-five you're never going to be anything but a loser?

Because I don't believe it, he answered himself. Even at my age, there must be someone smart enough to recognize my capabilities. I've been an insurance salesman, a junior account man in an advertising agency, an assistant buyer in a department store, a dozen other things, not necessarily in that order. But it all adds up to experience. All I need is the right chance in the right place. Maybe Harry Carson will be the answer. If he really will back me in that men's boutique, I know I can make a success of it. I love good clothes and I know about buying and promoting. All I need is the money.

As always, optimism returned. This time, things would be different. He'd be in his own business, not subject to the petty demands of a stupid employer who had no vision. This time he'd succeed and Mary would be happy, as she'd been in the early years of their marriage.

Smiling to himself, confident once more, he lit a cigarette and consulted her travel schedule. She'd been gone three days. Probably too late for mail to catch her in Tahiti, and the ship's brochure suggested that no mail be sent to the exotic port of Juku Alofa in Tonga. (Small wonder. They probably had no post office.) He'd write to her in Auckland, New Zealand. By the time she heard, she'd have been gone eighteen days. He hoped she'd miss him on every one of them. Using two fingers, the old hunt-and-peck system, he began:

Sunday, Feb. 13, 1977

Darling,

Sitting in your chair, at your typewriter, makes me feel closer to you, even though you're so many miles away. I try to imagine you on your way to Tahiti, to Papeete and Moorea and Tonga . . . those exotically named islands of sunshine and smiling natives. Tell me every detail about them. Do you feel like Mary Martin in *South Pacific?* Don't meet a handsome French planter and never return to me!

A lot of exciting things are going on in our home town this week, but I'm planning nothing much. If you were here, maybe we'd go to see Eva Le Gallienne in *The Royal Family* at the Curran. Or trot down to the U.S.F. gym to watch Charlton Heston and Lloyd Bridges and Rob Reiner and James Franciscus play celebrity tennis for the Muscular Dystrophy Benefit today. If you'd been here, I'd even have let you drag me to the symphony last night to hear Sarah Caldwell conduct during Women in Music Week! (That shows how much I miss you!)

I've been pretty much in the house since you left. Not that people haven't been kind about inviting this lonely soul to dinner. I just haven't felt like going. I did break down and say I'd go to Rae's for supper tonight. She's having a few

31

people for a "pre-valentine buffet" and I agreed to come, even though my heart is on the high seas.

Mostly, I'm getting facts and figures together for my meeting with Harry Carson on the 25th. He seems very high on the idea of backing me in the boutique and I've even been scouting possible locations. Seems to me that Sutter Street would be the best if we can find the space there. Of course, there are three or four other men's clothing stores there, but mine would be completely different, much more inventive, if Harry goes along with my ideas, as, of course, he must if we're to succeed.

Charlie Burke called yesterday and said to give you his love when I wrote, and to tell you that things are okay at the station and they'll be filling in with the interviews you taped before you left. I called Patricia and told her you and Jayne got off safely on Thursday and that the ship looked wonderful.

But not as wonderful as you, my darling. And not as wonderful as you'll look when you come sailing back to me.

All my love, Michael

He reread the letter. It was no literary masterpiece, but he was no writer. As in all things, he'd done the best he could.

* * *

On the day before they were to arrive in Tahiti, Mary realized how quickly she'd become accustomed to this strange new life at sea. The past eight days had given her a chance to learn her way around the ship and to settle into the easy routine. It wasn't difficult to see why people became infatuated with cruising. It was the most pampered, trouble-free (face it), mindless way to spend the long days and nights.

32

On the pillow at bedtime was the program for the next day, every hour charted if one chose to follow the schedule. There were deck games and exercise groups and dance classes in the morning. Bridge lessons and movies and bingo in the afternoon. Cocktails and elaborate entertainment after dinner, and late-night entertainment and dancing until all hours in the Soho Club, which turned out to be the ship's cabaret. One could swim or sun or read in a deck chair; play Ping-Pong or shuffleboard; have a massage and sauna, a shampoo and set. One could eat five times a day and order food in the cabin at any hour. And one certainly could drink. The British Bar began serving cocktails at ten o'clock in the morning and not a few people were there waiting when the bar opened. Nothing was left to chance. The daily bulletin even told you how to dress in the evening—casual, informal or formal, depending upon the activities offered.

Almost every evening she found an invitation under her door. At first, they were the formally engraved kind: "Captain Anthony Robin cordially invites you to the Captain's Reception at 6:45 P.M. in the London Lounge." But as she came to know more people, the engraved invitations meant for all passengers gave way to those specially typed on the ship's available invitation cards. People were constantly giving luncheon parties in the card room, tea dances in the Soho, cocktail gatherings in their cabins. The officers invited selected passengers to predinner drinks in their quarters, and she and Christopher quickly became part of the small "in" group asked to lunch or cocktails with the captain, with whom she was now on a "Tony-Mary" basis. At these select occasions in his quarters, Peggy Lawrence was very much the hostess, openly proprietary about the tall gray-haired captain, who was undeniably handsome in his immaculate white uniform with all the gold braid.

It was quickly taken for granted that she and Christopher were a twosome, and with good reason. They spent their days together, swimming and sunning, met for cocktails in the Trafalgar Room before dinner on the rare evening when they were not at a party, danced far into the

33

night at the Soho. Mary knew she shouldn't be spending all her time with him. People probably thought they were sleeping together. They were not, though Christopher made it plain that he hoped they would. So far, she'd been able to lightly turn off his hints, but there was a long way to go before they parted. She also worried that she spent so little time with Jayne and said so one morning after the stewardess brought breakfast to their cabin.

"I feel as though I'm neglecting you, baby. I almost never see you except at breakfast and dinner."

"Neglecting me? Don't be silly. You're living it up, and so am I. That's what a cruise is for, isn't it? To throw your inhibitions into the drink?"

Over her coffee, Mary stared sharply at her niece. Did Jayne also think her aunt was having a shipboard affair? It was true she came back to the cabin very late every night, sometimes after Jayne was in bed. Maybe the girl assumed she was in Christopher's cabin for an hour or two after the last bar closed. She wasn't. Often they left the Soho when the band departed and wandered up to the deserted sun deck. That's where they did their talking. That's where Mary learned her new friend was a widower and quite rich. He told her about his house in Sydney, his two married sons, about his life at home and his travels around the world. And it was here that she told him something of her life in San Francisco with Michael. She did not tell him of her doubts about her marriage, nor confide the ambivalent feelings about her husband. But Christopher was bright. He read between the lines, knew she was in the most vulnerable state of her adult life.

"I didn't think I had too many inhibitions," Mary said now. "But if I have, they're still with me."

Jayne looked amused. "Aunt Mary, I know you're not sleeping with Christopher. Maybe you should. It might be just what you need. I've been to bed with George Telling."

Mary was genuinely shocked. Not only by the fact that Jayne was having an affair with the young purser but that she could announce it so calmly. She also wondered why she was surprised. Jayne was almost the only young girl aboard. Mary had seen the way the officers looked at her, had been aware of the glances Jayne and Telling exchanged across the dinner table, had seen them wandering off by themselves after dinner. Still, she hadn't really thought . . .

She tried to sound unalarmed, matter-of-fact. "Darling, is that wise? I mean, you've only known him a week. And I don't want to see you getting a reputation as a . . . a . . ."

"The expression is 'crew chaser,'" Jayne said. "I know. We have a couple of them aboard. That pathetic middle-aged woman who carries the crossword-puzzle book around with her and is always asking the officers to help her with the difficult words. And your good friend Peggy. In a way she's a crew chaser, too. Even if it's the captain."

"Peggy's a mature woman. And Tony's a grown-up man. They have a long-standing relationship, Jayne. In fact, they hope to marry."

"*She* hopes to marry is more like it. George says Tony has been a bachelor too long. He's not going to give up this little dictatorship for a house in the Chicago suburbs where he'd live off Peggy's money and die of boredom at the country club."

Mary wanted to tell her that it wouldn't be that way, according to Peggy, but the trend of this conversation was getting off the subject. "I'm not concerned with Peggy and Tony," she said. "I'm concerned with you. After all, your mother left you in my charge. I'd feel responsible if you got into trouble."

Jayne finished off her scrambled eggs. "Dear heart, I'm not going to get in trouble. You didn't really think at twenty-one with four years of college behind me I was an innocent child, did you? I know what I'm doing. And I recognize a shipboard romance when I see one. Tomorrow or sixty days from now George Telling and I will kiss each other good-bye and go our own ways. And we'll have had a helluva good time. Believe me, Aunt Mary, I know what I'm doing." She paused. "Do you?"

Mary didn't answer.

"You don't have to pretend with me," Jayne said

35

gently. "Do you think for one minute I believed Uncle Mike's 'big deal' kept him from coming on this trip? I'll bet a million bucks you never asked him. You wanted to get away from him, didn't you? Good Lord, I can understand that! Fifteen years with the same man and never a night apart! Who wouldn't need a break?" She hesitated. "It's none of my business, but I wish you'd make it a *real* change. Have an honest-to-God affair. It would do you good. You'd probably be a lot more content with Uncle Mike when you got home."

"It wouldn't work that way for me," Mary said. "I don't think I could ever look him in the eye if I'd been unfaithful."

"Unfaithful is as much a state of mind as of body. Listen, just wanting to go to bed with Christopher makes you as much of an adultress as actually doing it. And you do want to sleep with him. You have a lousy poker face, Aunt M."

Mary pushed the tray away angrily. "You're quite mistaken. I have no intention of it. Christopher knows I'm married. Our generation doesn't take sex as lightly as yours. Maybe our emotions don't run any deeper, but our principles might. I don't like what you're doing, Jayne. I can't stop you. I can't become a watchdog. I won't spoil your trip and mine by following you around every minute, but I can't approve of the careless way you give yourself to strangers."

"*Give myself to strangers!* I don't believe you really said that! It sounds like something out of a nineteenth-century novel. Aunt Mary, you amaze me. I thought you were so with it, so today, and suddenly you've gone all over Victorian on me. I always thought you were the most broad-minded woman I know. I meant it when I said I felt you were my age. I always have."

Mary's eyes filled with tears. "Until now. That's what you really mean. Oh, Jaynie, I'm sorry. You have a right to your life. I just don't want to see you turn into a promiscuous, careless young woman."

"Like my mother."

The words caught Mary like a stab in her middle.

36

"I've known for a long time, Aunt Mary. About Mother and Daddy having to get married."

"You've known? How could you know?"

"Mother told me once when she was furious with me about something. I was about fourteen, I think. I remember her saying, 'If it hadn't been for you, I'd never have landed in this stupid marriage with your idiotic father. If I hadn't gotten pregnant I'd have had a glamorous life.' Words to that effect. Enough to let me know I wasn't exactly a planned-for child."

"My God! That's monstrous! How could Patricia do such a thing to you?"

Jayne shrugged her shoulders. "No matter. I brooded for a while but I got over it. The point is, I'm not stupid the way Mother was. Or still is. I'm not likely to get pregnant and if, God forbid, I did, I'd know what to do about it. She probably 'slept around' to be popular. I don't 'sleep around' in that sense, but I'm sensible enough to gratify my urges when I want to. Just as men do. A double standard doesn't make sense to my generation."

"Does fidelity make sense?" Mary's question came slowly.

"If it makes you happy, yes. If it doesn't, it's hypocritical."

"As simple as that."

"Yes, darling aunt, as simple as that."

* * *

Mary thought of that revealing conversation as she lay in a deck chair sunning herself after a morning swim. Tomorrow they'd be in Tahiti. Christopher knew the island well and promised to take her sight-seeing. Jayne already had plans for the day and Mary refused to think what they were. From the chair next to her, Christopher reached over and took her hand.

"If you weren't wearing those sunglasses, I probably could tell what you're thinking. Big thoughts?"

Mary smiled. "Fairly sizable but not awfully important."

"Such as?"

"Such as how content I am. How wonderfully removed from everything. How much I'm looking forward to seeing the place Gauguin loved."

"I'm afraid you'll find it changed. Gauguin would."

"Everything changes."

"Yes," Christopher said. "Everything and nothing."

Mary didn't answer. Instead, she sat up, pushed her glasses on top of her head and looked at the island of Moorea, which was clearly visible from the ship. They lay at anchor for the day in Cook's Bay, but Christopher had decided that they'd not go ashore.

"It's a waste of time," he'd said over late-night drinks. "Absolutely nothing there except the Bali Hai Hotel, which was started by three of your enterprising young business executives who went looking for a better life."

"Americans?"

He nodded. "Your twentieth-century explorers. Made a good thing of it, too. It's a lovely spot, but it's off-limits to cruise passengers unless you're on one of the ship tours, and God knows you want to avoid *those* organized expeditions!"

Mary had looked wistful. "I may have to join them, just the same, after you leave the ship in Sydney. I can't go sight-seeing on my own. Not even with Jayne. You're going to spoil me with personalized tours of Tahiti and Tonga. Not to mention New Zealand and Australia. What will I do when you go?"

"Maybe I won't go."

Sitting at the little table in the Soho, she'd stared at him in the half darkness. "Not go?" she repeated. "But of course you will. That's home."

"Well, I had this idea that I'd check out things at the office and if there's nothing crucial I might stay on the ship a while longer. I've already inquired, and I can keep my cabin until we get to Yokohama."

Mary felt a surge of excitement. "Really? You mean we could see all the other places together? Oh, Christopher, how marvelous!" She stopped. "But I don't want you to change your plans for me. You've seen this part of

38

the world many times. Even Red China. You've already managed to get in there."

"But not with you. I've never seen any of it with someone I care about."

They were coming dangerously close to a subject she was afraid to face. The thoughts she'd had the first time they met came flooding back: I mustn't let myself get involved with anyone. Being attracted to another man will distort my thinking about Michael. Yet the chemistry between her and Christopher was irresistible. Unwillingly, she kept comparing his confident, masterful ways with Michael's docile temperament, finding that she loved having her life ordered for her, feeling more feminine than she ever had.

"I don't want to be selfish," she'd said last night.

"Why not? I am."

This morning, looking at the craggy peaks of the French Polynesian island, she wondered whether Christopher would stay on the ship and knew she wanted him to. Wanted it very much.

February 26, 1977

Dearest Michael,

So far, it's been an interesting trip. The ship is full of characters and though most of them are on the geriatric side (one of my tablemates calls this the Three C's Cruise—canes, crutches and cardiac cases) there are some pleasant people aboard and Jayne is managing to have fun. So am I. You know how much I've always wanted to see this part of the world and it's almost living up to my expectations. I didn't leave the ship at Moorea, but had a pleasant day in Papeete, though Gauguin would never know it now! I drove miles around this lush, killingly hot island, stopping occasionally for a cold beer and lunch at the Hotel Tahara in Arue. Frankly, it was touristy, with Astroturf at the swimming pool and a quartet of elderly native musicians, old men and women with phony, toothless grins and greedy eyes. I must admit my high-flown dreams of Tahiti are now deflated. It's a plastic island, overpriced, overpopulated, and, for my money, overrated. Nonetheless, I can say I've seen it.

More to my liking, peculiarly enough, was Tonga, even though the heat was even more oppressive and the poverty sickening. Still the people seemed more friendly, standing by the roadside, shaded by their parasols, waving as I drove by. I was fascinated by the birds they call "flying foxes" which hang from the trees like yards of black crepe. (On the rare occasions when a white one appears it's supposed to mean a royal death. One came two weeks before the last queen, Salote Tupou III, died. Spooky, I call it.)

There is nothing to buy on these islands. They sell shell necklaces, wicker baskets, bad carvings and tacky cotton dresses. The same ones in every market, so they must have a production line somewhere! Probably suffering sunstroke, I bought two dreadful "at home" costumes off the fence near the pier. Eight dollars apiece and at whose home I'd ever wear them, I cannot possibly imagine!

In two days I shall be able to post this in New Zealand where we will arrive on what will be, to me, the 28th. I'm not sure what that is in San Francisco as we lost a day when we crossed the dateline. (They promise to give it back on the return trip.) The ship's newspaper coyly headlined the event with the words "February 24 canceled due to lack of interest."

I taped my first interview with a delicious old colonel who sits at my table in the dining room, another with a priest on Tonga. I'll mail them to Charlie when we reach Sydney.

Hope your meeting went well and that every-

one is taking care of you for me. Jayne sends
love, and so, of course, do I.

Mary

She frowned as she addressed and sealed the letter. It
would not be what Michael hoped for, but she couldn't
bring herself to say she missed him or wished he were
there. It was as impersonal as a letter to a friend, a travelogue which said little more than that she was alive and
well. Worse, it was a lie. For by implication she'd said she
was alone on her sight-seeing expeditions. I've never lied
to him before, Mary thought, but this time I have no
choice. What was that old Irish saying? Something about
"Words spoken you are a slave to; those not said you are
the master of." At least hers was a lie of omission. Not
like those unforgettable ones Michael had told her over
the years. She remembered them all. They began the day
they met.

Chapter 4

Mary met Michael Morgan two weeks after she arrived in San Francisco in June 1961. She was two months past her twenty-third birthday, uneasy about being a continent away from everyone she knew, terrified of the long chance she was taking by accepting the job at the San Francisco radio station and thrilled by the prospect of turning it into something nearer her ultimate goal.

The station was a network affiliate of the one in New York where she'd worked for five years, climbing from her first job as a girl Friday in the newsroom to executive secretary to the station manager. It was in this latter spot, a highly responsible one, that she met Charlie Burke, an old friend of her boss. Charlie came to New York every couple of months on business and he and Mary had fallen into the habit of having dinner together on the evenings he was free. They liked and respected each other. Theirs was a no-nonsense relationship. He told her frankly about his wife's drinking problem but he did not suggest that Mary might help him forget his troubles. Perhaps, she thought later, Charlie knew even then what a little Puritan I was.

For her part, Mary talked more freely than she ever had to anyone. She told him about the still-idolized brother, dead these fourteen years, about her parents, her married sister and the niece she adored.

"You'll marry and have your own kids," Charlie had said.

"I guess so. But first I'd like to see what I can accomplish on my own."

"A career woman instead of a wife? That's your choice?"

"I don't see why it has to be a choice. Lots of women manage both."

"I'm not so sure about that." Charlie was very serious. "It's tough handling two jobs. I know some working wives with real ambition, not women just supplementing the family income. They have a hard time deciding where the priorities are. The only way a career woman can succeed in that kind of double life is either to have a husband who's very secure in his own right or one who doesn't mind being dominated."

Mary had laughed. "That's old-fashioned propaganda. My Lord, Charlie, do you have such a low opinion of women?"

"Not at all. If anything, the low opinion is of men. Most of them think with their egos." He grinned. "Notice I said 'most,' not all. There are a few rare birds who wouldn't feel threatened by a bright wife." The grin faded. "I like to think I'm one of them. You know, Mary, if I were unattached, I'd be the perfect husband for you."

"Well, then, I'll just have to find a second Charlie Burke, won't I? Where might he hang out? In California?"

"More so than in New York, I suspect. This is a competitive city. We're much less nervous in the West."

"Okay. I'll move to San Francisco. Find me a job and I'll find the unthreatenable husband."

"Do you mean that?"

She was taken aback. She'd been rattling on blithely but Charlie apparently was prepared to take her seriously.

"I don't know. I've never really thought about leaving New York."

"Well, think about it. And don't take too much time. The assistant station manager at our place is leaving next month. I think you'd be damned good for the job."

43

Six weeks later she was in San Francisco and two weeks after that she met Michael. He was twenty-nine, separated from his wife, and a charmer. They were introduced at a cocktail party given by one of the girls at the station and the attraction was mutual and instantaneous. He immediately asked her to dinner and she didn't hesitate to accept.

Over coffee they exchanged facts about themselves. He told her he'd been born in Los Angeles, that his widowed mother still lived there and he had no brothers or sisters. He'd gone to U.C.L.A. until the Army grabbed him and shipped him to Korea. When he came home, he married his childhood sweetheart.

"It just didn't work out. We had nothing in common anymore. She's a nice girl. Successful, too. She's a fashion model in L.A. We parted amiably six months ago. I expect she'll get a Mexican divorce when she has time."

"I'm sorry," Mary said.

"Don't be. It wasn't a bad experience for either of us."

Much later she'd learn that was the first lie. A year after she and Michael were married, his mother told her about that first marriage.

"Linda's a nice girl," Mrs. Morgan said. "She really loved Michael, but she couldn't stand his irresponsibility. It made her terribly unhappy that he left everything up to her. She isn't a competent person the way you are, Mary. She didn't know how to handle him. It was a bitter thing, that separation. Linda felt she'd failed miserably. She hadn't, of course. She just wasn't mature enough to understand that some men aren't interested in taking charge. And some women need things demanded of them."

The conversation took place at a strange time in Mary's life, a time when she was beginning to realize that Michael had no compunction about twisting the truth if he thought it made someone happy to do so. She had just learned that he'd lied to her about what he did for a living. She could hardly believe it. During the year of their courtship and the year since their marriage, she thought Michael was a sales executive with United Airlines. That's what he told her when they met and that was the farce he

44

continued until she inadvertently discovered the truth. She'd accepted his explanation of his constant traveling. It made sense that someone in sales would be away three or four days some weeks, talking with travel agents, scouting business in various cities across the country. She hated his being away so much and was surprised that they paid him so little for such an important job. She asked him often why he didn't look for something better, something that would let him be at home every night.

"I'm a good salesman," he'd answered. "It's only a matter of time before I get into top management, honey. I know the pay isn't terrific, but it will be. I'm sorry most of the expenses are on your shoulders, but that won't be forever."

"I don't mind that. It's not important. I just want you to be even more successful, and I hate all the traveling you have to do."

"That's a young executive's life, babe."

She was proud of him and lonely without him and she believed implicitly in him and his future until the devastating day when one of the men at the radio station said casually, "Flew in from Denver last night with your husband, Mary. Helluva nice guy."

"Oh? You and Michael were on the same flight?"

"Sure. That's one of his regular runs, isn't it?"

She didn't understand what he meant, but she pretended to. "Yes, of course. He travels a great deal."

"Most of those guys do." The man laughed. "You've got a wild sense of humor. 'Travels a great deal.' That's a good one. What else does an airline steward do?"

Airline steward! She was stunned, but simply smiled, hoping her surprise didn't show.

On the way to their apartment—it was a smaller one then, a little walk-up just off Powell Street that Mary had found when she first arrived and into which Michael moved six months before they were married—she wondered what he'd say when she told him she'd learned what his real job was. Or maybe he planned to tell her now, on the theory that her co-worker might do so. How

45

had he managed so long not to run into anyone they knew? And why had he lied about his work?

He was waiting for her, arms outstretched, martinis ready and dinner on the stove. She ignored his greeting, dropped her handbag in the bedroom and came back to face him. She went straight to the point.

"Michael, I was talking to Winkie Kaufman at the station today. He says he came in on your flight last night."

"Yes, he did."

She waited but Michael did not go on. His back was to her as he stirred the martinis and poured them into chilled glasses.

"Why, Michael?"

"Why what?"

"Why have you lied about your job? Why did you pretend you were a sales executive? Are you ashamed of what you do?"

He put the glasses down carefully. "No. I thought you might be."

She was aghast. "You thought I'd be ashamed? For God's sake, Michael, what kind of person do you think I am? I wouldn't care if you were a street cleaner! I love you. It doesn't matter to me whether you're a big executive or simply doing an honest job of work. There's nothing wrong with what you do. It's a very responsible job. But it was wrong to lie about it. Wrong and snobbish." She nearly added, "And stupid, too." He must have known that sooner or later he'd be found out. How blind with love she'd been not to have sensed, long ago, that his hours didn't make sense.

He handed her a glass and she accepted it automatically. "I just wanted you to think I was important," he said. "I want you to be proud of me, Mary. I was afraid you'd be embarrassed if you had to say your husband was a flight attendant. I'm not going to be one forever, you know. This was just a way to get my foot in the door. In fact, I'm planning to give it up if I'm not promoted soon. I've stayed with this longer than I have with anything. I'm thirty-one and I know there's something better for me in the field of aviation. I thought it would make you happier if you believed I'd already gotten where I expect to be. I did it for you. That's the God's truth. Your happiness is all I care about."

She didn't know what to say. He should know happiness couldn't be built on deceit. Of all sins, lying was the one she found hardest to forgive. And yet, looking at him, loving him so, her anger disappeared. He was so eager to please her, so anxious to appear larger than life in her eyes. He was like an unhappy little boy who'd lied to his mother rather than risk her disapproval or lose her love.

"Michael, darling, I don't care what you do. Always remember that. Just tell the truth about it. Please."

He knelt and put his head against her breast. "You're so wonderful, Mary. So understanding. I will make good. You'll see. And I won't lie to you again. Not ever. You have my word of honor."

She'd cradled him, saying that was all she wanted, that she loved him more than anything in the world.

That night he made love to her more passionately than ever. And that night, for the first time, even while she responded ecstatically, a small corner of her mind opened itself to a disturbing ray of doubt. She tried to tell it to go away, that he'd seen how silly and superficial it was to lie in order to make himself a big man, that he'd never do it again.

And to her knowledge, he hadn't. In fact, he seemed relieved not to have to pretend, secure in the knowledge that what he did couldn't change her love for him. She refused to think, cynically, that knowing she'd provide for them both made Michael less ambitious, more relaxed about waiting for his "big break."

Slowly, unwillingly, his casual attitude began to annoy her. Wishing she didn't feel that way, she began to resent it when he refused jobs he considered "beneath him" or ones that involved traveling.

"I know you're unhappy when I'm away," he said. "So I wouldn't consider it again."

She said nothing because that's what she had said in the beginning. Like any young bride, she wanted her hus-

47

band beside her at night. Michael was only giving her what he thought she wanted: his presence. He couldn't see that his idleness had become more distressing to her than his absence. It's my own fault, Mary thought. I nagged him to stay home and now I hate it when I go off to work in the morning and he's still asleep. I hate it when I come home in the evening and find he's done nothing about getting a job.

He had, of course, had many jobs over the years, all of them low-paying and short-term. He'd long since given up even the gesture of offering any contribution to their joint expenses. He really didn't seem to mind being—in that old-fashioned phrase—a "kept man."

Fortunately, or perhaps unfortunately, as his prospects waned, Mary's grew. Five years after she joined the station, Charlie Burke suggested she might try a local show of her own if she was still interested. He knew, from the early days, where her ambitions lay.

"You still want to be on the air?" The question had come casually.

"You know I'd love to, but I might be the biggest flop in the history of broadcasting."

"You might. That's why I think we should test it. Think you could do it in addition to your regular duties for a few weeks? That way we could get an idea whether you'd attract enough sponsors to make it worthwhile for us and you. And if it didn't work, you'd still have your job. I know you need it."

She'd glanced at him sharply. They didn't have their quiet dinners anymore. But even when they talked privately she couldn't tell him about Michael's attitude, wouldn't have humiliated Michael or herself that way. Still, Charlie knew. They had many mutual friends, sometimes went to the same parties, and no matter how important Michael made his current job sound, Charlie was smart enough to know what it really was.

"Thanks, Charlie. Were you thinking of a daily or a weekly?"

"Weekly, probably. We'll hype it and see if it attracts listeners and sponsors."

She'd gone home bubbling with excitement when she told Michael. He'd been as pleased for her as she was for herself.

"That's wonderful, sweetheart! With your personality you can't help but be a smash! Imagine, my wife a big radio star!"

"Well, hardly," she'd laughed. "It's just a trial run. It might not take off at all."

But she'd known it would. She worked hard on her scripts, developed a format that wasn't exactly original, but she gave it a new twist. Instead of the stale "famous people interviews," she went looking for "real people" with lives and problems to which the listeners could relate. The research was time consuming but worth it. She found interesting middle-class housewives who did things outside the home; registered nurses who treated the terminally ill; volunteers who worked with retarded children; teenagers who couldn't get along with their parents. Her genuine interest in people drew out the best in a line of "unfamous" interviewees from divorced fathers who wanted custody of their children to adopted children who sought their mothers. She was ahead of her time in picking topics many people cared about and few radio talk shows selected. There were enough other programs to accommodate visiting actors and actresses, writers pushing their books and politicians wanting their say. She didn't care about those easy choices. She sought out, sometimes with difficulty, people whose lives were intriguing or inspirational and always "just plain human." She worked hard to find them and to make them articulate and involving. And the formula, so basically simple that it escaped other broadcasters, worked. Word-of-mouth about "The Mary Farr Morgan Show" quickly spread and sponsors became interested. Within three months, she was locally famous. It was back-breaking, handling the preparation and not neglecting her duties at the station. She worked late at night at home, preparing her shows, badgered everyone she knew for suggested guests, read every newspaper for human-interest stories she could follow up. She lost ten pounds and gained a confidence she'd never had. In six months she was firmly established and the show became her sole career.

Without being immodest about it, her success did not surprise her. She'd waited years for this chance and she had no intention of failing. She now was a San Francisco celebrity and even something of a national name through newspaper and magazine interviews. She brought a great deal of revenue to the station and her compensation rose accordingly until she was able to rent the big apartment on Taylor Street and have the luxury of a daily cleaning woman. It was not that she became rich or world famous, but she was satisfyingly successful, known and, most important of all to her, loved by thousands of people in and around her adopted city.

But the approval she wanted more than any other still eluded her. She called her parents in New York when Charlie offered her the first chance. Camille answered and listened curteously as Mary almost shyly told her what had happened.

"That's very nice, dear," her mother said.

"Well, of course, it's only a test. I might not be able to make it work."

"But you'll still have your regular job in case it doesn't."

Damn you, Mary thought. Couldn't you at least pretend to have some faith in me? Just once. Just once couldn't you show you care? I know you do. You must. I'm your child. She suppressed a sigh. "How's Daddy?"

"He's fine. Right now he's watching Walter Cronkite. It's seven o'clock here, you know."

"Yes, Mother, I know there's a three-hour time difference."

She waited for Camille to ask about Michael. The Farrs hadn't come to California for Mary's wedding, but she and Michael had made three trips back East. Each time they'd stayed at a hotel and visited with the Farrs in the big old apartment. There would have been plenty of room for them to stay, but the invitation did not come and Mary was too proud to ask. Her mother and father

50

had treated their son-in-law politely, but he was a stranger to them. They did not take easily to strangers.

"Michael's started a new job, by the way. He's working with a brokerage house here."

"I see."

Camille's two-word response spoke volumes. In the past three years Michael had had six jobs, and each time Mary had been foolish enough to call home and tell her parents about them. Each time he took a new position she pretended it was a step upward, but the Farrs were not fooled. They knew a man who changed jobs so often was not to be relied on.

"I'll tell your father your news," Camille said. "I know he'll be happy for you. We really should hang up now, Mary. These calls are very expensive and I hate to see you wasting your money."

Mary smiled bitterly at the other end of the phone. Why couldn't she be soft and loving? Other mothers would be thrilled to have their children call from California.

"It's not that expensive. We can afford it. Tell me, how's Patricia? And Stanley? And how's Jayne? She must be growing like a weed."

"They seem to be all right. Stanley's doing well in the hardware business and little Jayne likes the private school they insist on sending her to. I don't know why the public schools aren't good enough. They were for you and your brother and sister."

"Things have changed, Mother." Impulsively, she added, "New York has changed. Even your neighborhood. Have you and Daddy ever thought of moving here? The weather's so nice in California and living is easier."

"We're too old to be uprooted, Mary."

"That's silly. You're only in your sixties."

"We still like New York. Besides, I wouldn't want to be so far from my only grandchild."

Did she imagine the emphasis on the word "only"? Camille never mentioned it, but her daughter was sure she wondered why Mary and Michael had no children. My God, Mary thought, she makes me feel guilty about ev-

51

erything, including my unwillingness to give birth. I wonder if Patricia feels guilty that she stopped after one? Not likely. Patricia never feels guilty about anything.

"Well, give my love to Daddy."

"I will. Thank you for calling."

The stilted phrase made her angry. She had a thing about it, no matter who said it. It sounded so cold. Like signing a letter "Very truly yours." Formal and disinterested.

"I'll be in touch, Mother. Let you know what's happening."

"Be sure to do that. Good-bye, Mary."

"Good night."

"Good night" indeed, Mary thought as she hung up. Better it *should* be good-bye. They didn't care, these remote parents of hers. Why should *she?* Why was she the one who yearned for family ties? Most children complained of too many of them. She was lucky to have such independent, self-sufficient parents. To have a sister who lived her own life with barely more than an exchange of Christmas and birthday cards. I don't miss any of them, she told herself resolutely. I have my own life, my career, my apartment, a place I've made for myself in this community.

She realized she was thinking "my." Not "our." As though she wasn't half of a couple. A tear slid down her face. This wasn't the way she meant it to be.

But this was the way it was.

Chapter 5

Peggy Lawrence awakened early. For a minute she didn't remember why she felt so unusually happy and then it all came back to her in delicious detail. Last night, Tony had agreed that they'd marry when the ship had a three-day layover in Hong Kong. Almost a third of the passengers would be taking the special tour into China and the ship would be quiet. They'd slip off, have a quiet civil ceremony and honeymoon in one of the most glamorous cities in the world.

She was so excited she had to tell someone. She rolled over and looked at the bedside clock. Seven A.M. In another hour they'd be docking in New Zealand. Maybe Mary would be awake. She and Christopher planned to get an early start so Mary could get in as much sightseeing as possible before they sailed at midnight. God knows what they wanted to see in Auckland. The Ellerslie Racecourse? The War Memorial Museum with all those beat-up Maori relics? Or a look at the city from the top of Mount Eden? She'd never seen any of them. In most ports, she left the ship only long enough to pick up a few trinkets for people back home. Sometimes she didn't disembark at all. It really depended on what Tony wanted to do.

Everything depended on that. For three years she'd chased him shamelessly around the world. She knew what people said about her. The "repeaters," those who'd sailed before on the *Prince of Wales,* knew that the rich and elegant Mrs. Lawrence was hellbent on marrying the captain. They probably laughed at her behind her back, certain she'd never get him, thinking she made a complete ass of herself. She didn't give a damn. Any more than she cared that the crew and the officers were so deferential to her, so scrupulously correct in her presence because they knew that any lapse of conduct would be reported within minutes to "the Old Man." Now they'd see that she was smarter than any of them gave her credit for. Soon she'd be rid of all of them. Tony would take early retirement and live with her in the big house in Highland Park in the summer. They'd winter in her place in Naples, Florida. They'd go to England frequently to see his eighty-five-year-old mother and his brothers and sisters and nieces and nephews. The thought of her wonderful new life was too much to contain. She picked up the phone and dialed 302. A sleepy voice answered.

"Mary?"

"No. Jayne. Who's this?"

"Peggy Lawrence. Is your aunt there?"

Jayne opened one eye and saw Mary at the bathroom mirror putting on her makeup. "Yeah. Hold on a minute." She put her hand over the receiver and called out, "Aunt Mary, it's Mrs. Lawrence calling in the middle of the night."

Mary hurried to the phone, holding her finger in front of her lips. "Hush. She'll hear you."

"No, she won't. Anyway, who cares? Who calls at this hour? Honest to God, she acts like you're her dearest friend."

Mary took the receiver. "Good morning, Peggy. How are you?"

"Absolutely wonderful! I have such news! Can you come up for coffee?"

Mary hesitated. "Well, I don't know. Christopher and I are going ashore early . . ."

"Please, Mary. Just for a few minutes."

"Well, all right. I'll be up in about ten minutes."

54

Jayne was thoroughly awake now. She propped herself up in bed and pushed the bell for the stewardess. "You want breakfast, Aunt Mary?"

"No thanks, dear, I'll have a bite with Peggy."

"I don't know why you're so nice to that boring woman."

"She isn't boring. Well, maybe a *little,* but I feel sorry for her."

"Sorry! She thinks she's Queen Elizabeth!"

Mary shook her head. "That's a big, brave act. She's a frightened, lonely lady."

"Oh, come on!"

"No, she really is, Jayne. She's one of those women who can't live without a husband. I doubt she's had a happy day since Mr. Lawrence died." Mary finished dressing as she talked. "She's desperate to get married again. She doesn't know how to live alone. And I don't think she has that many friends here or at home."

"So she picks on you. How can you put up with it?"

"Sweetie, it's temporary. I'll never see her again after this trip. It doesn't kill me to spend a little time with her every day." Not when I have Christopher the rest of the time, she added silently. It's frightening how quickly I've made him part of my life. I mustn't. Even if he doesn't leave the ship at Sydney, I must get used to the idea of never seeing him again after Japan. He's not part of The Decision. I can't let him be. I don't even know that he wants to be. She picked up a sweater and prepared to depart. "You and George have plans for the day?"

"Nope. He has to stay aboard."

"Oh."

"Don't look so conscience-stricken. I'll be okay. In fact, you'll never guess what I'm going to do."

"What?"

"Go sight-seeing with Terry Spalding. He's even more lonely than the lovely Peggy. You know, I think it's a damn shame the way everybody ignores him because he's a little limp in the wrist. He's a sweet boy."

Mary smiled. For all Jayne's assumed sophistication, she was a softie, too. Spending a day with that lonely young man was a nice thing to do. Particularly when Jayne could have gone ashore with one of the other officers or even joined the three or four other young people aboard.

"You're a good kid, Miss Richton."

Jayne waved her off. "Might as well have two patsys in the family. Have a good time with Chris."

"Christopher," Mary corrected. "Never Chris. He hates it."

"Veddy soddy, old girl. Have a good time with Christopher."

I always do, Mary thought as she took the lift to Promenade. I love the way he takes over. I feel womanly when I'm with him. Even that thing with the interview. He respects my work, but to him it's something totally apart from us. She'd wanted to do him as one of her interviews.

"Come on, Christopher. Please do it," she'd begged a few days ago. "You're a wonderful subject and my listeners would be so interested. They're mad for antiques and decorating."

He'd only laughed. "Not a chance, luv. No Colonel Stanford, I."

She'd been defensive. "The colonel is a darling man. He gave me a wonderful interview."

"I couldn't agree more on both counts." Christopher had turned serious. "But that part of your life is your own, Mary. It doesn't involve me in any way whatsoever. I'm interested in the woman, not the radio personality." He'd looked at her steadily. "They are two separate people, aren't they? I mean, one could, if necessary, live without the other?"

If anyone else had asked me that I'd have unhesitatingly said no, she thought. To Michael, or even Charlie, she would have replied that she couldn't be complete without her work; that nothing could take its place. But to Christopher she said nothing. Simply smiled and said lightly, "Well, you're my first turndown. I suppose it had to come sooner or later."

They'd left it at that, Mary remembered, as she tapped

lightly at the door of Peggy's suite, but her silence had been disturbingly significant.

Peggy flung open the door and embraced her visitor. "Oh, Mary, thank you for coming up! Come in. Sit down. What can I get you?"

"Just coffee. Maybe a piece of toast. What on earth has happened, Peggy? You look positively radiant."

"I am radiant!" she gave the breakfast order to her stewardess, who hovered in the corridor. Then she closed the door and perched on the sofa next to Mary. "You won't believe it. Tony and I are going to be married in Hong Kong! Isn't that sensational?"

Mary leaned over and kissed her cheek. "I'm delighted for both of you! You'll make him a good wife, Peggy."

"Of course I will. That's all I know how to do—make a man happy. I'm a born wife, Mary. I'm miserable without someone to fuss over. I need to be married. I need to belong to someone. Without a husband, I'm only half alive."

"Yes, I'm sure you are. I couldn't be more pleased for you."

"I knew you'd understand. The others on this ship, well, I know they think I'm pretentious and possessive, but they don't know how lost I feel as a single woman. You realize what an important thing marriage is. You're so much more self-sufficient than I, but even so, you know how secure a wedding ring makes a woman feel."

Mary hesitated. "I'm glad you're going to be married, Peggy, but I think you're secure with Tony as it is. A piece of paper doesn't make that much difference when a relationship is as firm as yours."

"Oh, but it does! It makes all the difference! It's a public declaration that I'm loved and in love."

"And that means so much to you." It was a statement rather than a question.

"Of course. Every real woman feels that way. Even the young ones will learn that sooner or later. From the beginning, men and women were meant to marry, not just couple, like animals. I know that sounds hopelessly outdated. We're all supposed to be individuals these days, with identities of our own. But I never felt that way. Even though I've been sleeping with Tony for years, I never feel right about it. I always feel as though he might leave me."

"And marriage will remove that fear?"

Peggy looked almost apologetic. "Yes. Oh, I know that's silly. Plenty of husbands leave their wives, but that won't happen to us. I loved my first husband and he loved me. When he died, I thought my life was over. I really did. But it isn't. I want to live as I did before, married and happy."

As though one thing guaranteed the other, Mary thought. How amazed this remarkably naïve woman would be if she knew the thoughts that are constantly in my head, the questions and doubts. Right now, I feel that marriage is nothing but a legal burden or, at best, an act of duty. I could belong more to Christopher having an affair with him than I can to Michael being his wife. I want to be loved. But maybe I don't want to be married.

She glanced at her watch. "Do you think that coffee is coming soon? I have to meet Christopher at the gangway at a quarter past eight."

Peggy leaped to her feet and pressed the buzzer imperiously. "I'm so sorry! I can't imagine what happened to that silly girl. She's his stewardess, too." Peggy smiled dreamily. "Soon, I'll be bringing him his breakfast. He's going to leave the ship and we'll live ashore."

They were silent while the stewardess set up the breakfast table. After the girl left, Mary said, "Tony's going to give up the sea? It's been his life, Peggy. Are you sure he'll be happy?"

"Of course he'll be happy. He's only five years from retirement anyway." She poured the coffee. "I'll make him happy, Mary. I'll love him so much he'll *have* to be happy."

You'll love him the way Michael loves me, Mary thought. Too abjectly, too undemandingly. Will Tony react as I do, eventually smothering under the selflessness? Perhaps not. Perhaps he'll be delighted. He's quite used to being obeyed. She realized Peggy had asked her

58

something and she hadn't heard. "I'm sorry, Peggy, what did you say?"

"I said would you be my matron of honor."

"Me? I . . . I'm flattered, but we really don't know each other that well."

"There's no one else, Mary. Nobody's going to fly out from Chicago to stand up for me, and there's no one aboard."

"But, Peggy, I can't. I'm going into China while the ship's in Hong Kong. I'm sorry, really I am."

The woman looked as though she were going to cry. "You'll hate China. It's primitive and full of Communists. Hong Kong is such fun. Oh, please, Mary. It would mean so much to me. To both of us."

"I . . . I can't, Peggy. I'd love to, but I do want to see the People's Republic. And I promised Jayne and Christopher." Peggy had begun to weep. It was foolish. What difference did it make to this middle-aged woman whether she had an "attendant" at her wedding? But her distress made Mary waver. "Let me see," she hedged. "It's almost a month away. Let's see what happens." She hated herself for being so silly. Sillier than Peggy. But she couldn't bring herself to stick with a flat refusal. Peggy cheered up instantly.

"I knew you would! Thank you, Mary. You don't know how happy you've made me!"

* * *

"Absolutely and positively not," Christopher said. "You're not going to miss the trip into China for the sake of some dotty, midlife matron who's behaving like a bloody idiot. I won't allow it. If you can't see how ridiculous that is, my dear Mary, then I'm forced to make the decision for you. It's quite absurd, the whole thing."

She'd waited until the end of the lovely day in Auckland to tell him what Peggy had asked of her. It had been a glorious twelve hours. They'd driven to the top of Mount Eden and looked at the beautiful city below, laughing at the incongruous touch of five cows placidly

59

grazing among the tourists. They'd visited the War Museum and lunched at a "typical tea shoppe," browsed through a quaint, reconstructed section called "Parnell," where Christopher bought her a little painting as a souvenir of the day. Now they were dining elegantly at Ponsonby's, an expensive restaurant that had once been a firehouse and was as "gourmet" as any in San Francisco or New York.

Mary sighed. He was right, of course. China was the place she looked forward to most. Few people had been there and she knew she'd get several good interviews, perhaps not with the Chinese (though she hoped for that) but at least with some of her fellow passengers who would give their impressions of Canton. Or, as the Chinese called it, Kwangchow.

"I hate to disappoint her. She's counting on me."

Christopher gave an exasperated snort. "Good Lord, Mary, must you always behave as though the world will end if you don't live up to everyone's expectations? From what I've come to know of you in the past eighteen days, I'd say you have an obsessive desire to please. First it was to please your parents, who obviously didn't appreciate your efforts. Then you had to succeed in your job to prove Charlie Burke's faith in you. Don't deny it. I'm certain that was part of the motivation. I can tell, from the obligated way you speak of it. You fret that you might not be giving Jayne as much attention as you should. And heaven knows what debt you feel you owe your husband! Now it's Peggy, a woman you scarcely know." He paused. "I'm sorry, darling, I don't mean to be hard on you. You're a lovely, giving woman. But there's enough of the amateur psychiatrist in me to recognize that you have either a strong streak of masochism or an inflated ego that makes you feel you're indispensable. People who let the weak or greedy drink their blood sometimes have a need to play God. Very often they're enjoying a secret sense of power, believing they're sacrificing themselves."

The words stung. But they made her feel more confused than angry. What if Christopher was right? What if

60

all the efforts to please really were prompted by righteousness rather than compassion? He knew virtually nothing about Michael, yet he'd hinted at what might be true. Perhaps she stayed with him because it made her feel powerful to believe he couldn't live without her. She was quiet for so long that Christopher finally reached across the table and took her hand, stroking it in a now familiar gesture of tenderness.

"I didn't mean to hurt you. I just got so damned mad when you told me you'd even consider missing the trip of a lifetime for such an unimportant reason. Forgive me?"

"Of course. You're right. I know that. I just didn't have the heart to refuse her on the spot. I'll tell her I can't do it. She'll be just as married without my being there."

"Good girl."

"You do think you'll be able to stay aboard and go with us, don't you?"

"Ninety-nine per cent certain. Unless there's some dire emergency in Sydney. And I'm sure there isn't or they'd have called by now or sent a wireless. But even if the highly unlikely happened and I couldn't go, you still must do it. It's an experience you'll never forget. It's another world. A far cry from what you've seen in your Chinatown."

"I'm only sorry I'll have so little time in Hong Kong."

"Big deal. We can go back there anytime."

She felt her heart begin to race. It was the first time Christopher had spoken of the future as though he intended they spend it together. I must be terribly transparent, Mary thought. He must know that the thought of never seeing him again gives me nightmares. She half wanted to pick up the lead he'd obviously given, but she was afraid. Afraid he might ask her to leave Michael and marry him. Afraid because she wouldn't know how to answer if he did. She needed time. Perhaps I'm hoping for some miraculous revelation, she thought. Something that will tell me the right thing to do. His mention of a wireless reminded her that she'd had no word from Michael about the outcome of his February 25 meeting with Harry Gordon. It must have been inconclusive or he'd have let her know. Surely there'd be a letter waiting when she got back to the ship, but it would have been written long before. No news was good news, she told herself. Or was it?

They returned to the ship an hour before sailing.

"Meet you on the Promenade at midnight to watch us cast off?"

Mary shook her head reluctantly. "I think I'll turn in. It's been a long, wonderful day, but I'm sure you've had enough of my company."

Christopher didn't answer, but his small smile told her how silly that remark had been.

Jayne was already in the cabin when she returned. A small pile of mail lay on Mary's bed, and Jayne was busy reading her own. She looked up when her aunt came in.

"Have a good day?"

Mary nodded. "Lovely. What about you?"

"Not bad. Poor Terry. He was so damned grateful for company. Even mine."

Mary glanced at her letters, anxious to get at them. Mail from home was so important when you were traveling. It kept you in touch with the familiar, even the part you were running from. She forced herself to continue the conversation with Jayne. After all, she'd run out on her all day. Damn. There I go again, she thought. Thinking I didn't do my duty. Maybe Christopher's right. Maybe I do think I'm indispensable. This young woman is quite capable of leading her life without me. I've seen her no more than three times in the past fifteen years. Still, from force of habit, she made herself sound interested in Jayne's day.

"You like Terry Spalding, don't you?"

"I'm sorry as hell for him, Aunt Mary. I think he hates being the way he is, but he can't help it. You know, he took this trip to recover from a love affair. His boy friend decided to go straight. Or pretend to. He's marrying some older woman, would you believe! Terry's heartbroken. Practically suicidal. He told me the story of his life.

62

Classic. Possessive mother. Frail childhood. All that junk. He's only twenty-six and his life's been a living hell since Day One."

Mary shook her head. "That way of life is hard for me to understand."

"A lot of life-styles are hard to understand." Jayne gave her a knowing look. "Mother's, for instance. If she's always been so unhappy with Daddy, why in hell has she stuck around? Why didn't she split early, while she was still young enough to find somebody else?"

"Maybe she didn't know what to do, Jaynie. She's never been equipped to make a decent living. Besides, your father is a dear man. Maybe she loves him more than you realize."

"No way. She despises him. Poor Daddy. He's spent the last twenty-two years making up for a lack of contraception."

The coarse statement shocked Mary. At a loss for an answer, she said, "Mind if I look over my mail?"

"Be my guest. I'm done in. It's not easy playing Freud and Ann Landers all in one day. Good night, Aunt Mary."

"Night, dear."

Mary undressed and climbed into her bed. By the light of the night lamp she opened the letter from Michael written three days after she sailed. It sounded like him: boyish and open. No subtlety there. She wondered if he'd had a good time at Rae Spanner's Valentine party. For a brief moment, she felt a twinge of jealousy. Rae was one of her closest friends, a rich widow who entertained lavishly and usually had a cluster of younger men around her. But she'd always had a special fondness for Michael. Mary sensed this would be a golden opportunity for Rae to move in and try to get something started with her friend's husband. She wasn't above it, that was for sure. But Michael wouldn't. Or would he? Sixty-four days without sex was a long time for a man. She smiled ruefully. For a woman, too, she thought. But if Michael decided to go to bed with someone, he wouldn't pick one of their friends. He'd pick some total stranger. Someone she'd never know about.

What kind of thoughts were these? Was she already predicting Michael's unfaithfulness to justify the possibility of her own? Or was she searching for an excuse to break up her marriage with a clear conscience?

Impatiently, she discarded this train of thought, concentrating instead on the vaguely disquieting part of the letter about his meeting with Carson. "Harry must go along with my ideas." The phrase stuck in her mind like a warning bell. She knew what would happen. Michael would make all kinds of demands for autonomy in the business capitalized by Carson. He'd probably blow the whole deal with his inflated ideas of his own knowledge. She sent him a silent entreaty. "Be sensible, be realistic." She wanted him to succeed. His employable years were going by too fast. Whether she was around or not, he had to be self-sustaining.

Quickly she skimmed three other notes from friends, chatty little letters telling her what was happening in their circle. She looked for a letter from her parents or Patricia, but there was none. Not surprising. Pat had probably written to Jayne, and her parents never wrote at all. Well, I haven't done any writing either, Mary thought. Just a few postcards from Tahiti and Tonga.

She saved the fat envelope from Charlie Burke until last, knowing she'd enjoy it. There was a long letter on the yellow paper he typed on in the office. A little clipping fell out and she read it first. It was from the radio column in the *Examiner,* saying merely that Mary Farr Morgan was on an extended assignment in the Far East and her shows would be pretaped for the next two months. "Mary on tape somehow gives us a feeling of loss," the columnist wrote. "The shows are good, but we'll be glad to have San Francisco's 'voice of human interest' back, with all her warmth and spontaneity, in mid-April." Across the top of the column Charlie had scrawled, "See? *Everybody* loves you!"

Smiling, she began to read the long letter from her boss.

Dearest Nellie Bly,

You should receive this in New Zealand, the home of the Kiwi bird. You know about that poor thing. It can't fly. It did once, but when it stopped soaring, its wings became ineffectual—proving, as an elderly, impotent roué once said, that what you don't use, you lose. This, of course, accounts for the notorious reputation of sailors in port. (And lone passengers at sea? Ah, no. Not my Mary!)

Did I ever tell you that once, way back when, Tracey and I took a South American cruise? I was young and boringly introspective in those days and fancied someday I'd be a serious writer. I kept a full and alarmingly pretentious diary during that trip, recording "impressions." A few days after you left, I looked up that collection of musty reminiscences and found that the words I'd so painstakingly inscribed now sound as though they were written with a quill.

But for the sheer hell of it, I've copied my lofty thoughts about cruise ships, wondering if your feeling about them may in any way match my young condescension. If so, you would express them far better, with more simplicity than a twenty-two-year-old Charlie Burke managed. Promise not to laugh? Okay, here's what I wrote:

"It's especially fitting that they call a cruise ship 'she,' for she is pregnant with a thousand adult embryos who long to stay forever warm and sheltered in this great white womb. How lovely to be hidden from a harsh and noisy world which demands decisions and discipline. How easy to have each day neatly planned, each hour secure and unchallenging. Effortless is the life of the floating fetus, snug in the belly of the mother ship. Passengers? No. Prisoners of pleasure, swaddled in blissful boredom, floating undisturbed, figuratively curled in the prenatal position, silently begging never to be born.

"And when, indeed, they emerge into the daylight, they are as infants, force-fed five times a day. The bartenders are their wet nurses, the stewardesses their nannies, the captain their father figure, the other passengers their playmates.

"And play they do. They play 'dress up' at their costume parties, form secret societies with dirty passwords, give tea parties worthy of the Mad Hatter. The bars are their playpens, the swimming pool their wading pond, the outdoor games their recess activities. In ports, they dutifully take their airings in big perambulator buses. Restless and fretful, they suffer these lessons in geography, buy their toy souvenirs, squirm and complain and rush home to their sea-going nurseries.

"Rich babies with too much time and money. Old babies running from the specter of death. Hungry, hopeful babies in search of love or comfort or forgetfulness. Poor babes-at-sea. Poor, rootless, fading flower-children in a bed weeded of all things ugly, a bed watered with self-indulgence and fertilized with the manure of mindlessness.

"Have pity on them, these captives willingly suspended above the bright blue water. Ask them not to grow, for they do not wish to grow. Rather, let them sail on endlessly, forever amused and entertained in the ways little people demand—pampered and petted and, above all, never left alone. For, wrenched from this world of make-believe, they are buds that cannot bloom elsewhere, frail blossoms that, transplanted to the cruel earth, wither and die."

Now, my dearest Mary, can you believe your hard-bitten boss ever wrote such high-flown drivel? You can see I had the cynicism of the very young. the pseudo-superiority of the cruel, remote and misinformed observer. How clever I thought I was. How much above it all. How condescending.

I'm sure that your "great white womb" holds a very different kind of embryo. Or if not, you will not see it through such prematurely world-weary eyes. Tell me about it as it appears to you, my lovely friend. Tell me it is a delicious, light-hearted time and that you are surrounded by kind and gentle and loving people.

Your first tapes will tell me whether you've found them. I doubt not that you have. For they would come flocking to you.

Charlie

She dropped the letter on the floor by her bed, snapped off the light and lay back, listening to the shouts and noises of the ship's departure and thinking of what she'd just read. An odd kind of letter from home. One expected local and personal news, an account of the writer's doings such as she'd received from her other friends. Nothing so trite from Charlie. He was trying to tell her something, warn her, perhaps, that she dwelt temporarily in a make-believe land. She doubted he'd ever taken a cruise, or that the "diary" had been written more than twenty minutes before mailing. There'd always been a kind of ESP between them. Even thousands of miles away he must sense that she felt like another person. The "old Mary Morgan" would not have become infatuated with another man, would not have ignored the speculation of others or virtually abandoned the young woman in her charge.

Yes, Charlie somehow knew that on shipboard everyone became an irresponsible child. The pretended "youthful impressions" were his way of telling her to remember that she had to return to a real world, that she could not be one of those who floated undisturbed forever above the bright blue water.

It's as though I've told him about Christopher, Mary thought. As though he knows the temptations and is begging me not to be blinded by the unreality of this time and place.

Chapter 6

Sunday dinner with her parents was such a bore. Patricia looked around the living room of the Farr apartment and thought how accurate a picture it was of its occupants. Nothing had changed in years, except for the addition of a big, monstrously ugly television set that stared at her from a place of honor in front of the never-used fireplace. The wall over the couch was crowned by three hand-tinted photographs in oval gilt frames, pictures of herself and Mary and John as children, taken thirty-five years ago. She studied them with distaste. She'd been a smirking twelve-year-old, full of airs and graces. John, at seven, looked resentful. And five-year-old Mary had an air of false bravado, her chin lifted but her eyes shy. There were no later pictures of any of them, though there were several of Jayne in frames on the round table in front of the window. Jayne as a fat baby. Jayne at her first communion, her high school and college graduations. At least she has an ongoing life for them, Patricia thought. The rest of us have been halted in time, as though we all ceased to exist when John died.

My God, I'm beginning to sound like Mary! She always believed that nobody mattered but the boy; that they cared for nothing after they lost him. Perhaps she was right. After thirty years, they still spoke of him, endlessly retelling stories about his childish exploits now transformed into deeds of an angel who stayed on earth such a brief, sweet time. It was like living with a ghost more real to them than the children who survived. Patricia shuddered.

She looked at Stanley Richton, fifty, paunchy and balding and wondered how she could ever have let herself be seduced by him. Hell, she'd let herself be seduced by everybody, never dreaming she'd spend the rest of her life paying for it. But to end up with Stanley! Dull, devoted Stanley, who aspired to nothing more than running his crummy little hardware business and eventually retiring to some place like Sarasota where he could watch the baseball teams in spring training.

She felt like screaming. She was forty-six years old and nothing was ever going to happen to her, ever. All she had to look forward to was another thirty years of mediocrity. She'd end up as a grandmother and a baby-sitter. She who should have used her beauty as a wedge to wealth and happiness. She might have been an actress, or at least the chic wife of some rich and exciting man.

Even Mary, plain, boring Mary, had made something of her life. She had a glamorous career and was a celebrity, even if it was only in San Francisco. Mary had a handsome husband who looked ten years younger than he was. Mary was lucky. Imagine winning a twenty-five-thousand-dollar trip in a drawing! That was more money than Stanley earned in a year.

Patricia resented the fact that Jayne had been invited to share this windfall. She should have asked me, Pat thought. If she wasn't going to take Michael, it would have been much more appropriate to take someone near her own age who'd speak her language. But no. Mary had to invite a twenty-one-year-old, as though she felt more at ease with her niece than with her sister. Damn it, my kid has plenty of time ahead of her to travel. I've never been anywhere and I'm not likely to go. It wasn't fair. Mary had never even invited her to visit. Not once in more than fifteen years.

A wild idea came into her head. If Mary wouldn't invite her to San Francisco, she'd invite herself. Why not?

Mary'd always avoided asking the family because she said she had no guest room. She'd turned the second bedroom into her "office" and the convertible couch was "too uncomfortable." Baloney. Mary didn't want her. Well, Mary wasn't there, and Pat was sure that Michael would gladly sleep on the sofa if she wrote and told him she'd like to come for a visit. The more she thought of it, the better an idea it seemed.

She interrupted the boring conversation Stan and her father were having about the rate of unemployment in New York.

"We had a postcard from Jayne yesterday. Mailed from Tahiti on February the twentieth."

"Yes," Camille said. "We had one from Mary."

Stanley nodded. "Jayne sounds as though she's having a good time. Wonderful opportunity for her. Nice of Mary to take her. Travel is so broadening."

Patricia winced. She might not be intellectual, but Stanley's clichés drove her wild. "Speaking of traveling," she said, "I thought I might go to San Francisco and meet them when they return. It would be fun to see a ship dock."

Her husband didn't seem perturbed. "Well, we'll see. They don't get back until the twentieth of April. It's only the fifth of March, honey."

"I thought I might go early and stay at Mary's apartment. I've never been to San Francisco and it wouldn't cost anything except the plane fare. I'm sure we can swing *that*." Pat's voice was heavy with sarcasm.

"Patricia, I'm not sure that would look right." Camille was disapproving. "What would people say if you stayed in the apartment with Michael, unchaperoned?"

"Unchaperoned! For God's sake, Mother, I'm forty-six years old and Michael's forty-five! Besides, he's my brother-in-law! What the hell kind of foolishness are you talking?"

"Patricia! Don't speak to your mother that way!" John Farr was once again the stern parent. "Besides, she happens to be quite right. It would look very peculiar if you spent a long time in Mary's apartment when she isn't there. A day or two, perhaps, if Stanley agrees you may go. But no prolonged stay."

Rage boiled up within her. "You obviously have a wonderful opinion of me, all of you. What do you think I'm going to do? Climb into bed with my sister's husband? If I were going to do that, I could manage it just as well in two days as two weeks! You don't trust me, Daddy, do you? You never have."

"Have you ever given us reason to?"

"Oh, fine! Dandy! I'm never allowed to forget that I was pregnant before I was married. You're chewing on your old disgrace like cows with their cuds. Always living in the past. I'm the slut, Mary's the grind and your dead son is still alive and well and holier than any of us! Well, it's 1977! John's rotted in his grave and I've been a bored wife for a hundred years. Get that through your heads, will you?"

She ran from the room, leaving the others in uncomfortable silence. Finally, Stanley got to his feet.

"I'm sorry," he said. "Patricia's not herself these days. I think she must be going through 'the change.' I'd better take her home. Thanks for the nice dinner."

John and Camille didn't answer, and Patricia didn't return to say good-bye.

In the bus on the way home, Stanley said quietly, "Honey, you shouldn't have gotten so upset with your folks. They're old. Sometimes I think they don't realize we've all grown up."

"Have we?" Patricia asked bitterly. "It doesn't seem to me we're any different than we were twenty-two years ago. Same dumpy apartment. Same stupid friends. Same boring life."

"I'm sorry. You know I'd like to give you all the things you want."

She turned on him. "How could you? You have no idea what I want."

"Tell me."

Patricia stared out the window, thinking, What do I want? Excitement. The company of interesting people. A sable coat. A diamond the size of Elizabeth Taylor's.

72

Freedom. My beauty back. And my youth. God, I want another chance at life! Finally she said, "I just want a little holiday, Stanley. That's all. I know you can't get away, but there's no reason why I shouldn't go out and welcome Jayne home, is there? And if I'm going to make such a long trip, would it be so terrible to spend a little extra time beforehand? Mary doesn't have room for Jayne and me to stay on, but I'm sure Michael wouldn't mind if I slept on the couch in her office. I wouldn't be in his way."

"But what would you do all alone in a strange city?"

"Just walk around. Take the cable car. Go to Ghiradelli Square and the Cannery and Fisherman's Wharf. Have a drink at the Top of the Mark. See Chinatown and I. Magnin and Telegraph Hill. I've heard so much about San Francisco. I'd like to see it. Is that asking too much?"

She could be so appealing when she wanted to. Stanley never could resist her.

"No. I suppose it isn't," he said. "All right, honey. Write to Mike, if you want to. If he can spare his wife for two months I guess I can spare mine for two weeks."

She squeezed his hand. "Thank you, darling. I really love you, you know." Suggestively, she moved closer to him on the seat. "Wait until we get home. I'll show you how much."

* * *

On the afternoon of March 6, H.M.S. *Prince of Wales* moved slowly into the harbor of Sydney, Australia. Mary and Christopher stood at the prow on Promenade Deck, crammed in among dozens of other passengers who'd chosen this same spot for the magnificent view. Below them they could see the crew also clustered at the railing for a sight not to be missed. Everyone, it seemed, had a camera to capture this moment. It was a perfect day, with a brilliant blue sky and bright sunshine dancing on the waters and bouncing off the white sails of what appeared to be a thousand little pleasure boats coming dangerously

73

near the big liner. One or two reckless motorboat drivers kept cutting back and forth in their path, scaring Mary to death. It seemed to her that all of Sydney must be on the water that day. There could be no one left in the great buildings that made up the skyline of the city.

"That's the opera house on the left," Christopher said. "You probably recognize it from pictures. It took nineteen years to build and ended up costing $125 million American dollars." He laughed. "The original estimate was ten million."

Mary stared, speechless at the sight of the great building with its roof of huge "shells," actually glass and concrete vaults, the highest of which, she'd been told, measured two hundred and twenty-one feet, about the height of a twenty-two-story building.

"And on the other side," Christopher said, pointing to his right, "is our famous Harbor Bridge, the largest arch bridge in the world. We call it 'the coat hanger' and, incidentally, at night it's lighted only on the chic-er East Side. We, too, can be snobs, my darling Mary, even though a mere two hundred years ago this was a penal colony. See that little island, there? That's where the convicts were kept in 1788. As you say in your advertisements, we've come a long way, baby!"

She looked up at him, laughing. "It's beautiful beyond belief. I can see why you want to live here."

"Can you? That's good."

Mary looked away, pretending interest in the view. They'd been lovers for three days and three nights, and Christopher wanted her to leave Michael and marry him. Lying in his arms, happy despite her conscience, she hadn't been able to give him an answer. She'd told him at last about Michael, how devoted he was, how hard he tried to make her happy.

"I came on this trip to think about my life, my marriage," she said. "I thought that getting away for a few weeks would clarify it all." She laughed ruefully. "And now I'm more confused than ever."

"Because of me," Christopher said.

"Yes. Because of you."

74

"You do love me, Mary. And I love you. I can make you happy, darling. I'm the kind of man you should have. One who'll protect you and care for you and share a full life with you. You can't stay with Michael out of pity or concern for his future. He's a grown man. Perhaps the kindest thing you could do for him would be to make him stand on his own feet. He'll never do that, you know, as long as you're there to take care of everything."

"I know. I know that's true. But I don't know what he'd do if I left him. He . . . he loves me very much, Christopher."

He'd stroked her hair gently. "How could he help it? Sweetheart, I won't pressure you. You have to make up your own mind. About a lot of things. But I need you, too. As much, perhaps more, than Michael, but in a different way. I want a woman with intelligence and grace. I've wanted that forever, it seems. Someone who'll make her life mine. It would be a very different life for you, Mary. I realize that. You'd live in Australia and travel with me. There'd be no radio show, no job at all because I'd want you always at my side. But I believe the gains would be worth the sacrifices, my love. I want you to have your identity, but a different kind."

With her first glimpse of his country, those words came back to her now, just as the memory of that first night of love returned in vivid detail. They'd had a wonderful time in New Zealand, visiting friends of his in Wellington, a charming couple who lived in a typically upper-middle-class "British" house, full of chintz and flowers and fireplaces and sherry before dinner. They'd explored the tiny town of Picton set against great green hills and deep water, a funny little town of two spotless streets and a dear little park where children played around statues of Mickey Mouse and Donald Duck and everyone seemed cheerful and happy. She'd never known such a hospitable country, such warm and welcoming people. She even managed to do an interview with one of the ladies on the town's Hospitality Committee. How amazed her listeners would be to hear this lovely, cultivated woman describe life in this remote place, proudly explaining how the vol-

75

unteers in their cars met every cruise ship and took the passengers sight-seeing, refusing to let them pay for the "petrol," even though the hosts were of modest means.

"We're quite proud of Picton," her interviewee said. "We do hope more of you lovely Americans will come and visit us."

Mary had been thoroughly enchanted, almost euphoric as they sailed that evening through Queen Charlotte Sound and the narrow straits, the ship daintily picking its way so close to land that one felt able to stretch out a hand and touch the shore.

That night, she and Christopher sat over late-night drinks in the Trafalgar Room. They were the only people in the bar at the very top of the ship.

"Like having your own yacht, isn't it?"

Mary nodded contentedly. "Um. Fabulous. What are those lights over there?"

"Japanese fishing fleet. They're brightly lighted to attract the fish. And the brightest light of all is the 'mother ship.' "

The phrase made her think of Charlie's letter. "It's unreal. Like a picture postcard. There's even a full moon. Do you believe a full moon makes people go crazy?"

"I don't know. Is it supposed to?"

"That's what they say."

Christopher's hand tightened on her own. "Mary. Darling. Haven't we waited long enough?"

She hesitated for a second. In three days they'd be in Sydney. She might lose him forever. She would never know what it was like to be loved by him. In the soft light, she turned to face him. She felt certain and happy.

"Yes," she said, "more than long enough."

* * *

"Will you be all right this afternoon? I have to look after my business and break the news to my children and the office that I'm leaving again for another month."

She realized Christopher was speaking to her. She'd

76

been so caught up in her thoughts she'd almost forgotten that they were about to dock in Sydney.

"Of course I'll be all right. You don't suppose anything will change your plans?"

He shook his head. "It was virtually impossible before. Now it's absolutely impossible. I have one month to make myself indispensable for a lifetime. I love you, darling."

"And I love you." How easily and surely the words came, though uncertainty about the future remained.

"I'll be back to pick you up about seven. We'll go to dinner at Eliza's. It's one of our smarter restaurants. I want you to see how civilized Australia is, and we only have two days here. We have a lot of ground to cover."

When Christopher left the ship, she returned to her cabin to answer her mail. To friends, she dashed off brief postcards, smiling as she remembered reading somewhere that it didn't do to write long or frequent letters home when one was away, lest people think you had nothing better to do than spend time at a desk. She did write to her parents, telling them things they could have read in any travel brochure. She frowned as she set down the inane, almost impersonal words to John and Camille, thinking how sad it was that she couldn't confide in them or ask the advice she so desperately needed.

There was no one to give her such advice. Not even Charlie, although he, of all people, would understand. Instead, she told him how she'd loved his "diary" and how accurate he was, in general, about the attitude of people on long cruises. "Fortunately," she wrote, "there are a handful of attractive, mature, un-lost souls among all the 'babes-at-sea.' They, and the interesting ports, keep Jayne and me from jumping overboard to escape the mere monotony of the days aboard. I'll tell you about them when I see you, dear friend."

Will I? Mary wondered. Will I ever be able to tell anyone about Christopher? Only if I link my life with his. If I decide not to, I'll never be able to speak his name again. It would hurt much too much. It would never stop hurting.

The noises of a ship in port swirled around her, the sounds of disembarking passengers and arriving visitors, the babble of strange voices and odd accents. How interested Michael would be in all this, she suddenly thought. It's like a big party. And Michael adores big parties.

Resolutely, she began a letter to her husband. She'd put it off until last, wishing she didn't have to communicate at all with the man to whom she'd been unfaithful. It seemed to her that whatever she wrote would be revealing, as though Michael could read between the lines. That was nonsense, of course. He'd be delighted to hear from her. She'd probably have another letter from him when the Sydney mail was distributed. She began by thanking him for his letter and saying she hoped by this time he'd had a good meeting with Harry Carson about the proposed men's shop. She rattled on about Wellington and Picton and the tapes she'd made and sent to Charlie. Not a word about her fellow passengers, none of them. She didn't dare, lest some inadvertent comment about Christopher pique Michael's curiosity. Instead (was it a subconscious defense mechanism?), she devoted a whole paragraph to inquiries about Rae Spanner's Valentine party. Had it been fun? Who was there? Did Rae have a new young man in her life? Or was Michael her beau for the evening?

I don't even care, Mary thought. How terrible. I'm almost hoping he's having a fling with Rae. Anything to make my own indiscretion justifiable.

It was a bleak thought. My God, an inner voice said, how deceitful you've become, Mary Morgan! What a crazed, torn creature you are. Worse than when you left San Francisco.

But there was no turning back now. She'd begun her joyous affair. There was no way to retreat between here and Yokohama. Surprised by her lack of guilt, she realized she didn't want to. For the first time in her life she felt physically and spiritually complete.

* * *

Michael was depressed, an unusual state for him. Even in the worst of times he was an optimist. When one thing didn't work out, he was soon ready to think about the next. But on this March morning, a few days after his meeting with Harry Carson, his mood was pessimistic.

Not that Carson had canceled the deal. He'd spent two hours going over Michael's projection for the men's boutique, first reading it all the way through, his face expressionless, the fat, ugly cigar he chewed on staying unlit in his mouth. Each time Michael tried to interrupt with an explanation, Harry raised a big hairy hand to silence him.

"Lemme get the whole picture, Mike. Then we'll discuss it."

Michael had been forced to sit for half an hour in uncomfortable silence as the "money man" slowly read his proposal. At last, Carson put down the papers and grunted.

"Not a bad outline, Mike. Lot of things wrong with it, of course, but could be the nut of something good if we make some changes."

"I'm glad you like it, Harry."

"I don't like it. That is, I don't hate it, but I don't like it."

"What the hell does that mean?"

"It means you're not much further along than you were the day you made the first proposal, pally."

Michael stared at him. "What are you talking about? I've spent weeks getting all the data together—the operating overhead, the promotional costs, the inventory investment, the resources . . ."

Carson interrupted him. "And it's crap. You're smoking opium with this plan! French designer labels, custom-made clothes, advertising in *Vogue,* free drinks at five o'clock, delivery by limousine! What the hell do you think I'm going to invest in, a society tea party? Men don't want that junk. Give 'em decent threads, well priced. Keep the overhead down. Buy from the big resources at the right cost. Have plenty special sale days. Give me those things in a proposal and we might be able to talk business."

Michael felt his anger rising. "We might be able to *talk* it, but we certainly wouldn't *have* it! For Christ's sake, Harry, you're talking about a store no different than twenty-five others in this town!"

"That's right. The ones that make money."

"But there's too much competition!" He tried to calm down. "Listen, I'm not on an ego trip. I know this is the way to go. You've got to offer the public something special if you want to build a new business. You have to invest, innovate, experiment."

"Not with my money. I'm all for doing what's tried and tested. I got no interest in some snotty little shop that might appeal to a few fairies." Harry flicked the papers back at him contemptuously. "If you want to go home and draft a plan for an honest-to-God store that won't lose a bundle for five years before it gets in the black, if ever, I'll be glad to meet with you again. But don't give me this jet-set garbage. I'm not sinking my dough into a damned boutique that only friends of yours and your wife's would come into. I want volume, Morgan. And profit."

"You'd have them," Michael protested. "And don't underrate Mary's friends. She's a very influential woman in this town. Why, she'd plug the show on the air, interview people about it. Customers would flock in!"

Carson looked at him with disgust. "Counting on your wife to save your hide, huh? I hear that's your specialty. Well, forget it. I don't believe she can do it this time. And even if she could, I don't buy that as enough reason for starting a risky business. I'll tell you again, Morgan. You want to start a solid, no-frills men's store I'm interested in investing. But *my* way and *only* my way. You want to redo the plan my way or not?"

Michael had wanted to tell him what he could do with "his way," but instead he said, "I don't know, Harry. I'll have to think about it. It would be hard for me to head up something I don't believe in. I don't know that I could succeed with a premise I thought was wrong."

The other man threw back his head and barked a grating laugh. "Man, that's a good one! When did all

80

those high-flown ideals ever pay off for you? When did you ever make more than twelve thousand dollars a year in your whole life? 'Believe in something?' I'll tell you what to believe in—the almighty buck. I didn't get to be a millionaire by chasing rainbows, and neither will you. Copy what works. Search the world and steal the best. That's the only way to make money. And you *do* want to make money, don't you, Morgan? Or would you rather live on ideals and your wife's income?"

His face red above his tight white collar, Michael rose. "I'll think about it, Harry, and get back to you."

"Sure. The offer stands. On my terms."

Damn it, Michael thought now as he paced the apartment, I can't do it his way. I can't start another dumb clothing store and let Harry Carson destroy every valid idea I have for a shop that's in touch with the times. But it's his way or nothing. His way. Old-fashioned. Boring. Cheap. All the things I despise.

But what are the alternatives? Look for another backer? They're probably all the same, these rich old fools who don't know the world has changed. Try to find another idea? I don't have one. I've run out of ideas and I'm running out of time. I almost promised Mary this would work.

Hating it, he sat down and began to draw up a plan pedestrian enough for Harry Carson's approval. He'd swallow his pride, bitter medicine as it was.

Chapter 7

The morning after they left Sydney, Gail DeVries cornered Mary in the British Bar where eleven o'clock bouillon was being served for those who did not care to start the day with bloody marys or brandy milk punches.

"Come talk with me," the little white-haired woman said. "We never get a chance to visit except at dinner, and lord knows it's hard to get a word in between Beau and Peggy Lawrence!"

Mary smiled. She didn't know her well, but Gail seemed to be the kind of woman Mary would like to be thirty years from now: active, cheerful, a motherly sort who didn't indulge in self-pity or complaints and who took her advancing years in stride. She and Colonel Stanford were obviously fond of each other and enjoyed their annual trip. The arrangement apparently suited them well. Maybe, Mary reflected, it was a better arrangement than marriage. They led their own lives ten months of the year and looked forward to a fresh renewal of friendship each winter.

They seated themselves in a far corner of the bar.

"Would you like a drink?" Gail asked.

"No, thanks. I can't start this early. What about you?"

"Never touch it until cocktail time. Easy to fall into the trap of too much drinking on a cruise. You know, it fascinates me. People who wouldn't dream of having a drink before six o'clock at home are up here at ten in the morning, waiting for the bar to open. There's a different mentality at sea, don't you think? There's a kind of to-hell-with-it attitude that's pervasive. Maybe that's why so many people like it."

"My boss thinks it's a little like going back to the womb. That most of the passengers want to behave like infants—fed, amused, pampered, with nothing demanded of them."

"Your boss sounds like a smart man."

"He is. And a lovely one. When we get back, you must meet him."

"I'd love to. And your husband, too."

Mary took a sip of her clear soup, avoiding an answer. Gail looked at her affectionately.

"Look, Mary, it's none of my business and you can tell me to shut up and stop being a meddlesome old lady, but I think you have problems, and if talking about them will help, I'll be glad to listen. I don't know you very well, but I'm old enough to be your mother. I have daughters your age. Lovely girls. And the one thing I'm grateful for is that they feel able to confide in me. You may not want to, but if you do, I give you my word that whatever you say will never leave this table."

Feeling ridiculous, Mary's eyes filled with tears. She needed to talk to someone. Someone with experience and compassion who would listen and react objectively. Many times in the past month she'd thought of confiding in Jayne, but she couldn't. They were too close in their relationship and too far apart in their views about things.

"Thank you, Gail. Yes, I would like to talk. And I know you won't repeat what I tell you."

As though someone had carefully lifted a cork from a bottle, Mary began to pour out her heart. She told the older woman about Michael and her marriage, trying to explain the conflict within her.

"I feel so shallow, caring that he's not strong and successful. I don't even think it's all his fault. I've helped to make him that way, demanding nothing of him, hiding the fact that I blame him for becoming the person I helped

83

create. I'm not happy with him, Gail, but I can't stand the thought of what might happen to him if I desert him. It's all so mixed up. I don't know where my loyalties lie. Sometimes I think I might do him a great favor to push him out on his own. Maybe he'd find the right kind of wife for him, one who'd be dependent, who'd insist he support her. Maybe one who'd give him children before it's too late. Or maybe that's just a cop-out I've made up to let me live with my conscience. I don't know. Christopher says . . ." She stopped. "Christopher and I are in love. I'm sure you've guessed that. It's not just a shipboard romance. He wants me to marry him. I met his sons in Sydney. They were wonderful. I could see how happy they were that their father had found someone to care for again. I could have a good life with Christopher. I could even give up my work, much as I love it. But there'd be Michael. The memory of what I'd done to him. The realization of what I *have* done to him all these years. I don't know if I could live with that." She stopped, surreptitiously wiping away her tears. "I'm sorry. I shouldn't be slobbering all over you. You can't make the decision for me. Nobody can. It's just so good to say things aloud to another woman. I've told Christopher a little of what I feel, but it's not the same. Mostly I just go over it in my head, again and again, until I think I'm going mad."

Gail sat quietly for a moment before she said, "What would happen, Mary, if Michael suddenly did become successful at something? Would you be content with him then? Does your ability to live him hinge on this one thing? If he changed, could you care for him as you once did?" She paused. "Do you really want him to succeed? Or do you just want out of this marriage, no matter what?"

"I don't know. As God is my judge, I don't know. I can't tell the difference between love and responsibility anymore. I think I don't want him to be dependent on me, but maybe I do, in a crazy way. I must have wanted him to be in the past or I wouldn't have made things so easy for him. What is it with strong women and weak

84

men, Gail? Do we seek them or do they gravitate toward us? I know quite a few women who have passive husbands like Michael. They seem content with the arrangement. But I'm not. The balance is wrong. No matter what people say about equality between the sexes, marriage is like business—somebody has to be in charge. And I don't want to be in charge."

"And with Christopher you wouldn't be."

"No. He's strong and secure. But this didn't start because of him. I've been fretting about Michael and me for years. I took this trip to make a decision about us. I didn't know I'd meet someone else. Had no idea of it. Women who take cruises thinking they're going to meet a man are just plain stupid. The odds were a million to one I'd meet Christopher." She smiled sadly. "In a way, I'm almost sorry I did. This didn't start because of him," Mary repeated, "but it's become much more complex because he's shown me what I'm missing. When I left home, I thought it would be Michael or nothing. I thought if I couldn't have a good marriage with such a kind and loving man I'd never be capable of succeeding at any marriage. I never really said it even to myself, but I know I'd decided that if I divorced Michael I'd never marry again. That I wasn't cut out for marriage. That I couldn't give enough of myself, even though I wanted to. Now, I don't know. I wish this ship would sail on forever so I'd never have to come to grips with the decisions, either of them."

"You and Michael or you and Christopher?"

"Yes. They're separate but entwined."

Gail's eyes were full of sympathy. "I've been listening to you very carefully, Mary, as though you were my own daughter. You know I can't advise you. You're too sensible to expect I'll have the magic answer. But I wonder if you're hearing yourself. You say you can't give enough of yourself, but the fact is you do nothing but give. Maybe for selfish reasons, but I doubt it. I think you've spent your life trying to please other people. Maybe it's time to think about yourself. You seem so full of guilt in every direction, dear Mary. Why is that? Was it instilled in you early on, this feeling of obligation? You seem to feel it for

Michael and even for Christopher. What makes you so lacking in healthy selfishness?"

Mary thought of the early years, the almost fanatical desire to make her parents love her, the insane notion that she could replace their dead son. Even her career, though it was something she wanted, was in part dedicated to pleasing Charlie, to making him feel he'd been right in giving her a chance. Maybe I even took Jayne on this trip to please my sister, she thought. Or maybe I wanted to show off to Patricia by giving her daughter something she could never offer. God, I'm so addled! Much more of this introspection and I'll go out of my head! For a moment the anger at herself was directed at Gail DeVries. How dare she meddle in my life? What gave this old woman the right to stir up long-suppressed thoughts?

Instantly, she was sorry for her silent reaction. Gail was being kind. Sensible. She was only trying to make Mary see herself and work through to her own solutions. She wasn't prying. It was honest concern, not idle curiosity, that made her encourage the younger woman to talk. And Mary was grateful. Nothing was solved, but just hearing all her fears put into words made them less terrifying.

"I can't tell you how much I appreciate your letting me pour out this living soap opera," Mary said. "It must be a riveting bore for you. I'm sorry I went on so."

"Mary, don't. Don't say such a thing. I like you. I only wish I could help."

"You have. Just by listening."

"And I will, any time you want to talk. Think of me as your surrogate mother."

I wish you were my mother, Mary thought. If you had been, maybe I'd be a different person. No, that wasn't fair. She wasn't going to blame her messed-up life on her parents or her childhood. She didn't hold with all the psychiatric crutches. Intelligent humans should be able to cope with their own problems without whining that their formative years were to blame for their later troubles. Oh, some people truly needed help. She knew that. But most people grew up and lived through the heartbreaks that life

86

handed out and didn't expect things to be fair. I have to be one of those, Mary thought. I'm strong enough to sort this out if I'm disciplined and in control. Gail probably is right. I should coldly, clinically think of myself and stop worrying about other people, as though I'm a necessary woman, indispensable to their happiness and well-being. Self-preservation is the first law. I must start trying to obey the law.

*   *   *

As Mary was keeping secrets from her, so Jayne was not telling her aunt what had transpired in her life. Behind the flippancy was a young woman easily hurt and more insecure than the world ever would have imagined. The knowledge of the accident of her birth wounded her deeply, though she'd have died before she admitted it to anyone. Like Mary, she yearned to be loved. But unlike her, Jayne went seeking it, cynically telling herself that she came by her promiscuity naturally, a self-destructive inheritance from the mother she hated.

She'd slept with boys from her sophomore days in high school, but she didn't fall in love until her senior year in college. Russell King was a classmate, captain of the football team, class president, big man on campus. And, to her surprise and joy, this paragon returned her love. She wanted to marry him, but he insisted they wait. He was going on to law school, would have to work his way through, as he'd worked part time to supplement the football scholarship that had gotten him to college.

"I'll help," Jayne had said. "I'll get a job. We can live. It will be wonderful."

"No, darling. It would be terrible. Years of struggling to make ends meet. Me feeling guilty that you were paying the bills. You ending up hating me because you were supporting me. I couldn't live that way, Jay. It's not for me. Look. We're young. We have time. We'll see each other and be secretly engaged. The time will go fast and we'll have years ahead of us."

"I don't want to wait years! If you won't marry me,

then we'll live together. What's the point of all this sneaking around with dates and secret engagements?" She stopped suddenly. "It's your family, isn't it? Your bloody, uptight family. They'd disapprove if you were openly cohabiting."

Russell had been angry. "All right, part of it *is* my family! They're poor people but they've given me everything they could. They're old-fashioned and they won't change. And I'm damned if I'll repay them by rubbing their noses in a situation they can't understand and would be devastated by. Damn it, Jayne, they'd consider themselves disgraced!" He'd calmed down. "We can go on just as we are. They'll get to know you better. We'll ease into some arrangement sooner or later. Take it easy, babe. Things will work out."

"No, they won't. We'll drift apart. We're not kids. At least I'm not a kid. But I think you are." The words came slowly, disparagingly. "I think you're nothing but a damned mama's boy, still scared to death you'll get a spanking if you misbehave."

"Don't be ridiculous! I'm just trying to show some decency and consideration!"

"For whom?"

"For everybody! Including you! Please, Jayne, don't be childish. If we love each other, we can wait awhile. Think it over and you'll see I'm right."

"No, thanks. *You* think it over. And when you grow up, get in touch with me."

She'd expected him to call the next day, but he hadn't. She waited three weeks and called him, swallowing her pride and saying she loved him and she'd see him on his terms. But it had been different, somehow. They still talked of the future and she pretended she could wait, no matter how long it took, but inside she knew she had to do something to force him into action. He was the only man she wanted. The only one she'd ever want, and she couldn't budge him. Why should he budge? she asked herself one day. He had what he wanted. He slept with her whenever he felt like it. He lived comfortably at home with his parents, had a parttime job in a law office and went to school. Nothing disturbed him and nothing would. Unless she made it happen. She considered getting pregnant and rejected the idea. She wasn't her mother and Russell wasn't her father. He'd never fall into that trap. She wouldn't want him that way, even if he did.

No, the only way was not to see him. Let him miss her so much he'd change his mind. But she didn't think she'd have the willpower not to see him. That was when Aunt Mary's invitation came like a miracle and she leapt at it. She'd be gone almost three months. By the time she returned, he'd be so crazy for her he'd do anything she wanted.

Lying on her bed in the cabin the day after they left Sydney, Jayne reread the letter for the twentieth time.

> I wanted to tell you before you left, but I wasn't sure, myself, that what I felt for Pamela wasn't simply infatuation. I realize I haven't been honest with you for the past few months, but I didn't want to hurt you by telling you I'd met someone else until I was quite sure of my feelings for her, and hers for me.
>
> We decided last week to become engaged and be married in June. She's lovely, Jayne, and my family is delighted. Her father is the senior partner in one of the most successful law firms in New York and I will, in time, be joining it. Until then, we'll live in her parents' house in Greenwich, and she'll continue her course in psychology while I work toward my degree.
>
> Darling Jayne, I know you will be surprised by this, but not too disappointed in me, I hope. I would rather have told you in person, as I've told Pam about you, but as I said, I had to make sure of my feelings. I know how strong and sensible you are and although I'm conceited enough to think you may be sorry, I'm also aware that you, of all people, are realistic enough to want the truth from me, instead

of having someone send you a clipping of our engagement announcement from the New York *Times*.

I shall never forget the wonderful times we had, nor what a terrific girl you are. I would like to have you as a friend, always, and if you think that's possible, please call me when you return. I wish for you everything good in this world, and I know you will have it.

Love,
Russ

Bastard. She let the letter flutter from her fingers. Selfish, scheming bastard. Liar. Opportunist. Shallow fool. How could she have loved such a spineless wonder? It was all quite clear. His precious Pamela was a rich lawyer's daughter. There'd be no years of struggle, no working wife whose support would wound his precious damned male chauvinist pride. He'd been seeing this girl all the time he was sleeping with her, pretending love while he was coldly calculating his future. She couldn't even cry. She felt leaden with loss, even though the logical part of her tried to be glad she was rid of this egotist before it was too late.

Funny. It was almost as though she knew this "Dear Jayne" letter was coming. Until she shared the purser's bed, she'd been with no one but Russell since the day they met. If she hadn't sensed it was over, why had she started the tawdry little affair with George Telling, someone she didn't give a damn about? Instinctively, she must have been beginning to rebuild her confidence, proving to herself that she could enjoy and be enjoyed by another man. No. Not so. She'd felt guilty about it, unfaithful to Russell. Before New Zealand, she'd already broken it off with George. That nonsense about his not being able to go ashore in Auckland was just a lie invented for Mary's benefit. Choosing to spend her time with Terry Spalding was her way of staying out of trouble until she got home.

She hadn't really thought her romance with Russell was over. She'd honestly thought absence would do the trick.

The little fling with Telling hadn't been a presentiment; it had been an impulse brought on by the glamour and unreality of shipboard life. She'd truly believed, until this letter arrived yesterday, that her plan would work. What blinders women wear when they don't wish to see the truth about men! If a girl friend had told her she was in love with a young man who wouldn't marry her, wouldn't even live with her because it would distress his ·family, she'd have thought her friend the world's biggest damned fool. "If he's in love with you, he won't ask you to wait years," she'd have said to someone else. "He won't take a chance on losing you. It wouldn't matter to him who paid the bills as long as you were together."

That's what she would have said, lofty in her wisdom, to someone else. But we can't analyze our own situations with such reasonable objectivity. The men we love are always perfect. Of course they are, otherwise we wouldn't love them, would we? They're an extension of our good taste, a mirror image of our own perfection. They can't fail, because we've chosen them.

Like hell. They're lousy bastards, all of them. Insensitive, like Russell. She thought of the condescending words. "Strong, sensible, realistic" was she? He "wished her everything good" did he? He hoped to "have her as a friend." It was outrageous! How dare he sit there smugly writing his little kiss-off letter and probably thinking she should be grateful for having known him at all. Well, she wasn't grateful. She hoped he was miserable in his well-chosen, secure little future. She hated his guts.

Tears came at last. She didn't hate him. She wanted him. She would die, thinking of him married to someone else. If only she were there, instead of thousands of miles away, maybe she could change his mind. Suddenly she hated the ship. Sobbing, alone, she unreasonably hated even Mary, who'd brought her to this Godforsaken part of the world. If she hadn't left New York, this wouldn't have happened. She'd have fought for Russell. Used every trick she knew to keep him. She wished she were dead. There was no hope, no consolation, no future.

Slowly, she sat up. At least she had her pride. No one

knew how deep her feeling for him went. There'd been no one to confide in, thank God, so there was no one to pity her. I couldn't stand that, Jayne thought.

Taking deep breaths, she tried to compose herself before Mary returned to the cabin. She'd be the same flippant, nonchalant person the world thought she was. Maybe she'd take up with George again, or find some other attractive man aboard. But there were no attractive men. Mary had the only eligible, available one and he was a hundred years old. Fifty, at least. Forget it. A man was the last thing she wanted now. Maybe ever.

* * *

Terry Spalding was beginning to feel better. The pain of his lover's betrayal was slowly diminishing, as was the desperation that had caused him to take every penny he had in the world and spend it on this escape cruise. He'd never forget Paul. He'd never stop loving him. People didn't understand how deep the feelings between people of the same sex could go. He didn't expect them to. It was rare when you found someone like Jayne who sympathized without condemnation.

He was grateful for Jayne's friendship and he enjoyed her company although he didn't understand why she'd chosen to spend all her time with him this past week. She was a lusty, blatantly heterosexual girl who could have had any man on the ship. The officers were always inviting her to parties, asking her to dance, suggesting she go ashore with them. But since Auckland she'd seemed disinterested, preferring to spend her time with him. He was happy and thankful for that. He began to feel a strong attachment to her, not in any romantic way of course, but he'd developed a genuine fondness for her.

It won't last, he told himself realistically. Her devotion to me won't last. She feels sorry for me, that's all. But he hoped Jayne wouldn't find anyone else on this trip. She was the only thing that made it bearable for him. She was so amusing, so relaxing to be with. He could tell her anything and know she'd be interested and compassionate.

If I could spend my life with any woman, it would be Jayne, he thought. But that's out of the question for me. I'm not like Paul. I couldn't marry to provide myself with a cover of "respectability." That's what Paul did. In addition to wanting money and security, he wanted to appear "normal" for the sake of his business career in the brokerage house where he worked.

I couldn't do that, Terry thought. Thank God I don't have to. In the theater, it didn't matter what sexual persuasion you followed. People liked you for yourself, respected you for your talent, kept their noses out of your private life. Jayne would fit in to New York, I hope I'll see her. He stopped. What was he talking about? By that time Jayne would be married to some Brooks Brothers type and she'd have forgotten all about the "waif" she'd been so kind to.

But I'll never forget her, Terry thought. She doesn't know it, but she saved my life.

Chapter 8

"Well, now that you've had a quick look at my country, what do you think of it?"

Mary smiled lovingly at the long-legged figure sprawled in one of the deep leather chairs that flanked the picture windows of the Trafalgar Room. "You *know* what I think. Sydney is fabulous and everyone was so kind. It's lovely to meet people who actually like Americans. I've heard that in other foreign countries we're not so popular."

Christopher smiled back at the beautiful woman in the long, pale-green chiffon gown. They'd made a pact to dress for dinner every night, whether or not the daily program indicated "formal attire." He didn't give a damn what others wore. "I like to see you in evening clothes," he'd said. "I like watching you enter a room looking better than any other woman in the place." He thought now she'd never looked more desirable. "Australians are crazy about Yanks," he said in answer to her comment. "It's been that way since World War II. The British wrote us off. They had to, you know. There was no way they could protect us. But, as we say, you Americans came like the morning mail. We'll never forget it."

"I'm glad we did."

"To you, it's schoolbook history," Christopher teased. "You were just a kid. What, three, four years old when that war broke out? God, it seems impossible! I'm an old man compared to you. I'll be fifty-two in August. You're just a baby."

"Some baby! I'll be thirty-nine next month, for heaven's sake!"

Christopher widened his eyes in pretended astonishment. "As old as that! Fancy! And you're still a real Sheila."

"Sheila?"

"Sorry. I keep forgetting you don't speak Australian. 'Sheila' is our slang word for a good-looking woman."

"Why 'Sheila'? What's the derivation?"

"I haven't the faintest idea. English is our official language, but we've done weird things to it. There really are three kinds of English in our language. The original Australian is just about extinct. It's the tongue of the Aborigines and you never hear it except maybe in the outback. New Australian is the English you recognize, and Old Australian, spoken by most of the native-born, is called Aussie-English. It's full of slang words and expressions like 'Sheila' and some people think it's close to Cockney. I suppose it is, at that. We do say things like 'a bag of fruit' to mean 'a nice suit.' And most of the Australian you hear in the street is spoken through closed lips, with a definite slur."

"You don't talk that way."

"No, darling. I was educated in England, remember? But I can speak Aussie-English as well as the next bloke."

"Tell me some more."

Christopher considered. "All right. You're the kind of woman who makes any man take a 'dekko.' 'Dekko' means a look, not a twenties or thirties art form. And our waiter is a 'bloody little bottler,' which translates into someone who gives you particularly good service. I promise you I'll never 'bung on a blue,' meaning I won't get into a fistfight, particularly with a 'Pommy,' which is the word for an Englishman. I do know the derivation of 'Pommy.' Supposedly it comes from the letters P.O.H.M. which stood for 'Prisoners of Her Majesty' and which the

95

original convict settlers wore on their backs. Had enough?"

Mary was laughing. "No. Tell me more."

"I will not. You're turning me into the biggest fool this side of the black stump."

"The *what?*"

" 'The black stump' is an imaginary marker that designates the limits of unmeasurable distances. Therefore, the biggest fool this side of the black stump is the biggest fool in or out of this world. Simple, isn't it?"

"Absurd. I think I'd rather learn French."

Christopher sighed. "Such a difficult woman. Why couldn't I have taken up with a nice agreeable hero worshiper like Peggy Lawrence?"

"You don't have enough gold braid. Besides, I'd scratch her eyes out."

"Nicest thing you ever said to me." He leaned over and kissed her lightly.

Involuntarily, Mary drew back. "Christopher, don't. Someone might see."

"Let them. You don't think we're fooling anyone, do you? Darling, this ship is a floating small town. What the passengers don't see, the crew does. You don't honestly believe people don't know we make love in my cabin after lunch or that you sneak down the corridor late at night?"

Put so bluntly, the facts made her cringe. It was true. She wanted to believe that no one knew she was behaving in a way she'd never have believed possible: letting herself quietly into Christopher's cabin, sliding into bed beside him, forgetting for long, wonderful moments that there were any other hands than his.

"Don't look so ashamed. It's important and wonderful."

Mary nodded. "And frightening."

"It mustn't be," Christopher said. "You must never be frightened again. Promise me you won't."

She tried to look happy. "All right, I won't." Another lie. A little white one, the kind that made someone happy.

As though he read her mind, Christopher said, "At the race track, we call that a 'percentage lie.' You just want to please me, don't you? I know you're frightened, darling. Scared to death of the future. But it's going to be all right, Mary. No matter what, we're not going to lose each other."

* * *

Jayne awakened abruptly, wondering what had jolted her from her sleep. The radium dial of her bedside clock said ten minutes before two. The ship was pitching and tossing ferociously, almost throwing her from her bed. Something slid off the dresser and fell to the floor. She snapped on her reading light, worried about what was happening. I've heard that the waters of the Great Barrier Reef are rough, she thought, but this is ridiculous! Damn! A full ashtray had gone skittering off the dresser and landed upside down on the clean white robe she'd dropped beside her bed. What a mess! She glanced over to see whether her aunt was awake. The other bed was empty. Of course. It was always empty until nearly dawn when Mary came sneaking back into the cabin. Jayne always pretended to be asleep. Poor thing, she thought every night, I'm sure she's guilty enough without having to face me.

Jayne picked up the ashtray, secured the other dresser-top items firmly and knelt on her bed to look out the porthole. The waves were so high they crashed against the glass, but in the intervals between each onslaught, she could see a little boat bobbing precariously on the churning sea. She thought she was dreaming as she watched the small figure leave the boat and scramble onto the ship through the crew-deck entrance. What was going on in the middle of the night?

She turned as the cabin door opened. Mary came in, looking worried. "Are you all right?"

"Sure. It's kicking up a helluva fuss out there."

"I know. Half the ship is awake. Christopher and I were just about to leave the Trafalgar Room when it started. Peggy came in, full of dire warnings about cyclones at sea."

"She would. Madam Captain. There isn't going to be one, is there?"

"Of course not. It's just a bad storm. Probably be clear and beautiful tomorrow when we cruise Whitsunday Passage. Did you see the pilot boarding just now?"

"Is that who that was? What pilot?"

"The special one who's supposed to board in Sydney. He was home watching 'the telly.' He thought we sailed today instead of yesterday, so he missed us. Had to fly to Brisbane and board a few minutes ago in all this storm. He guides us through the Passage. Poor man. I don't know how he ever got aboard."

"It wasn't easy," Jayne said. "I thought I was seeing things." She looked out into the black, stormy night again. "There won't be much sleep for anybody tonight."

"No. Peggy says the waves are coming all the way up to Promenade." Mary sat down on her bed with a lurch. "Wow! This *is* rough! I was hanging onto the walls all the way back to the cabin."

"Maybe you'd feel safer with Christopher. Don't stay here on my account. I'm perfectly okay."

Mary didn't answer.

"I'm sorry, Aunt Mary. That wasn't meant to be a nasty crack. I just meant I think it's silly that we're playing games. I know you spend most of every night with Christopher. I'm all for it. I told you long ago I thought it was a good idea. You don't have to pretend with me. I'm glad you're happy." Her voice broke. "I'm glad one of us is happy."

"Jayne, what is it?" Mary forgot her own problems. "What's wrong?"

"Nothing."

"That's not true. You're miserable about something."

The sympathy in her aunt's voice got to her. Damn it, she hadn't meant anybody to know about Russell, but now it came pouring out, all of it, the whole story, told between choking sobs. Mary ached with pity for her, remembering how it felt to be that age, recalling how desperately in love with Michael she'd been, how she'd have been suicidal if he hadn't married her. She didn't think

98

the young took things so hard these days. Jayne seemed so independent, so self-assured. But human nature doesn't change, no matter what people say. Hearts ache in the seventies as they did in the fifties, as they have since the beginning of time. She staggered over to Jayne's bed and put her arms around the weeping girl.

"I'm so sorry, Jaynie. So terribly sorry."

Jayne wiped her eyes and tried to smile. "You can't win 'em all, to coin a phrase."

"Don't, honey. Don't try to be brave. You have a right to cry. I wish there were some words of comfort that weren't the old clichés. You know the answer—time. And some really nice young man who'll come along."

"Sure."

"I know you don't believe that now, but it's true." Mary hugged her. "Think you could get some sleep? Even with this rocking and rolling going on? Tomorrow will be a better day."

The girl nodded. "Thanks. Sorry I dumped all over you."

"I'm glad you did. Talking helps. I know that." She undressed and slid into her bed. Christopher was waiting for her. It was the first night since New Zealand that she hadn't been with him. He was probably disappointed, but she was too troubled to forget everything, even in his arms. Some nights it was better to lie quietly alone and try to make sense of things. In a little while she heard the sound of Jayne's even breathing. How wonderful it was to be young and resilient. Heartbroken as she was, Jayne's youth let her sleep, healing herself as she dreamed.

Not so with Mary. She lay awake all night, listening to the groaning and creaking of the ship as it fought the angry waters. Jayne would forget that selfish young man. In days to come she'd scarcely remember his name. If only I could do the same, Mary thought. There are two men in my life I'll never be able to forget. Because in a terrible, pulled-apart way I'm in love with both.

* * *

Michael picked up the mail and quickly skimmed it, happy to see a letter from Mary postmarked Sydney. Things took an unconscionable length of time to reach San Francisco from the other side of the world. He'd memorized the schedule. By the time he read her words from Australia, she was on her way to Bali. How he envied her that trip. He hadn't let her know how disappointed he was that she'd taken Jayne. Angry, really, though he didn't show it. Still, he didn't know how lonely he was going to be without her. In a way, he'd almost looked forward to the separation. It would be like being a bachelor again, he'd thought. And if some pretty young thing took his eye, well, what Mary didn't know would never hurt her.

But it hadn't worked out that way. He just hadn't been in the mood. Reading his wife's presumably lighthearted questions about Rae Spanner, he wondered what kept him from accepting her unmistakable invitation to stay on after the party. Rae was a damned good-looking woman and, he suspected, a sexy one. It wasn't his high moral character that kept him from cheating on Mary. He'd done that several times, unbeknownst to her, since their marriage. But they were always inconsequential adventures, most of them in Los Angeles when he went down to visit his mother, and they meant nothing to him. He supposed he was afraid that getting involved with Rae Spanner might lead to more serious trouble. She was not one to be brushed off, and rather than risk Mary's finding out, he'd pretended not to take her overtures seriously. He'd left the Valentine party early and had not seen her in the month since then.

In addition to his wariness about Rae, he'd been so damned caught up in trying to prepare a new proposal for Harry Carson that he'd hardly thought of anything else. He still hadn't finished it. It was boring and stupid to plan the kind of men's store Harry wanted. Michael hated the idea. He'd made a dozen false starts, knowing that anything so difficult to do must be wrong. But he had no choice.

He flipped through the bills, putting them aside, and

threw the advertisements and charity pleas into the waste-basket. At the bottom of the pile was a letter addressed to him in a handwriting he did not recognize. Surprised, he read Patricia's brief note. He barely knew Mary's sister, had seen her only on those rare visits to New York, spoken to her once on the phone. Now she was asking if it would be possible for her to come and stay at the apartment until Mary and Jayne returned!

"I'd so like to meet the ship when it docks," Patricia wrote. "I miss my child terribly and can't wait to see her and Mary again. And since I don't know San Francisco at all, I thought it would be fun to spend some time in advance of April 20. I wouldn't get in your way, Michael, and I'll be perfectly happy on your extra couch. But if it isn't convenient, don't hesitate to say so. I'll understand if the idea of a houseguest fills you with horror—even if it's a member of the family!"

She's right, Michael thought. The idea of a houseguest does fill me with horror. It will be a pain in the behind. But how can I refuse Mary's only sister? God, I'll have to take her sight-seeing and out to dinner, or prepare meals for her here! She'll get in my way just when I need to be alone to get this silly business started. Still, I can't say no.

He dashed off a letter saying he'd be delighted to have her and to let him know when she planned to arrive.

With alarming speed she responded that she'd come on March 25 if that was agreeable. He shouldn't bother to meet her at the airport. She'd take a bus to the terminal and a taxi from there, so unless she heard further, he could plan to see her that Monday afternoon and she was so appreciative and looked forward so much to her first vacation in years.

Michael couldn't believe it. He'd thought she'd come a few days before the ship returned and here she was planning to stay nearly a month! What's more, her arrival was less than a week away! He muttered a four-letter word. He'd have to give her the bedroom, of course, and he didn't look forward to sleeping on the convertible. For that matter, he didn't look forward to the whole damned thing. He supposed he could have made some excuse, but

Patricia knew the room was here. And Mary would be upset if he'd refused. She'd have a right to be angry since she paid the bills. It was really her apartment, Michael thought. He'd have to make her sister welcome.

* * *

Charlie Burke read his letter from Mary with pleasure and a sense of appreciation. She knew his diary was phony, written not only to satisfy the frustrated essayist within him but also to prepare her for the fact that most cruises were filled with boring people and she shouldn't be surprised if she found her fellow travelers less than stimulating. Apparently she had not. He wondered who the "handful of attractive, mature, un-lost souls" were. At least one of them must be a man.

He felt an unreasonable twinge of jealousy. He was fifty years old and married to a woman who'd live a long time, at least until she drank herself to death. Not that he wanted Tracey to die. He couldn't bring himself to wish that. But life with her was day after day, year after year of purgatory. A hundred times she'd told him she wanted to stop drinking, but of course she didn't. She made half-hearted attempts at psychiatry and gave it up after a few sessions; went to Alcoholics Anonymous meetings and quit after two weeks, saying they were a bunch of crazy extroverts who stood up and told the most disgusting things about their lives. She wasn't one of them, she told Charlie. She'd never been picked up drunk on the street or landed in the alcoholic ward of the City Hospital.

No, he'd thought, you haven't. Maybe it would be better if you had. Maybe it would shock you into realization of how sick you are. Instead, you drink quietly and steadily at home, knowing I'll come and find you either passed out or incoherent. Or, on more than one occasion, raving mad and violent.

She'd been younger than Mary when she became a heavy drinker. A pretty woman in her early thirties. They'd been married almost ten years when she went into her depression and began to seek forgetfulness in the

102

bottle. The doctors said she brooded over her inability to have children. She had three miscarriages in the first five years of their marriage, and they told her she could never go full term.

"Some women can't handle their barrenness," the doctors said. "They feel utter failures, to themselves and their husbands."

"But I don't care whether we have children," Charlie had protested. "I've told her that over and over. I've even said we could adopt if she wants babies so badly, but she refuses to listen to the idea."

"I know. These cases are beyond reason. Maybe analysis . . ."

Charlie had finally persuaded her to try it, but it didn't take. He knew it wouldn't. It couldn't, unless the patient really wanted it, and Tracey only went to please him. Just as she went to AA to please him, knowing full well she didn't believe in it. He gave up long ago, accepting the fact that this was their cross and they'd have to bear it. Unreasonably, he also felt some guilt for her condition. It wasn't only her childlessness that tore them apart, it was Tracey's feeling of inadequacy in other ways. She saw him become more and more successful in his business and felt herself being left behind. She didn't mix well with the wives of his associates and whenever they went to a business party she got drunk immediately, having fortified herself for the ordeal with several hefty shots of scotch before she left the house. She embarrassed him terribly at such times and there were terrible scenes when they got home. Eventually, he stopped taking her to these gatherings, an action which both relieved and angered her.

"I know I'm not smart enough for your friends," she said bitterly. "I'm just a dull, dreary housewife."

He'd lashed out sometimes. "You wouldn't be, damn it, if you'd stay sober! You think I've left you behind. Well, if I have, it's your own fault. You're as bright as any of those wives, except *they're* not falling-down drunk!"

She'd cry, then, and beg him not to leave her, she loved him so, she couldn't live without him. Charlie was always remorseful and apologetic. She couldn't help the way she was. It was despicable of him to say such cruel things to her.

It had been going on for five years when he met Mary and fell silently, hopelessly in love with her. He loved her in that fashion still. It was hard to be her friend, her mentor, when he wanted to be her lover. Yet there was comfort in seeing her every day, in watching her bloom into the personality he knew she could become. Half a loaf, but he settled for it. He even tried to like Michael, though he was convinced the man wasn't good enough for her. If he makes her happy, he's a good choice, Charlie tried to believe.

But Michael *wasn't* right for her. Charlie recognized that even before Mary told him a little of it. They seldom spoke of it these days. It was a taboo subject, just as his feelings for her were off limits in any conversation. He'd always felt that someday she'd meet someone who'd be all she deserved, and he wondered what would happen when that time came. Would she stay with Michael, out of pity and conscience, the way he stayed with Tracey? Or would she have the great good sense to grab at happiness while there still was time?

Funny. She mentioned no man in her letter, but Charlie felt this strange certainty that there was one. Good luck if there is, sweetheart, he said silently. Don't let him get away.

He opened the package of tapes that had arrived along with the letter and put the first one on the portable machine that was a duplicate of the one Mary carried. He listened with satisfaction to Colonel Beauregarde Calhoun Stanford. It was a wonderful interview. You could fall in love with this courtly gentleman of the old school, even forgive him his "chauvinist views," which he didn't recognize as such because he obviously adored women and wanted them on a pedestal to be worshiped.

Nice job, Charlie thought. He put on the second tape. Mary had interviewed her cabin stewardess, an unmistakably lower-class English girl with youthful charm and enthusiasm. She described life at sea, what it was like "below decks" in the crew dining room where a half-

104

dozen languages were spoken, and in the bar where the staff obviously had a rollicking good time when they were off duty. She told, under Mary's skillful prodding, how wonderful it was to see the world and be paid for the privilege and how most of the youngsters aboard signed on for that very reason and would leave the ship after their contracts were up.

Good. A real "Upstairs, Downstairs" approach. Charlie was equally pleased with the interview with a Catholic priest on Tonga who spent his life helping the poor on the island, running a school for the children, assisting the adults in setting up meager farms to support their pathetically modest needs. And the lady in Picton was just fine.

The fifth tape was an interview with the English captain. The man spoke fluently of his long naval background, beginning with his experiences on a British cargo ship in World War II as a young sailor and moving easily into the more glamorous life he now lived. Charlie listened carefully. Mary seemed intensely interested in everything Anthony Robin had to say, expressing surprise that he'd never married, laughing indulgently when he replied that the ship was all the woman he could handle and the sea a demanding mistress.

Was this the one? Charlie wondered. Maybe. Maybe not. Mary's seeming fascination with his story might indicate that she had more than a professional interest in the man. On the other hand, she gave the same rapt attention to everyone she talked to. It was the secret of her success. People knew she cared. The interviewee was flattered by it and the sincerity of her interest came across to the listener. Probably he was only imagining there was something different in the way she spoke to the captain. Of course he was. Mary wasn't the kind to go chasing after the officers on a ship.

He snapped off the machine. Nearly two hours had passed as he sat listening to her voice. It was the best two hours he'd had since she left.

Chapter 9

Bali was a dream. Everything was as Mary had pictured it—the beautiful, graceful people in their exotic and brilliantly colored clothes; the ornate, golden temples of Balinese Hinduism; the breathtaking sight of Gunung Agung, the ten-thousand-foot peak towering above the rice paddies. It was unbearably hot, but they didn't mind. She and Christopher went ashore in a ship's launch, laughingly fended off the noisy souvenir sellers and tourist guides at the pier and found their own pixyish cab driver who took them to Ubud, a microscopic village forty kilometers from the main town of Benoa.

In a tiny art gallery, they drank coffee and bought a painting and, almost shyly, Mary asked the owner if she'd consent to talk into the machine for the American radio. Politely, the woman agreed. In halting, charmingly broken English, she told them something of life on the small Indonesian island. Under Mary's questioning, she described the food and its preparation, with emphasis on the steamed rice called *nasi,* a word also used to mean food itself. She spoke reverently of her religion built around Sanghyang Widi, the Supreme Being of the Balinese, portrayed as a symbolic male figure with flames shooting out from his body. She described feast days and offerings to pacify evil spirits and, her eyes shining, the beauty of Balinese dances and drama, all rich with symbolism. Enchanted, Mary listened, interrupting only when the woman seemed to falter, and at the end she impulsively kissed the smooth cheek of her obliging "guest."

"The people in America will be so interested. We can't imagine this kind of peaceful, gentle life."

"Not always peaceful in Bali. Sometimes Agug spit fire."

Mary looked questioningly at Christopher.

"She means a volcanic eruption," he said. "Mount Agug and Mount Batur erupted in the early sixties. Wiped out whole villages and killed thousands in eastern Bali."

"Gentleman is correct. But our mountains the home of gods. We look *up* for help. Not out to sea like some peoples." She smiled. "We look up for love and protection. Always *up*. Bali once a flat land but gods raised mountains to live in. Agug most holy of all."

"Thank you," Mary said. "You've been wonderful."

The woman bowed. "You come back. Always welcome."

Christopher answered for them. "We'll be back, madame. You can count on it."

* * *

Jayne was already in the shower when Mary returned carrying her painting, a lovely piece of batik and her precious tape. In a moment, the girl emerged, wrapped in a towel.

"That island was like a sneak preview of hades! I've been standing under ice-cold water for ten minutes! Nice day?"

"Perfect. I even got a great interview. Did you have fun?"

Jayne nodded. "I went ashore with Terry. Took a drive and ended up having a late lunch at the Hong Kong restaurant. It was so funny. Nobody spoke a word of English, but Terry had five pretty little Balinese waitresses hanging around the table watching him eat. They looked like they'd like to kidnap him."

Mary was noncommittal. "He is a handsome young man."

Jayne stepped into her bra and panties. "You know," she said thoughtfully, "I'm not sure Terry's gay. That is, I know he's gay, but I think he could be bisexual. He was flirting like crazy with those girls. I think he's even turned on by me."

Mary tried not to show her dismay. Since the night of the storm, Jayne hadn't referred to her broken romance with Russell and Mary considerately hadn't reminded her of it. But now she said, "Jayne, you're not getting any silly ideas about Terry, are you?"

"You mean like maybe trying to get him into bed? I've been thinking about it. Why not?"

"That's not the answer to your unhappiness. And you might create more for him."

The girl raised her chin in a defiant gesture that reminded Mary of her own youthful rebellion. "It might be the best thing I can do for both of us. Terry's never slept with a woman. It could change his whole life."

"Darling, be sensible. You're not the first woman who's ever thought she was the one to change a man's sexual preference. Unfortunately, it rarely works." Mary tried to sound light-hearted. "There's a little bit of conceit in that kind of thinking, my dear. As though only you in all the world could be so fascinating that Terry would 'see the light.' "

"I'm not sure that isn't true."

"Jayne, it isn't the answer for you," Mary said again. "You're hurt. You're confused and rebounding. You won't get even with Russell this way. Don't do it."

"What have I got to lose? My God, I'm not talking about marrying Terry! It's just an experiment. I've never tried it before." She sounded angry.

"You don't experiment with people's psyches! It's too much like playing God!"

Jayne didn't answer. Mary looked at the half-clad young body. How beautiful she was. Beautiful enough, perhaps, to stir even Terry. But it was no good. Mary knew other women who married gay men in the honest belief they could "reform" them. Strangely enough, some of the marriages lasted, though she wondered how they did. How could a woman share her husband with another man? Bad enough to fight a female rival, but a male would be impossible competition. She was being silly. Jayne had no intention of marrying the boy. She wasn't that foolish. But there was little doubt she was going to try to seduce him. It could be a disaster for both of them and yet there was no way to stop her. The more I argue against it, Mary thought, the more she'll be determined to do it. I just have to hope that Terry isn't as curious as she is.

* * *

Peggy Lawrence was furious. Damn Christopher Andrews! He was the one who'd talked Mary into going ahead with her plans for China instead of staying in Hong Kong to act as Peggy's matron of honor. The man had Mary twisted around his little finger and she couldn't see what a fool she was making of herself. Peggy had seen enough of these shipboard romances in the past three years to know they ended as abruptly as they began. Andrews was smooth. No doubt about that. And Mary was totally taken in. The whole ship was gossiping about her infatuation. Angry when Mary told her she couldn't do her the favor she asked, Peggy had told her just that.

"You're really making a spectacle of yourself," she'd said coldly. "Everyone knows you're a married woman. Besides, what kind of example do you think you're setting for your niece? Really, Mary, I'm shocked by your behavior!"

Not knowing whether to be upset or to laugh at the incongruity of Peggy's criticism, Mary chose to be calm. "I really doubt that Christopher and I are of that much interest to anyone. We're not children, after all. As for Jayne, she's a young adult, quite capable of making her assessments. I'm sorry to disappoint you about the wedding, Peggy. I know that's why you're upset. But it's not really Christopher's fault that I'm going to stay with my original plan. One of the main attractions of this cruise was the chance to go into China."

Despite her reasonable tone of voice, Mary was disturbed. It wasn't just the fact that she was being talked about, though she hated that. And heaven knows it wasn't as though she was doing anything Jayne thought even mildly shocking. Peggy's words had stirred up feelings she was continually trying to suppress. She tried not to think of Michael, alone at home, believing in her, trusting her implicitly.

And less important but not to be ignored was the fact that after this blow-up she'd have to face Peggy every day for another month. Discounting shore trips, that meant another twenty or so strained dinners at the same table with a woman who disapproved of her. Maybe after they were married Peggy and Tony would dine in his cabin. No, that wouldn't work. Part of the captain's duties was to preside at his own table of VIPs. It's a stupid arrangement, their getting married in the middle of a trip, Mary thought with annoyance. If Peggy weren't so hungry for a husband, she'd have the good sense to wait until Tony had shore leave. And how dare she criticize me anyway? If there's a spectacle aboard, she's it! Wrong. The truth was that Tony and Peggy were both free agents. Questionable taste as it might be for the captain to have his lady love aboard, there was no adultery involved, as there was with her.

Christopher was furious when she reported the conversation to him on the way to Singapore.

"That bloody bitch! How dare she talk to you that way?"

"Don't get so upset or you'll make me sorry I told you. We still have to look at her at dinner between here and Yokohama."

"Maybe I should try to get us a table for two."

"Christopher! Don't you dare! Good lord, if there's talk now, think what that would do! Besides, I'm traveling with Jayne, remember? I can't just waltz off and leave her."

"I could get a table for three."

"No. It's out of the question."

He looked at her, half amused. "You can be a very determined lady when you choose to, can't you? I'm quite sure you're used to making decisions and having them obeyed. All right. In this I concede, but don't think you're setting a precedent with me, my love! I'm stronger and tougher and meaner than you, even if I'm not as pretty."

* * *

"Gin."

Colonel Stanford turned a baleful eye on the woman across the card table. Gail DeVries smiled innocently.

"I've been having a great run of luck on this trip, haven't I, Beau? Let's see, we've played gin rummy every morning since San Francisco and you now owe me forty-seven dollars and fifty cents. I think I'll let you spend it on me in China."

"I don't think there'll be anything worth forty-seven dollars in China. Besides, little lady, I'm not sure they're going to let us in. You saw the brochure. They're recommending it only to people in good health, without handicaps."

"So? We're in good health and neither of us has a handicap."

"You don't think old age is a handicap?"

Gail bristled. "I certainly do not! We're not infirm, either of us. And as for all that warning nonsense about lots of walking and very few public toilets, who cares? I mean to go into China, Beau, and I certainly don't intend to let longevity stop me! My lord, the Chinese are supposed to revere old people!"

"The Chinese, maybe, but what about the Occidentals? They're the ones who'll decide whether we're up to making the trip."

"Well, I'm not going to let some whippersnapper of a young tour director decide whether I can go or not!" Gail was vehement. "I don't know if I'll ever get this way again, and I don't intend to miss it. I won't let you miss it, either. For heaven's sake, Beauregarde, you're not going

111

to die in Canton!" She smiled. "It would be much too inconvenient."

She delighted him. How lucky he was to have a friend like this enthusiastic, cheerful woman. Other men his age were sitting in rockers on their children's front porches or, worse still, withering away in some old folks' home. But he had his trip with Gail to look forward to every year, and his weekly correspondence between times to keep him feeling alive and interested. His children and grandchildren didn't understand. To them, old people were stereotypes, useless, ancient things to be tucked quietly into a corner and given a decent amount of respect and attention. They were also sure he was squandering their inheritance on these expensive trips. Crazy kids. They didn't know there'd be plenty left for them if he died tomorrow.

Of course, all that silly talk about being buried at sea was just part of his conversational patter. He knew cruise ships had their own morgues aboard. They had to, on long voyages such as this. He'd never seen it, but he'd heard they had a place for three or four bodies. Statistically, it was to be expected that with a passenger list of primarily elderly people, they had to be prepared for the possibility of death aboard, and for handling the deceased until they reached the next port from which the unfortunate one could be shipped home. Gail knew how to handle that for him if it happened. They'd exchanged that information on their second cruise. She knew what to do if he died. And he knew what to do for her. Of course, the odds were it wouldn't occur. They were lucky, both of them, to be so robust. They'd probably take quite a few more trips together. He hoped so. It was a lifesaver for both of them, in more ways than one.

"All right," he said, packing up the cards and score pad. "China it is. Mary is going, isn't she?" Gail had told him what Mary had confided in her: that Peggy wanted her to stay in Hong Kong for the wedding.

"Yes, thank goodness, she's going. Christopher put his foot down. But her niece has decided against it. She and Terry are going to take in the sights in Hong Kong."

"I see. Well, I suppose it will be gay for the young folks."

She raised her eyebrows. Was her old friend deliberately making a play on words? They'd never discussed Terry. She wasn't sure whether Beau knew about him. Homosexuals were something he probably gave no thought to, and they'd never discussed Terry's "condition" as she thought of it. For that matter, she realized, Terry was a good deal less obvious than he'd been at the start of the trip. The jewelry had disappeared and he seemed, somehow, more confident, even more, well, manly. Maybe Jayne was having a good influence on him. Gail frowned. She certainly hoped that nice child wasn't deluding herself. In San Francisco, Gail had met many young men like Terry, friends of her granddaughters'. She knew about the "gay community," but she wasn't sure Beau had that much knowledge of it. He was not an unsophisticated man, but his life in Atlanta was different. She doubted, even now, he realized what Terry was. She wouldn't tell him. It might not sit well and she wouldn't want to upset him or have him upset Terry. She liked that boy. He was sweet and sensitive. She wished he were different. He and Jayne made such a handsome pair.

* * *

They'd arrive in Singapore on the twenty-first, just two days from now, and Jayne and Terry were making their plans for the shore excursion. There's such a change in him, the girl thought, as she listened to him reading from the information booklet the ship provided in advance of every port.

"We have to have a drink at Raffles," Terry said. "A Singapore Sling, naturally. In honor of Somerset Maugham. And we'll go to Chinatown. Do you know you can still see old women with bound feet from their youth? And we should have dinner at the open market on Orchard Street. How are you with chopsticks?"

"Terrific. No self-respecting New York girl grows up

113

not knowing how to eat with chopsticks. Next to kosher delis we specialize in Chinese restaurants."

Terry laughed. "You make everything such fun, Jayne." He sobered. "When I came aboard, I never thought I'd have fun again."

"You feel better about Paul."

He swallowed hard at the mention of the name, but he was glad Jayne was always so direct. It was one of the things he liked best about her. "Yes, I feel better. I'm still hurt, but I've come around to feeling angry, too. That's healthy, I guess."

"You bet your damn boots it's healthy!" Jayne looked at him affectionately. They were still friends, nothing more, but she hadn't forgotten what she'd said to Mary in the cabin. At the time, it had been almost an effort to shock. She wasn't sure she'd meant it seriously. But now she was genuinely devoted to Terry. If she got him into bed, it would be more than an experiment. It might well be a loving experience. Terry was sensual, as she was. She looked at the lean, hard young body under the thin cotton shirt and felt genuine desire. But what about him? As though to test him, she said, casually, "How about Bugis Street? I hear that's where the action is after midnight."

He wasn't deceived. He knew what was in her mind. Bugis Street was famous. Or notorious. That's where the "girls" paraded their wares, moving up and down the wide alley, past street cafes, looking for clients. Some of them were female prostitutes, often accompanied by their pimps, openly inviting the willing sailors who flocked to Bugis Street. But there were even more who weren't girls at all, but who were also looking for business. Men "in drag" were a large part of the passing parade. Terry had heard all about them from friends who'd been to Singapore. There was even a changing room in the shape of a corner cafe. Young men disappeared into this shuttered structure and reappeared minutes later wearing extravagant female attire, clinging dresses slit to the hip, luxurious wigs and makeup. Bugis Street was decadence personified. Anything you wanted was there, yours for the taking at a gesture. Jayne knew about Bugis Street too. She was probing.

For a minute he resented it. If he wanted to pick up a young man, it wasn't her business. But he didn't. Not that he might not be happy to find a replacement for Paul someday, but when he did, it would be a civilized long-term arrangement. He wasn't one for this tawdry kind of chance encounter. He looked directly into Jayne's eyes.

"I think we should see Bugis Street," he said. "Together. I hear it's a unique spectacle."

Her eyes gave him a warm, approving response.

* * *

After Patricia announced her impending arrival in San Francisco, Michael dashed off a letter to Mary. With luck, she'd receive it before the ship left Hong Kong on March 29. In his note, he made light of the visit he dreaded.

> I can't say I really relish putting up with a female guest for such a long stay, but she seemed so anxious I couldn't very well say no. Anyway, I made a reservation for her and Jayne at the St. Francis for the night of April 20, in the devout hope they'll go home next day. I'm sure, fond as you are of Jayne, you'll have had plenty of her by that time. I'm damned sure I'll be glad to see the last of your sister, no matter how little trouble she is. And I certainly don't want anybody around to spoil our first night together after so long!
>
> Harry Carson and I are still talking about the boutique and I'm making a few minor changes in the plan. I'm sure it's in the bag and things will be rosy from there on.

In his mind, it was all true. He did feel unable to refuse Patricia's request. And he was eager to have Mary home. It seemed forever since he'd been to bed with her, and

115

though their love life wasn't that great after fifteen years, it satisfied him. Most of the time.

As for Harry, well, he'd decided not to knuckle under to Harry's stupid demands. He'd make minor changes in the plan, but not many. If that fool didn't like them, he could go to hell. But Harry would go along in the end. Michael was sure of it.

When Patricia arrived less than a week later, he was stunned. Either he hadn't paid her much attention before or she'd undergone a transformation. In any case, she was a beauty.

"Michael!" She kissed him on the cheek. "It's so good to see you!" She stepped back and looked him over appraisingly. "I'd forgotten how handsome you are. My sister's a lucky woman."

He felt himself blushing like a schoolboy. "Good to see *you,* Patricia. How was the trip?"

"Fabulous. I felt as though I were running away from home." She gave a throaty laugh. "As a matter of fact, I am. Not literally, of course. Don't get nervous that you'll be stuck with me forever. But it's marvelous to have a change of scene! And you're a darling to take me in."

"Happy to have you here." To his own surprise, he found it was true. She was as ebullient as she was good-looking. *She'll be nice to have around,* Michael thought. *I didn't realize how empty this place has been.* He felt suddenly comforted. It was like having a part of Mary here, a gayer, more enthusiastic Mary. He couldn't believe Patricia was seven years older than her sister. She didn't look a day over thirty-five. The shining blond hair fell to her shoulders and the makeup, though too heavy, was skillfully applied to a perfect, unlined skin. Obviously, she worked hard at looking young. The effect was just a little cheap, he realized. A little out of keeping for a woman her age. But it was dramatic, and combined with the good figure and the pantsuit, which emphasized the extraordinary length of her legs, it made for a woman any man would turn to stare at as she passed.

"Let me show you to the bedroom. I'm sure you'd like to unpack."

She held up a long, well-manicured hand in protest. "Now don't give me an argument. I'm not taking your room. I know Mary has a couch in her office and that will suit me just fine. All I need is a place to hang up a few things."

"Nonsense. Mary would kill me if I let you sleep there. Not that it's all that uncomfortable. I mean, I don't mind it, and you're our guest."

"Well, if you're sure. . . . But I do feel I'm inconveniencing you terribly, Michael."

"Not for a minute."

"You're very sweet. I can understand why Mary's so crazy about you."

Again, he felt vaguely uncomfortable and didn't know why. Hell, she was only being pleasant. Grateful that he allowed her to impose for such a lengthy stay. But he felt a surge of physical excitement. She was the most provocative woman he'd met in years. Patricia could make a banal conversation sound like an invitation to seduction. Ridiculous! Was he crazy, having such thoughts about his sister-in-law? It was disgusting. She'd slap his face if she could read his mind. He'd been too long without a woman, that was all. More than a month. He'd better sneak out one of these nights soon and find himself something. After all, a man had his needs. Maybe Rae. No. Better a stranger. There was that cute little secretary in Harry Carson's office. She gave him the eye every time he went in. Sure. Why not? If Mary left him alone so long she couldn't expect him to live like a monk. Next week when he went to see Harry, he'd see what else he could accomplish.

Chapter 10

"I wish you were going into China with us."

Jayne, busily inspecting the mound of things she'd bought the first day in Hong Kong, shook her head. "Terry doesn't care about it. He wants to do the restaurants and night clubs and, of course, shop. Did you ever, in your life, see such a city for encouraging bankruptcy? We've been here eight hours and I've already bought enough stuff to open my own boutique on Madison Avenue!"

Mary looked with interest at the array that covered Jayne's bed: a palm-sized transistor radio, a camera, yards of silk fabric, an exqusite mandarin coat, assorted pieces of ivory. One lovely piece, in particular, caught her eye. It was a delicately carved ivory figure of a Chinese woman, a superb nude with carved flowers in her hair and a bouquet of them held against her breast. The gleaming figure rested on a teak base about twelve inches long, as though it were reclining on a bed.

"What's that fascinating thing?"

"Isn't it wonderful? They call it a 'doctor doll.' Unfortunately, it's a reproduction of the antique ones, but I love it just the same. Do you know about them, Aunt Mary? In the old days, Chinese ladies wouldn't undress in front of their doctors, so they had these dolls and could

118

point to the spot where their complaint was. Terry bought it for me."

"It's beautiful." She hesitated. "I didn't know Terry was interested in female nudes."

"He is now," Jayne said. "In fact, he has been ever since we left Singapore."

There was no mistaking her meaning. So she did it, Mary thought. She actually seduced him. She admitted to herself that she was curious, but she'd bite off her tongue before she'd ask her niece to tell her more.

"Come on," the girl said, laughing. "You know you're dying to hear about it. Don't be so bloody tactful. I don't mind telling you. It's been great, Aunt Mary. For both of us. It's like introducing a child to the mysteries of the birds and bees. He's struck dumb by the magic. Oh, the first time was a little awkward, I admit. But since then, it's as though he can't live without me. And believe me, I don't mind. He's a beautiful person, spiritually as well as physically. God, when I compare him with that insensitive Russell. . . ."

Mary didn't know what to say. Apparently she'd been wrong in her fears that Jayne would only further confuse herself and Terry by trying to have an affair with him. Obviously, it had worked well. So much for my curbstone psychology, she thought. Jayne's instincts are better than my limited knowledge. The girl was looking at her, waiting for a reaction.

"You still disapprove."

"No, darling, I just don't want to see either of you hurt by this."

Jayne's face softened and her voice became almost a whisper. "We won't be. I think it's the best thing that ever happened to me in my whole life. I didn't know a man could be so gentle, so worshipful and still so virile. He's tried before, Aunt Mary, but never with someone who cared for him. You know, he cried that first night. Actually wept. I held him in my arms for hours, soothing him as though he were a child. He's happy, and so am I."

Mary kept still. This was wrong. She still felt it. Jayne was the mother Terry was looking for. He was acting out

119

a fantasy. No, I mustn't think such things! I have to believe she's the one-in-a-million woman who can change a young man like Terry. And I can only pray that they'll say good-bye in San Francisco without having done some terrible emotional damage to each other. She looked at Jayne, radiant in her new-found happiness. At least for the moment she's forgotten how miserable she was. That's something to be grateful for.

"Be careful, darling," Mary said. "That's all I ask."

"You mean don't get pregnant?"

"No, I mean take this for what it is—a very special moment in time that both of you will remember with gratitude and affection. You're both getting over bad love affairs, finding consolation with each other. Don't read more into it than that, Jayne dear. Don't try to continue it when the trip ends."

Her aunt's lack of belief in miracles stung the young woman. Mary didn't know what she was talking about. She hadn't been there during those hours of lovemaking, hadn't seen the joy in Terry's eyes. She was spouting textbook psychology and it infuriated Jayne.

"I hope you're going to take your own advice," she said. "Speaking of 'special moments in time,' I trust that's how you look on your own affair with Christopher. You do have a loving husband at home, as I recall. Or had you forgotten?"

The bitter outburst did not anger Mary. "I haven't forgotten," she said quietly. "Perhaps it's because I haven't forgotten that I'm so concerned about you. I don't want to see you make the same mistake I did."

"Don't tell me Michael was ever gay!"

"No. Of course not. But he also wanted someone to cling to. Someone always there to soothe and comfort and protect. You're very like me, Jayne. Perhaps that's why I love you so much and fear for you at the same time. You could fall into the same trap I did, choosing someone who needed your strength, a man who made you feel superhuman. You're strong, as I am. And our strength is our weakness where men are concerned. We mother them, excuse them, feel some misguided obligation to take care of

120

them. It's wrong, Jaynie. We end up unhappy and unful-filled, and guilty because of our feelings."

Her niece stared at her. "I didn't know," she said. "I didn't know how you felt. I always was kind of sorry for Uncle Mike. I thought you dominated him because you liked having a pet on a leash. I didn't know you felt empty and miserable. I'm sorry, Aunt Mary. You always seemed so much in charge of your life. I thought you had everything you wanted. Funny. I never thought you had problems of your own. All I saw was a career and a fancy apartment and a good-looking man who adores you. It never occurred to me that wasn't enough. I can see now why you're so attracted to Christopher. He's everything Mike isn't, I suppose—successful, demanding, unmanage-able. What are you going to do about him?"

"I don't know. He wants me to marry him."

"And you want to."

"Yes, I do." It was strange to say it aloud for the first time. "But I don't know whether I can. I didn't tell you, but I came on this trip to think about whether or not I wanted to go on with my marriage. I was uncertain even before I met Christopher. He hasn't changed my thinking that much. I mean, I'm not one of those women who predicates her future on the next man. Even if there'd been no Christopher, I'd still have to decide by the time I got back whether I wanted to stay with Michael or set him free."

"Set *him* free?"

"Yes. I'm not sure that marriage to me isn't worse for him than marriage to him is for me. I've helped make him more dependent and helpless than he already was. I didn't want to. Not consciously. But I did. I'm torn between thinking it would be the greatest kindness I ever did both of us, or the greatest disaster."

Jayne looked at her with pity. "You still love him, don't you?"

"In a way. But I can't respect him, maybe because I can't respect myself. All my life I've wanted to be *some-body*, Jayne. I watched my mother, your grandmother, sublimate herself to her husband. She's no more than a mirror image of my father. I saw your own mother throw her life away because she couldn't resist flaunting her beauty. I never had beauty, Jayne, but I made up my mind somewhere early on that I'd be more in control of my life than either of those two handsome women. I'd find a man who adored me because I was competent and smart. One who'd love me because he needed me." Mary gave a little laugh. "Well, I did. And I have no right to blame him because he succeeded at that. He shouldn't pay for my conceit." She paused. "And Terry is too nice a boy to pay for yours. He needs you. He worships you. He's even discovered that with you 'normal sex' can be good. But that won't be enough for you in the long run, I'm afraid. And probably not for him, either."

"I'm not going to marry him, Aunt Mary. I'm not going to marry anybody."

"I'd hate to think you meant that. About not marrying anybody, I mean. When it's right, marriage is the best state of all."

"Do you know any that are right? Would you call your parents' marriage ideal? Or mine? How about your own? And what do you think Peggy and Captain Robin's chances are when they do that dumb thing here? No, I'm not going to marry Terry or anybody else. I'll love someone and live with him. Terry, maybe. But no marriage. Marriage is strictly for procreation and I want no part of that."

Mary sighed. Jayne had a right to be disillusioned about marriage. The knowledge of her own conception was enough to make her cynical about matrimony and its aftermath. Yet Mary was romantic enough to believe it could be good. It would be with Christopher, she thought. I know it would.

"Well, let's hope we both come out of our situations intact," she said finally. "You're a sensible girl, Jayne. Use the brains God gave you. That's all I ask." She managed to smile. "And I'll try to use the ones He gave me."

"Right." Jayne obviously was glad to end the discussion. "You and Christopher going on the town tonight?"

"No. We're having an early dinner aboard. We have to

122

get up at five o'clock. Breakfast is at six and we leave by train at seven. Which reminds me, I must put my jewelry in the safe-deposit box at the purser's desk. We mustn't wear any into China. Nothing but a wedding ring and a watch."

"Why? Will it be solen?"

"Not by the Chinese. I'm told you could leave all your money lying out on the dresser and if any of it was missing it would be because somebody in the tour group pinched it. The Chinese are very honest. And very moral. The Party doesn't allow them to be anything else. It's just that it isn't good taste to be overdressed in The People's Republic." Mary self-consciously fingered her new ring. "Look what Christopher bought me today."

Jayne stared at the jade and diamond ring and whistled. "That's some gorgeous! It must have cost a fortune even in Hong Kong."

"It did. I didn't want to take it, but he insisted."

"An engagement ring?"

Mary looked troubled. "He'd like it to be, but I wouldn't accept it on that basis. I can't. Not now. Maybe not ever."

The sadness in her voice tore at Jayne's heart. "Think about your own happiness, Aunt Mary. Please. And Christopher's too. He's a very, very nice man. As nice as you are a woman."

Mary tried not to cry. Damn it, all she did these days was puddle up! She blinked back the tears and nodded. "I'll try," she said. "I'll really, truly try."

* * *

Dressing for dinner, Christopher thought about the day. A lovely day. Lovelier even than Mary knew. He'd been afraid she might get suspicious when he left her for a couple of hours that afternoon, but she unquestioningly accepted his lie that he had to meet some business associates.

"Don't worry about it," she said. "I won't get lost. In fact, I think I'll head right back to the Ocean Terminal

123

where we're docked. I'm dying to explore all those shops. Floors of them! A whole arcade full of gorgeous things right at the bottom of the gangway. What bliss! I'll meet you aboard later. Good luck with your meeting."

He'd put her in a cab, made sure the driver understood his instructions and watched her disappear. Then he took another and headed for Queen Mary Hospital. He'd not felt up to par since Singapore. Nothing serious, he was sure, but since that damned heart attack five years ago he took no chances. Queen Mary's was the center of Western medicine in this part of the world. He'd simply have a precautionary check.

On the way back to the ship he felt wonderful. The doctors diagnosed it as nothing. Maybe a touch of indigestion. Or too much wine every night at dinner. He was fit as the proverbial fiddle and delighted he'd gone to make sure. In the cab, he smiled to himself. Maybe it's a good omen, he thought. The Queen Mary Hospital was the setting for Han Suyin's book *Love Is a Many Splendored Thing.*

* * *

Terry stepped out of the shower, dried himself and walked, naked, to the closet. He opened the door and stood looking at his reflection in the full-length mirror on the inside. He'd never been vain about his firm young body though he'd often been complimented on it. His earliest memories were of his mother parading him, nude, in front of her women friends.

"Isn't he adorable, my little man? What a handsome fellow Mummy's precious is going to be!"

He'd only been four or five at the time but he remembered his embarrassment even then. In an instinctive gesture he'd tried to cover himself and he could still hear the ladies laughing as Theresa Spalding had picked him up and carried him out of the room, cuddling him to her. Damn her! Terry thought. She even named me for herself. Or as close as she could come.

It was years, many years, before he saw her as the

destructive influence she was. In his childhood and adolescence, he'd hated the father who abandoned them when Terry was seven. It was a hatred fostered by Theresa, who reminded him over and over that Maurice Spalding was a cruel and unfaithful man who left his wife and only child to marry another woman.

"You're all I have, baby," she said. "Promise you'll never leave me. No one could ever love you as I do. You're my life."

He'd thought she was wonderful and stayed with her most of the time. At ten, he was playing bridge with her and her cronies. He went with her when she bought her clothes, hovered around when she cooked dinner, sat with her in the evenings watching the ugly, cathedral-shaped television set. They were one of the first in his mother's group to have the new TV, bought with the alimony check Maurice sent every month, year after year.

He'd read and studied enough to know now that his formative years almost predictably led him to compare all women to his mother and find them wanting. In high school, he had a few dates, but he found the giggling, overperfumed girls nauseating and he soon stopped seeing friends his own age. The girls were repulsive and the boys thought only of them or of football and basketball, neither of which Theresa would let him play lest he get hurt.

He didn't go to college. Maurice's money didn't stretch that far. After high school he got a job ushering in a movie theater and there he met other young men like himself, all of whom wanted to be actors. He decided he wanted that, too. Since Theresa wouldn't accept a penny from him, he used his small salary to pay for lessons at a drama school. He got a few small parts in local productions. He also took his first step into the gay community where, after a few chance encounters, he met Paul and fell desperately in love with him. Terry was twenty-two, still living at home. Paul was thirty, making a name for himself in the brokerage business and able to afford a nice apartment where he and Terry met several evenings a week. Terry never stayed overnight. Theresa would have disapproved. Theresa, in fact, disapproved of Paul, not

125

because she knew what he was, but because she saw him as a rival for Terry's time, a serious threat to her own monopoly.

"I do wish you'd take out some nice girls, Terry darling, instead of spending all your time with that dreary young man."

"I don't know any nice girls, Mother."

"Of course you do! What about that pretty little Jo-Anne Peterson? Her mother's a dear friend of mine. I'm sure Jo-Anne would love to go out with such a handsome boy!"

He couldn't tell her that Jo-Anne was a tramp. Everybody knew what a nymphomaniac she was.

"She's not my type. Honest."

"Nonsense! You've never had a date with her. How would you know?"

She nagged and prodded until Terry finally agreed to call Jo-Anne. Not that Theresa wanted him to be interested in any girl. It was her way of trying to pry him away from Paul. He called and Jo-Anne agreed to see him. They went to a movie and he took her home.

"Why don't you come in? The family's away for the weekend. We could have some fun."

The idea made him sick. "No thanks, Jo-Anne. I'd better get home."

"Why? Mama waiting up for you?"

"No. She's visiting my aunt."

Jo-Anne leaned against him in the car, letting her hand run languidly across his leg. "It's true what they say, isn't it, Terry? You really are queer."

For some inexplicable reason, the condescending tone enraged and excited him. He'd never been with a woman, but now he got out of the car, opened the door on her side and almost dragged her out and into the house.

"I'll show you how queer I am!"

It had been terrible. He'd been awkward and fumbling, and though the aroused girl tried to help him, he could do nothing. He felt dirty and degraded, unable to look at her as he got into his clothes. Jo-Anne lay on her bed, laughing at him.

126

"Don't worry," she said. "The first time's the hardest." She giggled at the vulgar double entendre. "I mean, it'll be better next time."

He hadn't answered, but he knew there'd be no next time. Not with her. Not with any woman, the clutching, panting things.

A year later, Theresa Spalding died of cancer. Terry didn't attempt to notify his father. He left that to the lawyers. She left him the house, which he sold, and he moved in with Paul. For three years he was very happy. The career progressed slowly, but he didn't particularly care. He had a few thousand dollars in the bank and all his expenses paid by Paul.

And then in January, Paul told him he was getting married.

"I have to, Terry," he said. "You don't understand. I'm in a very macho business where the social side means a lot. I have to entertain and mix with my associates and their wives. I'm thirty-four and they're beginning to wonder why I'm single."

Terry was hurt and angry. "You mean they're beginning to suspect you're a closet queen," he said spitefully.

"If you want to put it that way."

"Damn you! How can you do this to me? It's been four years, Paul! Nobody but you."

"I'm sorry, Terry. Will you be all right?"

"What the hell do you care? You'll never want to see me again. I might embarrass you in front of your precious straight associates!"

"No, I won't see you. You're right about that. But I still care what happens to you. Do you need money?"

"No. I don't need anything. God help you, Paul. I hope you know what you're doing. And God help that poor stupid woman who's marrying you."

"She knows. She's older and very worldly, but she's made it a condition that I don't see you."

Devastated, Terry had booked himself on the cruise that left a week later. He was at loose ends. All he wanted was to get as far away from San Francisco as possible, from everything that reminded him of his lost love.

127

For days on end he'd done nothing but think. He saw his mother as she really was—a sick, possessive, destroying woman. He saw Paul, who cared more for himself and his career than he did for Terry. And he saw himself, empty, caring for nothing.

Somehow Jayne had changed all that. She was at first a friend, the first woman friend he'd ever had. She was casual, undemanding, sympathetic. His affection for her became deeper and when he sensed she wanted to go to bed with him he was both grateful and afraid. What if it turned out to be another hideous experience like the one with Jo-Anne? Why should he even risk it? He didn't like women that way.

But when it happened, that crazy, half-drunken early morning when they came reeling back from Bugis Street, he'd found that a woman could be ardent but tender, slow in bringing him to a pitch of excitement and able to share his astonished pleasure without threatening to devour him.

Afterward, he'd wept with relief and she'd held him steadily until, to his further surprise, he made love to her again. And every night since then. Only four nights, but they were a revelation.

Standing in his cabin, he wondered whether he was in love with her. He loved her, but that was different. He didn't know how he'd continue to feel. If he met some man tomorrow . . . he couldn't predict what would happen.

But for now, he was happy.

Chapter 11

At Shum Chun, the border, the tour group from the ship stepped off the train that had brought them from Hong Kong into this secret, mysterious world. The hundred and twenty tourists were divided into small groups, each assigned two guides, a young Chinese man and woman wearing blue Mao jackets and baggy pants. Mary and Christopher, Gail and Colonel Stanford were assigned to Group 7, instructed to wear their identification badges at all times and to follow their male guide, Mr. Li, who carried a placard bearing the number 7 on a long stick high above his head. His teammate, Miss Lu, shepherded them solicitously past the unsmiling border guards in green shirts with red lapels, blue trousers and the perennial Mao caps. But only the soldiers were grim-faced. Everywhere else, the visitors saw welcoming faces and a graciousness none of them expected.

Excited and curious, they crossed a long, covered bridge, passed immigration and entered the railroad station for the long walk through customs and money-changing areas before boarding the train that would take them to Kwangchow. It was a time-consuming, leisurely procedure that took them past endless reception rooms filled with white slip-covered chairs and couches and beautiful old teak furniture. At one point, they had a "tea shop" where sheets of propaganda material were distributed.

On the surprisingly comfortable train, they settled into chairs with footrests, drank tea from lovely covered mugs and accepted box lunches of small, delicious sandwiches, hard-boiled eggs and fruit. Mary looked with dismay at her ornamented cardboard container.

"Aside from the box, which is beautiful, I'm disappointed. It's like an American picnic!"

Christopher, busily snapping pictures of rice paddies, water buffaloes and straw-hatted farmers in the fields, smiled as he leaned across her to the window.

"Don't worry. You'll eat enough unidentifiable food in the next three days to satisfy you for life."

She looked up at him. "In the briefing on the ship they told us we weren't allowed to take pictures from the train, or photograph the police or military."

"They also told us we'd have to carry our own bags, and I'm sure you noticed ours were put on trucks to cross the border. The Chinese are anxious to please their 'foreign friends.' You'll see." He sat back down beside her. "There's a strange psychology here. For example, if there's something you want to do and you're refused permission, you just write a letter home saying you weren't allowed to do it. Next day, like magic, you'll suddenly receive the permission."

"You mean they read the mail?"

"That would be a fair deduction. And monitor the phone calls as well."

"Who'd make a phone call from China, for heaven's sake?"

"Anybody who wanted to have good service. The phone and cable service from here is better than in most parts of the Orient."

Mary shook her head. "Weird. So far, nothing seems as primitive as I expected. Unless maybe it's the fact that I've counted only three pieces of farm machinery in the last hour and a half. I thought their agricultural production had speeded up, but so far the rural area looks like a twelfth-century painting come to life."

"Give 'em time. They've only been 'liberated' since 1949. And the rural farm communes weren't set up until

'58. We'll see one of those tomorrow. 'Lokang,' it's called."

The two-hour train ride ended at another beautiful railroad station, spotless, modern, flanked by trees and dominated by an enormous portrait of Chairman Mao. They were efficiently settled into creaking buses which jolted their way to the Tung Fang Hotel. En route, Mary realized she saw no cars or taxis on the broad streets of Kwangchow; just thousands of bicycles ridden by men and women of all ages.

The hotel was another surprise. From the outside, it looked as modern as any in America, but once inside the doors, it became a fascinating combination of yesterday and today. There were, of course, no bellmen. She was prepared for that. She knew that in this new China there were no servants, that no one would carry a bag and that room service was unknown. Here, all were equal. Tipping was forbidden, as were gifts. They'd been told they might offer their guides a small gift, but nothing more important than a picture postcard from their home towns, or perhaps a souvenir lapel pin picked up for twenty-five cents in Australia or New Zealand. She was not, however, prepared for the room to which she was directed. The "old wing" in which she was housed was built in 1961 but it looked as though it had seen a hundred years of wear. The floors of her room were bare, and the paint job sloppy. The screens to the balcony were ill-fitting and the plumbing workable but antiquated. She hadn't expected luxury, but she was surprised by the griminess of the tub and the thin, worn towels. No matter. She could shower and dry herself and live for three days without a face cloth, which no one had told her to bring. On the ship, she'd been told to take cleansing tissue, medication, instant coffee, an alarm clock and liquor if she wanted a drink. None was sold in China. She wished they'd also mentioned light bulbs. There were two small lamps in her room, each of them with a bulb that couldn't have been over twenty-five watts.

In spite of this, she was intrigued by her quarters. The Chinese gave great thought to the amenities, if not the

131

modern necessities, of life. Her room was large and faced onto a garden and a busy badminton court. On the dresser was a thermos of hot, boiled water, a delicate tea set; a bottle of Pearl River Orange Drink and one of Yuchuan beer, both warm. Close by were White Cloud cigarettes and a small box of matches. The desk was equipped with hotel stationery and a notice that her room was priced at twenty-two yuan a day, about twelve dollars. Under the twin beds were rather worn-looking slippers and over each bed heavy mosquito netting. She'd forgotten this was semitropical country and later she'd find the netting claustrophobic. A couple of mosquito bites were better than smothering. She only wished her briefing had also included the advice to bring bug spray. The room smelled of something unidentifiable. Bug killer? Disinfectant? Incense?

Mary sank into one of the armchairs and thought that even if she couldn't do an interview with the Chinese, she could do a half hour of impressions on the train trip and the hotel alone. And probably three or four more programs on the rest of her adventure. It was wonderful to have a purpose in life. Her work was her passion. The thought brought a little frown to her face. Much as she loved Christopher, could she really be happy giving up this job she adored? It was a disturbing thought. Tiny as her career was, it held her to San Francisco, perhaps as much as did her obligation to Michael. Don't be a fool, she told herself. You can't have it all. Something has to give. Something has to . . . There was a light tap on her door.

"Ready?" Christopher called. "The troops are gathering at the bus. We're off to the Children's Palace."

She opened the door. "Welcome to the Ritz. How's your room?"

"About the same, but we weren't expecting Paris accommodations, were we? God, the terrible tourists are at it already, complaining that the bus is uncomfortable and the rooms are bad! You should hear them in the lobby."

"I don't want to. I have a feeling they'll get worse."

132

He looked around. "It's not bad, really. Bed looks comfortable enough."

"Except for that damned netting. I've never slept under such a contraption and I don't think I'll be able to."

Christopher gave her an exaggerated leer. "Ever made love under one?"

"No."

"Neither have I, but I'm willing to try."

She pushed him out the door. "None of that. The bus awaits. Anyway, we're in a moral country. I'm sure the Chinese wouldn't talk that way."

In the empty hallway he kissed her. "The hell with that," he said. "I'm not Chinese."

* * *

The Children's Palace was enchanting, fascinating and somehow frightening.

"It's identical to those pictures of Pat Nixon's visit to China," Mary whispered as they were greeted by a gathering of small boys and girls waving bright red pompoms. "They must be programed in exactly how to greet visitors."

"In many things," Christopher said quietly. "Wait. You'll see. There's something scary about it."

She realized what he meant. The Kwangchow Children's Palace was an "educational center" for youngsters from seven to fifteen, set up, according to the eternal propaganda release, for "varied extracurricular activities to help the children develop themselves morally, intellectually and physically." It held ten thousand children at a time and received an average of six hundred thousand a year, every afternoon and on Sunday morning and each day during summer and winter vacations. On the surface, it was beautiful. The tiny gymnasts performed beautifully, the dancing class was delightful and the singing group was sweet. But in addition to the cultural parts, there was heavy emphasis on electric games and shooting, boys simulating war maneuvers and a playground called "Route of Long March for Little Red Army."

"They're like tiny robots," Gail DeVries said under her breath. "All following Chairman Mao's revolutionary line. Think of it. Thousands of them, millions of them, being brainwashed to obey orders. It makes one quite nervous, thinking of the future."

At dinner that night, Mary sat next to their female guide and was delighted by her. She was a young woman of twenty, attractive despite the fact that like all the Chinese girls she wore the regulation uniform and no makeup. Mary kept mentally comparing her to Jayne, who was almost the same age. It was like comparing creatures from two planets. Miss Lu was idealistic and dedicated to her political philosophy. Though she was outgoing, free with information and full of questions, she seemed surprisingly innocent and untouched.

Hoping she wouldn't be thought rude, Mary questioned her about her life. She was unmarried, of course. By government decree, young people couldn't marry until they were twenty-two.

"Most girls wait until they're twenty-five or twenty-six," Miss Lu said. "And most men until twenty-eight or thirty."

Was that to discourage large families?

"No, to give us more time for study."

She explained that separations were rare in marriages and could be obtained only with government approval. Chinese women could get the birth-control pill. "But only the married ones, of course," she told Mary almost primly. Life was good in China today, Miss Lu said proudly. "Wait until you see the commune tomorrow. Even the peasants are determined to carry out Chairman Mao's directives, with class struggle as the key link. We adhere to the Party's basic line and make greater contribution to the socialist revolution and construction. The Lokang People's Commune is led by the Party Central Committee and headed by Chairman Mhua Kuofeng," Miss Lu recited. "We follow the policy of self-reliance and hard struggle."

Life was good, Mary repeated in her head. Perhaps, in comparison to what it had been. But how would little

134

Miss Lu know the wretched past? She wasn't born until years after the liberation. She wished she could show this young woman a world Miss Lu couldn't imagine. Maybe not a better one, in many ways, but one that would fascinate her as this one fascinated Mary. Miss Lu was looking at her, smiling happily, her glass of rice wine raised.

"Bottoms up!" she said.

Mary grinned. "Bottoms up!"

* * *

There were twenty-seven thousand people in the commune, which was eighteen miles and an hour and a quarter of torturous ride from the hotel over rough roads in a bus that had long since lost its springs. They were received ceremonially by the leader, fed tea, dried leechee nuts and wrapped prunes in a hall dominated by huge pictures of Mao, Lenin and Marx, conducted on a wearying tour of orchards, fruit-preserving factories and the community hospital.

The high point, for Mary, was a visit to a private family in their tiny brick house with a bare stone floor and wooden benches for the guests. Mary felt a little uncomfortable, as though she were prying, but the husband and wife and one remaining daughter who lived there seemed proud and pleased to have been chosen to entertain the foreigners. She looked around the main room with its bare light bulb hanging in the center, its photographs of the family of ten, its eternal picture of the Chairman, and she wondered how she dared complain about anything. Through the interpreter, the head of the house spoke cheerfully of their well-being. He had a wristwatch and a radio now, and his wife had a sewing machine. He earned 450 yuan a year, about $300, working from seven-thirty in the morning to five in the afternoon with a lunch break and a morning recess. He had six days off every month, two days in every ten, and his food and housing were free. His children, after working two years, could apply for the university, and he paid twenty cents per person per month for the family's medical care. Some of his sons wanted to go into the army, he said, but there were too many applicants. Not all volunteers could be accepted.

Going back on the bus, Mary was thoughtful.

"Incredible, isn't it?" Christopher said.

"Totally. Their philosophy isn't for me. Couldn't be. But I can see how it's right for them. In a way it's enviable, thinking first of the good of others. Imagine putting yourself after the state and the commune. Imagine believing so much in *anything*. What must it be like to be so grateful for so little?"

He took her hand. "Depends on what you think is 'little.' Enough to eat is sometimes a lot. So is a roof over your head. And protection for your health, and hope for your children. Success is measured by different yardsticks, my love. In the minds of these people, they're achieving success."

* * *

Everything seemed to conspire to keep him from becoming the success he should be, Michael decided as he left Harry Carson's office. The man was a damned fool who couldn't see beyond his nose. What did he want for his money, anyhow? A dumb manager who'd say "yessir," that's what he wanted. Some stupid slave who'd never venture an idea. Some idiot who'd do things the way Harry wanted them done.

He'd gone to Carson's office feeling optimistic. He'd revised the plan for the men's boutique, taking out some of the things that bothered Harry but leaving the general idea of a super-chic establishment intact. He couldn't bring himself to give his potential backer the kind of unimaginative, boring men's clothing store the man wanted. But he had compromised, hadn't he? He'd toned down some of the fancier things and he was sure Harry would meet him halfway.

The night before, he'd read the plan to Patricia and she'd thought it was wonderful.

"It's brilliant, Michael! It will be the talk of San Francisco!"

"Cross your fingers. I'm dealing with a square character who doesn't understand what's happening today. I hope to God he buys it."

"He will. How could he not? You have a real flair for this kind of thing. Not that I'm an expert, of course, but I am the modern consumer. I know a shop like that would attract me. I'd insist that Stanley buy all his clothes there. And there must be thousands of women like me, not to mention thousands of men who have the same kind of elegant taste you have. Why, it's more imaginative than anything in New York! I've never seen anything as original on Madison Avenue or Fifty-seventh Street or even in the men's department in Henri Bendel. Don't worry. Your Mr. Carson can't help but see how good it is."

He'd been enormously pleased and suddenly confident. It was true that Patricia wasn't a businesswoman. He suspected she really wasn't even too bright. But what she said made sense. She was the modern shopper. Women like her influenced what men bought. Even if the boutique was too chichi for some men, their fashion-conscious wives would push them there. That was an important point. He'd have to make sure he stressed that to Harry.

But he never had a chance. The tough businessman read through the revised proposal as he had the first one, refusing any comment during the process. When he finished, he leaned back and lit a cigar. Michael waited hopefully.

"You, Morgan, are the biggest damned jackass this side of the Rockies. What are you wasting my time for? I told you what I wanted. So why do you come back with the same jerky plan?"

"It isn't the same plan! I've made a lot of changes. Look, Harry, I know it's right. I was talking to my sister-in-law last night and she said . . ."

Carson snorted. "She said you were a genius, I suppose. Frankly, I don't give a damn what your relatives think. Or what *you* think. I'm a businessman and I know what *I* think. And what *I* think is that this is a piece of

137

arrogant crap and I wouldn't put a plugged nickel into it!"

"Harry, you've got to realize . . ."

"I know what I've got to realize, pal. You can't take orders, for one thing. You're stubborn as a mule with a brain to match. When are you going to wise up, Morgan? If you're so smart, why ain't you rich?" He shoved the papers across the desk. "It's been nice meeting you. Hope you find a sucker dumb enough to go along with this."

Michael hesitated. He could still salvage it. If he backed down and agreed to plan it Harry's way, he probably could talk himself into one more chance. No, damn it, he wouldn't! He wasn't going to knuckle under to this bully. He wasn't going to fawn and meekly agree to something he didn't believe in. There'd be other men with vision. Or maybe he could swing it by himself. No. That was out of the question. He didn't have a dime of his own.

"You're the one who's dumb, Harry," he said as he gathered up his papers. "You'll see that when I get the boutique going."

Carson didn't look up. He'd already dismissed him.

Patricia was waiting when he let himself into the apartment. She'd been there four days and already felt at home. Michael had been lovely to her, taking her out every night to some elegant restaurant for dinner. They'd been to Ernie's and Lehr's Greenhouse and Emelio's. It was expensive and lovely and she wished it would go on forever. It was fun dining in beautiful places with an attractive man, a far cry from fixing dinner every night for a boring husband who wanted to eat at six o'clock and watch television for the rest of the evening.

And she was flattered that Michael had discussed his big proposal with her and complimented her on her insight about the appeal of the shop to women. Stanley never discussed his business with her. Not, God knows, that she gave a damn about nuts and bolts.

She was sure Michael was coming home with good news. She'd surprise him by cooking dinner in the apartment. They'd celebrate his success over an excellent meal

138

and a good bottle of wine and she'd listen to him carefully as he told her every detail of his triumph. She looked at the carefully set table with the candles ready for lighting and checked the coq au vin on the stove. Everything was perfect.

Everything except Michael's face when she greeted him in the foyer. One look and she knew before he said it.

"Carson didn't buy it."

Patricia looked stricken. "I can't believe it. The man must be crazy! What happened?"

"He called it a piece of arrogant crap." Michael sounded defeated. "Maybe it is, Patricia. Maybe he's right and I'm just a stupid, impractical dreamer."

She was indignant. "Nothing of the sort! It's a wonderful idea. He's the one who's wrong. Not you." Without thinking, she put her arms around him and held him close. "You're ahead of your time, that's all it is, Michael. The world's not smart enough to see what you do. Don't worry. You'll find someone who appreciates you. You were just dealing with the wrong person. The right one will see how terrific your ideas are."

The words were like balm to his battered ego. And the warmth of her, pressed against him, was like being enveloped in a voluptuous cocoon. He held her close, felt the ripe figure under the thin cotton shirt, and realized she was trembling. As though he couldn't help it, he found her mouth and kissed it deeply.

"I . . . I cooked dinner for us," Patricia whispered.

Michael put his lips against her ear. "I don't want dinner, do you?"

Wordlessly, she shook her head.

Chapter 12

Standing alone in her cabin at midnight, Peggy watched the ship sail out of Hong Kong toward the Japan Inland Sea and Kobe. Life was wonderful. She turned the gold band on the third finger of her left hand and said, aloud, "Mrs. Anthony Robin. Peggy Lawrence Robin." Beautiful.

Almost until the last minute, she hadn't been sure Tony would go through with the marriage. She could admit to herself now how frightened she'd been the evening before they docked. Tony had come next door to her suite, looking worried.

"Peggy, we have to talk."

She made him a drink. "Yes, darling?"

"You know I love you." He'd fiddled with his glass. "But I'm still not sure we should get married right now."

She'd felt as though she'd turned to ice. She could feel herself shivering inside but she managed to sound calm.

"Why not?"

"It's not practical. I don't want to take early retirement, and if we get married I'll be away months at a time. Most of the year. It wouldn't be fair to you, you sitting at home while your husband is at sea."

She stared at him wordlessly.

"I know," Tony said. "I agreed to leave the ship, but I can't, Peggy. Try to understand. It's my life. In another five years I'll have to step down. But right now I'd miss it so much I'm afraid I'd make you miserable with my unhappiness."

"I'd make you happy, Tony. You don't know what it's like to have a wonderful, settled life. We'd travel whenever you wanted to, but it would be play, not work. We'd live in lovely houses and enjoy interesting friends."

"*Your* houses. *Your* friends."

"Darling, they'd be *ours!* You wouldn't be bored, I promise you."

"Yes I would. I'd be useless. An aging ex-sea captain living off his rich wife. I couldn't stand it."

She'd been frantic. The thought of not being married to Tony was unbearable. She had to belong, any way she could.

"All right, dearest. If you feel so strongly, we'll have to work this out so we'll both be content. We'll go ahead with our plans, get married day after tomorrow as we've arranged, and you'll continue to work as you want. I won't insist you leave the ship if it makes you so unhappy."

"Peggy, be reasonable! Five years of almost constant separation? It wouldn't work."

"We don't have to be separated. We can go on for the next five years as we have for the past three. I'll make the trips with you. I don't care where I am, as long as we're together."

Tony sighed. "You don't understand. I couldn't have my wife aboard. It's against all regulations."

"I wouldn't expect to share your cabin. I'd keep this one."

"For God's sake be rational! You'd still be my wife! We don't even allow crew members to sail with their spouses! Even a dining-room waiter and a stewardess who marry can't be on the same ship together. It's a company rule. As for the captain having his wife in the next cabin, it's unthinkable."

"Then we'd keep it a secret. Nobody would have to know we're married. I could keep on being Mrs. Lawrence, the constant passenger."

Tony shook his head. "I don't understand you. In the first place, the news would get out through the grapevine. If it didn't, you'd be sure to tell someone. You couldn't keep that to yourself. And if you could, what would be the point of marriage? We might just as well go on as we are. Our affair is no secret." He began to get angry. "I've often wondered why I haven't been called on the carpet before this. The line doesn't like this kind of thing. God knows if you weren't such a good customer, guaranteeing them a hundred thousand dollars a year, they probably would find a way not to have a reservation for you!"

She began to weep. "I want to be your wife. I don't care if nobody else knows. I'll know. I'll feel safe and protected. I can't stand being alone, Tony. I don't feel like a whole woman. It's me. How I feel inside. Can't you understand?"

He spoke more gently. "No, Peggy, I really can't. To be a secret wife seems like nothing to me."

"Then believe it means *everything* to me! I swear to you, on my mother's grave, no one will know we're married. Please, Tony. Please, please do this for me."

"I can't. It's not the kind of life you should have. I really think, dear, after this trip you shouldn't book any more cruises. I'll see you whenever I have leave. We'll be together ashore. And if you still want to marry me in five years, I'll be a happy man. I won't stop loving you, I promise. But you'll have to make a separate life while I'm away."

She became hysterical. "Why don't you say what you really mean? It's not my life you're worried about is it? It's yours! You don't want to be tied down. You want to be the glamorous captain, flirting with all the hungry widows, strutting around giving your damned little orders! You don't love me. If you did, you'd want me to be your wife even if nobody knew but you and me. You'd want to own me, as I want to be owned. Tony, if you don't marry me, my life is over. I don't want it anymore. I couldn't live away from you."

"Sweetheart, don't talk nonsense. I love you dearly. I'm

142

not looking for anyone else. I'm just trying to be sensible. It's only a matter of postponing our plans."

"For five years? At our age?"

"They'll go quickly, darling. We'll see each other often. You can't stay on the ship, Peggy. It's a futile life for you. You drink too much, have too many hours to kill. It's too confining. I promise you, it will be better my way."

"Get out," she said. "Leave me alone."

"We'll have a good time in Hong Kong."

"No. I don't want to see you again."

He tried to make a joke of it. "That's going to be pretty hard to avoid, love. We're almost a month away from San Francisco. Or are you planning to fly home?"

"Never mind what I'm planning. Just go."

He rose to leave. "See you in the morning."

Peggy didn't answer.

At 3:00 A.M. the phone by his bed rang. He could hardly make out the words but he recognized the voice.

"Peggy? What's the matter? Are you sick?"

She sounded very far away. "Just . . . wanted to say good-bye. Love you."

"What's going on? Peggy! Answer me!"

"Too tired . . . very sleepy . . ."

He slammed down the receiver and called the ship's doctor. "Get to Mrs. Lawrence's cabin on the double!" Tony pulled on a robe and raced next door. Thank God she hadn't locked herself in. He knew what had happened. Peggy had tried to commit suicide. Jesus! He'd never forgive himself!

Later, when the doctor brought her around, a weary Tony went back to his quarters from the ship's hospital, silently thanking God she was alive, and resigned to the fact that now he'd have to marry her as she'd planned. He'd leave the ship after this trip. Better that than living in fear that next time she'd succeed in taking her life. He couldn't handle that. Not for the sake of another few years in his job.

He'd ordered the doctor and nurse not to mention this unfortunate incident to anyone. Lucky for all of them, he thought, that it happened in the middle of the night when

143

their hurried rush down to Adriatic Deck could be managed with no one around. Even the night stewards were dozing in their service rooms. He supposed he should have known Peggy would get her way somehow. Perhaps it was just as well. Better, in the long run, he consoled himself, than facing a lonely old age in some little house in Southampton watching ships commanded by younger men sail in and out of the harbor.

* * *

The doctor yawned and stretched. It was 6 A.M. and Peggy Lawrence was sleeping normally.

"Cup of coffee, Doctor?"

He took the cup the nurse offered. "Thanks."

"Will she be all right?"

"For God's sake, Martha, you know it was a fake! She didn't take enough pills to kill a two-year-old."

"Just enough to scare hell out of the captain."

"Exactly."

"I don't understand it," Martha said. "The scuttlebutt is they're getting married in Hong Kong. Why would she pull such a stunt?"

"Maybe the Old Man tried to back out."

The nurse looked thoughtful. "Well, he's hooked now. Did you hear him while we were working on her? 'Peggy, darling, you must live! We're going to be married in Hong Kong. Everything will be fine.' "

"Yeah, I heard him. I'll bet you fifty dollars Mrs. Lawrence did, too."

Tony had been frantic, Peggy thought now, as she remembered the scene. Some people would call it underhanded, pretending she'd taken a lethal dose of pills, but it was the only way to show him how much he loved her. It was for his own good as much as for hers, this justifiable means to an end. He'd been so close to throwing away their future. She couldn't let him do that. Men were such babies sometimes. They had to be figuratively hit over the head to do the sensible thing. He'd see that she knew best.

And he'd never know what a good actress she was. He'd always think she preferred death to life without him.

As the ship headed slowly toward Japan, Peggy put a hundred-dollar bill into one envelope and a fifty into another. She addressed them to the doctor and nurse. "A most inadequate expression of my appreciation" she wrote on the cards she enclosed.

There was nothing like a little cash to make sure the captain's orders were carried out. Or to make sure the captain never knew the truth.

* * *

Jayne lay snugly in the curve of Terry's arm, listening to the departure noises outside. "I hate leaving Hong Kong," she said.

"Not sorry we didn't go to China?"

"Not a bit, though Aunt Mary said it was marvelous. She came back looking like a basket case this afternoon. Must have been some strenuous trip! Every minute programed, from official dinners to a look at the pandas in the zoo. She skipped the acupuncture operations but she said those who went were stunned. Apparently, they did a heart by-pass and a brain operation with the patients conscious and waving at the audience! Can you imagine?"

"I'd rather not."

"That's how she felt. So she and Christopher went to the ivory-carving factory instead."

"How did Gail and Colonel Stanford hold up?"

Jayne giggled. "Apparently, better than most. They told the Chinese they were a hundred years old and got super VIP treatment. Aunt Mary said the Chinese practically carried those two around while the rest of them had to manage as best they could. They're marvelous, aren't they? I hope if I live that long I'll have as much pep as they do. It's kind of a shame they don't get married."

"Why?"

"Why what?"

"Why is it a shame they don't get married? I think they have a great arrangement. They'd probably turn into two

145

old, bored people if they saw each other every day. She'd hate his snoring and his dentures in a glass by the bed. And he'd be fed up with her daily reports of success or failure on the john in the morning."

"Terry! You're terrible!"

"I know." He reached for her. "But you're wonderful. I'm going to miss you when this trip is over."

She lay close to him, feeling the beat of their hearts. "I'll miss you, too." There was a little silence before she said, "Terry, what are you going to do when you get back?"

"Do? I don't know. Look for a job, I guess."

"Will you see Paul?"

He disentangled himself and lay on his back, staring at the ceiling. "No. That's over. I told you. He doesn't want to see me ever again. I don't fit into his life."

"Will you find . . . I mean, will you look for . . ."

"Another man? I don't know, Jayne. I'm not sure now. You've made me take a step on a different road. At least I know I'm bisexual, if not thoroughly hetero. I'm not over Paul. Maybe I never will be. Most people never quite forget their first love. But it doesn't hurt so much anymore." He propped himself up on one elbow and looked at her. "Because of you, I can function. I don't mean just sexually. As a person. You've made me grow up. I think I can make it on my own now."

"Can you? Or would you like to find out what the therapy would be like on dry land?"

"What does that mean?"

"How would it grab you if I stayed in San Francisco for a while? The little I saw of it before sailing appealed to me. Maybe I could get a job there and stay a few months. There's nothing to take me back to New York anymore."

"No more Russell King, you mean."

Jayne sat up and lit a cigarette. "That's right. No more Russell King. You've helped me get my head on straight too, Terry. You've shown me what a thoughtful, considerate man really is. Let's face it. I don't want to lose you. Oh, I don't want to marry you. I'm not going to marry

146

anybody. But maybe we could find a little apartment, share expenses, live together, at least until we're sure our broken wings are mended and we can fly back into the cold, cruel world alone." She laughed. "How's that for a poetic proposition?"

He sat up beside her. "Are you serious?"

"Totally."

"I'm not sure I'm in love with you, Jayne."

"Did anybody mention love?"

"I might hurt you. I don't know how I'll feel when I get back to reality. This isn't reality, you know, this shipboard life. I wouldn't want to get you into something . . ."

"Would you rather send me back to nothing?"

"Come on. You're being dramatic."

"Not really. I hate living with my parents. My dad is a poor, dull, dominated man. And my mother is a selfish bitch."

"Jayne!"

"Don't look so shocked. She is. Motherhood—especially unwilling motherhood—doesn't change a devil into a saint. She's made life hell for my father. And not so terrific for me. It's a terrible household I live in. I was planning to find a roommate and get an apartment in New York anyway. Why not in San Francisco?" She smiled. "I promise I will not discuss my toilet problems with you. And I know you have your own teeth. You snore a little, but I can put up with that."

He laughed. It was a crazy idea. Totally unexpected and probably impractical. But why not? They knew all there was to know about each other. They were congenial and physically compatible and there were no illusions on either side. Maybe it made sense. He still had a few dollars and he'd find work. Jayne would get a job. Her aunt would help her, if necessary. It was worth a try. They had nothing to lose. At least they weren't pretending. He wasn't insanely in love and neither was she, but at this stage of their lives they needed each other. If they were lucky, it might grow into something.

"You're sure?" Terry asked again.

"I can't see anything against it, can you?"

"No. Not as long as we know it's a friendly experiment."

She held out her hand. "Deal?"

Terry shook it firmly. "Deal," he said.

* * *

Charlie Burke shifted uncomfortably on his seat in the Fairmont Tower cocktail lounge. It was embarrassing to hear Mike Morgan go on about what a jerk Harry Carson was and how the fool had let a million-dollar opportunity slip through his fingers. Charlie didn't know Harry Carson, but he thought the man was probably right. Michael's idea sounded, even to his unknowledgeable ears, like a sophomoric dream. It isn't a plan, Charlie thought; it's an ego trip. Mary's husband sees himself as the suave proprietor of a fancy store, dispensing charm and fashion authority to a waiting world. His superior attitude grated. The guy was a four-flusher, nothing more. How in God's name had Mary put up with him all these years? And now Michael was going to ask him for money. He knew it, even before the man got around to the subject. He also knew he wouldn't get involved with this stupid scheme. Not even for Mary's sake.

"So, I thought, what the hell," Michael was saying, "if Carson's too dumb to know a good thing when it falls in his lap, there are plenty of smarter people around. I figure on forming my own corporation and offering shares to my friends. I'd hold fifty-one per cent of the stock, of course, but three or four other chums could get in on the ground floor for a few thousand dollars apiece. I wanted to give you a shot at it, Charlie. You've been damned good to Mary, and we'd like to show our appreciation."

"I see. Does Mary know?"

"Not yet. I just got this brain wave a couple of days ago. She was in China, so I couldn't call her, but I'll probably get her on the phone, ship-to-shore, on her way to Kobe." He grinned. "I know she'll think it's a great idea. She'd never forgive me if I didn't offer you a piece of the action. Mary's devoted to you, you know."

148

"Mary's a very loyal woman."

"You better believe it." Michael took a sip of his scotch. "A lot of other women wouldn't have the faith she has. She's always had confidence in me, and this time I'm going to prove how right she is. Hell, Charlie, this one shop is only the beginning. We could have a chain of them. Los Angeles. Dallas. Chicago. New York. All the major markets. It's a gold mine."

More like a pipe dream, Charlie thought. Even if he got the idea going, Michael didn't have enough discipline to give it the kind of backbreaking time and effort needed to start a new business. He'd lose interest in a few months and be off on some other wild tangent. And that would be the end of it. Assuming it ever got started, which it probably never would.

"I appreciate your coming to me, Mike, but I'm afraid I can't take advantage of the offer. You see, I have pretty heavy expenses these days. Tracey's spending a few months in a sanatorium, for a rest, and it costs the earth. I'm really strapped for cash."

"Tracey's in a sanatorium? Hey, I'm sorry." Some "rest," Michael thought. She's drying out again. Poor old Charlie. To have to put up with that! "I know hospitals are killers," Mike went on, "but maybe that's all the more reason you should look for additional income. The boutique will pay off in six months, at the outside, and you'll be able to pick up some extra money."

"Sorry. I just can't swing the initial outlay."

"The bank will lend it to you. No problem."

Damn him, why doesn't he stop? Charlie fumed. There was no end to his nerve. Mary will die when she finds out he's going around to their friends trying to put the bite on them for this idiotic scheme.

"Wish I could get in on it, Mike. Good of you to think of me, but I'm old-fashioned. Hate owing money. I know that's out of step. Everybody borrows these days. I understand it even makes you a better credit risk to have a bank loan." He gave a little laugh. "But I'm square. I don't like to live beyond my means."

Michael shrugged. "No problem. I won't have trouble
149

raising the money. Rae Spanner's already in for twenty-five thousand. A couple of other investors, plus my own share, and I'll be off and running. Refill, Charlie?"

"No thanks. I have to go back to the station this afternoon. We really miss Mary. She sent some terrific tapes, by the way. I suppose you know that."

"Yes. She said she was sending you some."

"Sounds like she's enjoying the trip. How are you making out, Mike?"

"Me? Fine. Oh, I miss Mary, of course, but her sister's staying at the apartment. Jayne's mother. She's a nice woman and a helluva good cook."

Charlie was surprised. "Oh? I didn't know Mary's sister was here. That should make it pleasant for you."

"It sure does. Patricia's good company."

"Listen, Mike, I have to leave, but maybe we can get together soon. I'll want to hear how you're doing on your project, and I'd like to meet Patricia."

"Right, Charlie. You run along. I think I'll have another one before I go home."

"Well, let me at least get the check."

Michael waved him off. "Wouldn't hear of it. This is on me. You buy next time."

Going down in the elevator, Charlie shook his head. Mike Morgan. Always the big shot. Offering deals. Picking up checks. Keeping up the façade of the charm boy. I wonder what he had to do to get twenty-five thousand dollars out of that man-eater Rae Spanner. Plenty, I'll bet. Poor Mary.

Michael ordered another scotch, flirting mildly with the waitress as he did. Not that he intended to do anything about her. He had enough on his hands these days. Yesterday, Rae Spanner had made it very clear what the conditions of her investment were: a little drop-in "visit" every afternoon from five to seven.

"You needn't worry," she'd said. "Mary will never know. Frankly, Michael, I don't think your scheme is worth a damn, but I've always had a yen for you. It's worth a few thousand."

150

He'd been genuinely shocked. "Listen, Rae, I've never yet sold the body. I'm offering a straight business deal."

She'd been amused. "*Are* you now? Well, so am I. My money for your affection, to put it delicately. A fair exchange on a temporary basis. Take it or leave it, Michael."

My God, he'd thought, has she no pride? She knows I don't give a damn for her. Oh, she's attractive, but I couldn't fall in love with her. And what if Mary found out? He'd almost laughed aloud. Why was he worrying about Mary finding out about Rae? If he wanted something to really squirm about, it should be his ongoing affair with Patricia.

Rae was waiting for his answer. "Well? What about it?"

He'd tried to find some face-saving way to agree. "Rae, you don't have to invest in my business to have me go to bed with you. I've been dying to, for years. Let's forget the money. I'm flattered as hell that you'd like me to drop in from time to time. Now that I know how you feel, I will."

He knew she wouldn't buy it. She needed strings attached. As he expected, she shook her head.

"Dear boy, that's much too indefinite for me. I'd rather have you in my debt. That way I know I can count on you. The money means nothing to me. I won't even miss it. Let's just say you're taking out a loan, with yourself as collateral."

He managed to smile. "A very discreet loan."

"Naturally."

"And the length of the loan?"

"That," Rae said, "will be up to me. Let's just call it 'payable on demand,' the way the banks do."

Chapter 13

"I have a surprise for you," Christopher said.

"I'm not sure I can stand another one." Mary spoke softly, not to be overheard by the people at the next table in the cocktail lounge. "I'm still stunned by Jayne's plans to stay in San Francisco with Terry. She's making a terrible mistake and I don't know how to stop her."

"You can't, luv. She's legally of age. It's her parents' problem, not yours. Besides, those kids have another three weeks to go. They might change their minds before then."

Mary shook her head. "You don't know Jayne. She's like me. Stubborn."

He smiled. "I've noticed that."

Mary didn't answer. It wasn't stubbornness that kept her from saying yes to Christopher. It was fear. Fear of uprooting her whole life, changing everything about it. Was she never going to get over this feeling that no one was better equipped to make decisions? Christopher was no Michael. He could take charge. Insisted on taking charge. Wasn't this what she'd always wanted? Why was she so fearful? Was her concern for Michael or more for herself? It was no good living with a failure. It was agony, watching him try to prove himself to her and knowing he'd never make it. Maybe I'm masochistic, she thought. Maybe I can't be happy unless I'm suffering, agonizing over someone weaker than I. Disgusting! I see this same quality in Jayne and hate it for her just as, deep down, I hate it for myself.

"Hello, there." Christopher recalled her to the present.

"What? Oh, darling, I'm sorry. I was a million miles away."

"Several thousand, at least. Don't you want to hear about my surprise?"

She'd almost forgotten. "Of course. What is it?"

"I've arranged for a car to pick us up in Kobe and take us to Kyoto. We have twenty-four hours, and you can't miss seeing the spiritual home of the Japanese. I forbid it."

She smiled. "*Do* you now?"

"Yes, I do. There are a couple of hundred Shinto shrines and fifteen hundred Buddhist temples. And wait until you see the shogun's palace. The art work is fantastic! We're going to stay at Tawaraya. An authentic Japanese inn. None of your tourist stuff. God, it's all so beautiful, Mary! And we're shot with luck, getting there at cherry-blossom time." He looked at her balefully. "You don't want to go."

"I do! Of course I do! Bear with me, Christopher. I have a lot on my mind."

"I know. And not just Jayne. What do you hear from Mr. Morgan?"

"Nothing. I don't understand it. I thought surely there'd be a letter in Hong Kong."

"The mails are not entirely dependable, my dear. Perhaps he sent it too late."

"Yes. Knowing Michael, that's possible."

"Or," Christopher said slowly, "maybe he's doing very well without you."

She looked at him sharply. "I hope so."

"Do you, Mary? Do you really? Or is it important to you that Michael draw on your strength? Is that why you won't commit yourself to me? Are you afraid I don't need you enough? I do, you know. Not in the way your husband does, but equally as much. Maybe more."

"I don't want to think about it, Christopher."

"I'm afraid you must, darling. In less than a week we'll be in Yokohama. That's the point of no return. When I leave the ship, I have to know whether you're coming back to me. It's your decision, my love. I'd like to make it for you, but I can't. You know what I have to offer. You know what you have at home. I've said all I can say."

Mary took his hand. "I love you. I want to come back. I just don't know whether I can."

"Not good enough. You can. It's whether you want to. *Really* want to, I mean. Not just say you do." His fingers tightened on hers. "You have to trust someone sometime, my darling."

She tried to sound cheerful. "Let's talk about something else. Isn't it incredible that Peggy and Tony actually got married? I didn't believe he'd go through with it, even though I said I did. I thought he'd back out. Everybody did. Peggy said it was just a nice quiet ceremony and they . . ."

"Shut up, sweetheart," Christopher said gently. "Stop trying to run away from the inevitable. You can't postpone it much longer. You must make up your mind."

"I will." Mary said soberly. "I promise you, by Yokohama I will."

* * *

Michael sat by the phone, debating whether to call. Mary would be so disappointed that the deal with Carson had fallen through. He didn't know how to tell her. He'd been so sure of it when she left. So certain that at last he'd be everything she wanted. In a panic, he thought this might be the last straw. These past few weeks she'd been surrounded by affluent men able to take their wives on long, expensive trips, dress them in Diors and diamonds, assure them security as wives and widows. Had Mary been comparing them with him? She didn't need him. She earned a good living. He'd kept their marriage alive on dreams and promises and on the deliberate appeal to her compassion. But he'd always thought that one day he could deliver. Damn Harry Carson. There was no way to start a business without him. Everybody he'd approached in the past forty-eight hours had turned him down. Even Charlie, who might have done it for Mary's sake. Only Rae had come through, and her lousy twenty-five thousand wasn't enough to get the enterprise going.

What a mess he'd gotten into! Like some damned male whore, dutifully turning up these past three afternoons at Rae's. It made him sick to his stomach, but a bargain was a bargain. He hoped she'd soon tire of her little game. She'd have to when Mary got home. He thought of returning the money and telling Rae to go to hell. But he hung on, hoping he could add to the stake. So far it hadn't happened, and it looked as though it never would.

And why in God's name had he gotten himself involved with Patricia? The first time it happened was just a reflex. He'd been so depressed. He'd needed comfort and forgetfulness. He hadn't meant it to go on, but how was a man to resist? Patricia was there, openly inviting him to make love to her in his own bed. Mary's bed. The woman was as hungry as he. More hungry, judging by the disparaging things she said about her husband. He felt rotten about the affair, even as he enjoyed the hours with her. But Patricia should be more ashamed than he. Her own sister's husband! And she seemed to have no conscience.

"We're not hurting Mary," she'd said at one point. "What's the big deal? She won't be deprived. You're terrific." She laughed. "Mike Morgan, the envy of the locker room!"

The crudeness made him cringe. It was one thing to have some young, willing bedmate. It was not even so terrible to cheat with one of Mary's "friends." But Patricia was different. Mary would die if she found out. Not that she would, of course. It would never enter her mind that her husband and her sister were sleeping together. Damn these women! He was extraordinarily virile, thank God, but how long could he handle two of them?

He needed to talk to his wife. Mary would be consoling, understanding about Carson. Of course she would. He could get rid of Rae, and Patricia would soon leave, in

155

any case. Resolutely, he placed the call and sat back waiting for it to be completed.

Mary was at dinner when the maître d' told her she had a ship-to-shore call. She went to the phone at the bar in the dining room.

"Mrs. Morgan? Radio room here. We have a call coming through from San Francisco. Would you like to take it in your cabin, madame?"

She'd hurried down to 320 and in a few minutes the phone rang. She heard the radio operator telling San Francisco to go ahead, Mrs. Morgan was on the line. Michael's voice came through with surprising clarity.

"Darling, how are you? How's the trip?"

"Michael? Is anything wrong?"

There was a second's hesitation. "Did you get my letter in Hong Kong?"

"No. What is it?"

"Nothing. I just told you that Patricia's here for a visit."

"Patricia? There? Why?"

"She wanted a little vacation, and to be here when you and Jayne returned. Don't worry. We're getting along famously. How are you?"

"I'm fine. So is Jayne." How easy it was to lie. "What happened with Harry Carson?"

There was silence on the line.

"Michael? Are you there?"

"Yes. Everything's signed, sealed and delivered. Carson's wildly enthusiastic."

"Oh, Michael, I'm so happy for you!"

"Yeah, me, too. I told you I'd pull it off."

"It's wonderful! I'm so proud of you! You must be working very hard, but it's a good feeling, isn't it?"

"Sure is. Thought you'd be pleased."

"I'm delighted. I was so afraid he'd back out."

"You been having a good time?"

"It's been fascinating. How's Charlie?"

"He's okey, but Tracey's in some sanatorium, drying out, I guess. We had a drink a couple of nights ago."

"Poor Charlie. Give him my love. And try to see him

156

as often as you can, Michael. He must be down in the dumps."

"Right. Well, I'd better hang up. The phone bill will look like the national debt. Just wanted to hear your voice, darling. I miss you. You must never go away again, unless I'm along."

"Yes. Take care of yourself. Give my love to Patricia. I'm sure Jayne sends hers, too."

She was trembling as she put down the receiver.

Her tablemates stared at her inquiringly when she returned to the dining room.

"Everything all right at home?" Gail DeVries asked.

"Fine." She didn't look at Christopher. "My husband just called to tell me he has a wonderful new business deal."

"Well!" Colonel Stanford said. "That's cause for celebration!" He beckoned to the wine steward. "I think we-all better have us a couple bottles of champagne and drink to his success."

*   *   *

Michael sat looking at the telephone. Why had he lied? He'd meant to tell her the truth, counting, as always, on her sympathy. But when he heard her voice, he couldn't do it. What was the point of spoiling her trip, anyway? Time enough to give her the bad news when she got home. But somehow he felt worse about deceiving her this way than he did about the infidelity. He should have come right out with it. Hell, what was he worrying about? Mary wasn't concerned about him. She was quick enough to go off and leave him. She always did what she wanted. Deliberately, he courted his anger. She was so bloody efficient, so damned lucky. Like falling into that job. He'd always thought Charlie Burke had more than a professional interest in her. For all he knew, they might have been sleeping together all these years. It wasn't fair. It was his rotten luck to be around women who always came up smelling like roses. His mother had been self-sufficient. So

157

had his first wife. And so, of course, was Mary. They enjoyed taking care of him. So let them.

He got up and began to pace the room, full of self-justification. They used him, these women. They took advantage of his amiability to satisfy their need to dominate. He gave them more than they gave him. He saw himself as the victim of sharks, the prey of devouring females.

"Something wrong?" Patricia stood in the doorway.

"I just talked to Mary."

"Oh. I suppose she was upset when you told her about Harry Carson."

"I didn't tell her. That is, I told her everything was okay. That the deal was on."

Patricia's face was expressionless.

"Damn it," Michael said, "what was the use of telling her the truth now? What could she do about it out there in the middle of the Pacific?"

"Nothing. You were right. Dear Michael. You're so sweet, so considerate not to worry her. How many men would have that strength? Most of them are babies, thinking only of themselves. Take Stanley," she said bitterly. "If such a thing happened to him, he'd make my life miserable with his whining. He'd be impossible to live with. But you're different. You think of your wife first."

He looked uncomfortable. "I haven't thought too much of her since you've been here. That hasn't been so considerate."

"Nonsense. Call it fate. Call it whatever you want. Something made me come out here to you just when you needed a woman to comfort you." She held out her arms. "I needed comfort, too, you know. The kind you give me."

He held back. "Come on, Patricia, don't tell me you're frustrated. Not a woman like you."

She laughed. "I don't know whether that's an insult or a compliment. *A woman like me?* What kind of woman do you think I am?"

Michael didn't answer.

"You're afraid of hurting my feelings, aren't you, darling? Don't be. I know what I am. Sexy. Selfish. Uncon-

158

ventional, to say the least. But in a healthy way, Michael. Just as you are. We're two of a kind, my dear. Danger stimulates us. Tell the truth—isn't illicit lovemaking more exciting than the legal kind?"

For a moment he wondered whether Mary had confided in her. Did she know how dutiful and routine her sister had become in bed? No. Mary wouldn't talk about her feelings to anyone. Not even to him. She was a good wife. Patient, faithful, loving in her own way. But she didn't have Patricia's lustiness, her blatant sensuality. Mary wouldn't know about illicit love. Patricia, he suspected, knew plenty about it. He was sure he was not the only one who'd given her "comfort" in the years of her dull marriage.

She moved close to him now, rubbing the back of his neck, letting her hands move invitingly down his spine. I'm going to die from all this, he thought half humorously. Rae in the afternoon and Patricia whenever she can turn me on. For God's sake, I'm forty-five years old and I'm trying to live the sex life of a boy of twenty! And yet, almost with pride, he found himself responding.

* * *

The talk with Mary had been painful. She'd been wide-eyed when Jayne told her what she and Terry planned when they returned to San Francisco.

"I know you don't approve, Aunt Mary, but you must believe we know what we're doing. I told you before, I don't intend to marry him. There are no strings. We can break it off any time either of us feels like it."

Mary sighed. "Jayne, it's not that simple. You'll be emotionally involved, both of you. You're asking for trouble. You know so little about Terry."

Jayne was defensive. "I know everything about him. I certainly know as much about him as you do about Christopher."

"I haven't decided to link my life with Christopher's. Besides, my dear, I'm almost twice your age. I like to think I know a little more about the realities than you do.

Jaynie, try to see this objectively. You know Terry's past. For now, he's fascinated with you. You're a new experience. Maybe he really does believe you've changed him, but what about tomorrow or a year from tomorrow? He could go back to being what he was. You'd be terribly hurt."

"No. We've discussed that. He's not sure what will happen. Neither am I. But who is? We're happy together, Aunt Mary. He adores me. He really does. And I love him. Not the way I loved Russell. More tenderly, because I know he needs me."

Mary was in despair. "Don't do it, Jayne. I beg you. Don't repeat my mistakes. It's wrong to tie yourself to a dependent man. You're strong and patient and good, but you can't handle this. Its not enough to be a tower of strength. Believe me. I know. You end up feeling cheated and glued to your bargain out of pity and false pride. There are millions of women like us, settling for a half-life because the men they chose can't get along without them. Don't be one of us. You don't know what a vacant existence that is."

It was like talking to a wall.

"I know you're only saying what you believe, Aunt Mary. I know you're trying to protect me. But you're assuming it's going to work out that way. How do you know Terry won't become a famous actor? I could end up living with a star." Jayne sounded reasonable. "But let's assume the worst. Let's assume Terry never makes anything of his life and I support him. That's not so tragic these days. Millions of women of my generation do that without being miserable about it. Times have changed. We don't expect a man to go out and kill a boar for supper, any more than we want him to drag us by the hair of our heads to his cave! We're willing to share responsibilities. We want to. You grew up seeing things differently. I know what you mean about the way some women feel. Even the ones who only manage the family budget, not those who've gone after real careers. They're women of your time, Aunt Mary. Not mine. They have a stereotyped idea of what a man should be, and if he doesn't live up to that conditioned image, they feel they've missed something. I don't buy that."

"What do you buy, Jayne? Being a mother to your lover? Or are you going to turn into one of those hard-bitten dames who think it's amusing to have a man they can boss around?"

"Neither. I want a career of some kind, but that won't necessarily make me a barracuda, will it? It hadn't made you one."

Mary made one last try. "Darling, you're going into something with impossible odds. Forget all we've said. Even if you believe the basic man-woman relationship has changed, which I don't, what about Terry's homosexuality? Won't you be plagued with doubts about him? Every time he's out, won't you wonder whether he's found some man?"

"Do you worry that Uncle Mike has found some woman?"

There was nothing more to say, Mary realized. No way to keep Jayne from getting into this perilous situation. They have to learn the hard way. They don't believe terrible things can happen to them, these naïve, opinionated young people. That's how it's always been. It's human nature. If Michael's mother or his ex-wife had tried to warn me about marrying him, I'd still have been positive it would be different with us. Just as Jayne is positive she and Terry can make a go of their arrangement. I wouldn't have listened either.

"All right. There's no point in discussing it further. I can see that. I don't know what your mother and father are going to say, but that's up to them and you to settle. If you decide to stay in San Francisco, I'll help any way I can—job-wise, apartment-wise, whatever. At least you'll know I'm there."

Jayne looked at her evenly. "Thanks, Aunt Mary, but will you be there? What about Christopher?"

The words came almost as a shock. She'd been so embroiled in Jayne's plans, she hadn't thought of her own. It was possible she wouldn't be there. For a moment, she'd forgotten that.

"I don't know about Christopher," she said slowly. "I wish to God I did."

Watching Mary as she returned to the dinner table after her call from Michael, Jayne wondered whether the good news from home would make Mary's decision easier. She seemed numb, somehow, and she didn't look at Christopher as she joined in a toast to her husband's future. Michael's okay now, Jayne thought. She can leave him with a clear conscience. Why doesn't she look happier?

* * *

Peggy fussed around the captain's cabin, rearranging the fresh flowers, checking the liquor supply he kept for cocktail parties, straightening the pictures of his mother and the rest of his unknown family in England.

It was the next best thing to taking care of him in their own home, she thought. She could hardly wait for that, though it might not come as quickly as she'd hoped. Frowning, she interrupted Tony, who was going over some papers at his desk.

"Are you sure you won't be able to leave the ship in San Francisco?"

He didn't look up. "I told you, Peggy. I can't just quit on the spur of the moment. They'll have to find someone to take over my command. That means I'll have to stay on at least until we get back to England."

"But that's so far away! Back down the coast, through the Panama Canal, all the way across the Atlantic. It will be weeks before you're free."

"Don't complain. It should have been five years."

"Should have been?"

He didn't answer.

"Tony! Answer me! What do you mean, 'should have been'?"

He looked up angrily. "Don't give orders to me! I give the orders! And you know damned well what I mean. If you hadn't blackmailed me into marrying you in Hong Kong, I'd have had the time I wanted. I'd have married

162

you gladly then, but no, you couldn't wait! You had to rig that damned fake suicide, didn't you? Make me feel you'd die if you didn't get me. Well, you've got me, in a manner of speaking."

She was outraged. That damned, sniveling doctor had told him. Taken her money, thanked her in his supercilious manner and run straight to the captain. No wonder Tony had acted so strangely the past couple of days. He'd been so loving and gentle on their brief honeymoon, but he'd turned horrid in the last forty-eight hours. Now she knew why. He was furious, knowing he'd been outsmarted. She felt a rush of fear. What if he decided to dissolve the marriage? Maybe he could divorce her, claiming fraud. She didn't like the sound of that phrase "in a manner of speaking." Peggy looked meek and repentant. It was the only way to handle him.

"Darling, I'm sorry. But it wasn't a fake. I just didn't know how many pills to take. I meant it, Tony. When I thought I was losing you, I didn't want to live."

He acted as though he didn't hear her.

"Please, believe me," she said. "You can't hate someone for loving you so much. I'll do anything you want. Anything to make you happy."

"Anything?"

"Yes, I swear it, darling. Anything you say."

"All right, Peggy. In that case, I'll tell you what you'll do. You'll get off this ship in San Francisco and go back to Chicago. You won't take any more cruises. Whenever I have leave, we'll spend it together, wherever you like. And that's the way we'll live for the next five years. The way I wanted it in the beginning."

"Tony! No! You can't! You promised!"

"No man is expected to stand by a promise made under the conditions you set up. I love you, Peggy. Strangely enough, I do. But I can't let you run my life. I'm going to stay with the ship until my retirement. You'll be my wife, and like the wives of other sea captains you'll be with me when I'm ashore. Later, we'll live the way you want to."

She stared at him. "You expect me to be alone for five years?"

"You won't be alone. I'll be with you some of the time. Many another woman has made that adjustment for much longer. Besides," Tony said sardonically, "you have what matters to you. You're a wife with a living husband. You belong to somebody. That's what really counts, isn't it?"

She began to cry, but she knew tears wouldn't help. This was an ultimatum. Take it or leave it. What choice did she have? He'd divorce her if she didn't go along with his decisions. Five years. It was a long time. But meanwhile, she would be Mrs. Anthony Robin. She'd have the security that meant so much to her. She'd be a married woman. The world would know she was wanted by a handsome, glamorous man. She'd not be one of those pathetic divorcées or widows, aimlessly adrift. It was better than nothing. Much better. And certainly she could change his mind before the five years were up. Peggy finally managed to smile.

"All right, darling," she said. "Your happiness is all I care about."

Chapter 14

As soon as Jayne left the cabin that evening, Mary pushed the "on" button of the tape recorder and began to speak into the microphone.

"Good morning, friends. This is Mary Farr Morgan. There'll be no interview as such today. Instead, I'd like to share with you an unforgettable interlude. Try to capture a moment in time. Imprison a picture in your heart as one is imprisoned in mine.

"I'm sure most of you have a mental picture of Japan. I know I did. I visualized a small, bustling country rapidly becoming Westernized. In the years since World War II, we've bought Japanese cars and TV sets, seen pictures of Tokyo, a traffic-jammed city bigger and more crowded than New York, with American-style night clubs populated by young men and women in modern dress.

"Well, I haven't seen Tokyo yet. Probably it's as we imagine. But there's another, quieter Japan that still exists, and I've just returned from it. For the past twenty-four hours, I've been in the gracious city of Kyoto.

"Forgive my sentimentality, but I think that wherever I go I shall never forget the feeling of having been plucked from the hurried, noisy world of the twentieth century and transported back to a culture whose roots go deep into Japanese soil. More than a thousand years deep. I won't bore you with statistics. Suffice to say that from 794 to 1869, Kyoto was the capital city of Japan and today is its fifth largest city with a population of nearly one and a half million.

"More interesting to me—and, I hope, to you—is the fact that Kyoto is still the cradle of Japanese civilization, the repository of its legends and the dramatic reminder of its sophisticated past. Not sophisticated in the world-weary sense, but in the elegant, unpretentious way that genuinely sophisticated people are, assured and elegant, conscious of their quality with no need to flaunt their riches.

"I arrived at night, under a full moon. I was driven through streets incredibly adhering to a modern, check-ered design laid out in the original plan more than eleven hundred years ago. And I came at last to an oasis of san-ity called Tawaraya, the inn made famous in the writings of Elizabeth Gray Vining, the American tutor of Crown Prince Akihito.

"Believe me, I could spend our whole half hour describing this inn managed by Mrs. Toshi Sato, whose family has run Tawaraya for eleven generations, or three hundred years. There are nineteen rooms, each with bath. And what rooms! Done in the traditional manner with sliding doors overlooking private gardens which are softly lighted at night. The main room is sparsely furnished with a low teak table and quote chairs unquote which really are pillows with rush backs and separate, kidney-shaped armrests of antique brocade. The no-color walls are bare except for one beautiful hanging. And precisely to its right, on the floor, is a perfect flower arrangement of two graceful blossoms in a wicker basket.

"I dined, solicitously served by a dignified elderly Japanese woman in traditional dress. I'm sure she was amused by my ineptitude with chopsticks and my thor-oughly baffled expression when confronted by pressed seaweed and other exotic and still unidentified dishes, but she was much too polite to show it.

"Later, I explored details I'd been too entranced at first to discover. The bath was a miracle unto itself. The sleek, oversized wooden tub has a cover to keep the water hot.

166

One soaps and rinses and then steps, rather gingerly, into the near-scalding water to relax. But the tub is not the only wonder of the perfectly appointed bathroom. There are stocks of kimonos and slippers, tissues, a comb and brush, razor, shampoo and body lotion, and several toothbrushes. And there are modern concessions which I almost wished weren't there. A portable hair dryer and, in the main room, a small television set. I found myself resenting their intrusion into this old-fashioned world, and I wanted to say, 'Don't. Please let me pretend I'm a pampered woman of a hundred years ago with smiling retainers to bring me tea and arrange my room for the night.'

"Dear friends, promise you'll never ask for an Occidental bedroom in Japan! Don't miss the ceremonial joy of watching the maid take your two flowered mattresses out of a secret closet in the wall and stack them on the floor, carefully covering them with thick padding. She adds clean white sheets, top and bottom, a striped blanket and over that a bright-pink quilt. Two small pillows are propped against one of the rush-back chairs which suddenly serves as a backboard. A standing paper lamp is set next to the bed and a calm descends that drives tension and pressures far into the still, moonlit night. You will rest as you never have before."

Mary snapped off the machine and sat thinking of the night as it really was. Whatever would happen to her and Christopher in the days ahead, they had this euphoric memory to share. This was a world made for lovers. A private world, civilized and tranquil, where even the movements of love had a slow, graceful, dreamlike quality.

Almost reluctantly she went on to describe the next day in Kyoto. The breathtaking beauty of the gardens, all water and stone and cherry-blossom trees in full bloom.

("The Japanese don't plant flowers in their gardens," Christopher said. "Flowers die, but trees live forever and grow more beautiful with age.")

She described the shrines she visited. The glorious

Shinto temple where she saw a baptism, called a "purification," in progress. Another where, for a few pennies, one bought a slip of paper with one's fortune. If the fortune was bad, you simply attached it to a tree outside the temple where it fluttered with hundreds of others, blowing its ill omen away, into the soft spring breeze.

With her listeners, she wandered through the seventeenth-century shogun's summer palace, stunned by the beauty of the intricately painted screen-walls, the decorative gold leaf that had endured for centuries, the "nightingale floors" that squeaked as one walked, as they'd once squeaked to warn the guards of intruders. On the area where the shogun's concubines lived, the "harem" scene was re-created with mannequins in authentic dress.

"Every night," Mary said, "each of the shogun's concubines offered him a cup of tea. The one he accepted was the lady chosen to be with him. The others had to wait their turn!"

("From this came the expression, 'You're not my cup of tea,'" Christopher solemnly explained. "Idiot!" Mary said. "You made that up!" He'd laughed. "Sure. But what a considerate rejection.")

The tape was coming to a close as Mary told of her experience with the famous "Bullet Train," known in Japan for its electrified smoothness and speed.

"I decided to take it back to Kobe to meet the ship, which sailed at six o'clock. My ticket was on the four-fifteen train and, knowing it was only a thirty-minute ride, I knew I had plenty of time. Unfortunately, at the station my guide informed me the train had been indefinitely delayed by, of all things, an encounter with a kite string! It didn't come into the Kyoto station until five o'clock and I nearly had heart failure racing up the dock to catch my floating home before it left for Yokohama! I made it. But barely!"

How they'd laughed, she and Christopher, at the idea of the super-streamlined train, the pride of Japan, stopped by a kite string. They were still laughing as they raced down the long dock toward the gangway. But the laughter turned to fear as Christopher suddenly stopped halfway and leaned against a post, his face gray. Mary ran on a few feet before she realized he wasn't following. She turned and rushed back.

"Christopher! What is it? What's wrong?"

He'd shaken his head and smiled. "Nothing. Just a little winded. I'll be okay in a second. Don't worry. They won't leave without us."

"I'm not worried about that! I'm worried about you!"

"It's okay." In a minute he straightened up. "See? Just had to catch my breath. The old boy ain't what he used to be."

"You're sure? Shouldn't I get a doctor?"

"Nope. I'm fine. Come along. We only have ten minutes."

No account of that terrifying episode went onto the tape. No mention of the fact that her "guide" was the charming, knowledgeable man she loved. She wished she could tell the world what it meant to spend this time with him. Poor Christopher, she thought, smiling. I can't even give him credit for some of the trivia I picked up. Like the reason the Japanese bow when they meet someone is because it's considered rude to look another person in the eye, and bowing is a graceful way to avoid such discourtesy. She ended her report with that little piece of information.

"Perhaps, more than anything, that simple gesture, so misunderstood by Westerners, symbolizes the courteous formality and the adherence to tradition one feels in this land. It also points up the vast difference between us. For as Americans, we condemn a person who 'can't look you in the eye.' In Japan, it is just the opposite.

"So, until you and I figuratively 'look each other in the eye' in San Francisco, this is Mary Farr Morgan saying 'Sayonara' from the other side of the world."

She put the tape in its container and addressed it to Charlie. Tomorrow evening she'd mail it from Yokohama. A part of her life was going to the States. And another part was going back to Australia, hoping she'd join him there. She thought of Michael's call. She knew what she was going to do. Tonight she'd tell Christopher.

* * *

He lay on his bed, resting. The pain was gone now, but it had scared hell out of him back there on the dock. It was like the time before. A searing poker in his chest. Stupid damned doctors in Singapore! They'd told him he was fine.

Christopher propped himself up on the pillows. Well, he probably was. It might not had had anything to do with his heart. After all, he wasn't a kid. He couldn't make those wild sprints along two city blocks without running out of steam.

He sat up gingerly. Sure. He was fine. No point in seeing that silly little med student who passed for a doctor on this ship. In another day or so he'd be home. He'd have his own specialist check, just to be sure. Ridiculous to get so frightened every time he had a twinge. His doctor told him that if he lived sensibly he'd be good for another twenty years. Racing like a track star was hardly sensible. He wasn't infirm, but he had to be cautious.

Perhaps he should tell Mary his history. No. If she wasn't going to marry him, there was no point. And if she was, it was selfish to worry her needlessly. He had no intention of dying soon. If he thought that, he'd never have proposed, would never let her give up everything to be with him. He was all right. Everything was all right. He was certain she'd marry him. Why wouldn't she? That damned husband of hers was finally on his feet. She need have no guilts about "abandoning" him. She must realize that after the phone call, though they hadn't discussed it. Her "helpless child" needed her no more. Christopher sighed with pleasure. The conscience-haunting hurdle that stood between them was gone. And Mary loved him. If he needed reassurance, it had come in Kyoto. They'd go back one day and recapture that particular ecstasy. Meantime, so many ecstatic days lay ahead.

170

* * *

"Christopher will never understand. And I can't say I blame him." Jayne stared at her aunt, who was slowly dressing for dinner. "My God, Aunt Mary, I've never heard such an inverted rationale! First you can't leave Uncle Mike because he's a failure and now you have to stay with him because he's a success! I don't get it. I really don't. I'm beginning to think you're some kind of masochist!"

Mary turned slowly from the dressing table to face her niece. She looked drawn and unhappy even while she tried to sound light-hearted. "The same thought crossed my mind," she said. "All I need in my spring wardrobe is a hair shirt."

Jayne persisted. "Why are you doing this? Why are you going back to him? Don't you remember anything you told me weeks ago? I thought the whole purpose was to decide whether Michael could live without you. You led me to believe that you stayed with him only because he depended on you. Well, he's all set now. He doesn't have to lean on you, financially or emotionally. You're scot-free, Aunt Mary, and a super guy wants you. You could be happy, be the kind of woman you say you always wanted to be. And you're going to turn it down? I think you're crazy!"

"I don't blame you. I think maybe I am." Mary nervously twisted the jade ring on her finger. "How can I explain it to you?"

"Try."

Mary took a deep breath. Later she'd have to try to make Christopher understand. As Jayne said, he never would. How could he? She didn't really understand herself. She wasn't even sure that what she was doing was right. Maybe if she talked it out with Jayne, it would be clearer in her own mind. A kind of dress rehearsal for disaster, she thought mirthlessly. A practice session before I try to make Christopher see what I must do.

"I haven't forgotten what I told you," she said. "It was all true, Jaynie. It still is, I suppose. The respect I lost for

171

Michael hasn't magically come back just because he's finally pulled off one of his impossible dreams. I haven't fallen in love with him again. But the thing of it is, everything he's ever done has been in an effort to make me proud of him. All the lies about his jobs, all the bravado about the big deals in the offing, all this was done to please me. To make me glad I married him. He loves me very much. More than I love him. He's never cared about being a success, except that he knows it's important to me. Now that he's broken his back to be what I wanted, could I possibly leave him? Wouldn't that negate everything he's tried to do? Wouldn't it make all the years of trying and failing meaningless? How can I walk out on him when he's done the very thing I felt I needed? Not the thing *he* needed. The thing *I* needed—his success. I can't let him feel it's all been in vain. I can't pat him on the head and say, 'Good boy, Michael. Now you don't need me anymore. Good-bye.' My God, Jayne, that would really destroy him! To have worked all these years toward an end that someone else wants and then be rewarded by desertion! I could have justified it more, in my own mind, when he was a failure. I could have convinced myself that he didn't care enough for me to try to make something of himself. I could have told myself he's a hopeless goof-off. But he's delivered what he believed I wanted. I believed it myself. Am I to repay all this pathetic striving by selfishly turning away from him? I can't. I want to, but I can't!"

Jayne stared at her, speechless. She really believes that, the girl thought. She honestly feels she has an obligation. That Michael doesn't care about himself. That his motivation has been her approval and nothing more.

"You're wrong, you know," Jayne finally said. "You're still doing the same number with a different twist. You still think he needs you. That this new career means nothing without you. Maybe you're afraid he won't make a success of it unless you're there. You still must be indispensable, mustn't you? I'm sorry, Aunt Mary, but I think you rather enjoy being a martyr. You must get your kicks out of self-sacrifice. I don't doubt you believe what you're saying, but it's dumb. Really dumb. Hell, it's more than

172

that! It's sick! Why does everything have to depend on you? What is this wild ego of yours that makes you think Michael can't make it without you? He's a grown man, for God's sake! And what about Christopher? Doesn't it haunt you to know how unhappy he's going to be?"

Mary didn't fight back. "Everything you're saying is probably true, but I have to live with myself. I can't help how I feel. I know Michael isn't strong enough to be alone. Christopher is. In a few months Christopher will have forgotten me, but not standing by Michael would destroy him. I made my bed. I'm going to have to try to be content in it."

Jayne snorted. "I never heard such hogwash! I could throw up! You're not doing anything admirable, Aunt Mary. You're still pampering an ego that won't stop. You may believe all those flimsy excuses about making Michael's efforts worthwhile, but I have my doubts. I think if you really told the truth, you'd admit that you don't *want* a strong man. That the thought of being second fiddle to Christopher scares hell out of you. That you can't stand the idea of giving up your career and your feeling of importance. I don't think it's Michael who's taking you back to your old life. I think you *like* your old life! I don't think you could live without it!"

Mary took the verbal beating without anger. For all she knew, Jayne might be right. She did love her work. She did love the attention it brought her. She couldn't deny that. As for the ego, the indispensability where Michael was concerned, maybe that was true, too. She didn't know. She only knew she couldn't deliver this final blow to a faithful, loving man who was trying to please her. Couldn't do it even if it meant giving up one she desperately loved.

"I know how I must sound," she said quietly. "In your place, I'd feel just as disgusted. Maybe I'm guilty of everything you say. Probably I am. But I won't be the first woman who stuck out of loyalty. Misguided, maybe. But still loyalty. There are principles involved here, Jayne. I'm not patting myself on the back, but I can't be as selfish as I probably should. Your mother and I were brought up to

173

believe in the sanctity of marriage. I'm sure, in a different way, she's not been any happier than I. But she's stayed with your father, hasn't she? She hasn't walked out because she's bored."

"Now you're really being ridiculous! Mother hasn't walked out because she has no place to walk to. You said so yourself. God! Don't point her out as the model of a perfect wife! She's cheated on Dad since Day One!"

Mary's voice was almost a whisper. "And I've cheated on Michael."

Jayne sighed. "That's part of it, too, isn't it? You're feeling guilty as hell about this affair. Probably beating yourself up because you've been having a wonderful time while Michael's been home trying to get his damned project off the ground. Aunt Mary, get with it! This isn't the Victorian age! Everybody strays from the reservation. You don't honestly think Uncle Mike's been a paragon of virtue all these weeks, do you? If you tell me that, I'll faint. I swear I'll absolutely faint!"

In spite of her distress, Mary laughed. "I can't imagine you fainting no matter what." She sobered. "I envy you, Jayne. I really do. I think I'm a strong woman, but next to you, I'm Jell-O. You're so certain of things. Everything is so neatly black and white. You're not afraid of anything in the world, are you?"

"Only of being maudlin."

Involuntarily, Mary recoiled.

"I'm sorry, Aunt Mary. I didn't mean to say that. But I can't stand what you're doing! Think about yourself. You talk of being 'unfulfilled,' of having made terrible mistakes, of not wanting to see me get into a situation like yours. Yet when you have a chance to escape, you won't. All this bull about loyalty and principles. What is it? Don't you see what you're going to do to Christopher? What you're going to do to yourself? No, of course you don't. You only see this fancied obligation to Michael. Don't do it. I beg you. You'll be sorry the rest of your life."

"You mean damned if I do, and damned if I don't."

"No. I only mean damned if you don't tell Christopher

you're divorcing Michael and flying back to him as soon as you can."

"I can't, Jayne. I want to, but I can't."

"Then you don't really want to. You prefer to suffer rather than take a chance on someone else."

It was very much what Christopher had said to her. You have to really want it. You have to trust someone, sometime. I do trust, Mary though. I know Christopher would take care of me. I trust Michael to be faithful and loving. It's my own emotions I don't trust. I don't even know when I'm lying to myself. I don't know what's true anymore.

I just know I have to go back and find out.

*   *   *

She'd never seen anyone look so bewildered and hurt. Then the look changed to incredulity.

"Mary, what are you saying? You're going to throw away everything we could have together because of this distorted thinking? It's not possible! It's upside down! My God, I could almost have made myself accept the fact that a woman like you wouldn't desert a helpless dependent man. But to believe that you owe him some kind of thanks for finally succeeding! It's incredible. I won't allow it."

"I know. It seems sick. But I do owe him, Christopher. He's spent the past fifteen years trying to please me."

"And what happens in the next fifteen? Or the next thirty?"

Tears came to Mary's eyes. "Don't you think I've thought of that? Don't you know how hard it is for me to do this?"

"No." His voice was harsh. "I don't know that at all. All I see is some kind of warped feeling of obligation that isn't credible. You're doing a terrible thing, Mary. You're destroying two lives, yours and mine, for the sake of one that doesn't sound worth worrying about. What kind of man has to be constantly propped up to keep going? What kind of man would have let you take care of him all these years? Damn it, don't you see what he is? What he'll always be?"

"You don't understand." The words came from her choked throat. "I love you, Christopher. But I can't love at someone else's expense. Women feel differently than men about things like this. Michael is my husband, for better or for worse."

"Like hell! Michael is your child. And that's what you want, isn't it? A child to mother. Too bad you never had any. Or maybe it's just as well. You'd have smothered them, too!" He stopped, instantly remorseful. "Oh, God, darling, forgive me. I'm beside myself. I don't know what I'm saying. I can't believe this. I don't know how to stop you from making this terrible mistake. I want you so much, Mary. I love you more than I've ever loved any woman. I can't lose you. It's wrong. Hideously wrong."

"I have to do it, Christopher. I have to go home and give him a chance. It has nothing to do with my feeling for you. I'll love you the rest of my life, but I must do this."

He rose from the chair on the upper deck where they sat under the stars and walked to the railing. With his back to her he said, "Yokohama tomorrow. I had such hopes."

Mary closed her eyes. I wish I were dead, she thought. I can't bear it. She felt Christopher return to her side.

"It's our last night, darling."

"Yes. Oh, Christopher, I . . ."

"Hush. No more to be said. You go home and decide about your life, sweetheart. Our life. You'll hear from me. I'm not going to take this decision as final. I realize you think you must stay, but I'm betting that when you get there you'll see you're free to leave. That you've paid your dues. Fifteen years of them. That you've done everything a loving woman can do. And more. When you see that, my dearest Mary, I'll be waiting. You know where to find me."

"Don't wait," she pleaded. "Make a life for yourself with someone else. I want you to. I want you to be happy."

"You'll come to me," Christopher said. "It may take a while, but you'll come." He pulled her to her feet. "Meantime, my love, we have one more chance to be together before our temporary separation. And that's what it is, dear heart, a time for the unfinished business you must complete. I know you must. You'd never know peace until you did." He smiled sadly. "My wonderful, darling Mary. What rotten luck she's such a loyal, compassionate woman."

"An old-fashioned idiot, you mean."

Christopher gently stroked her hair. "Yes," he said, "that, too. But I wouldn't have you any other way, dearest. Even if it means letting you find out for yourself what I already know."

"That I'm wrong for Michael?"

"More importantly, that you're right for me."

Chapter 15

Patricia poured a cup of coffee for Michael and handed it to him across the breakfast table. She'd been a guest in her sister's apartment for ten days, her brother-in-law's lover for nearly that long, and she hated to think of it coming to an end in another couple of weeks. I wish I could stay in San Francisco, she thought. I love this city. I could get a little apartment and see Michael now and then when Mary was at work. Forget it, she told herself. Who'd support her? Not Stanley. Not Michael, who didn't have a penny of his own. And she certainly wasn't going to start trying to earn a living at this late date. Maybe Jayne, she thought suddenly. Maybe the kid would like to work here and share an apartment with her mother. She decided to try the idea out on Michael.

"What would you think if I could talk Jayne into staying in San Francisco and the two of us took an apartment?"

The horrified look in Michael's eyes was her answer, though he quickly tried to cover his dismay.

"I don't know," he said casually. "Do you think you'd want to live here permanently? What about Stanley?"

"To hell with Stanley."

"He's your husband, Patricia. Even if we've chosen to ignore the fact." Michael looked uneasy. "Besides, I think you'd be bored here. All your friends are in New York."

"I make friends easily. Anyway, *you're* here."

Michael began to feel nervous. "Look, Pat, this whole business ends the minute Mary comes back. You do know that, don't you? I mean, my God, there's no way in the world I could see you after she returns!"

"Really? You couldn't see your sister-in-law?"

"You know what I mean."

"You bet I know. The cat's on her way home and playtime is over for the mouse. It's easy enough to dump me, Michael, but what are you going to do about your friend Rae?"

He was visibly startled. "What about Rae?"

"Oh, come on! Do you really think a woman like Rae Spanner could keep a triumph like that to herself? She called here yesterday, pretending she'd like to give a party for Mary and Jayne when they return, and saying how anxious she was to meet me. She was about as subtle as a see-through blouse."

"How did she know you were in town?"

"She said somebody named Charlie Burke mentioned it. And then she said she was amazed that you hadn't told her." Patricia imitated Rae's boarding-school voice. " 'I can't imagine why dear Michael didn't tell me himself. He drops by every afternoon. We're in a business venture together and we've become *very* close.' " Patricia laughed. "I got the picture. She's lent you money and she's extracting her pound of flesh."

Michael flushed. "All right, it's true, but I can't imagine why she'd want you to know any of that."

"Oh, Michael, you are naïve! Don't you see? She wants me to tell Mary."

"Tell Mary!"

"Of course. You don't really think she's going to settle for some temporary arrangement, do you? She's after you, dear boy. After you for keeps. Don't tell me you didn't suspect that."

He was growing angry. "What makes you so damned sure? You've never even met her. It seems to me you're

179

jumping to a lot of conclusions based on one telephone call"

Methodically, Patricia ticked off her reasons on the fingers of one hand. "Okay. Number one, Mary's mentioned her over the years. I know she's rich and single and used to buying what she wants. Number two, I know you'd do anything to get money to start your own business. Number three, I'm a street-smart girl from New York. I've heard that proprietary tone of voice before. Women understand other women, Michael. I know her type. I saw through that phony phone call even before she said more."

"Said more? What more?"

"Just a few little things. Like wasn't it too bad that someone as brilliant and attractive as you didn't have a rich wife to set him up in business. And how marvelous it was that Mary at least could do well enough to let the two of you live comfortably. And how she wondered what Mary's reaction would be when she came home and found you hadn't raised enough capital. She's a barracuda. If I were you, I'd pay her off and deny everything if she starts trouble. If you're lucky, Mary won't find out what's been going on there."

"You're not going to tell Mary, are you?"

Patricia grinned. "What's it worth to you?"

"Exactly what does that mean?"

"Is it worth your helping me talk Jayne into staying in San Francisco and getting a job to support her devoted mother? And is it worth an occasional visit to me while Mary's at work?"

He stared at her and then, unexpectedly, began to laugh. "That's funny! Oh, God, that's funny! Talk about your boomerangs! You'd really do that, wouldn't you? You'd threaten to tell Mary about my involvement with Rae, which isn't nearly as ugly as my involvement with you. And I'd be in the middle, wouldn't I? Because you know I'd never tell her about us." Michael stopped laughing. "It's hard to believe you and Mary are sisters. She's so damned honest and you're as devious as they come.

180

Jesus, how could the two of you have come from the same parents?"

Patricia was unperturbed. "It happens that way, lots of times. Saints and sinners out of the same womb. Not that I think Mary's a saint. Not by any means. She's been self-centered since the day she was born. I don't think she could make a real commitment to anyone."

"She certainly made one to me!"

"Nope. With you she made an arrangement. She found herself a nice, big, handsome guy who wouldn't get in the way of her ambitions. That's not a commitment, Michael. A commitment means putting yourself in someone else's hands. Has Mary ever done that? Has she ever depended on you for a roof over her head and food in her mouth? Has she ever made you feel like a man? Hell, I've cheated all over the place but I've made more of a commitment to Stanley than Mary has to you."

"Shut up!" Without thinking, he reached across the table and slapped her hard across the mouth. Patricia hardly blinked. She simply put her hand to her face as though to cover the red fingermarks that appeared.

"Nice going," she said slowly.

Michael was horrified. He'd never hit a woman before. The act sickened and yet, strangely, excited him. Violence had never been his thing but he suddenly understood how it aroused all kinds of passions. Looking at Patricia, he realized she understood it, too.

Wordlessly, she rose from the table and walked slowly toward the bedroom.

In silence, Michael followed.

* * *

Mary lay on her bed as though life had left her body. It was five o'clock in the afternoon and the ship was in port at Yokohama. Since five o'clock that morning, when she'd crept back to her cabin from Christopher's, she'd not left the room, had eaten nothing and spoken to no one except Jayne. The girl had gone now, to explore the city with Terry. She'd been reluctant to abandon Mary.

181

"Are you sure I shouldn't stay wtih you? I don't mind. There's nothing much to see here."

Mary shook her head. "No. You run along. I'm okay."

"You're not okay. You didn't see Christopher at all today. You didn't even say good-bye to him."

"I said good-bye to him last night, Jayne. We agreed not to see each other again. Too anticlimactic."

Too painful, you mean, Jayne thought. Too terrible. It was awful. She didn't tell Mary she'd run into Christopher on deck at lunchtime. He looked gray and devastated as he beckoned Jayne to a corner of the lounge.

"How is she?" he asked.

No need to ask whom he meant. "Lousy," Jayne said. "She hasn't gotten out of bed all day. Won't eat a thing. Hardly speaks. Why are you letting her do this? It's dead wrong for both of you. You know that. Can't you make her see what a stupid sacrifice this is?"

Christopher shook his head. "I can't force her to go against her conscience. I can only hope that she'll get home and see how wrong she is. I'm waiting for her. She knows that."

She wanted to shake both of them: Mary for being so stupid and Christopher for being so damned noble. I don't understand that generation, she thought. Who brainwashed them into all these ideas of duty? They're intelligent people and yet they're living by some outmoded code of conduct they find impossible to ignore. It was too bloody civilized. Where was the anger, the bitterness Mary should have felt? Where was the command Christopher should have exerted? Why did he take this lying down? Was there no fight in him that he accepted this with almost pious resignation?

He seemed to read her mind. "You're wondering why I don't raise hell, aren't you?"

"Frankly, yes. You're a strong man."

"And your aunt is a strong woman. It takes superhuman strength to do what she's doing, Jayne. She doesn't run away from her obligations, even if you and I think they're false ones. Don't mistake what she's doing for weakness or stupidity. And don't mistake my acceptance

182

for lassitude. I'd fight for her if that would help. But it won't. I'd only add to the unhappiness she already feels. She's left me no choice but to wait and hope that she can come to me without lingering doubts and guilt. That's the only way it can ever work for a woman like Mary. For me too. I fell in love with her for what she is. It would be childish of me to expect her to change."

"Do you think she'll ever see how undeserving of all this Michael really is?"

"Yes," Christopher said, "I think she'll see. I only hope it's in time."

Jayne looked at him curiously. "You mean you'll wait only so long."

"I'll wait as long as I can, but one never knows about tomorrow. Accidents happen. Sickness happens. Who can tell?" He pulled a note pad out of his pocket and scribbled on it. "I'd like you to give her my son James' address and telephone number. Mary knows where to reach me, but in case she should want to contact me while I'm on a business trip or something, give her this, will you? I travel a lot, but James always knows where I am."

"Will you be in San Francisco soon?"

Christopher shook his head. "No. I think I'll avoid it for a while. I'll write to Mary at the radio station. She knows that, but tell her again, will you? And tell her I love her more than anything in the world, though she knows that, too."

Looking down at Mary, who lay deathly still in her bed, Jayne took the scrap of paper out of her pocket.

"I saw Christopher this morning," she said. "He asked me to give you this. It's his son's address and phone in Sydney. In case Christopher's away when you're ready to reach him."

Mary opened her eyes and took the paper wordlessly.

"He said to tell you again that he loves you more than anything in the world."

A look of pain crossed Mary's face, but she said nothing.

Jayne made one more try. "Please, Aunt Mary, won't you . . ."

"Go away, darling. Please, just go away."

With Jayne gone and Christopher on his way to Tokyo to catch a flight back to Sydney, Mary finally gave way to her tears. She seldom cried, but now she sobbed uncontrollably, not even trying to stop. Let it all wash away, she thought. Let all the heartache and longing run out through my eyes. If only it would. If only she'd stop wishing she were free and on the plane with Christopher to start a whole new life. If only she'd never taken this trip at all. No. That she wouldn't wish. Not to have known Christopher was far worse than losing him. Not to have experienced mutual love and desire would have been to be cheated out of the greatest emotion of her life. I have that to cherish, she thought. Those memories to savor. The knowledge of his love to give me strength. I need strength. People think I'm so strong. Even Jayne, who knows more about me than most, thinks I'm made of steel, a woman who may bend but never break. But I'm not. Just the opposite. Perhaps because I cannot bend, I will break into a million tiny pieces that can never be put together again.

It seemed so long ago that she'd stood on the deck and watched San Francisco disappear and thought about The Decision. Who'd have thought Michael would make it for her, pulling her back to share the success she wanted for him? And who'd have thought she'd go so unwillingly, so reluctantly, hating every step of the way?

She turned her head to the wall. She pictured Michael, exuberant with delight at her return, anxious to tell her every detail of his accomplishment, eager to take her to bed.

God, how will I go through with it? How will I pretend to make love to my husband when it's someone else I want? Won't he know? Won't he sense the change in me? Will I be able to play out this charade, thinking always of Christopher?

I suppose I should feel ashamed of my unfaithfulness, but I don't. I love Christopher. I love him still. When Michael's arms are around me, I'll be remembering another man's. When my husband tells me how wonderful

184

life is going to be, I'll be thinking only of the one I could have had. It's not fair to Michael. But I've never been fair to him. Not really. Just as he's never been fair to me.

Angrily, she pounded the pillow. Nothing was fair. Everything was too late. Michael had come to manhood too late. And she'd come too late to love.

*　*　*

It was not until they were well at sea, on their way to Hawaii, that Mary finally found strength to dress and come out of the cabin. Late in the morning she wandered up to the British Bar and found Gail DeVries having a cup of consommé. The older woman cheerfully beckoned her over to a corner table.

"Where have you been hiding for three days? I rang your cabin the morning we arrived in Yokohama, but there was no answer. Beau and I were going up to Tokyo overnight and we thought you might like to join us."

Mary had heard the phone ring a couple of times after Jayne left, but she hadn't answered. She didn't want to talk to anyone except Christopher, yet she was terrified that if she did speak to him again she might not be able to go through with her agonizing decision.

"That was kind of you, Gail. I'm sorry to have missed it. I haven't been feeling too well."

"Nothing serious, I hope."

"I think you can imagine what it was."

Gail sighed and nodded. "You've let him go."

"Yes. Jayne thinks I'm the world's biggest fool. I'm not sure I don't agree with her. I've probably made the worst mistake of my life. I must be crazy. Nobody in his right mind would throw away such a chance."

"You're not crazy," Gail said. "Do you think you're the only woman in the world who felt compelled to stand by someone who needs her?"

"That's just the point. Michael doesn't need me now. For the first time in forty-five years he's independent. He's done something on his own, with no help from me. He's going to have an identity of his own."

185

"Fair enough. But it wouldn't be a complete identity unless he shared it with you, would it?"

"I suppose not," Mary said. "Deep down, I guess I think I owe him that satisfaction."

Gail patted her hand. "Why don't you admit it, Mary? You know it's more than that. You're not sure that Michael will make it even now. A new business venture is a risky thing. Aren't you afraid he'll fail again and there'll be nobody to pick up the pieces? Nobody but strong, dependable Mary? Isn't that part of it?"

Mary gazed out the window for a long moment. "Yes. That's part of it. I haven't even wanted to admit it to myself. I lied when I said Michael doesn't need me anymore. I know, in my heart, he'll need me more than ever now. It will be hard for him, more frightening than he'd ever admit. There'll be bad moments in the months ahead until the shop is on its feet. I can't desert him when he'll need all the support and reassurance he can get."

Gail shook her head. "Mary, Mary," she said despairingly. "Dear child, for a modest woman you have an inordinate sense of indispensability. Must you take perpetual care of every wounded bird? I don't mean to be hard on you. I know you're miserable enough without a lecture from me. I know what you're going through. I've been there, my dear."

Mary looked at her inquiringly.

"Isn't it boring," Gail said in quiet amusement, "how people always want to tell you their own stories instead of listening to yours? I suppose that's why psychiatrists are better than friends; the paid listener doesn't interrupt with his own experiences. Well, I've committed the unpardonable sin of bringing this conversation back to myself, so I might as well go on. Before I married Mr. DeVries, I was terribly in love with another young man." Her expression grew gentle. "Even now, I remember how wonderful he was. But I felt I had a duty to marry my husband because he was well off, whereas the one I loved had no money at all. You see, Mary, I supported my parents when I was young. My father was an invalid, barely scraping by on a pension, and my dear mother had three other children to care for. At sixteen, I was the breadwinner. Imagine, almost fifty years ago I was a typist, earning twelve dollars a week and taking care of six people. I had to make a decision. Marry the penniless one I loved and leave my family to shift for itself or marry Mr. DeVries, whom I liked and who would take care of the people who needed me. Obviously, you know which road I chose."

"How sad for you," Mary said. "How brave."

Gail smiled. "It wasn't brave. It was selfish. It was simply as though I had to do it or never know a moment's peace. And it worked out. I was very happy with my husband. I even grew to love him. We had a good life and nice children. I was glad I'd done my duty, when I saw my parents living comfortably and my brothers and sister educated and successful. I suppose I felt very saintly. But in retrospect, I can see that it was an unhealthy decision. I missed the great love of my life, Mary. I'm older now and hopefully wiser. If I had it to do all over again, I'd realize that nobody appointed me God. My family would have managed. But I didn't believe they could. I felt that with my defection they'd go under. I never thought that if I died they'd go on somehow. I didn't see that my vanity was more important to me than a solid sense of self-preservation."

Gail looked compassionately at her younger friend. "My story has some of the elements of your own. Or so it seems to me. The situation is different but the motivations are recognizable."

"Yes. You're saying I'm not necessary to Michael's survival any more than you were to your family's. But it's different, Gail. When this trip started, I was coming to the conclusion that he'd be better off if I kicked him out of the nest. Now I feel I have to support him emotionally if not financially. It's a matter of decent, civilized behavior."

"You're quibbling, my friend. It all comes down to the same thing. There's a streak of martyrdom in us, I suppose, though I find that most distasteful to contemplate. But the main flaw in our character is an overwhelming and exaggerated view of our role in life. In business, it's called autonomy or, more kindly, leadership. The com-

187

pany will collapse, the president thinks, if he doesn't make every decision. In private life, it's a compliment to ourselves and an insult to others."

"I can't see it that way. I wish I could."

"I know." Gail was sympathetic. "Perhaps you'll always be glad you did what you thought you had to do. I only hope that you don't wake up one day and wonder how your values could have gotten so mixed up when your intentions were so good. I don't want to think that, when you're older and time is racing by, you may feel some bitterness for the sacrifice you made. It will be too late then. There'll always be a hole in your life that not even self-righteousness can fill." She paused. "I know you'll never disappoint your husband. I hope he never truly disappoints you."

Mary smiled. "*Truly* disappoints me? Gail, it's happened a hundred times. The big deal that's always going to come through. The big job that never pans out. It's played like a broken record. Until now. Now it sounds as though he's really gotten his teeth into something. I don't think it will be the same kind of disappointment."

"I didn't mean that kind of letdown. I hope your Michael is always the devoted, adoring man you picture him to be. Constant failure has a funny effect on people sometimes. A man who can't succeed in business very often has to prove his manliness in other ways."

"Like running after other women, you mean? No. Not Michael. I don't think that would happen." A note of bitterness crept into Mary's voice. "Michael's too dependent to risk losing me through unfaithfulness. At least, he has been until now. Who knows what he'll be like when he has something to be proud about? But I don't think he'll disappoint me, Gail. Not that way." She hesitated. "And I couldn't really be outraged if he did, could I? I've no right to point a finger. Not anymore."

A voice behind them said, "Now what are you two pretty little ladies up to? You look mighty serious!"

They smiled up at Beauregarde.

"Girl talk," Gail said. "None of your business. I just told Mary we wanted her to go to Tokyo with us."

"Yes. I'm sorry I missed it, Colonel Stanford."

The old man snorted. "You didn't miss much. Biggest damned crowded place I ever saw. And the prices! Lord, I never saw prices like that in New York City! Little people in the streets. Big numbers on the menus."

"What kind of nonsense is that?" Gail said tartly. "You never worry about spending money. It's your children who're worried." She stood up. "Speaking of money, you're late for our gin game, Beau. I mean to liberate some more of your cash."

"She does, too," Beau said indulgently. "I think her daddy must have been a Mississippi riverboat gambler."

Mary watched them affectionately as they moved to their card table. Lovely people. They were what growing old should be. Not self-centered retreat or querulous hostility, but continued *joie de vivre* and a lively curiosity about new places and people. They were enjoying every day left to them, giving off love, and sharing, if it was wanted, the kind of wisdom that comes only with a lifetime of experience.

She thought of Gail's unexpected confession of her own lost love and the way she'd come to terms with it, not without regret but with realistic acknowledgment of why she'd done what she had. Not many women would admit they'd married for money. And not many would have analyzed their motives as dispassionately as Gail, seeing the flaws in their logic but rejecting self-pity. It was a lesson in discipline and self-control, a gentle reminder that most lives are not storybook perfect. She felt a rush of affection for Gail DeVries, once again comparing her to Camille Farr and wishing she could talk to her own mother as she could to this comparative stranger. She envied Gail's daughters a mother so worldly wise and independent, so understanding of human frailties and so full of the saving grace of humor.

I hope I'll see Gail when we get home, Mary thought. I won't burden her with my problems, but it would be good to have another woman to turn to when the weight of my world gets too heavy to handle.

For the first time in days, she felt better. The burden of

loss was still with her. Even the thought of Christopher brought unwilling tears to her eyes. But she'd survive. She'd take it day by day, step by step, remembering that the life line between her and Australia stretched strong and firm to take her back, when and if she felt free to go.

Meanwhile, she'd do the best she could. She'd let Michael know she was proud of him. She'd show him she trusted him and depended on him. Perhaps now she'd be able to put all of herself into her marriage as Gail had done, since that was the course she'd decided to take. Put up or shut up, she told herself. You've made up your mind to go home, so give it everything you've got. Don't even think about that life line, because if you do you'll be only half-hearted in your effort to be content as Michael's wife. You must make yourself believe it's the only possible choice and it's going to work. Otherwise, it never will.

She was not a religious person but she believed in some kind of Presence and she spoke to it now. Help me, she said silently. Help me do what's right. Give me peace and dignity. Show me how to accept these past few weeks of my life with gratitude and serenity, remembering them as a wonderful, impossible dream.

Chapter 16

Patricia dashed into the apartment full of high spirits, her eyes shining with excitement. She was hardly inside the door when she burst out with her news.

"Guess what? I found an apartment!"

Michael, sprawled on the living-room couch, reading the evening paper, sat bolt upright.

"You *what?*"

"I said I found an apartment. For Jayne and me. Three rooms on Fillmore Street. A furnished sublet. We can have it for only six months while the owner is away, but that's great. By that time we'll be settled and can find a permanent place."

"You're out of your mind!"

"Not at all. I know exactly what I'm doing. I told you before," Patricia said patiently. "I have it all figured out. Jayne will get a job. Eventually, I may find a little something to do, too. The apartment isn't expensive and we can manage."

Michael stared at her. "I don't believe this! You're taking a hell of a lot for granted. What if Jayne doesn't want to stay in San Francisco? What if she can't get a job or, more likely, isn't willing to support you? Has it ever occurred to you, Patricia, that Jayne may have other plans? And what about Stanley? I can't believe he'll not lift a finger to stop you. You're his wife!"

191

Patricia didn't stop smiling but there was an edginess in her voice. "This is where I came in, I think. We've been all over this before. I told you, to hell with Stanley. It's a matter of supreme indifference to me whether he likes it or not."

"Well, for God's sake give him a chance to express an opinion! Maybe he'll take to the idea of living in California. Maybe he'd be happy to move out here, too. If you're so bound and determined to stay, it's a hell of a lot more practical to set up housekeeping with your husband than to expect a young girl to take care of you."

"I'm bored with Stanley," Patricia said calmly. "I've been bored with him for twenty-two years. I don't want him here and I don't intend to go back where he is. I'm going to enjoy the rest of my life, Michael. As for Jayne, I can talk her into the idea. Remember, you promised to help."

"You have no conscience about saddling that girl with a mother to support?"

"None. I've taken care of her for twenty-one years. She owes me. Besides, if I'm lucky I'll find a man. One who can marry me. A rich man, of course. That's what I always wanted. Then I'll be off her hands. It may take a year or two, but she can afford to give me that much. She hasn't given me much up to now."

"My God! You'd really do that. You'd sponge off Jayne."

"What's so terrible about that? She's my daughter. My flesh and blood." Patricia began to get angry. "I don't think you're in much of a position to talk about sponging off people!"

"*Touché.*" Michael smiled wearily. "Okay. Let's call a truce. It's none of my business. But I still think you're moving too fast, Pat. Why don't you wait until Jayne gets here? It's only a couple of weeks now."

Mollified, Patricia calmed down. "All right. Truce. But I've put a deposit on the place and I am going to take it."

"I'm sure you will. Just do me one favor, will you? Don't tell Stanley until we've all had a chance to talk, you and Jayne and Mary and I."

"That won't change my mind."

"I'm sure it won't, but it will be a more acceptable thing if Jayne believes she had some hand in the decision."

Patricia shrugged. "Makes no difference to me. The outcome will be the same."

When she left the room, Michael sat back and took a deep breath. He was playing for time. He couldn't afford to antagonize Patricia. But it was unthinkable that she'd move to San Francisco. He knew she'd never leave him alone. All that big talk about finding a rich man to marry her! What craziness was that? Didn't the woman know there weren't that many eligible men, rich or otherwise? And that those who were available would marry a woman who was very rich or very young? Patricia was neither. She looked good for her age. No question about that. But she was no competition for a twenty-two-year-old, which was what any rich, free man wanted. Youth was everything. Even money didn't speak as loudly as it once did. Look at Rae Spanner. She was attractive and loaded, but the only way she could get a man was to rent one.

The thought of Rae left a bad taste in his mouth. He hated those afternoons with her. She was getting more and more possessive and even less discreet. He'd faced her, angrily, when Patricia told him about her phone call. At first she pretended innocence.

"I didn't tell her anything, Michael darling. I can't help it if your sister-in-law draws inferences from simple statements."

"Simple statements! You practically spelled out our arrangement! You want her to tell Mary about us, don't you? That's the whole plot. You want Mary to leave me, so you can have a chance."

Rae laughed. "I must say that's about as conceited a conclusion as anyone could reach. Really, Michael! Do you think I'm madly in love with you? I'm not. You're a good lover. Period. Why on earth would I want Mary to divorce you? I like things just the way they are. I wouldn't have you as a husband on a bet. Support you? No way. You're worth twenty-five thousand dollars as a

193

loan for value received. And not a penny more." Her eyes narrowed. "Sometimes I'm not sure you're worth even that. You haven't been exactly an enthusiastic participant in this deal. Let's say you're competent but scarcely imaginative in bed. Quite the opposite from what you are in business. There you have imagination but no skill."

Michael was furious. "What the hell does that mean?"

"Oh, darling, I know Harry Carson! He told me how insane your business ideas are. Like a child playing at storekeeping. You're never going to raise any more money, Michael. You're not smart enough. You won't be realistic. Everybody knows that—Harry and Charlie Burke and half of San Francisco. You're a dreamer. An amiable, nice-looking, dinner-party decoration. Good in bed when you want to be. But a go-getter? Never. You should be glad you have a wife to pay the bills. And friends like me to pretend they're making a profitable investment."

For a moment he was speechless. How dare she? How dare this rich tramp talk to him like that? He wanted to kill her. But when he answered, he sounded cool and assured.

"If you think the deal's so hopeless, Rae, let's call it off right now. I still have your money intact. It's only a fraction of the stake anyway. I don't need it. You see, you and Harry Carson are wrong. I'm already well financed for the shop."

He was lying and Rae knew it, but she simple raised her eyebrows and said, "Really? That's marvelous! I'm delighted to be misinformed!" She feigned distress. "I do apologize to you, dear. I was simply angry when you accused me of saying irresponsible things to your sister-in-law. I didn't. Obviously, she made up a whole story out of fragments of a conversation. Let's forget it. We've cleared the air. I believe in you. I know my money's safely invested, not that I give a damn." She came close, touching him. "Come to bed, Michael. It's a lovely, rainy afternoon."

He calmed down. The only financing he had was still safe and he would get more somehow. He had to. Hopefully before Mary came home and found out he'd lied. But he didn't want to make love to Rae that day. He knew he probably couldn't, even if he tried.

"I don't have time," he said. "I'd like to, but I have to meet a guy in half an hour. He's a money man from Chicago. Very interested in the boutique."

She pretended remorse. "You're still angry with me. I told you I'm sorry."

"I'm not angry. I honestly have to meet this fellow. I'll see you tomorrow."

"Promise?"

"Of course. I'm a man of my word."

Remembering it now, Michael shuddered. It was so ugly, the whole business. But you did anything when you were desperate. He could understand, a little, why women sold themselves. Money was the most important thing in the world. With it, you had confidence and power. Without it, you were nothing.

* * *

"Aunt Mary's birthday is day after tomorrow," Jayne said. "I think we should organize something."

"Like what?" Terry looked baleful. "She'll murder us if we trot out a cake and have the musicians come to the dinner table and sing 'Happy Birthday to You.' You know how she cringes every time they do that to somebody else. And she's been through every kind of gala known to man since we came aboard—the mandatory ones dreamed up by the cruise director and the impromptu kind put together by our fellow travelers."

Jayne made a face. "They're terrible, all of them. I can't stand all the organized fun the ship seems to think we enjoy, like those awful costume parties with people making fools of themselves. Remember that vulgar Mrs. Juniper, who stuffed a pillow over her stomach and carried a sign saying 'I should have danced all night'?"

"She wasn't as ridiculous as Mrs. Fletcher, who wrapped himself in toilet paper and came as a 'high roller.'"

"How about the Smiths, who hopped in as a pair of Australian kangaroos?"

"Or the Kitridge family, who covered themselves with pots and pans and came as 'A conducted tour of the kitchen'?"

They began to laugh hysterically. "Why do people make such asses of themselves?" Jayne said. "Certainly not to win those silly cuff links and bookmarks for prizes!"

Terry shook his head. "Beats me. At least Gambling Night was kind of fun and the prizes were good. Christopher won that nice crystal vase for accumulating the most chips at the end of the evening, remember?"

Jayne nodded. "He gave it to Aunt Mary."

Silence fell between them. "I don't think she's going to feel much like celebrating her birthday," Terry said.

"I know. She's turned down all the invitations we've gotten so far for the rest of the trip—the Jeffersons' Balinese lunch party in the card room; the Endicotts' 1920s tea dance. She doesn't want to do anything since Christopher's gone." Jayne slammed her fist on the arm of the deck chair. "Damn them! Why are they being so silly? I don't understand Aunt Mary. She's such a fool!"

Terry, who knew the whole story, shook his head. "I don't understand it, but I can't criticize people for the way they choose to live. I've had too much criticism in my own life. People do what they think is right for them, Jayne. Even if the world doesn't agree. Your aunt knows herself better than you know her. You have to respect her feelings, even if you don't share them."

"You're right. It's just that I love her a lot. I don't want her to be unhappy. God knows what she's going to find when she gets home."

Terry looked puzzled. "What she's going to find?" he repeated. "I thought everything was under control. Your uncle has his business deal wrapped up. And your mother is there, waiting for you and Mary. You sound as though she's in for some kind of shock."

"Maybe she is. I hope I'm wrong, but I have a bad feeling about things, Terry. If Uncle Mike has lied to her, she'll go out of her mind. I don't know that he has, but if so it won't be the first time. And as for Mother, I've been nervous about that ever since I heard about it."

"Nervous? Why?"

"She's not your basic good influence. My mother has the morals of the proverbial alley cat. She's been alone in that apartment for weeks with Uncle Mike. If she hasn't seduced him by now, he's a bloody saint."

"Jayne! What a God-awful thing to say about your mother!"

"You don't know her. Unfortunately, I do. She can't keep her hands off anything in pants, even when she's home. I can imagine what she's like three thousand miles from my father, alone night after night with a good-looking man."

"Come on," Terry said, "you don't mean that. He's her brother-in-law. She wouldn't do that to her own sister."

"I'd like to think that," Jayne said. "I'd sure like to think it for Aunt Mary's sake." She gave a little shake, as though to brush off bad thoughts. "Anyway, we still have the birthday to celebrate on the tenth and we haven't solved it."

"I can't think of any party that hasn't been given on this floating palace. We've whooped it up on every deck from Promenade to Adriatic, from the Soho Club to Colonel Stanford's cabin. If there's a nook or cranny on this ship that hasn't been used for a celebration, I sure don't know it."

Jayne stared at him in delight. "That's it! You've just come up with the answer!"

Terry looked blank. "I have?"

"Sure. We've partied all over the passenger area, but we've never had a bash below decks. In the crew quarters! That's what we'll do for Mary. Have an after-hours party with the staff!"

Terry hesitated. "I'm not sure that's such a terrific idea. The passengers aren't even supposed to go there. It's against regulations. Anyway, I don't know if Mary would enjoy it. And supposing she did, how would we arrange such a thing?"

197

Jayne was excited by the idea. "No problem. I'll get Lars, the bartender in the Trafalgar room, to set it up for us. He loves Aunt Mary. She and Christopher were his regulars. I know he'll do it. We'll buy the booze and get mounds of caviar, and after the bars close we'll get a little group to go down and celebrate the birthday with the 'real people.' Aunt Mary will love it! We'll get Gail and the colonel and you and me. I'll tell Lars to invite Ron, and Geoffrey from the Soho bar, and George and Walter, our table waiters, and our cabin stewardess and the manicurist and hair stylist from the beauty salon. It'll be a ball!" Jayne was bubbling. "The only thing we have to be careful of is not to let Peggy know anything about it. 'The Eyes and Ears of the World' would tell the captain, and all those adorable people would be in trouble."

Terry continued to look doubtful. "I don't know, Jayne. It's risky. It might be terrible down there."

"It isn't. It's super."

"How do you know?"

She looked faintly embarrassed. "Well, I went down one night. The night before we got to Singapore. Before you and I . . . Anyway, I was up in the Trafalgar late and Lars asked me if I'd like to go to a crew party. It was tremendous. Lars has a great cabin. He's decorated it with sheepskin rugs from New Zealand and he has the best stereo I've ever heard. And a million tapes. He even showed me how the crew hides things they're smuggling home to England. The customs people give them a hell of a going over in every port, but they have all sorts of secret spots for cameras and tape recorders and antiques they pick up."

Terry didn't say anything.

"What's the matter, luv? Do you still think it's a terrible idea to have Aunt Mary's party there?"

He looked unhappy. "It isn't that. I mean, I guess it would be fun. It's . . . well, did you sleep with Lars?"

For a moment she looked at him in surprise. He was jealous! Terry, the young man who'd never loved any woman, was actually jealous! She felt elated. He loved her. He really was "cured" and she'd done it. Gently, she reached for his hand. "No, I didn't sleep with him," she said.

Terry was almost petulant. "You had a thing with George Telling when we first came aboard."

Jayne wanted to laugh, but she managed to stay very serious. "Yes, I did. A very brief thing. I guess it's par for the course for impressionable young females. All that starched white and gold braid and the romantic atmosphere of a ship at sea. But it didn't last, as you well know. George is nice, but he's dull. He's also quite conceited. I suppose he's so used to every unattached woman making a pass at him that he responds automatically. I felt like I was just one of a long list to be checked off as impersonally as he reviews the boarding cards. I don't like being an anonymous body. I've slept around a little. You and I haven't made a secret of our past. But I've always cared for the person I was with, Terry. Just as you did. George Telling could never fall in that category and I knew it. That's why I cut it off so fast. It was cheap. And dumb. And I don't like being either."

Terry brightened. "How do you like that? I was actually jealous. I might as well confess it. I was."

"You're kidding! You? Jealous?"

"Yes. And you know something else? I liked it."

* * *

"What a smashing idea!" Gail DeVries said when Jayne told her the idea for Mary's birthday party. "I love it. So will Beau. What do we do?"

"We meet in the Trafalgar at midnight and sneak down the service elevator back of the bar. I thought it would be more fun if it was a surprise, so I'm not going to tell Aunt Mary. I'll get her up there on some pretext or other. And, of course, don't mention it to you-know-who or she'll tell 'our leader.' "

Gail understood. "Not a word to Mary or Peggy. And I'll warn Beau. I think we ought to go through the formalities at the dinner table, though. Just so Mary won't suspect there's anything else, and Mrs. Captain won't decide to dream up something on her own."

"Good idea. Aunt Mary will hate the cake and the serenade, but she'll live through it."

"Yes," Gail said. "She's been living through much worse. My heart aches for her."

"Mine, too. Do you think she's doing the right thing?"

"There's no right or wrong in this, Jayne dear. There's only what her conscience dictates. Nothing any of us can do about that."

Gail turned brisk. "Well, now, I have only two problems. One is what kind of gift to give that darling Mary."

"And the other?"

The other woman laughed. "The other is how to keep Beauregarde Stanford awake until twelve o'clock at night!"

* * *

Every evening when Mary walked in to dinner she felt a pang, remembering the first time she'd met Christopher. They'd removed his chair and place setting after Yokohama and the table was now an uneven seven with Gail, rather than Christopher, on her left. She was glad they hadn't put some stranger at the table. After so many weeks, they'd almost become "family." She'd grown very fond of Terry, despite her reservations about Jayne's plans to live with him. She loved Gail and Beau, tolerated George Telling and felt sorry for Peggy Lawrence Robin.

Peggy had confided, with a great show of bravado, the change in her plans. "Tony and I have agreed he'll finish his time with the line," she told Mary. "It's quite the most sensible thing to do. And, of course, he'll have a great deal of leave to spend with me."

"But I thought . . . That is, it will be years . . ." Mary floundered.

"Time goes quickly," Peggy said, "And it would be wrong of me to ask him to cut short a brilliant career."

She's lying, Mary thought, but I give her credit for putting a good face on things. At least she has what she wants. A ring on her finger. "Captain and Mrs." on her calling cards. To her, that's security, as necessary for her peace of mind as food for her body. Mary had heard about the "suicide attempt." The whole ship had, though she was sure Peggy didn't know that. She felt pity for the woman. How humiliating to be laughed at behind one's back. Thank heaven Peggy had no idea she was a joke among the passengers and the crew. Perhaps I am, too, Mary thought. Maybe everyone is laughing at the middle-aged married lady who had such an overt affair with a man they think abandoned her in Japan.

It didn't matter. Nothing mattered now except getting home and getting on with the business of her old life. She was anxious to see San Francisco again, to plunge herself into work. It would be hard, pretending to Michael that nothing had changed, but she'd made her choice and now the best thing was to rediscover the old Mary Farr Morgan. If, indeed, she still existed.

On the night of her birthday, she was horrified to see her table in the dining room decorated with an elaborate centerpiece from which rose brightly colored balloons. Oh, no! They weren't going to make a fuss! She didn't think anyone knew. Jayne. Of course. Jayne had told them. I'll kill that child, she thought.

She found half a dozen gifts heaped in front of her place. Laughing, protesting, she opened them, while George Telling ordered champagne. Jayne had given her a delicate gold chain, and Terry's gift was an exquisite Japanese fan. From Gail she received a large piece of beautiful silk with instructions to have it made into something as lovely as the wearer. Also enclosed was the card of Gail's own dressmaker in San Francisco, with a note saying it was good for "one gown for Mrs. Michael Morgan." From Colonel Stanford came a carved rose-quartz figure of a Chinese goddess to remind her of their trip to Kwangchow. And Peggy had given her an ornate jewel box from the gift shop aboard. It was hideous, emblazoned with the ship's insignia, but Mary exclaimed over it and smiled fondly at Peggy as she read the message: "Happy birthday from Tony and Peggy Robin. May we share many other happy cruises."

"I'm quite overwhelmed." Mary said. "I don't know
201

how to thank you. You must be depleted Singapore and Hong Kong! And," she added quickly, "our own marvelous shop!"

There was caviar and wine and a trio from the band played that awful song and half the dining room joined in singing it. Mary yearned for dinner to be over so she could escape to her cabin. She wondered whether there'd be a message from Christopher. He'd always teased her about being an Aries. "I love Aries women," he said. "They're so totally unpredictable." But there was no word from Christopher. None from Michael, either, which surprised her. He always made a great fuss over birthdays and anniversaries, buying her costly gifts which were put on their joint charge account and ultimately paid for by her. He probably had some expensive, useless present awaiting her return.

At last, mercifully, dinner ended. Peggy asked her to join Tony's table in the lounge, but Mary declined apologetically. "Another time," she said, lightly. "I've had all the birthday I can stand! But I love all of you for being so kind."

Jayne followed her down to the cabin after dinner, helping her carry her packages.

"That was nice," Mary said. "Very sweet of them, though I know you tipped them off, you rat!"

"Sure. I love birthdays."

"Wait until you're thirty-nine and tell me how you feel about them then!"

"Pooh! Thirty-nine's not old." Jayne handed her a small package. "I didn't think you'd want to open this in public," she said quietly. "Christopher gave it to me the morning he left."

Mary's hand trembled as she took the box. "Thank you."

"Listen, I'm going up to meet Terry. Will you join us in the Trafalgar a little later for a drink? Gail and the colonel are coming up. It's a private celebration. Just the good buddies."

"Oh, Jayne, I'd rather not. Make my apologies, please."

"Aunt Mary, you can't stay in your shell. Besides, I promised Gail and the colonel you'd come. It would be mean of you to disappoint them after they've been so nice!"

Mary sighed. "All right. I'll be up in a little while."

"Great! See you later. No more fancy fuss, I promise."

She waited until Jayne closed the door to open her package. Inside was a jade heart pendant surrounded by diamonds, a work of art very like the ring she wore. There was also a note in Christopher's hand.

"My darling, this little gift says everything. It is my heart, yours to keep forever. I know I shall see you wear it one day. Until then, I close my eyes and think of it lying close to you, as I wish now and always to be. I adore you. Christopher."

She held the heart against her own and believed she felt it throb with the love of the man she'd sent away.

Chapter 17

Jayne nudged her aunt. "They just called 'B-twenty-two' and you didn't cover it on your card."

Mary looked up, startled. "What?"

"If you're going to play bingo, the object is to cover the board and win the money." Jayne's voice was half-impatient, half-amused. "The pot's fifty dollars for this game."

"Right. Sorry." Obediently, Mary did as she was told. "It doesn't matter, actually. I've never won anything in my life." She smiled. "Except this trip, of course." She put down the card and looked at her niece. "What on earth are we doing here, anyhow? Tomorrow we're in Hawaii. Practically the end of the trip and this is the first afternoon we've spent in the lounge playing this silly game."

"Beats me. It was your idea." Tactfully, Jayne didn't remind her that most of her afternoons in the past weeks had been spent with Christopher, doing more interesting things than playing bingo. She did say, "At least it's better than your staying in the cabin day and night."

Something of the old, spirited Mary returned. "That's an exaggeration! Didn't you see your ancient aunt kicking up her heels at her birthday party night before last? That was fun, Jayne. There really is another world on the crew deck, isn't there? It's like 'Upstairs Downstairs' with a 1977 setting."

Jayne grinned. "Except it's the *Prince of Wales* and not Eaton Place. And the staff's a lot more hip than Mr. Hudson and Mrs. Bridges. You did have fun, didn't you? I'm glad."

"I had a wonderful time. Much to my surprise, frankly. I loved the whole thing—sitting on the edge of Lars' bunk, listening to that wild stereo music, guzzling champagne and eating caviar. And looking at those great kids. It was the best birthday I ever had, Jaynie, and it was all thanks to you."

"It was good to hear you laugh again."

"I know. I've really been a drag this past week. I'm sorry."

"Hey, I understand! You have a right!"

"No, I really haven't. I've been a bloody bore, crying over what's done. I'm going to get my act together. Scout's honor. Other women have. I will, too." She thought of Gail DeVries, who'd also given up the man she passionately loved. Of course, years had healed that hurt, but Gail had made the best of things, had found a life in which she was content, one that justified her choice. *I'll never be that strong,* Mary thought, *but I'll get over this. I'll make it work. It's too important not to work.* "Gail and the colonel had a marvelous time at the party, Jayne. I'm so glad you asked them. They got right into the swing of things. You'd never guess they were old."

"They're not. They think young. I hope I can be like that at their age."

"Yes," Mary said. "Me, too." She looked at the little old ladies around them, intent on their hour of bingo, the most exciting part of their day. "I hope I can be productive till the day I die. Even when I'm too old to work, I want to be active and interested, enjoying everything, the way Gail does." She put down her card. "Come on, let's get out of here. Let's take a few laps around the deck and get the old blood pumping. Okay?"

Jayne sighed with relief. "I thought you'd never ask."

They were on their second lap when the deck steward stopped them. "Mrs. Morgan, they've been looking everywhere for you. Could you go down to the hospital, please, as quickly as possible?"

"The hospital? What for?"

"It's Mrs. DeVries, madame. She's been taken ill and she's asking for you."

"Ill? How ill?"

"I don't know, but Colonel Stanford is there. He sent the message to find you."

Jayne looked concerned. "Want me to go with you, Aunt Mary?"

"No. I'll let you know what's happening. See you in the cabin later."

Without waiting for the elevator she ran down the four flights from Promenade to Adriatic and rushed through the corridors to the ship's infirmary. Beau was in the waiting room, pacing back and forth, his face gray with anxiety.

"Mary! Thank God you're here! She's been asking for you."

"What is it? What's happened?"

"I'm not sure. An hour ago, we were in the middle of our afternoon gin game and she suddenly got this terrible pain in her chest. She didn't want to see the doctor. You know her. But I insisted. She's inside, and they sent word a few minutes ago that she wanted to see you."

Mary managed to sound calm, though she had a hideous premonition. She patted Beau on the arm reassuringly. "I'm sure it's nothing. Probably indigestion. What did she have for lunch?"

The old man passed a shaky hand across his eyes. "I don't recall. Soup, I think. And, oh yes, they had franks and beans. I remember telling her that junk food would kill her."

Mary acted unconcerned. "See? What did I tell you? Probably gas pains. Don't worry. I'll check it out and be right back."

She went down the hall, looking for the doctor, and met the nurse coming out of one of the rooms.

"I'm looking for Mrs. DeVries. She called for me. How is she?"

"Oh, I'm glad you're here, Mrs. Morgan. She's been anxious to see you."

Something in the girl's voice alarmed Mary.

"What's wrong with her? It isn't serious, is it?"

The professional mask appeared. "I think you'd better speak with the doctor. He's inside. I'll get him."

One look at the man's face confirmed Mary's worst fears even before he spoke to her.

"Mrs. DeVries is very ill, Mrs. Morgan. She's had a heart attack."

"Will . . . will she be all right?"

"I don't know. We're doing everything we can, but of course our facilities are limited here. Thank God we'll be in Hawaii tomorrow morning. If she can just hang on until then . . ."

"Hang on! You mean she may die?"

"There's a strong possibility she won't make it through tonight. I can't say for certain, one way or another, but if we can get her to the hospital in Honolulu she'll have a fighting chance. It depends on what happens between now and eight o'clock tomorrow morning."

Mary leaned against the corridor wall for support. "A helicopter," she said. "Can't we get a helicopter to lift her off this afternoon and fly her to Honolulu?"

"Too risky. I wouldn't dare move her. She'd never survive the trip."

Tears began to run down Mary's face. "Oh, my God! She can't . . . she mustn't . . ."

The doctor took her by the shoulders. "Mrs. Morgan, you must get yourself together! She's conscious and very brave and she wants to talk to you. Don't stay long. I shouldn't let her see anyone, but she's adamant. And under these conditions . . ." He shook his head. "Anyway, don't stay more than three minutes. And try not to let her get excited. I'll be right outside the door if you want me."

Gail looked very small and frail in the hospital bed, an oxygen mask over her face. She feebly indicated to Mary that she wanted it lifted off, and when Mary hesitated she gestured almost imperiously. Gently, Mary raised the mask.

"Gail, you shouldn't talk."

The cheerful voice was almost a whisper and the words came haltingly but precisely, as though she'd organized them.

"Mary, dear. Not going to make it. Saw my husband. Same thing." She fought for breath. "Tell Beau call my children. Can't face him. Tell him not be sad. You neither. Be happy, Mary. Wanted to tell you . . . you did right thing. Don't you regret it." Gail's breath became more labored. "Better put that . . . damned thing . . . back. . . ."

Hurriedly, Mary replaced the mask and Gail drew a deep breath. A little smile touched her face and she looked almost happy.

"I love you," Mary said. "We all love you. You'll be all right, darling. We'll get you into the hospital in Honolulu and you'll be fine. You and Beau will take another cruise next year."

The eyes thanked her as they denied it, then they closed gently. Mary rushed for the door, calling the doctor. In a moment he looked up from Gail's still form and shook his head.

"I'm sorry, Mrs. Morgan." He took her arm. "Really sorry. You'd better go now."

"Is she . . ."

"It's over. I was afraid she'd go fast. That's why I let her talk to you. She couldn't make it. I think she knew it, too."

Mary began to tremble. "Yes, she knew it." Mechanically, she moved toward the door. "I'd better tell Colonel Stanford."

"Wouldn't you rather I did that? He's an old man. The shock . . ."

"No. He's strong but he'll need me."

She didn't have to say the terrible words. When she walked back into the waiting room, Beau let out one terrible cry of pain and took her in his arms. Together they wept, the man who'd lost his dearest companion, and the woman who'd benefited by her wisdom and gained strength through her example. They stood, locked in sorrow, almost unable to believe the swift stroke of fate that overwhelmed them. At last, Beau stepped back and wiped his eyes with a great white handkerchief.

"Did she say anything, Mary?"

"She said you shouldn't be sad, Beau. Her last thoughts were of you. I think she didn't want to put you through those final moments. That's why she didn't call for you. She loved you too much."

"I loved her. Very much. She was my best friend."

"I know. In many ways, mine too. She's the mother I wish I'd had."

Beau nodded. "She cared about you a great deal, Mary. We talked about you a lot. She hated to see you so sad, but she felt you'd done the right thing. I remember her saying that if you were her daughter she'd be proud of you for your courage and your loyalty." He began to weep again. "God knows she knew about those qualities. She had them in abundance. I can't believe she's gone. I just can't believe it."

Mary put her arm around his shoulders. "She'll never be gone, dear. She'll be with you on all the cruises in the future."

He shook his head. "No more. No more cruises for me. I'm an old man, Mary. I'll stay home where I belong."

"She'd be furious if she heard you say that. She wants you to be happy. It was the last thing she said. She wants us both to be happy. We have to try, Beau, for her sake. She never let anything stop her. I know she expects the same of us." She led the old man out of the waiting room. "Let me walk you back to your cabin. Try to get some rest."

"No rest. I have to call one of her daughters. I have the numbers. Will you stay with me while I call?"

"Of course. Do you want me to do it for you?"

"No. I've met them. They're lovely girls. I have to break the news myself. See what they want done." He sighed. "They're strong women, Gail's children. Like their mother. Like you, Mary. You're all stronger than we are. Your sex is more compassionate than mine, but more realistic, too. You know about birth and death. Women

209

handle those things better than men. I like to pretend that women need protecting, but I know in the end they're the protectors. We lean on them, just as I'm leaning on you."

Mary brushed the tears from her eyes as she and Beau walked slowly toward his cabin.

"We lean on each other," she said gently. "We support and are supported. That's what friends are all about."

And lovers, too, she thought suddenly. Michael needs me too much. And perhaps Christopher needs me too little. And I? Maybe I've never met the man who understands the happy medium. Maybe I never will.

* * *

Jayne burst into tears. "It isn't true! I can't believe it! I saw her only this morning and she was fine!"

Mary hugged her. Death was incomprehensible to the young. Unacceptable. They acknowledged its existence, but not for themselves or anyone they cared for. Jayne has never had contact with it before, Mary thought. For that matter, neither have I. No, that isn't true. I remember my brother's death. I was never allowed to forget it. But I didn't grieve. I was old enough to understand but I didn't mourn. With the callousness of childhood, I suppose I was almost glad he was gone—the perfect one, the center of attention, the rival for my parents' love. One mourns selfishly, for oneself. For what is lost. For the things one took from the departed. John Jr. gave me nothing in eight years. Gail gave me hope and understanding in the brief time I knew her. For the first time, I know the overwhelming pain that comes with another human's death, the deprivation one feels knowing you'll never talk again to someone you need. I made her a surrogate mother and she believed in me more than my own ever has.

"Jayne, darling, listen carefully," she said at last. "Colonel Stanford and I have spoken to Gail's daughters in San Francisco. There's no point in their flying to Hawaii to meet the ship tomorrow. Beau and I are going to fly back with . . . with Gail. We leave tomorrow after-

210

noon at two twenty-five. I couldn't let him make the trip alone."

"I'll get ready."

"No, there's no point in your going. It would be easier if you stayed aboard for the last week and brought my things off the ship with yours. I'll meet you a week from tomorrow. I can't fly with all the luggage I brought for the cruise. You won't mind packing for me, will you? Someone on the ship is going to pack for the colonel so neither of us will have to worry about luggage on the plane. Gail's daughters will meet us at the airport. They're making the arrangements there. They sound like wonderful women."

"They must be devastated."

"Of course. Any child would be."

Jayne looked out the porthole without answering. I wouldn't be, she thought. Oh, I'd feel sorry, I suppose. I'm sorry when anyone dies. But my mother wouldn't be missed the way Gail will be missed by her daughters. I'm certain of that. It must have been wonderful growing up with a woman so warm and caring. I never had that. Neither did Aunt Mary. Neither, for that matter, did Mother. And Terry had too much mother. Maybe that's why we've all turned out as we have. Early influences count. They do mold us, one way or another. For good or evil. In emulation or rebellion.

"Have you told Uncle Mike you're flying home?"

"Yes. I just sent a radiogram saying I was arriving on the evening of the thirteenth. There was no need to go into explanations."

Jayne smiled without humor. "Mother will be furious, being kicked out of the apartment a week early."

"Nonsense. For that matter, she can stay right where she's been these past weeks. It won't make any difference. That part of it might even work out well. It will give us a chance to visit before she goes back to New York. We haven't really spent much time together in the past fifteen years."

"Lucky you."

"Oh, come on, Jaynie. She's not so terrible. We all

211

have our faults. Maybe we'll find we've both mellowed. Maybe we have more in common than we know."

"Yes," Jayne said. "Maybe you have."

* * *

Michael read the radiogram with surprise. "Mary's flying home tomorrow night," he said. "She'll be in at nine-fifteen."

Patricia was startled. "Why on earth is she doing that? Will Jayne be with her?"

"She doesn't say why she's coming early." He read the message aloud. "Feeling fine. Arriving San Francisco April thirteen, United Flight number ninety-six nine-fifteen P.M. Jayne staying aboard. Explain when I see you. Love. Mary."

"I don't get it. She doesn't sound as though she's upset."

Michael raised his eyebrows. "Why would she be upset?"

"How do I know? Maybe she's heard you don't have the deal after all. Or maybe she's heard about you and Rae. Or possibly somebody tipped her off about us."

"I doubt any of those things. Nobody but you knows anything about the deal. And Rae certainly wouldn't tell her about that mess. As for us . . ." He stopped. "Patricia, you wouldn't be a big enough damned fool to . . ."

"Tell Mary I've been sleeping with you? Hardly. What would be the point of that?"

"None. But I don't get the point of a lot of things you do. Like planning to stay in San Francisco without discussing it with Stanley or Jayne."

"That's a little different from telling your sister you've had an affair with her husband. For God's sake, Michael, what do you think I am? Give me credit for a little sensitivity. I might make love to my brother-in-law but I'm not crass enough to talk about it."

"Bully for you."

"And there's no need to be sarcastic! I didn't rape you.

212

You've seemed to enjoy playing house these past weeks. *Any* house."

"All right. I've been a bastard. I admit it. But strangely enough, I love my wife."

"Sure. Like I love the Bank of Northern California."

"Damn you!" Michael's face flushed with anger. "You're a bitch! All I want is to see you out of this house!"

Patricia shrugged. "I'm going. As soon as Jayne gets back."

"No. Tonight. I'll call the St. Francis and tell them to move up your reservation. You can stay there until Jayne gets back and you straighten things out with her."

"Michael, don't be ridiculous. I'll move my clothes and bunk in the office when Mary gets here. My God, what do you want to do, make her really suspicious? She'd think it was odd that I suddenly checked into a hotel alone after staying here for weeks." Patricia laughed. "Or do you think my presence in the next room will inhibit your performance with your wife?"

"I just want you out! I wish to God you'd never come! Boy, do I wish you'd never come! And believe me I'm not going to encourage you and Jayne to stay in this town!"

Patricia wagged a finger at him playfully. "Naughty, naughty! Remember our little conversation."

"You're bluffing. You'd never tell Mary about Rae and me."

"Want to bet?"

He stormed out of the room. Why was Mary coming home early? Even if she was bored, why was she spending the money on air fare when there was only a week of the cruise left? She must know something. Maybe Charlie Burke had told her how Michael had tried to hit him up for money and she put two and two together and figured Carson was out of the picture. Or maybe Rae wrote her about the loan. Even Patricia might be lying. Who knows what that warped character might have done? But it was true that Mary's wire had not sounded upset. She'd said she was fine, so he wouldn't worry about her health. And she'd signed it "love." He was sure she didn't know about

213

his extramarital affairs. And if it were merely the business deal, she could wait one more week. What the hell could bring her flying home? Well, he'd soon know. Worse, he'd soon have to tell her the truth about another aborted dream.

PART II

Chapter 18

The airplane flew swiftly and steadily toward San Francisco. Outside was black nothingness, but within half an hour they'd be on the ground, she and Beau, bringing Gail home to her children. Mary turned to look at the old man who sat stiffly, dry-eyed, in the seat beside her.

"You all right?"

He nodded. "I was just thinking how unpredictable everything is. I've been so sure, the last few years, that it would be Gail coping with my death on one of these trips. It worried me, I must admit. Her having to bring me back. All that talk about being buried at sea was just so much nonsense, of course. They don't do that. They take you off at the first port and send you home. And if it happens in some heathen country, it's a mess. So many complications and clearances. I was afraid Gail would have to go through that. She'd have managed. She could handle anything. But I didn't want her to." The colonel sighed. "I'll miss her, Mary. Doesn't seem like much to go on living for now."

She took the gnarled hand in her own. "I told you before—Gail wouldn't want you to feel that way. You have your children and grandchildren, Beau. You still have your health and your independence. Life doesn't stop, dear. It just stutters now and then."

He summoned up a little smile. "I know, but as you get

older it takes longer and longer to get over things, which is bad because you have less and less time to spare. I'll be all right, little girl. I've had a good, long life. Nothing to complain about. A few rough spots here and there, but who doesn't have those?" He looked at her affectionately. "Don't fret about me. You have problems of your own. Gail told me. I hope you'll let me know what's happening to you, Mary. Maybe you'd even come to see me in Atlanta one day. We'd make you mighty welcome."

She squeezed his hand. "It's a promise. I'll stay in touch if you'll do the same."

"Never was much of a letter writer, but you'll hear from me. And I'm no substitute for Gail, but if you ever need me . . ."

Mary felt a lump in her throat. No more tears, she commanded herself. She'd shed so many in the past weeks. Tears for Christopher, tears for Gail and Beau, tears for herself. It was a new and unwelcome experience. She was not a woman who cried easily, and rarely over sad things. She was much more touched by happy events: sweet solemn weddings; the accomplishment of a handicapped child in the Kennedy Special Olympics; the reunion of returning soldiers with their loved ones after Viet Nam. A hundred joyous things moved her. She suffered but seldom wept over tragic ones. She felt deeply inside, but outwardly she was slow to weep. Perhaps the tight rein she kept on deep emotions during low moments was why she let herself go in the richly sentimental ones. Perhaps the unshed tears were always there, just below the surface, but she was too proud or disciplined or stubborn to let them flow. Until lately. Lately, it seemed, her pillow was always wet. Mary swallowed hard. She wouldn't break down when she saw Gail's daughters. Later, maybe, when she was home in her own bed.

A chill came over her. Michael would be in that bed, too. Michael would be at the airport, his happy, unsuspecting face turned eagerly toward her. Michael would be waiting for her to share his joy. Their joy.

She stared out the window. I'm right to go home, she told herself again, trying to believe it. I had no choice.

Gail knew that. Even Christopher did. Where is Christopher now? Is he sitting alone, thinking of me? Is he trying to explain my convoluted reasoning to his sons? Is he back in his own social sphere, surrounded by attractive women who are delighted to have him home?

The musing brought physical pain. I mustn't be a dog in the manger. I can't expect him to go through life alone, moping over me, rejecting another love, hoping for what may not, probably will not, happen.

And yet she was ridiculously, childishly jealous. She wanted him to yearn only for her as much as she yearned for him. She wanted him never to forget, because she'd always remember.

* * *

In the waiting room, two groups who did not know their connection with each other watched nervously as the clock on the wall ticked off the last minutes before the arrival of Flight 96 from Honolulu. In one corner, Gail's daughters and their husbands sat quietly, handling their shock and sorrow with well-bred restraint. In another, Michael, Patricia and Charlie Burke talked among themselves, curious about Mary's premature return, pretending to be delighted.

Only Charlie truly was. He didn't understand the arrival by air, but since Mary's message said she was fine he wasn't worried. On the contrary, it was a bonus to have her home a week early. He'd missed her more than he'd imagined. For more than fifteen years he'd grown used to seeing her nearly every day, and the two months since her departure had seemed an eternity. They had so much to talk about. Her trip. What had happened at the radio station since she'd been away. Even his troubles with Tracey. His wife wasn't getting better in the sanatorium. Usually she came out of these "visits" looking and feeling like a new woman. For weeks she'd be sober and reasonable before she slipped gradually into her old ways. But this time was different. The years of drinking were taking

218

a terrible physical toll. She was sober but ill. The doctors would not even give an anticipated date for her release.

Ashamed of the knowledge, Charlie admitted to himself that he did not miss her. It was peaceful to go home to a quiet house knowing there'd be no scenes, no hysterics. It was a relief to attend social functions without having to explain Tracey's absence or, worse still, her behavior when she accompanied him. He was tired of it. Terribly tired after twenty-five years of this difficult marriage. Hating himself for it, he dreaded her return. Dreaded it as much as he welcomed Mary's. Like an ardent young man, he wished he were alone to greet her, without Michael and that extraordinary sister. Two such different women, he thought. Patricia was loud, brassy, arrogant. She clung possessively to Michael as though he were *her* husband. Charlie glanced at her speculatively. She exuded an air of intimacy in her glances, her touch. Michael looked decidedly uncomfortable. Was something going on there? Good God, that was unthinkable! And yet it was strange that Michael called and asked Charlie to come to the airport with them. Almost as though he needed protection, an "outsider" to make the reunion go smoothly. Rot! Charlie told himself. He was imagining things. Michael was simply being considerate. He knew Mary would be happy to see her "boss," who was like one of the family.

"Another couple of minutes," Michael said. "The flight is on the ground. She should be coming through the gate soon. I hope she's all right."

"Of course, she is!" Patricia sounded petulant. "Her wire said she was fine. Really, Michael, you'd think Mary was made of spun sugar! I don't know what you're so fidgety about. If she was sick, she'd have said so."

"That's right," Charlie said. "I'll bet she just got cabin fever after two months on that ship and decided to cut out the last week at sea. After all, she saw everything she wanted to. The trip from Hawaii would only be a bore."

"Apparently Jayne isn't bored," Michael said.

Charlie smiled. "It's not a disease of the young. Jayne's probably found herself a beau she can't bear to leave. When I was her age, I was constantly interested in everything and everybody." The smile broadened. "I was also constantly in love."

Patricia looked at him coyly. "And now?"

"Now I'm an old married man. Creeping up on old age, though I can't say I feel it." He laughed. "I don't feel old, but I sure as hell feel married. Just like you two."

He added the last words deliberately, watching for a reaction. Michael looked away, pretending nonchalance, but Patricia stared at him boldly. You've made a pretty good guess, haven't you? her eyes said. So what? What are you going to do about it?

Nothing, his look said in return. I wouldn't hurt Mary, even if you would.

"She's coming!" Michael started forward and then stopped. "She's holding on to some old guy's arm. Who the hell is he, do you suppose?"

Patricia laughed. "Some old fogy she picked up on the plane, no doubt. You know Mary. Very big on waifs and strays."

A well-dressed woman standing nearby heard the remark. She turned and stared with distaste at Patricia before she and her sister moved forward to greet Colonel Stanford.

* * *

"How the hell was I to know they were the woman's daughters?" Patricia kicked off her shoes and sank down on the couch in Mary's living room. "Make us a drink, Michael. That airport scene was too much! My God, Mary, who but you would fly home with a perfect stranger in a pine box? I think you're crazy to cut a week off your trip for that. You hardly knew the woman or the old boy she traveled with."

Mary leaned back in her chair and closed her eyes wearily. She felt drained. Gail's daughters had been wonderful. They and Beau couldn't stop expressing their appreciation, courteous even in their grief, but it had been an ordeal. There'd hardly been time to explain in the midst of introductions and words of thanks. She'd simply turned Beau over to these loving hands, kissed him and said she'd see him later. There was nothing more she could do. Gail's children would look after him until he was ready to return to Georgia. Just as they'd look after their mother through the last hours they had her.

"Beau Stanford is a lovely man," Mary said. "Anyone would have done as much. I didn't do it for Gail. I did it for the colonel." She corrected herself. "No, that's not entirely true. I wanted to do it for her, too. She was a very special lady. Like a mother to me on that trip."

"A mother?" Patricia echoed. "What did you need a mother for? Isn't the one you have enough to drive you crazy?"

Mary didn't answer.

"I think it was a wonderful thing to do," Charlie said. "Sad for the old boy. It must have been a terrible shock."

Patricia sighed impatiently. "For God's sake, Michael, what are you doing? Distilling that booze? I've never seen anybody make such a production out of mixing four drinks!"

She sounds so proprietary, Mary thought. As though this is her house. As though Michael is Stanley, whom she can order around. She wished suddenly that Patricia weren't here. Not that she wanted to be alone with Michael. Quite the contrary. She dreaded the moment when they retired. Michael wouldn't expect anything of her tonight. He could see she was exhausted. She simply didn't want to talk privately with him, didn't know how she could summon up the enthusiasm he'd expect as he told her about the boutique. I wish I were back on the ship, she thought. Back in Charlie's "watery womb." How will I ever be able to talk easily and naturally about the trip when Michael and I are by ourselves? I'm such a bad liar. He'll guess something happened to change my life.

"I think I'll run along. You look done in," Charlie said. "I hope you don't plan to come in to the station for the rest of the week. No need to. We didn't expect you back so soon anyway."

"I'll be in. I've missed it, Charlie. I'm anxious to see everyone. And I have some more tapes." She stopped.

221

"No, I haven't. That is, I left them aboard for Jayne to bring with my luggage. Well, I'll come in anyway to see the gang."

"Want to have lunch tomorrow?"

"Love to. You can fill me in on the gossip." She rose and kissed him on the cheek. "Thanks for coming to the airport, Charlie. It was good to see all my family there."

When the door closed behind him, Patricia held out her glass to Michael for a refill. When he went into the kitchen for more ice, she looked at Mary.

"Poor Charlie. Nothing as sad as unrequited love, is there?"

"What are you talking about?"

"Oh, come on, Mary. That man's crazy about you."

"And I'm crazy about him."

"Does Michael know?"

Mary looked at her with annoyance. "There's nothing to know. Charlie is my oldest and dearest friend. He loves me. I love him. It is possible to love without being in love, Patricia. What we feel for each other is not, never has been and never will be physical. Michael knows that as well as Charlie and I do."

Patricia spat out a four-letter word. "Your intentions may be pure," she said, "but you give Charlie Burke the slightest come-on and he'll leap at it. Take it from me. I know the look. He may be a 'gentleman' but he'd sure as hell like not to be."

"Don't be absurd." Mary hoped she sounded convincing. Of course she knew Charlie was in love with her. Had been for years. But she denied it to her sister just as she denied it to herself. At one time, she'd imagined herself half in love with him too, but she'd never come between a husband and wife even if she could. She'd long since dismissed all thoughts of such a thing and now it was utterly out of the question. Since Christopher. Christopher made the difference. In this and everything.

Michael came back with Patricia's drink. He turned to Mary. "You want another, darling?"

She shook her head. "No, thanks. I had a couple on the plane. More than my quota for one evening."

222

"I know," Michael teased. "You're such a lush."

"Probably why Charlie Burke is so fond of her," Patricia said lazily. "She's such a contrast to his wife."

Mary went lightly past the barb. "How is Tracey, Michael?"

"Not good, I hear. She's been in the hospital for weeks and there's no telling when she'll be out. They say her liver is affected. Not surprising. It's a wonder she hasn't caved in before this. Damned shame. I hope nothing happens to her. Charlie would take it hard."

Patricia's voice dripped sarcasm. "I *bet* he would."

Michael turned on her. "My God, Patricia, you have a rotten mind! There never was a more devoted, faithful man than Charlie Burke! Jesus! You think nobody's happily married, just because you hate your own life! Well, let me tell you, there are some men who love their wives and suffer when they suffer, and Charlie Burke is one of them!"

Mary stared at him. She'd seldom heard Michael so violent. He sounded as though he hated Patricia, as though he'd like to harm her physically as well as attack her verbally. I suppose she has been a trial all these weeks, Mary thought. It really was colossal nerve of her to park herself on Michael for such a long time. He's probably fed up. Small wonder. She thought of Jayne's dislike of her mother. Probably she has reason, Mary decided. I've seen so little of Patricia these past fifteen years that I'd almost forgotten how abrasive she is. Un-insultable, as well, as she quickly proved. Michael's angry words didn't seem to bother her at all. She smiled as one would smile at a child having a temper tantrum.

"My, my! Aren't we the loyal friend! You mean always stick together. I didn't know you were so fond of Charlie."

"Well, I am! So is Mary. We're very close to him."

"That's nice." Patricia sounded indifferent. "By the way, Mary, you haven't said much about Jayne. Has she had a good time?"

"Yes, I think so. I mean, I'm sure she has." Mary was relieved to be off the subject of Charlie Burke but hesitant about discussing Jayne. She was certain Patricia knew

223

nothing of Russell King's defection and probably had never heard of Terry Spalding. It was up to Jayne to tell her mother about those things. Her aunt had no intention of discussing the girl's plans.

"Were there any interesting young men aboard?"

"One or two."

"I hope they weren't sailors!" Patricia laughed. "Every movie about cruises always has some dashing young officer in pursuit of the resident beauty. Jayne's so impressionable. She didn't get mixed up with the crew, did she?"

"What do you mean, 'mixed up'?"

"Now just what do you think I mean? Was she sleeping with the staff?"

"Patricia!"

"Don't sound so shocked. You don't have children. These days, girls much younger than Jayne know what it's all about. I know *she* does. She's been carrying on with Russell King for years."

Mary didn't answer that. She merely said, "I'm sure Jayne will tell you all about the trip when she gets home."

"I have something to tell, too, haven't I, Michael?"

"Don't involve me in this, Patricia."

She looked injured. "I'm not involving anybody except myself."

"And your daughter."

"What are you two talking about?"

Patricia gave her an innocent smile. "I've decided it would be marvelous if Jayne and I stayed in San Francisco. New York has changed so much I really can't stand it anymore."

Mary was stunned. "Move here? Permanently? You and Jayne? I don't understand. What about Stanley?"

"He'd hardly miss me."

"But how would you live?"

"Well, Jayne could certainly get some kind of job. I'm sure you'd help her. And rents here are less than New York. I found this darling place I know we can afford. I've even put a deposit on it."

Knowing Jayne's plans with Terry, Mary was aghast.

For a moment she thought of telling Patricia that her daughter already planned to stay in San Francisco, with Terry, but in the next breath she decided against that. For all she knew, by the time the ship docked they might have changed their minds. But one thing was certain: Jayne would never consent to live with her mother, much less support her. It was foolish of Patricia to make such arrangements without discussing them with the other people involved. Foolish and selfish as always. She didn't give a damn what suited anyone else.

"Patricia," she said patiently, "I don't think you should move so fast on this. You have no idea whether Jayne would go along with that idea. And you're hardly being fair to Stanley, making such a big decision without even telling him what's in your mind. He *is* your husband. You can't just walk out on him with no warning."

I know whereof I speak, Mary thought bitterly.

Patricia was unconvinced. "I told you. Stanley won't give a hoot. Or, if it comes to that, he's perfectly free to move to San Francisco. I don't care one way or another." That was a lie. She never wanted to see that boring man again, but leaving a loophole sounded more convincing. "As for Jayne, why wouldn't she be pleased? I had a letter from a friend in New York. She told me Russell King has dumped Jayne for some rich lawyer's kid, so I'm sure she'd be glad not to go back. Anyway, I've been looking around. There seem to be a lot more eligible young men here than there are back East." Patricia was pleased with herself. "I've thought it through very carefully. Change is good. It keeps you young. I was getting in a terrible rut. I didn't realize how deep a one until I came here."

There was no use arguing with her. She'd made up her mind. Anyway, the discussion was academic. When Jayne arrived and told her mother about Terry, that would put an end to Patricia's plans. Without Jayne to support her, Patricia couldn't leave Stanley. And unless Jayne had a change of heart, she intended to share a place with Terry. Mary looked at her watch, stood up and yawned.

"I'm exhausted. It's after midnight. I simply have to get

to bed. You two stay up and talk if you like, but I'm turning in."

Patricia gave Michael an amused look. So much for your amorous ideas, she seemed to be saying. Michael rose when Mary did.

"It's time we all packed it in," he said. "You've had a long day, darling. An emotional one, too. You need a good night's rest."

Mary smiled gratefully. She kissed her sister on the cheek as she started toward the door. "Are you all right on the office couch? Anything you need?" Then she smiled. "Silly of me. You must be quite used to that awful convertible by now. I hope you haven't been too uncomfortable, Patricia."

"I've been very comfortable. Couldn't have asked for better accommodations."

Alone in their bedroom, Michael began to take off his clothes. Mary found a robe and gown and headed for the bath. Her husband looked up, surprised.

"Since when have you started undressing in the bathroom?"

She stopped short. She didn't want to undress in front of him, fearful it might precipitate the overture she dreaded.

"Force of habit," she laughed. "I've been rooming with Jayne too long. I got used to changing in the bathroom on the ship."

Michael looked amused. "Seems a little prudish somehow."

"I know. Silly. But I just don't take to the picture of two females prancing around naked in one room."

"How about a male and a female?"

"Husbands and wives are different." She quickly stepped out of her dress and underthings and put on the gown and robe, aware that Michael was watching her with a puzzled expression.

"You act as though you're almost afraid of me."

"Don't be ridiculous! I'm just so damned tired, Michael. I hardly know what I'm doing."

"I'm not going to try to make love to you tonight." He

sounded almost hurt. "I'd like to, but I know you're not in the mood."

She didn't answer.

"Is something wrong, Mary? You seem different. Keyed up."

"Nothing's wrong, dear. I'm just done in. I'll be fine tomorrow. I want to hear about everything, especially the plans for the boutique, but I don't want to fall asleep in the middle of it. You don't mind, do you?"

"No, of course not. I can wait."

She brushed her teeth and fell into bed without even bothering to take off her makeup. Minutes later, Michael slipped in beside her. He kissed her lightly and said, "Good night, love. Sleep as long as you can. I'm so glad to have you home."

"Mmmm. Good night, Michael dear."

She turned her back to him and lay still. She was bone-weary but wide awake, almost too tired and far too troubled to fall asleep. So much to think about. So strange, somehow, to be here in this big, familiar bed with her husband beside her. He made her feel guilty with his devotion and understanding, his blissful ignorance of what was going on inside her head. And yet he sensed something. She wasn't surprised. She knew she was a terrible actress. How long could she sustain this role of the pulled-together, organized, happily married Mary? And what of Patricia? Of Jayne and Terry? Even Charlie was in her thoughts. So were Beau, and Gail's children. God! It was like a kaleidoscope of ever-moving, frightening images, with the central figure of Christopher weaving in and out among the pictures in her mind.

Much, much later, when Michael's regular breathing told her he was asleep, she crept quietly out of bed and went to the window. There it was. San Francisco. The place where she'd once been happy and where the restiveness had slowly begun to take shape. She'd tried to run, tried to think, and it had solved nothing. She was unhappier than ever.

For God's sake get yourself together, she thought angrily. You're here. You made The Decision. Get your own life in order, Mary Farr Morgan, and stop trying to play God. Other people's problems aren't yours. Not Jayne's or Patricia's or Charlie's. They'll have to work them out for themselves. You have enough to do to muddle through your own.

Chapter 19

Christopher sat alone at the desk in his study, a mass of color photographs taken aboard the ship spread out before him. He'd ordered a copy of every one in which he and Mary appeared, even the group shots at their table in the dining room and the ones in the lounge where they were sitting with boring strangers whose names he didn't remember. As long as he and Mary were in the picture together he'd bought two, one for her and one for himself, as though he knew they'd end up keeping separate albums. What will Mary do with hers? he wondered. How will she answer when her husband asks about the man who is constantly at her side? Probably she won't show them, but maybe she'll look at them secretly and remember.

Idly, he shuffled through the glossy prints. Pictures of them at the captain's reception for all the passengers and others taken at small parties in his quarters. Glimpses of them laughing at the participants in the masquerade parade and the ceremonial shenanigans that went on when they crossed the equator and "King Neptune" ordered some unlucky first-timers daubed with paint and thrown into the swimming pool. Mary had been afraid they'd grab her, but Christopher had reassured her. The victims were pre-chosen, usually members of the crew who had to suffer such embarrassment while the paying guests looked on.

He smiled at the sight of Mary at the railing, wide-eyed as they sailed into the harbor at Sydney. How she'd loved it! She'd been so at home with his children and they'd adored her. It had been wonderful seeing her in his place and more wonderful still when he'd told her he'd arranged his affairs to stay aboard with her until Yokohama. It was one of their most joyous nights, rich with love-making and the knowledge that they still had time together. Time. Christopher shook his head. It hung heavily on one's hands when the days and nights were lonely. Only a little more than a week since he'd seen her. And it seemed a year.

He went back to the pictures. He and Mary bargaining with the Balinese who came out in their funny-shaped boats to bob alongside the ship, offering to sell canes and carvings to the incoming visitors who shouted back at them from the decks high above the water. Mary in a swimsuit grinning at him from an adjoining deck chair; smiling up at him as they walked down the gangplank in Singapore; eager and solemn as they left the ship in Hong Kong en route to China. Mary everywhere, looking beautiful and young and in love. Studying the dozens of prints, it seemed to him that the ship's photographer had been omnipresent. He knew a good thing when he saw one, Christopher thought. He knew every picture he took of Mary and me was a guaranteed sale.

He set the pictures aside and idly toyed with other souvenirs of those blissful days: the silly little stuffed kiwi bird she'd bought for him in New Zealand; the tiny figure of a Balinese goddess carved of boar tusk and picked up for a dollar on the dock; a set of enameled Chinese pendants brought back from Kwangchow where there was little else to buy; a handful of wooden toothpicks from the inn in Kyoto, each a small masterpiece in itself, carved at the top with the exquisite detail the Japanese put into even the most mundane objects. Sentimental trinkets, monetarily valueless but precious in the recollections they evoked.

One memory was uncomfortable. Christopher frowned as he recalled the frightening attack he'd had on the dock in Kobe. It had been slight but ominous and as soon as he returned to Sydney he'd phoned his doctor, who was also one of his oldest friends. He'd been told to get right over to the office for a look-see. As Christopher buttoned his shirt after the examination, Charles Grahame had looked at him appraisingly.

"I can't find any further deterioration, Christopher, but you look like hell. For a man just back from a restful sea voyage, there's a bloody lot of strain in your face even under that tan. What have you been up to?"

Christopher, relieved that his heart was no worse, smiled. "I've been falling in love, Charles old boy."

"Oh? And trying to perform like an eighteen-year-old, I suppose."

"Right. I felt like an eighteen-year-old."

"Who's the lady?"

"An American. She lives in San Francisco. Has a little radio show there." He paused. "I asked her to marry me, Charles."

The doctor leaned back in his chair and pushed his glasses up on top of his head. "And?"

"And she won't. She can't. She's already married."

"I must have missed the article that said they outlawed divorces in the States. Or is this a one-sided passion?"

"No. She loves me too. She just can't bring herself to walk out on a weak husband. Presumably he's charming and devoted and utterly dependent." Christopher threw himself into the chair opposite the doctor's desk. "In point of fact, it's even more complicated than that. It's a nightmare."

"Want to talk about it?"

Christopher hesitated for a moment and then he said, "Yes, if you don't mind. I need to tell someone. I've been trying to understand it myself. One minute I do, and the next I don't."

He told Charles everything. The meeting, the instant attraction, the weeks of falling deeper and more passionately in love. He tried to explain Mary's feeling of

231

pity and loyalty toward Michael as a failure and, later, her belief that she needed to be there when he finally was about to achieve the success she felt he wanted only for her sake. It sounded almost irrational as he set forth the facts. There was no adequate way to describe Mary's compassion or the torment she felt over her wrenching decision. No way to explain to another man how he tried to understand the workings of a woman's mind, pretending to comprehend and sympathize even when he couldn't. Christopher finally stopped, his voice trailing off in confusion and despair.

The doctor shook his head in amazement. "Good God, no wonder you look as though you've been through the wringer! Your Mary is either a saint or the biggest damned fool on two continents. As for you, where in hell is your backbone, man? Are you telling me you just walked away? That you accepted this like a broken dinner date? I've known you for thirty years, Christopher. You're strong, successful, intelligent. Why are you behaving like a lily-livered fool? For Christ's sake, go get her! Can't you see she's just begging you to be masterful?"

Christopher shook his head. "You don't understand. It wouldn't work unless she came to me voluntarily, without guilt. She has to work her way out of this herself."

"Balls! You're so in love with this woman you can't see the reality of it. Listen to me carefully, Christopher. I'm no psychiatrist, but every doctor has to treat the mind as well as the body. I hear a lot of stories all day long, meet a lot of men and women. I think I've picked up enough understanding of human nature to dare to give you some advice, not only as your doctor but as your friend. You've never met a woman like this one. She's probably much more aware than you are that this strength of hers is something she really doesn't want. Strong women, for the most part, want to be dominated. Not ordered around as though they have no intelligence, or physically battered by some insensitive oaf, but they're always looking for a leader. Sometimes it's subconscious. Sometimes they know it but don't know what to do about it. But in all cases, they know they need a man stronger and smarter and more solid than they. A man they can respect. A person to depend on. They can't make the step toward that man, but they're always hoping he'll take matters out of their hands and demand they put themselves under his protection." Charles leaned forward and looked Christopher in the eye. "I'll stake my reputation on the fact that Mary is one of those women. She doesn't *want* you to listen to reason, Christopher! She wants you to ignore her misguided maternal instincts toward her husband and refuse to take her emotional decision as the right one. You love her. She loves you. Life is short. For God's sake, friend, will you realize that you know what's best for her and hop the next plane to San Francisco?"

Christopher stared at him through the long, unusually impassioned speech. He'd never heard Charles so vehement and intense. What if he's right? What if Mary is silently begging me not to respect her wishes? What if they're not her wishes at all? He shook his head. Could he have been so wrong in the way he handled this? Was Mary disappointed that he hadn't behaved in the forceful way Charles suggested? No, she was much too intelligent for that. She believed in what she was doing. He had to respect that belief.

"Maybe you're right," he said slowly. "Maybe a lot of women do think that way, consciously or not, but I don't think Mary does. You don't know her, Charles. She has so much character, such a strong sense of obligation. She'll have to come around through her own process of reasoning. I can't just turn up on her doorstep and demand she leave her husband, even though I believe she wants to. She's her own person. She can't be made to obey, or even enticed into hurting someone."

Dr. Grahame sighed in despair. "She's hurting *you*, isn't she? Worse than that, she's hurting herself. If you love her so much, isn't it your damned duty to see that she's happy? Or are you afraid of the responsibility?"

Christopher thought of Jayne. Jayne also thought he'd behaved like a spineless ninny. He remembered their conversation the day he left the ship. The girl hadn't said much, but he hadn't wanted to hear even the few things she did say. He'd been too busy spouting about Mary's strength and obligations and excusing his acceptance under the guise of respect for Mary's feelings. Were Charles and Jayne right? Was he, in his own way, as weak as Michael? Maybe Mary felt he was. Maybe she had doubts about his ability to give her the protection the doctor was so sure she wanted.

"I don't know," Christopher said. "I wish I knew whether you were right. If I was sure you were, I'd go to San Francisco and force a confrontation with Mary and her husband. Clear the air once and for all. I don't know how long I can live in this limbo, wondering what will happen now that she's home."

Charles played idly with a paper clip on his desk. "I can't force you to do anything," he said almost indifferently. "I can only tell you what I believe, as your friend."

"And as my doctor? Can I expect to offer Mary a long life with me? That figures into this, too. I've never told her about my heart attack."

"As your doctor I can't give guarantees. Not even the unqualified assurance you'd like. But I can say, Christopher, that if you continue to live with moderate good sense you should have an average life expectancy. As far as I can see, the doctors in Singapore were right. And I don't think you had another incident in Kobe. You probably were responding to too much food and wine, too much excitement and, most significant of all, too much anxiety. Your heart attack is behind you. Sometimes it's a good thing—a warning to take better care of yourself. I wouldn't dwell on the health aspect, if I were you. Certainly not in terms of Mary."

"At least that's reassuring." Christopher grinned. "Let's hope I don't drop dead on the way out of your office."

"Try not to. It's beastly for my reputation."

They shook hands at the door. "Let me know what you decide," Charles said. "And don't wait too long. You should have another twenty years or so at least, but they go by mighty fast. I hope you're going to enjoy them with your American."

Sitting at his desk a week later, Christopher thought of

his doctor's advice. He still didn't know what was fair to Mary. He was eager to have his first letter from her. He hoped she'd mailed one from Hawaii. If so, he'd have it in a day or two. Its tone, after a week's absence, should tell him what he wanted to know. He deliberately hadn't written to her. He'd put all he felt into the little note that was enclosed with the jade heart and now he waited impatiently for the response. Knowing nothing of Gail's death, he assumed it would be still another week before Mary reached San Francisco. He'd have a letter waiting for her at the office when she returned. Hopefully a letter of love that would acknowledge her own.

*　*　*

The apartment was very quiet when Mary awakened the next morning. She still felt desperately tired. It was eleven o'clock, but it must have been after four before she fell into an exhausted sleep. For a minute after she opened her eyes the room seemed strange, big and empty after the close confines of the cabin. Then everything came rushing back. Beau's sad face as they parted at the airport. Charlie's gentle welcome and Michael's flash of intuition in the bedroom. Patricia's crazy scheme. It was all jumbled in her head as she forced herself into consciousness.

She slipped on her robe and wandered out into the other rooms. Neither Michael nor Patricia was around and she was glad. The longer she could postpone any serious conversation with them the better. In the kitchen she found a breakfast tray set up and a note from Michael propped up on it.

"Darling," it said, "I didn't want to wake you. Had to leave for a business meeting. Patricia's gone on some errand of her own. Charlie called at ten to remind you of lunch. See you this afternoon. I love you. Michael."

She heated the coffee on the stove, drank a glass of orange juice and called the radio station. The switchboard operator was delighted to hear her voice.

"Welcome home, Mrs. Morgan! Was it wonderful?"

"Thanks, Susan. Glad to be home. Yes, it was terrific."

"Your tapes were fabulous! Mr. Burke let us hear them. Gosh, I'd give anything to make that trip! You're really lucky."

"I know." Would this gabby young woman never shut up? "Is Mr. Burke there?"

"Oh, sure. I'll connect you. You coming in, Mrs. Morgan? We're all dying to hear about everything."

"I'll be in, Susan. Will you please put Mr. Burke on?"

The girl caught the impatience in her voice and resented it. What was wrong with Mrs. Morgan? She was always so nice, so friendly with everybody. It would be a crying shame if she'd suddenly gone all high-hat just because she had a ritzy cruise. Susan assumed her professional manner, hoping Mary would notice that she, too, could be cool.

"I'll put you through to Mr. Burke's office. One moment, please."

The change in tone did not escape Mary. Damn. Susan was a darling child, and she'd hurt her feelings with her obvious reluctance to chat. She started to say something more friendly but the switchboard operator had already connected her with Charlie.

"Mary? Good morning. How do you feel?"

"Not too bad. A little jet lag, I guess. We're still on for lunch?"

"Absolutely, if you feel up to it. I'm looking forward. Michael doesn't mind if I steal you the first day, does he?"

"I'm sure he doesn't. In fact, he's already gone out. A meeting with Harry Carson, I should think."

There was a small silence on the other end of the wire.

"Charlie? Are you there?"

"What? Oh, sure. Where would you like to meet? You want to come to the office or go straight to the restaurant?"

"I'm such a late starter this morning, I'd better meet you there. Julius Castle as usual?"

"Perfect. One o'clock?"

She agreed and hung up, feeling a little better. It would be good to have a real visit with Charlie. Last night didn't count. They weren't alone, and anyway she'd been so tired she hardly knew what she was saying. In the intimate atmosphere of Julius Castle they could really talk. It was their favorite place, an attractive restaurant with good food and a wonderful view. And sufficiently out of the way so that few tourists found their way down the bottom of the hill on Greenwich Street to a restaurant favored by the "in" people of San Francisco.

As she dressed, she realized how strange she must have seemed last night. She'd told her husband and her sister and her best friend almost nothing about the trip and they hadn't pressed her for a "travelogue." They knew how tired I was, Mary thought. And how distraught over Gail. They were being considerate, waiting until I was ready to talk about the people and places I've seen these past sixty days. She stared at her reflection in the mirror as she put on her lipstick. Or can they see the change in me? Do they sense what's going on inside and feel as though a stranger has returned? I do feel remote from them, from everything that was once so familiar. I'm preoccupied with myself, with my future. Perhaps they are, too, she suddenly thought. Michael was unusually agreeable when I begged off from hearing about the boutique. It's not like him to be so patient about discussing one of his schemes. And there was that pregnant pause this morning on the telephone when she told Charlie that Mike probably was seeing Harry Carson. An uneasiness came over her. Something was wrong. There was something Michael didn't want her to know. Whatever it was, Charlie must know it, too. Maybe Patricia as well.

Now that she looked back on it, it was as though everyone was carefully waltzing around things they didn't want to reveal. Patricia's attitude toward Michael was odd. She'd noticed it last night, and this morning in retrospect it seemed even more peculiar. It was more than proprietary. Almost as though she had the upper hand and could make Michael jump when she snapped her fingers. His reaction confirmed it. Michael was always angry and defensive when someone tried to boss him. He hated authority. Of course he did. That's why he never stayed long

237

in any job. And, Mary thought ruefully, why he's so attached to me, because I've never made demands on him or made him feel threatened.

But how could he feel threatened by Patricia? She was a domineering woman, but she had no weapons to use against Michael. Mary paused, the lipstick halfway to her mouth. Or did she? Did she know some secret Michael was trying to keep? Patricia was a devious woman. Always had been. Look at the way she was planning to dump poor Stanley and stay in San Francisco, demanding her daughter support her. She probably had this in mind even before she arrived. The excuse to meet the ship was very likely only a subterfuge to put a continent between herself and the husband she detested. And Jayne was merely a convenient means to an end.

Lord! I'm going crazy! My imagination is running away with me. I'm reading all sorts of implications into the simplest things. Michael was simply being sweet to me, as he always is. And I'm fantasizing that business with Patricia. Her attitude toward Michael is only what her attitude is toward everyone: arrogant and demanding. Why *shouldn't* Michael resent her? She's been too much underfoot for weeks. Well, she'll soon be on her way back to New York. Another six days and she'll find out Jayne has no intention of living with her. She'll come up against the only one who won't knuckle under: her own daughter.

And Charlie? There was no change in Charlie. If he seemed more subdued and introspective than usual, he was entitled. He must be out of his mind with anxiety about Tracey. Pathetic woman. If anyone ever had her finger on the self-destruct button it was Tracey Burke.

I see ghosts in every corner because I'm so haunted by my own fears, Mary told herself. Nobody here has changed. It's I who am different. And will never be the same.

* * *

"I hope Aunt Mary and the colonel are all right. God, what a terrible mission!"

Terry patted her hand. "They're all right, Jayne." He settled himself comfortably on the blanket they'd spread out on the white sandy beach. "I'm sorry Mary had to miss seeing Hawaii. It's so beautiful. I'm glad we flew over here to Kauai for the day. No wonder they call it the 'Garden Isle.' Do you suppose Eden was something like this?"

Jayne looked at him tenderly. He was like a beautiful boy, graceful and sensitive. Though she was younger by five years, she felt protective of him. He'd had a terrible life, really. She was glad she'd been the one to bring him some feeling of belonging, some sense of his place in the scheme of things. They'd be all right. Things would work out. She'd be lover, confidante and friend to him, as he was to her. We are an unlikely pair, Jayne thought, without regret. A couple of misfits who can't make it alone but might struggle through together.

"Eden?" she said in answer to his question. "Maybe. What we're wearing is damned close to fig leaves. I know that!"

Terry laughed. "You're beautiful."

She made a face at him. "You're ugly, but I suppose I have to put up with you."

He looked troubled. "Maybe you shouldn't, Jayne. Maybe we're crazy, thinking of taking an apartment at home. It might not work out. I wouldn't want to hurt you."

"Why do you keep saying that?" She ran her hand lightly across his chest. "Aren't you afraid I might hurt you?"

"No. You never would. You're like your aunt. You care about other people."

"Don't you, Terry?"

"I haven't cared about many in my life. Only two, really."

She lay back and stared up into the cloudless blue sky. I'm one of the two, she thought. And the other is Paul. But Paul was faithless. I never will be. She thought of Mary's warnings. Was she drawn to Terry because she wanted to mother him, to feel omnipotent because he needed her strength? Would she end up, as her aunt feared, feeling lonely and unfulfilled, the victim of her own attraction to the weak and helpless? No. She loved Terry in a way she'd loved no other man. She felt peaceful with him, confident they were products of a strange and merciful destiny. Still, she felt a twinge of fear. Terry wasn't as convinced as she. But that was natural. He'd lived a different kind of life. He was making a far bigger step than she. Bigger, perhaps, than even he realized.

"Terry?"

"Hmmm?"

"Do you want to call it off? Our plans, I mean. If you do, if you have second thoughts, I'll understand. I don't want to push you into something you're not ready for. Maybe we should take this step by step. I could live alone in San Francisco for a while at least, and so could you. We'd see each other and decide whether we wanted to live together. Would that make you happier?"

He rolled over and took her in his arms. "No, I don't want to call it off. Not as long as you're patient with me. I've never spent all my time with a woman, Jayne. Except my mother, and that was a sick thing. I love you. I can't live alone. I want to be with you."

They made love there on the deserted beach. It was romantic and unreal, as idealized as one of the South Pacific movies that had been filmed nearby. But we're not acting, Jayne thought dreamily. We were meant to find this life together.

Only when they dressed and prepared to leave did she remember one small, disturbing sentence. I can't live alone, Terry had said. Was that because he eagerly anticipated their life together or because he was afraid of his old temptations? She pushed the thought from her mind. It was unworthy of consideration. Terry was too fine to use her as a shield. He was through with his old life. She'd opened his eyes to a new one. She put her hand in his as they walked toward their rented jeep. "We'll have some surprises for the folks back on the Mainland, won't we?"

Terry's fingers tightened on hers. "Yes," he said softly,

"tongues will wag. It won't be easy. I'm thinking of your family, for one thing. What will they say about all this?"

"I don't care what they say. I don't care what anyone says. People aren't important. Nothing's important but us. We know what we are, Terry. We know what we feel."

He stopped and kissed her. "Darling Jayne. You make everything right."

"And I always will, as best I can. As long as you want me, I'll want you. Nothing and nobody can change that."

Chapter 20

Rae Spanner's housekeeper opened the door when Michael rang the buzzer at ten-thirty that morning. She'd already alerted her half-awake employer that Mr. Morgan was on his way up. The doorman had called on the house phone. In the evening he wouldn't be announced, Tessie thought with distaste; the evening shift knew him well from his daily five o'clock calls, visits whose purpose probably were no secret to the whole staff of the apartment. It was shocking. Everybody knew Mrs. Spanner's reputation. Too many young men had left the apartment in the early hours of the morning, having obviously spent the night. That was bad enough, but the regular afternoon visits from Mr. Morgan were disgusting. How could she? Mrs. Morgan was supposed to be one of her best friends. The housekeeper shook her head. Sometimes Tessie felt as though she lived in a brothel. A high-class one, to be sure, but a brothel all the same. Someday this wickedness would catch up with Mrs. Spanner, and Tessie only hoped she wouldn't be around when that day came.

"Good morning, sir," she said politely. "I've told Mrs. Spanner you're here. She'll be right out. Would you like some coffee?"

"No thanks, Tessie. I won't be staying long." He gave her that charming smile of his, the one that made her feel like a conspirator. "Not as long as usual."

Despite her impersonal manner, Tessie blushed. He meant he and Mrs. Spanner wouldn't retire to the bedroom a few minutes after he arrived. How could he be so brazen!

Rae appeared in one of her lacy negligees, looking elegant even at this hour, and obviously surprised to see Michael.

"Well! What on earth brings you here this morning?"

He glanced at Tessie, and Rae followed his look. She'd almost forgotten the woman was still in the room.

"That will be all, Tessie," she said. "I'll ring if I need you." She settled herself on the couch and patted the pillow beside her. "Sit down, Michael. What's going on?"

"Mary's home. She came in by plane last night."

"Oh?"

"A friend of hers, a woman she met on the cruise, died of a heart attack. Mary accompanied the body back from Hawaii."

"You can't be serious! A woman she barely knew?"

"That's Mary."

"Yes." Rae's voice was amused. "That's Mary. Bighearted Mary. She would cut her trip short for such a pointless reason. So she's home. How is she?"

"She seems all right. She was terribly tired last night, of course, and still asleep when I left this morning. We really haven't had a chance to talk."

"I see." Rae calmly lit a cigarette, waiting.

Michael was nervous. "You know what this means, Rae. I can't come here anymore. Not the way I have been, I mean. You know that. You knew this arrangement had to end when Mary came back."

"Did I? I don't remember saying that. All I recall is our making a business deal. A loan with payment on demand. There wasn't a time limit on it as far as I know."

"For God's sake, don't be crazy! You know I can't keep coming here when my wife is in town!"

"Why? Is she going to quit her job? When does Mary ever get home before seven? If you like, we can move the hours up a little. If it would help, we could make it four-thirty to . . ."

"Stop it! How can you want somebody who doesn't want you?"

"It's easy, dear heart. It happens all the time. In fact"—Rae smiled cynically—"it's been my experience that people have a way of wanting what they can't get much more than they want what's offered. I suppose that makes me quite human. You now present more of a challenge than ever, Michael, and somehow that makes the game more interesting."

He stared at her. "I don't believe you! You're incredible! You'd actually *prefer* to have this affair going on right under Mary's nose, wouldn't you? It isn't enough we've made a fool of her when she wasn't around. You'd enjoy it more if you could see her, pretend to be her friend and laugh at her behind her back. God, have you no conscience?"

Rae was unperturbed. "Probably not. I find this kind of thing rather stimulating." She sat up straight and her tone was steely. "Don't be a child, Michael. You've gotten yourself into something complicated and this time you're not going to get off the hook."

"I'll get off the hook!" He pulled his checkbook out of his pocket and began to write furiously. "Here's your money, Rae. I've had it in a separate account. Here's a check for twenty-five thousand. Take it, and good riddance!"

Slowly, deliberately, she took the check and tore it into tiny pieces. "You can't cancel this kind of debt so easily. The money is incidental. It's the interest payments that count. You've been paying off the interest in a very unusual way, Michael. I think Mary would be more fascinated by that than she would be by the loan."

He looked at her through narrowed eyes. "That's blackmail!"

"Not unless I choose to use it." Rae smiled. "And if you continue to be a good boy, I won't."

She had him and he knew it. If she wanted to make trouble, she had more than her canceled check made out to him. She had Tessie and the whole damned staff to testify to his visits. She even had Patricia, if it came to that.

244

She'd been clever all right, letting Patricia know by in-direction what was going on. In a panic he tried reasoning with her.

"Listen, Rae, I know you could blow the whistle on me anytime you feel like it, but what's the point of going on with this? You're too attractive a woman to hold a man by threats. You don't need to. You're a realist, too. Good lord, do you really think I could make love to you under these conditions? You know what will happen if I con-tinue to come here because you demand it. I'll be no good to you at all."

"It's a possibility," she conceded, "but I'll take my chances. I like going to bed with you, Michael, and you like going to bed period. So let's see how satisfied you are at home before we decide whether or not you can still be a lover to me. Maybe it won't be such an unwelcome diversion in the future. Especially when you tell Mary that you flunked finance. I wonder how she'll react to that?"

He was stunned. "What the hell do you mean?"

"Well, you have lied to her once again, haven't you? A woman like Mary might take her disappointment in you very much to heart. She's not tough, Michael. Not the way I am. Her emotions very much influence her actions. How do we know? Maybe she'll be so hurt she won't sleep with you. Then you'll be very glad to have this soft bed to run to."

"You really are crazy! You don't know Mary if you think she'd punish me for something I can't help."

Rae shrugged. "Maybe I'm wrong. It's just a wild guess. But it isn't the first time you've failed her. There's bound to be a breaking point, even for her. She might be fed up, my dear. Even angels must find their wings too heavy sometimes. She's hovered over you for a lot of years. Even our saintly Mary must know she doesn't need you. How long do you suppose she'll go on thinking it's her duty to be your protectress-in-residence?"

He was furious. "What kind of game are you playing? Do you really think you can brainwash me with that crap? I know Mary. She loves me. She understands me. But you

. . . you're like all the others. God almighty! You and Patricia! Two of a kind! Both of you thinking there's nothing in life but sex!" He stopped abruptly, horrified at what he'd admitted.

Rae smiled. "Patricia, too? My, my, you *have* been busy! That's amusing, Michael. It really is. I love it! You going all over virtuous and all the time you've been sleeping with Mary's sister!" The smile turned to laughter. "Go away," she said. "You're too idiotic for words! You're worried about *me* when you have a real bombshell sitting under your own roof? That's funny! I mean you are the jackass of the world!" She stopped laughing and stood up. "Run along, Michael. You have a few things to sort out, I'd say. Oh, and why don't you take a couple of days off? I won't expect you until day after tomorrow. I imagine you'll need the time."

He let himself out of the apartment. How had he gotten so involved? He hadn't meant to, not with either of them. Things just happened to him that way. He was too easygoing, too susceptible. Damn Rae Spanner! She was wrong, of course. Mary wouldn't turn away from him just because a business deal fell through. She never had. Still, she'd acted strangely even before she left on that trip. And last night, that business of starting to undress in the bathroom as though she wanted to be invisible. It wasn't natural. A woman who'd been without her husband for two months wouldn't . . . Hell, what was he thinking? That fast-talking Rae had gotten him all muddled. Mary didn't know the Carson thing was down the drain. And even when he told her, she'd sympathize. In every way.

* * *

Patricia rang the landlady's bell at the house on Fillmore Street. There was no real reason for her to visit the apartment on which she'd put a deposit, but it wouldn't hurt to let Mrs. Delaney know how enthusiastic she was. It would still be nearly a week before she could sign the lease and she didn't want the woman to give the place to someone else. She'd been reluctant enough to hold it as it was. Patricia smiled brightly when Mrs. Delaney opened the door.

"I hope I'm not disturbing you, but I just had to have another look at that adorable apartment!"

The woman was suspicious. "Why? You having second thoughts, Mrs. Richton? You did put a deposit on it, and I'm holding it in good faith. I could have rented it a dozen times since you were here. And for more money, at that."

"No, no! I haven't changed my mind! I just want to take a few measurements. You said it would be all right if I had some things of my own sent on from New York." Patricia laughed. "Heavens! Change my mind? On the contrary, I can't wait to move in! My daughter will be here in less than a week. She's been on a sixty-nine-day cruise to the Orient, you know. The minute she arrives, we'll come over and sign the lease."

Mrs. Delaney seemed mollified, but then she said, "A sixty-nine-day cruise? Your daughter work on the ship? She's not an entertainer, is she? I don't rent to theatrical people."

Patricia looked shocked. "An entertainer? Certainly not! She's my sister's guest on the voyage. A graduation present after college." Patricia put on her haughtiest air. "Perhaps you've heard of my sister—Mary Farr Morgan. She has a very popular radio program here in San Francisco."

Mrs. Delaney was impressed. "Mary Farr Morgan is your sister! Well, think of that! I never miss her! She's wonderful! I'm sorry, Mrs. Richton. Naturally, I didn't know you were related to Mrs. Morgan. Do you think she'll come here to visit? I'd love to meet her."

"I'm sure she will. We're very close. In fact, that's why I'm moving to California, to be near my only sister."

"I understand. It must be lonely for you, being a widow."

"Yes. Family becomes very important at a time like that."

"Well, you go right along and have another look

around." Mrs. Delaney gave her the key. "It'll be a pleasure having you here."

As she walked up the two flights of stairs, Patricia idly wondered why she'd said Stanley was dead. Maybe because I feel as though he is, she thought. She'd only talked with him once since she'd been in San Francisco and even then she'd made the call. Stanley was too miserly to use long distance. He'd sounded rushed, worried about the money she was spending, emphasizing that she should get the charges from the operator and pay Mary for the call before she left.

Patricia had sighed at the pettiness of the man. "Don't worry. I will. It's very cheap to call in the evening."

"I don't want you imposing, that's all. It's enough you're making such a long visit. Your mother and father don't understand it. Tell you the truth, dear, neither do I."

"Is it so terrible for me to have a vacation once in my life? God knows you never take me anywhere!" She wanted to tell him it was a permanent vacation, but she controlled herself. "Anyway, I'm enjoying it. How are the folks?"

"Fine. Everything's fine. But we miss you and Jayne. I can't wait for April twenty-first!"

"I know. Well, I'd better hang up now."

"Yes. Have a good time."

"I will."

Yes, Patricia mused as she wandered through the sunlit living room of the apartment, Stanley really is dead. The walking dead. And if I stay with him I'll die of boredom. But I'm not going to stay with him. I'm going to live here in this clean, cheerful place. I'll start fresh, make a wonderful new life.

She could hardly wait for Jayne to return. She'll love it as much as I do, her mother thought. This is an exciting city for a young girl. Then a sickening thought struck her. What if Jayne decided to stay in San Francisco alone? She easily could. I've found her an apartment and there's no reason why she needs me. I'm an unnecessary expense. No. I'll make her see how much more comfortable it will be if I live with her. I'll do the cleaning and cooking and take care of things like dry cleaning and shoe repair. I'll make it sound like she has a live-in housekeeper who gets no salary. Well, maybe a few dollars here and there, but not as much as she'd have to pay an outsider.

It was a weak argument, but Patricia was not one to be deterred by logic. I'll talk her into it, she decided confidently. And Michael will help me convince her. He knows he has to. She'll buy it. I'll be pathetic, if necessary. She knows how miserable I am with her father. Yes, Jayne will break down. Underneath that independent attitude she has guilts. All daughters have. Patricia smiled. All except me.

* * *

Charlie was waiting at the restaurant when Mary arrived.

"Am I late?"

He glanced at his watch. "Nope. Right on time. I was early. Full of anticipation, you might say."

"That's nice. *You're* nice, Charlie. I'm so glad to see you! Last night hardly counted, I was so punchy."

"Terrible thing. You going to the funeral?"

Mary shook her head. "No, it's private. And honestly I hate funerals."

"Who loves 'em?"

"Lots of people. My mother, for one. She has everything planned for hers and Dad's. Right down to what they'll wear. They've even ordered their tombstones engraved, with just the last date blank."

"Good lord!"

"It's funny. I mean strange. I've noticed whenever I interview old people they're eager to talk about death. Preoccupied with it, as though they enjoy the details. Isn't that odd, Charlie? You'd think the older you get the less you'd want to discuss it. Most times it's just the opposite. Kids have a greater horror of it than old people. Could it be that God gives you a kind of protective acceptance when the prospect gets terribly close?"

He shoved her drink gently toward her. "I think we could talk about more pleasant things on such a beautiful April day."

"Do you believe in God, Charlie?"

"I suppose so. Some kind of force, whatever you choose to call it—fate, destiny, something. Do you?"

Mary took a sip of her vermouth. "Yes. I mean, I don't think there's nothing except what we see here. I don't know about heaven and all that, but I'm sure we're put here for some reason. It would all be too ridiculous otherwise." She smiled. "Well, enough of that! Tell me what's been happening."

"I'm sure you have much more interesting things to tell. How was the trip? It sounded great."

"It was a dream. An absolute dream."

He looked at her searchingly. "Your tone doesn't go with the words. Something wrong?"

With her finger, Mary stirred the ice in her glass. "A few little things. Nothing that time won't take care of."

"Want to talk about them?"

"Not really. Not yet, anyway. Maybe later. I really do want to hear about the shop."

"Well, everybody loved your tapes. You have a sack of mail from your fans."

Her eyes lighted up. "Honest? Any from overseas?"

Charlie frowned. "Overseas? Not that I recall. Why would there be? It's a local show, remember?"

She seemed flustered. "I . . . I just meant I thought maybe I'd heard from some of the people I met while I was away. You know. The lady in Picton. Somebody like that."

"Maybe. I don't know, honey. I didn't go through the mail that closely." He paused. "What is it, Mary? You're jumpy as a cat. You must have a lot on your mind. Why don't you spill whatever it is? I've always been a pretty good listener, haven't I?"

Mary touched his hand lovingly. "The best. The best listener and the best friend. It's just that I'm not the most coherent explainer right now. I'm pretty mixed up."

"It's Michael, I suppose. We both know you went away to think about him and you. Did you think?"

"Of course. A lot."

"And?"

"As I said, I'm still mixed up. I can't talk about it until I'm clearer, Charlie. Not even to you. You understand, don't you?"

"Sure."

"I haven't even had a chance to talk to Michael."

"I assumed not."

Mary's eyes widened. "What does that mean?"

"Nothing. I just meant I know you were exhausted last night and he left early this morning. When would you have talked?"

She nodded. "Right. God, I *am* jumpy! Everything seems ominous to me. Every damned word and gesture seems scary."

"You're probably still tired. Have you considered that?"

"Yes. That must be part of it. But not all." She looked troubled. "One of the things that has me terribly worried is Jayne."

"You didn't get along together?"

"It isn't that. We got along beautifully. She's wonderful. Remarkable. It's just that she's about to make a terrible mistake and I don't know any way to stop her."

She told Charlie about Jayne's plans with Terry. "He's a delightful young man," she said, "but it's wrong. She's too young to handle such a complex situation. Women twice her age can't cope with it. It frightens me to death, knowing she believes she's the revelation Terry's been waiting for. What if he goes back to his friend Paul? Or some other man? What will that do to her? And what's Patricia going to say about all this? Not only does she expect Jayne to take an apartment here with her, but can you imagine what will happen when she hears about Terry's past? Jayne will tell her, you know. That child is too honest and too filled with evangelical zeal not to! And Patricia will hit the roof! She'll be furious, not only for

251

Jayne but for herself. And God knows what she'll say to Terry!"

Charlie did not interrupt throughout the long recital except to order them both a second drink. When Mary wound down, he looked half annoyed, though his voice was gentle.

"Mary, why are you torturing yourself about this? Jayne isn't your child. I know you love her like your own, but she's Patricia's responsibility."

"But I feel responsible. If I hadn't taken her on that trip, she'd never have met Terry Spalding."

"Now that's plain silly! She's a grown girl. You didn't push her into the guy's arms. You really aren't making any sense. Blaming yourself for taking her on the trip! I never heard anything so lame-brained!"

"It's true, all the same."

"So it's true! My God, Mary, if we all went around blaming ourselves for every innocent move, we'd spend our lives saying *mea culpa*. Do you want me to feel guilty because I talked you into a job in San Francisco where you met Michael Morgan? Blaming yourself for Jayne's possible mistake is like blaming me for your unhappy marriage! What's going on in your head? You don't seem like the same woman who left here two months ago. You're behaving like a character in a soap opera! Where's the calm, pulled-together Mary the world admires? Where's that sensible woman I've always loved?"

The words came out of Mary like a stifled scream. "That calm, confident person doesn't exist! She never existed! I'm damned tired of being dependable and contained! I'm fed up with never being allowed to fret over the things other women worry about! Never permitted to be irrational or emotional! I'm not those things, Charlie. I've spent years pretending to be, but I'm not. I have my fears and my wants and needs like everybody else. Only nobody listens. Nobody wants to think I could have a problem . . . or worse yet, *be* one!"

The tears streamed down her face as she searched in her bag for a handkerchief. Charlie handed her his.

"You make me ashamed." he said quietly. "Ashamed

252

of myself. Ashamed of us all. You're right. We take you for granted, don't we? We expect your knees never to buckle. We load our problems onto you and get annoyed when you react to your own in a very human, very understandable way."

Mary wiped her eyes. "No, I'm the one who's ashamed. Flying off the handle that way. You're right. I'm being stupid about Jayne. She's not my responsibility and this thing is not my fault. I don't know why I'm carrying on so about it."

"Maybe because it's only symptomatic," Charlie said. "My hunch is that real as Jayne's difficulties are, they're only part of what's bothering you. I know you still have your future with Michael to sort out. And I suspect there's something more, Mary. Something you've only hinted at." He held up his hand. "No, don't tell me what it is. You're not ready to talk about it yet. When you are, I'll be here, and I promise I'll listen with more understanding than I did a minute ago."

"Charlie, what the hell's the matter with me?"

He didn't pretend not to understand what she meant. "You want me to play curbstone analyst? Okay. I'll tell you what I think. You practically said it yourself a moment ago. You've spent your whole life trying to be what you think everybody expects. You've tried to be the successful son your parents lost; the mother your husband requires; the enviable image the women of this town look up to. I think you're always acting a part, Mary dear. Not that you're not good and kind and dependable. You are. But you're not perfect. You're fallible and mortal, a fact it's taken you thirty-nine years to discover. Something, or some *things*, have happened to crack that perfect shell, and the realization is throwing you. It's too much, too suddenly. Too much you think is demanded of you. Too much you demand of yourself. Why don't you consider yourself for a change? A good, gutsy dose of selfishness might be the best thing in the world for you. Hell, Mary, even the best actress in the world can't play a role seven days a week, three hundred and sixty-five days a year without taking time off!"

She silently considered his words. "I'm not sure I know what my real self is. I think I lost it somewhere along the way. Jayne thinks I have a martyr complex. Maybe she's right. Maybe I'm one of those terrible people who enjoys suffering in silence. God knows I do enough of it." She smiled sadly. "Until today, that is. I haven't been very silent today. I'm sorry to load all this onto you, Charlie. It must be a bore."

"There you go again, apologizing because you're behaving like an ordinary person. Mary, don't you know people are pleased to be asked for advice? It's like compliments—it's as important to know how to receive them as it is to give them. You never ask for help, never go to your friends and say 'Look, I'm in trouble. What should I do?' Do you have such a low opinion of yourself that you think you're not worth helping? Or such a high one that you think your friends aren't qualified to help?"

"Neither," Mary said. "There hasn't been any one to go to, Charlie. Only you. Isn't it strange? I don't have a single close woman friend. Not one I can let down my hair with. Jayne is the closest I've come in my whole life to a woman with whom I can talk freely. Jayne. A child. Young enough to be my daughter."

"What about your sister? Were you never able to talk with her? Not even when you were young?"

Mary shook her head. "Not really. Patricia's never been interested in anyone but herself. I remember once, years ago, trying to talk with her about our parents. About the way they cared for nothing after John Jr. died. She thought I was crazy. No, there's never been a woman I could confide in." She paused. "Except Gail DeVries. I did talk openly to her, I'd almost forgotten. I was looking forward to seeing her when we got home, thinking she was someone I could always go to for advice, like a mother who was sensible and caring. Is it possible that for a moment I blocked her out because I'm so sad that she died?"

"Are you sad or are you angry with her for leaving you just when you needed her most?"

Mary looked shocked. "What a terrible thing to say!

254

Angry because someone died? Charlie, how could you think that of me?"

"Because very often people do almost hate their loved ones for dying. It's a kind of desertion. A rejection. They have a spontaneous, unreasonable anger, as though they've been betrayed. I hope you do feel that way about Gail. It would indicate that you're coming around to the degree of self-interest that's healthier than the patient understanding you've cultivated all through your life. Your willingness to forgive and forget is going to destroy you, Mary. I want to see you angry and rebellious, striking out against the unfairness of things, not accepting them as though you had no right to feelings of your own. *You* matter! *You,* Mary Farr Morgan, are important! Let the others survive—Jayne, Michael, Patricia, me. We drain you, Mary. We bleed you dry, hand you our troubles and make you the brunt of our selfishness, and you accept it, as though it's some God-imposed duty. I want you to stop it. I want you to think of nothing but what makes you happy, no matter who else you may think you hurt."

Charlie stopped abruptly. He'd been on the verge of telling her not to overlook, once again, Michael's failure. To warn her that the man was going to let her down again, and to beg her not to put up with it still another time. But he couldn't do that. It was not his right. She'd find out soon enough. He looked at her, a world of longing in his eyes. There was something very important she was not telling him, something he sensed he didn't want to hear. Once again, as he had when he listened to the interview with Captain Robin, Charlie wondered whether she'd fallen in love with the man. Or if not with that man, some other. I want her to be in love with me, he thought. Subconsciously, all this advice about being happy may be my way of asking her to be with me when Tracey goes. And Tracey is going. She can't last more than another few months, if that.

God! What a monster I am! How can I even think such things when my wife is lying desperately ill? But she's not my wife anymore. She's a creature in another world, bound to me by the laws of this one. I've done all I can.

Now I'm trying to hand Mary a dose of the medicine I've prescribed for myself, advising her to take whatever happiness she can while there's still time. Hoping she'll decide to take it with me.

"Mary?"

She looked at him with the glazed eyes of a sleepwalker.

"I didn't mean to be tough on you," Charlie said. "Whatever I said was said because I love you. You know that."

"Yes, I know that. I love you, too."

He nodded. Sure, she loved him. Hadn't she said he was her only friend? That will have to be enough, Charlie thought. It's better than nothing at all. No. Like hell it was. Men and women weren't meant to be friends. They were meant to be lovers or acquaintances, and nothing in between.

"Promise me you'll get all this out in the open," he said. "Whatever it is, stop bottling it up inside. Tell me, tell the people involved, tell *anybody*, but for God's sake stop trying to solve your problems alone! Nobody can, Mary. Everybody needs to talk out what's driving them up the wall. Even if you don't listen, even if you don't respect the advice, lay it on somebody!"

"Seems to me I've been laying it on you for the past hour."

"Not all of it. We both know that."

"No. Not all of it. Some of it. Some you already know." She sat up straighter. "Enough of this. Really. I appreciate your advice and I'll try to take it. It just isn't easy to start being somebody else after nearly forty years of living with yourself as you think you are." She was the old, sympathetic Mary again. "Tell me about Tracey. Is there anything I can do?"

Chapter 21

Eighteen steps forward and eighteen back. Michael counted them as he paced the living room, awaiting Mary's return from lunch. Three o'clock. Damn it, where was she? Probably telling Charlie Burke the story of her trip, giving him the play-by-play account she'd been too "tired" to tell last night. It wasn't natural. Nobody came home from such a long, exciting trip and barely talked about it. It was as though she was avoiding any personal conversation. The thought crossed his mind, as it had before, that she might somehow have heard the bad news about the boutique and didn't want to face the meaning of it.

Michael frowned. Well, what *was* the meaning of it? Deals fell through every day. That was business. She'd understand that; she was a businesswoman herself. Rae was wrong. Sure, Mary would be disappointed for him but she wouldn't let it come between them. That wasn't her style. Rae didn't know her the way he did.

Rae. The memory of the morning meeting returned like another dark cloud. The woman was insane, tearing up his check, refusing to let him go. He supposed, in a way, it was a compliment, some sort of testimony to his sexuality, but it was flattery he could live without. Damned nymphomaniac! Sooner or later, Mary would find out about his borrowing Rae's money. And what he had to pay for that loan. Maybe he should tell her first. She'd be hurt, but she'd realize that he'd been driven to it out of desperation, and now was trapped by this insatiable woman. Mary was realistic enough to see how such things happened and how little they meant. Maybe she'd even get him out of it. If Rae knew that Mary knew, the hold would be broken.

He cheered up. Things would settle down now that his wife was home. There'd be some sticky minutes when he told her, but she'd appreciate his honesty. It would be more acceptable to her than being lied to. She could forgive anything except lies. They insulted her intelligence, she often said. She hated being made a fool of by people who thought she believed the transparent fabrications they invented. Yes, the truth was best. It wouldn't be pretty, but he'd be relieved.

He heard her key in the door and called out.

"Hi, honey. I'm in the living room."

She came in, put her handbag on the table and sank wearily into her favorite chair. Michael gave her a light kiss on the forehead before he took the chair opposite hers.

"Still tired from the trip?"

Mary nodded. "Jet lag. I guess. It'll probably take a day or two."

"Sure. How was your lunch? How was Charlie?"

"He's fine. Well, not really fine. He's worried about Tracey, of course. I'm afraid she's terribly sick. Poor woman. Poor Charlie. It hasn't been easy for either of them." Mary sat up straighter. "Well, enough of that. Tell me about your meeting. I assume it was with Harry Carson. I'm sorry I was so bushed last night, Michael. I'm really anxious to hear everything."

"I didn't have a meeting with Carson today."

"Oh? He canceled?"

"No. That is, not today. He canceled about three weeks ago, actually. Pulled out of the deal."

It took her a moment to understand. "Three weeks ago? But you called me on the ship a couple of weeks ago. You said everything was fine. What happened?"

"Carson's an idiot. The man's impossible! He doesn't want a man's boutique; he wants a mama-papa clothing store, for Christ's sake! I broke my back working up a plan that made sense in today's market and he wanted to water it down to nothing. I'd be nothing more than a damned small-time haberdasher! If he doesn't understand what's happening in men's fashions, that's *his* hard luck. I told him to take his money and stuff it! If he wants to set up a shop that could have come straight out of the thirties, he can get himself another boy. I'm not about to get myself involved with an operation that has no future."

Mary was speechless.

"You don't have to look so horrified," Michael said, defensively. "Hell, *I'm* sorry it didn't work out, too, but it was just one of those things. We agreed to disagree. That's show biz, honey. Nothing's certain until it's signed, sealed and delivered. I couldn't live with Carson's ideas. I'd have been miserable every day of my life."

She didn't seem to hear him. "You lied to me. You knew it had fallen through when you made that call." Mary spoke in a monotone, as though she couldn't believe it. "You deliberately let me think everything was fine. Why did you do that, Michael?"

"I did it for you, babe."

"For me?"

"Sure. Actually, I planned to tell you the truth. That's why I made the call. But when I heard your voice, I thought, Why should I spoil the rest of her trip? There's nothing Mary can do about it from thousands of miles away, so why not let her enjoy the cruise?" He looked wounded. "It seemed the only decent thing to do. I thought you'd appreciate it. God knows, it wasn't easy to pretend things were fine when I was so low. But I didn't see why both of us should suffer. I was being considerate, that's all."

"Considerate!" She began to laugh hysterically. "You thought you were being considerate?" Her body shook with laughter. "My God, you don't know how funny that is! It serves me right. It really serves me right!" Without warning, the laughter turned to tears. Mary buried her face in her hands and began to cry. What a fool I am! she thought as the tears flowed. What a blind, blundering self-righteous moron! I despise the part I was playing: the wonderful little wife, returning against her wishes to stand by the man who'd done it all for her. And it was a joke. A sick joke that changed the course of my life. She began to quiet down. But it's not my fault, she realized suddenly. If what I thought to be true really had been, I'd have been doing the right thing. Instead, I've been used again. Considerate? Michael wasn't being considerate. He'd been afraid to tell her, postponing it as long as he could. As always, he hated unpleasantness. He was buying time, hoping for a miracle, sure he could smooth it over when we were face to face. Or maybe counting on some magical solution turning up before I got here.

I hate him, Mary thought. I hate his unreality and his inflated ego and his injured air. I hate him for making a fool of me over and over again. I hate myself for letting him. She raised her head and looked into Michael's distressed, puzzled face.

"Hey," he said gently, "don't take it so hard. Look, I admit it's a bad break, but something else will come along." He came over and crouched by her chair, his eyes on a level with hers. "Take it easy, honey. Don't go to pieces this way." He reached out for her. "Don't cry, please. I can't stand to see you so upset."

She pushed him away roughly. "Don't try to smooth it over. It's too late for that."

He went back to his chair. Damn. This was worse than he expected. He knew she'd be disappointed, but he hadn't anticipated this loss of control or the physical rejection. It made him uneasy to see her this way. Mary was always so cool about things. It wasn't like her to get hysterical over a bad break. Desperately, he tried to salvage something.

"Hear me out," he said. "I know I have a good idea about that shop and I've decided to finance it independently. I've already raised twenty-five thousand dollars from one investor. It's just a matter of finding a couple of more angels. I can start on a shoestring. Borrow on my life insurance. I don't know whether you'd be willing, darling, but we do have a few thousand in our joint savings. Maybe . . ."

She was in control now, coldly in control, almost objective about this latest horror. "No, I'm not willing. I've worked hard for that nest egg, Michael. I won't risk it on one of your crazy schemes. I can't think of anybody in his right mind who'd invest in your adolescent dreams. You're insufferable. Your childish delusions about your own worth have made you a liar and a parasite and a cheat. Anyone who knows you at all would know they were throwing their money down the sewer if they gave it to you. You have an investor? He must be as infantile as you."

Rage boiled up in him. How dare she? Hadn't he tried to be what she wanted? Was it his fault people were too stupid to recognize talent when it was offered? Parasite? Damn her! She was the one who wanted a fancy apartment and nice clothes. She was the one who wanted him to be successful, just so *she* could be proud of him. He'd spent fifteen years trying to please her, and this was the thanks he got. Condescension and insults. He wouldn't stand for it. Crazy schemes, were they? An infantile investor? He'd show her who was the childish one. Uncaring, he struck back.

"Your friend Rae Spanner doesn't think I have childish delusions! She's given me twenty-five thousand to put into a shop and she's no stupid woman when it comes to money!"

Mary stared at him. "Rae Spanner? You asked Rae for money? How could you, Michael? How could you go to our friends?"

"What the hell's wrong with going to our friends? This is a solid business proposition. I just offered to let them in on the ground floor. Rae was smart enough to recognize a good thing. Not like your wonderful Charlie, who turned me down!"

Mary closed her eyes for a moment. Charlie, too. Both of them knowing this was another of Michael's pipe dreams. She was ashamed for him. If a smart moneyman

261

like Harry Carson thought Michael's ideas were impractical, the others would know they were. Charlie wouldn't go along, even for her. But Rae? Rae was smart, too. Too smart to throw away that much money, even though she easily could spare it. Rae wasn't given to charity. She wanted something in return. And if it wasn't money to be made on her investment, it was something else. Something more than friendship. And Rae Spanner wasn't that good a friend. She had bought herself a new "diversion." I don't care, Mary thought dully. God help me, I don't even care. When she spoke, her voice was dispassionate, almost curious.

"Rae Spanner lent you twenty-five thousand dollars? What did you use for collateral, Michael?"

The flush that started from his collar and rose to his forehead was all the answer she needed.

"Don't tell me," Mary said. "I think I can guess."

Michael began to stammer. "Listen, Mary, I . . . I know it was stupid. It's meaningless. You know that. I was desperate. I couldn't stand the idea of telling you I'd failed. So when Rae . . . when Rae offered . . . well, I just thought . . ."

"You just thought what?"

"I don't know. I don't know what I thought. All right, it was dumb. I've admitted that. I'm sorry. Sorrier than I can tell you. But it was for you, Mary. All of it was for you."

She was incredulous. "My God!"

"I know that sounds crazy, but it's true. I've always wanted you to have the kind of life you deserve. Have I ever asked you to live on what I could earn? Have I ever asked you to give up your job and be a real wife, one who'd be willing to struggle with me, no matter how little we had?"

"No. I wish you had."

"Wish I had!" It was Michael's turn to laugh. "Now who's being funny? You've pushed me ever since we met. You've made me feel inadequate, inferior, always wanting in your eyes. You wish I had? Like hell, you do!"

"Yes, I do. I never wanted to be the stronger one. I

262

didn't want to support us. I thought, under the circumstances, it was what any wife would do. God knows I never meant to make you feel less than a man. As for my working, you never offered me an option, Michael. You just assumed I'd take care of things while you wandered through life, chasing your ridiculous dreams. Yes, I wish you'd told me to lean on you. Yes, I wish you'd demanded your dignity. You're a man, not a child. Why haven't you acted like a man?"

"Because you didn't want one!" He was furious. "You're a castrating female, but I loved you. All I cared about was your well-being, your happiness. I thought you'd be miserable if I didn't go along with your life-style, admire your damned efficiency! I thought love and devotion were the best things I could give you. I was afraid to offer you less than you'd become used to. And what's my reward? Being called a parasite and a cheat because I have too much pride to kiss the rear end of a stupid bastard like Harry Carson? To be spat upon because I debased myself to get money out of Rae Spanner? It was for you, Mary. Can't you understand that? I was trying to live up to what you wanted!"

She put her hands over her ears. "Stop it! I don't want to hear any more. No more excuses. No more pretending. No more trying to make me feel guilty because you're too vain and shallow to think of anyone but yourself. I can't stand this life. It's destroying me. It's destroying both of us." She looked at him, wild-eyed. "You twist everything, Michael. You always have. You don't care what I want. You don't even *know* what I want."

He stared back at her. "All right. Tell me. What do you want?"

Slowly, she let her hands fall into her lap. He believes what he's saying, she thought. All those things about me. All those things about himself. She kept her eyes on her wedding ring, turning it slowly around and around on her finger.

"I want a divorce, Michael."

It was as though she'd struck him. "A divorce! What are you saying? I love you. And you love me. God al-

263

mighty, every married couple has arguments, but they don't run to the divorce court! I was wrong about Rae. I'm sorry. And I was wrong not to tell you about Carson. But I meant well. I meant to succeed for your sake. You can't penalize me for one little lie and one mistaken infidelity. Not after all these years, Mary. Things will come right. This venture isn't the only game in town. I'll take any kind of job. I'll manage to pay the bills somehow. I'll provide for you, if that's what you want. Anything. I can do it, if I try. Marv, you can't do this to me!"

She felt light-headed, as though everything was drifting away. The anger had left, but the determination remained.

"I know you meant well," she said. "I'm civilized enough to forgive the thing with Rae. One mistake like that doesn't spell the end of a marriage these days." Hypocrite, she thought. Of course you can overlook the unfaithfulness. You were unfaithful yourself. With a twinge of conscience, she put Christopher out of her mind. "I don't want a divorce because you slept with someone. Or even because you lied about Carson. I want it because you can't help the way you are, any more than I can help the way I am. We just don't belong together, Michael. We've never been right for each other. We never will be. Funny. It's taken years for both of us to say what we feel about the other. All these years and no real communication until the end."

"You're wrong," he said desperately. "Mary, you're wrong. It's all out in the open now. We can start over in a healthy way. It hasn't been such a terrible marriage, has it? We never fought. We can make it work again. We can even make it better."

She shook her head. "I don't think we can. I don't know whose fault it's been. Mine. Yours. More likely both. We went wrong somewhere, a long time ago. I didn't ask enough, or too much. You offered too little or too much. I'm not sure. All I know is that we didn't understand each other's needs. We were too busy trying to please, and we were going at it the wrong way."

"But that can change! *I* can change!"

"No, you can't. Neither can I. It's not possible. I can never be the wife you need, the clinging vine who'll leave you no choice but to get out and support her. Maybe I could have done that once if you'd asked me. But not now, Michael. I'm not that love-struck girl anymore. I'd be too frightened, too unsure to do today what I might have been able to do fifteen years ago when I was young and anything seemed possible. I'm sorry. Truly sorry."

The color had left his face and he was trembling. "I love you," he said again. "Doesn't that mean anything?"

She wanted to run from the room. How could she do this to him? How could she abandon a man who depended so much on her? What would happen to him? I can't think about that, Mary told herself. He'll survive. There'll always be someone to take care of Michael.

"It means a great deal," she said. "I know you love me, in your way. I love you, too, in mine. I think we'll always love each other. But that isn't enough. We need mutual respect. And a feeling of security. We don't have that anymore. And after this, we could never get it back."

He seemed to sag. "You're determined about this. You really want me to leave."

She clutched the arms of her chair. "Yes. Yes, I do. Today."

"Today? You want me to leave today? I . . . I don't know where to go."

Go to Rae, she wanted to say bitterly. Or use her money to live on for a while. No. That was despicable of her. She no longer hated him. But she had to cut it off, now, while she still had the force of reason.

"Perhaps you could go to your mother for a while," she said gently. "It might be wise, for many reasons, to go down to Los Angeles." Damn it, I'm still planning his life for him, she thought. Will I never stop?

"Can't you give me a few days?" Michael asked. "Just time enough to make some plans?" He saw her expression and shook his head. "I know what you're thinking—that I'll hang around and try to make you change your mind. I won't. I promise you. I'll just stay until I find some kind of a job and get a room. It shouldn't take too long. I'll

265

sleep on the office couch. Patricia can go to a hotel or, better still, go home." He smiled bitterly. "Ironic. I wanted her to move out when I heard you were arriving. I thought she'd disrupt our second honeymoon. I didn't know she'd mess up our separation."

Mary said nothing. It was terrible to see him beg. Beg for love. For forgiveness and another chance. Even for a place to sleep. She felt like the most heartless creature who ever lived, but she couldn't let him stay. Better the quick amputation than a painfully slow severing of the last shreds of their marriage.

"It's best you leave today, Michael. Do you . . . do you need some money?"

He gave her a long look. "Right to the end, huh? Always Lady Bountiful. No thanks. I'll manage." He moved toward the door. "I'll just take a few things now," he said politely. "You won't mind if I come back later for the rest?"

"Michael, I'm sorry. Believe that."

"Sure. Not to worry."

She listened to him moving around the bedroom. She'd never done anything so cruel, never felt so selfish and remorseful. But she couldn't back down, no matter how much she pitied him. He'll be better off without me, she thought, I truly believe that. And I can't take it anymore. It wasn't the failure or the lies. It wasn't Rae. It wasn't even freedom to go to Christopher. She didn't know where she was headed. All she knew was that despite the sadness, she felt an enormous sense of relief. It was as though she realized for the first time how smothered she'd been by Michael's need of her. She'd been like a drowning person fighting for air, and even now, even in this terrible moment, she was ashamed to recognize that she felt as though she was coming up into a clean, healthy atmosphere. Michael sucked out the very breath of her life with his attachment to her. It had to come. It had taken a specific shock to finally move her toward this act of self-preservation. It was selfish, perhaps heartless. But it was necessary. She had to cut the cord that held them together, sever the life line that sustained something not worth keeping alive. It was, Mary thought, an emotional mercy killing, agonizing but inevitable.

Half an hour later she hadn't stirred from her chair. She heard Michael moving around in their bedroom, slamming closet doors, opening and closing the medicine chest. Then he came back, one-suiter in hand, and stood looking at her.

"I'll be in touch."

Mary nodded. "Where will you be staying?"

"I got a room at Stanford Court."

Unthinkingly, she reverted to practicality. "Stanford Court? Michael, isn't that fearfully expen . . ." Mary's voice trailed off. It was so dumb of her to say things like that now! No wonder Michael smiled almost condescendingly.

"Don't worry. I won't charge it to you."

"I know. That was stupid of me. I'm sorry, Michael," she said again. "I really am. Sorry about everything." She felt miserable. She'd hurt him enough without reminding him once again that he took luxury for granted.

Her apology wiped the smile from his face. "I'm trying to understand you, Mary. I keep having the feeling something has happened to change you so drastically. Something *I* didn't do, I mean." He waited for an explanation, but she didn't respond. Michael sighed. "Look, I want to ask you just one favor. Don't rush into a divorce, will you? Things have happened too fast. You've been home less than twenty-four hours. You want a separation. Okay. But don't take any final steps for a while. Let's give this a little time. Maybe we don't have to destroy something we both cared about a lot. I'll buckle down and try to be more realistic. I see, now, the mistakes I made. I can change, Mary, whether you believe it or not. Give me a chance to prove that to you. Please promise me you'll think this through before you do anything legal about it. It's the only thing I ask of you."

She couldn't refuse. Even though she knew things would never change, she had to pretend to give him that chance. In a strange way, she wanted to. She hadn't ended her marriage in order to go to Christopher. Perhaps that's what she would do in time. But not now. At this moment she was too confused, too unhappy to think of the future. All she wanted was peace. Some kind of orderly, undramatic life. Later she'd know what to do about Christopher, but love of him wasn't the primary motivation in the step she'd taken.

"I won't do anything in a rush," she said. "You have my word."

"Thank you," Michael said quietly. And then he was gone.

She sat quietly in the gathering darkness, wondering what it was all about. It was cumulative, she supposed, the way most things are. Like suicide. People didn't kill themselves because of one unhappy moment, but rather because slowly, perhaps over a period of years, misery built in their minds until a final word or act or thought tipped them over the edge. That's how it was with her marriage. It wasn't this latest lie or Michael's admitted unfaithfulness. It wasn't even the knowledge that on the other side of a world a wonderful man waited for her to be free. It was the gathering of a hundred lies, a thousand trivial deceptions, a lifetime of vague uneasiness and uncertainty about so many things. She felt, again, the sad-happy sense of release, the pleasure of being alone, with no one to make demands on her. She'd write to Christopher and tell him what had happened. But she'd also have to tell him she needed more time. Time to be sure of what she was and what she really wanted. At this period she craved solitude. She felt as though she'd escaped from all the pressures, loving and otherwise, that addled her brain and tore at her emotions. Perhaps I'm incapable of giving, in the true, unselfish sense, Mary thought. Not material things. Not even love. She'd given Michael the former and Christopher the latter, but she was suddenly full of doubts as to whether she could wholly and gladly give herself.

I'm so tired, she thought, I want to sleep, to blot out everything and everyone.

A voice in the foyer put an end to those thoughts.

"Anybody home?" Patricia sounded revoltingly cheerful.

Oh God, Mary thought. I'd forgotten all about her! "I'm in the living room, Patricia."

Her sister breezed in, snapping on a lamp as she entered. She was, Mary realized, a little drunk.

"What are you doing sitting here in the dark? Let's put on some lights. Start some music. Have a little drink." Patricia looked around. "Where's the head of the house?"

"Michael's not here."

"Oh? He must be having a big day. He was ready to leave when I went out this morning."

"He's been home since," Mary said. She couldn't bring herself to tell what had happened. Not quite yet. "Where have you been?"

Patricia unsteadily poured herself a drink at the bar. "Well, first I went over to the apartment. Jayne's and mine. Made a lot of character with the concierge when I told her who my famous sister was. And then I did some window shopping and had lunch. And then"—she flopped on the couch and grinned at Mary—"then guess what I did."

"I haven't the faintest idea."

"I called your boss, good old Charlie. And I invited him out for a drink."

"You called Charlie? What on earth for?"

"To ask him to give Jayne a job! And you know what? He said he would! Isn't that great? She'll be a receptionist. A hundred and forty a week to start. We can get by on that. And who knows? Maybe the kid will turn out to be a star, like her aunt. History could be repeating itself!" Patricia was triumphant. "How about that piece of news? Jayne will be thrilled! I know she will. Maybe she'll even realize her mother isn't as dim-witted as she thinks!"

Mary was dismayed. "Patricia, I really don't think you should take Jayne's life in your hands like this. There was no need to go to Charlie. I thought you'd wait until Jayne got back and you could discuss it with her. I could always have gone to Charlie then, if she decided she wanted to . . . to stay here and live with you."

"What's wrong with having it all set up? I know she's going to love the idea." A mean little smile crossed Patricia's face. "What's the matter? Are you jealous that I contacted your admirer and had a few drinks with him? Or maybe you're mad that you can't take credit for getting Jayne the job."

"Don't be ridiculous! What do I care if you see Charlie Burke? Or, for that matter, who speaks to him about Jayne? I simply think you take too much for granted. You can't tell people where and how to live, Patricia. Not even your daughter. She's grown up. She'll make her own decisions."

"Well, thank you very much!" Patricia's voice dripped sarcasm. "I'm delighted to hear you're such an expert on children, having had so many of your own!"

Mary was too exhausted to argue. "Skip it," she said. "Jayne will be home in five days. You two can thrash it out then."

"Right." Patricia sounded thoroughly satisfied, her victory assured. "When's Michael coming back?"

It was no longer possible to stall. "He isn't. He's left for good. We've agreed to separate. Michael's gone to Stanford Court."

"What?"

"You heard me. He's moved out."

Patricia seemed to sober up instantly. "What happened, for God's sake? This morning he was happy as a lark!"

"I don't want to go into it, Patricia. Not now."

"He told you about the Carson fiasco, didn't he?"

"Yes. That and several other things."

Patricia nervously lit a cigarette. "What other things?"

"It doesn't matter." Why didn't Patricia stop questioning her? She'd told her she didn't want to discuss it. Why didn't the woman have some consideration? Patricia was acting very strangely. Her stare seemed to penetrate Mary, as though she was trying to discover what was in her sister's mind. Oh, hell, there'd be no peace until she gave Patricia some kind of answer. "He's also borrowed money from Rae Spanner and had an affair with her." Mary's tone was leaden.

"Anything else?"

Mary gave a rueful little laugh. "Isn't that enough?"

270

Then she looked grim. "It isn't just the deal, or even Rae. We haven't been happy for a long while, Patricia. A separation may be a good thing. We need to be alone, each of us, to think things through."

Patricia breathed more easily. Thank God Michael hadn't told Mary anything about them. She pretended sympathy. "I'm sorry. This must be very hard on you, dear. I'm glad I'm here right now when you need me. A good woman friend is important at a time like this, and we've always been friends, as well as sisters. Don't worry. I'll stay with you until Jayne comes. And even after that, I'll be nearby. It must have been fate, my deciding to move to San Francisco."

Mary was appalled. She didn't want Patricia around. She wanted to be alone. Totally, restfully, peacefully alone. And she'd never confide in Patricia. Never in a million years. It was absurd for her sister to act as though they were close.

"I thought . . . well, that is, it would seem better somehow if you stayed in a hotel until Jayne arrives, Pat. I'm not very good company." Mary hesitated. "Not that I don't want you, but I know I'm going to be dull company for a while. It's difficult for you, too, I'm sure. I mean, there's only one bath and you must be awfully uncomfortable on that couch. I feel terribly inhospitable. I wish I had a guest room. Anyway, I insist you be my guest at a hotel until the ship arrives."

"Nonsense! Do you think I'd leave you alone, in your state of mind? I'm perfectly fine here. Don't worry about the cramped quarters. Michael and I managed just fine. It would be silly of you to spend your money putting me up for five days in a hotel. It costs the earth! Now you just relax. I won't get in your way. I'll keep the house tidy and cook you good dinners and we'll have lots of time to talk."

"But . . ."

"No buts about it! What's a family for if not to stand by when one of them needs help? It will be my pleasure, Mary, dear. A small enough gesture to repay your hospitality these past weeks. Now you go have a nice, hot bath and climb into bed. I'll bring you a tray. You need rest after what you've been through. Men! Such ingrates! You've done so much for Michael. Now *you* deserve some consideration! You just do whatever you want and don't worry about me. I don't need to be treated like a guest. I'm quite at home here."

It was no use. Patricia wouldn't be moved with the kind of lame excuses Mary had given. And Mary couldn't bring herself to say, Go away. All I want is to be left alone.

"All right, Patricia. Thank you. I think I will go straight to bed. But don't bother about dinner, please. I'm not hungry. I don't think I could force a mouthful of food."

"I'll just do something light. Maybe a nice cheese soufflé. You run along and get comfortable. You look done in. I'll take care of everything. You'll see. It will work out fine. It will be just like it was when we were kids at home."

Mary smiled at her helplessly. God forbid, she thought.

Chapter 22

As the ship edged its way gently toward its berth, Peggy Lawrence Robin watched from the window of her suite on Promenade Deck. Tony was busy, of course, supervising their arrival in San Francisco. Nervously, she smoothed back her long blond hair, done in the classic chignon she preferred, tucking in the stray tendrils and wondering, as she did so, why it was so important to look her best. Nobody would be there to meet her. She and Tony would have one evening together ashore before he left on the next cruise down the coast of California and through the canal to England. He was going home and happy about it. Happy to be free again, relieved to be rid, even temporarily, of a wife he didn't really want. The awareness filled Peggy with bitterness. She'd frightened him into marriage, but only because she believed he loved her as much as she loved him. The past weeks had shown her otherwise. The devoted, passionate captain of the past three years had turned into an almost indifferent companion. They'd spent less time together since their wedding than they had before. Tony seemed to invent excuses not to be with her. She kept her suite next to his, of course, but she was more often alone in it. Gone were the intimate dinners in his cabin. Since Hong Kong, he'd been at his table in the dining room every night, explaining that he had VIPs to entertain, leaving her, since Hawaii, with only Jayne and

Terry and the purser for company at the big table for eight. She was bored and angry, and yet she was still pleased to be Mrs. Anthony Robin. She knew it was an obsession with her, this business of being a married woman, but it mattered, terribly. Even though she returned alone to Chicago, she'd come back as a woman some man wanted. Better, by far, to have an invisible husband than to be one of those rootless widows or divorcées she despised. In a few years she'd live with Tony. She could wait. Once he settled down and knew his seafaring days were over, he'd be content with her.

At least I know where I stand, she thought. I'm better off than Mary, who clearly was unhappy about returning to her husband, though she pretended not to be. She had nothing but scorn for Mary. "Miss Goody-Twoshoes." The woman was an idiot to let that rich Australian get away from her when it was obvious she was in love with him. Happily married women did not fall in love. Mary would be the type to go back to her marriage out of some idiotic sense of duty. I'll probably see her on the dock, Peggy mused. She'll come down to meet Jayne. It will be interesting to get a look at the unknown Michael Morgan, who'll undoubtedly be with her.

From her window, Peggy could see Jayne and Terry leaning over the railing, holding hands and talking animatedly as they looked toward the waiting crowd on the pier. What an odd couple they were! That combination had been the source of endless speculation ever since Singapore. It was hard to believe that Terry Spalding was attracted to a woman. And harder still to understand what a good-looking girl like Jayne saw in this delicate young man. And yet, crew gossip said they were sleeping together.

Peggy shrugged. Who cared? It was just another shipboard romance. She'd seen a hundred of them, though she had to admit that this one was more off-beat than most.

She put the last of her jewelry into the case she'd carry off the ship. Adieu to cruising, she thought with a tinge of regret. But *bon jour* to the status that more than took its place.

* * *

"I see her! I see Aunt Mary." Jayne jumped up and down like a child. "Over there, Terry!" She pointed to a slim woman in a neat navy suit. "And there's Mother, next to her! Good God, I never thought I'd be glad to see my mother, but I really am! I can't wait to introduce you!" Jayne's eyes sparkled. "I wonder where Uncle Mike is."

Terry tried to make out the features of Patricia Richton, still a blur from this distance and this height. As he came closer to meeting Jayne's mother, he grew increasingly nervous. What would the woman say when she heard her daughter's decision? She must know about me, he thought. Mary must have told her. But he doubted that Mary had gone into any detail about the future he and Jayne planned. She'd leave that up to them. Ridiculously, he scanned the crowd, half expecting Paul to be there. Insane. Paul didn't even know his former lover was on a cruise. It had taken all Terry's willpower not to tell him before he sailed, or to send him a postcard en route. He wondered whether the man he'd cared so much for had missed him, or was even curious as to his whereabouts. Probably not. Paul would be much too involved with the woman he must have married by now. The thought of Paul's wife left a bad taste. He pushed the mental picture aside. I mustn't think of him ever again. He's part of the past I want to forget. That's over and done with. I have Jayne. Darling, wonderful Jayne. She's given me something to care about, something to live for. He felt suddenly happy as he joined his excited companion in waving enthusiastically toward her family below.

For the first time in five days, Mary felt a little surge of pleasure as the ship nosed gently against its moorings. She'd be so glad to see Jayne again, to hear that incredibly understanding voice and see the affectionate smile. What a contrast she was to Patricia! It was as though Jayne was the elder and more dependable of the two. Patricia had driven Mary mad these past days. She was so damned solicitous, so overbearingly proprietary, so patently phony in her new role of "big sister," Mary could hardly wait for her to leave.

Yet, even while she was filled with joy at the prospect of seeing Jayne, the sight of the *Prince of Wales* engulfed her in a longing for Christopher and all the days and nights they'd spent together. In her purse was a letter from him which had arrived at the office yesterday. It was a tender, loving, undemanding message meant to be waiting for her when, as he thought, she stepped off the ship this afternoon. She hadn't written to him since her return. She'd made four or five starts but abandoned every one. She desperately wanted to communicate with him but was afraid to say too much or too little. I'll write tomorrow, Mary thought. Tomorrow night when Patricia's gone and I'm finally alone and can calmly and quietly tell him all that's happened. He'll be sad about Gail's death and the terrible blow it's been to Beau. He'll be happy Michael and I have separated. But how will he feel when I ask him to wait a little while longer for my decision? How much understanding can I expect from him or any man? Can I put into words the crazy, ambivalent feelings I have, not about him but about my whole life? I want him. And I'm scared to death of another marriage. It's as simple and complex as that.

There'd been no word from Michael since the day he left. He'd arranged to come by for more of his clothes at an hour he knew she'd be at the station. Patricia had been home when he came, and reported that Michael seemed well and was still at Stanford Court. He had no job yet, but he was "looking." What is he living on? Mary wondered as she listened in silence to Patricia's account of the visit. That's not my problem, she thought in the next breath. I can't worry about Michael anymore. He has to learn to worry about himself.

Patricia's eyes widened as the big, white ship, all flags flying, came closer to its destination. What a gorgeous floating hotel! Again, she felt jealous of Mary and Jayne. Someday I'll sail off on a boat like that, she thought. I don't know how or when, but I will. My life's going to change from now on. I feel it. At last, it will have some glamour. Now that I'm free, I can make it happen. There'll be some man, somewhere, who'll give me all the wonderful things I've dreamed of—the clothes and jewels and trips I was meant to have.

God knows who it would be. She hadn't met him yet. It certainly wasn't Michael, who'd never have a penny to his name. Or Charlie Burke, who was polite but obviously disinterested in her. I'll find him, Patricia thought. Through Jayne I'll probably meet a lot of attractive men in San Francisco. A young, pretty girl was a perfect lure. Her new beaus would have uncles or fathers interested in her still-beautiful and available mother. Stanley would be out of the picture soon. She'd be unattached and enchanting. She smiled at the thought, forgetting for a moment where she was or why she was here. She was almost surprised to feel Mary nudge her.

"There she is! There's Jayne up on Promenade! See her, Patricia? She sees us! She's waving!"

She followed Mary's finger. Yes, there was Jayne waving madly with her right arm. The left one, Patricia could see, was linked through that of a young man beside her.

"Who's that she's with?"

"That's Terry. Terry Spalding. He and Jayne became good friends on the trip."

"Oh? *How* good?"

Mary was evasive. She still had told Patricia nothing of Jayne's plans. She supposed she kept hoping they'd changed since Hawaii. Not that she didn't like Terry. She liked him very much. She simply couldn't shake the conviction that Jayne was going to do something she'd regret.

"They're very fond of one another," Mary said. "He's a nice young man."

"Live here?"

"Yes, I believe San Francisco is his home."

Patricia seemed pleased. "Perfect! He'll know a lot of people. It will make it easier for both of us to get into a social life." She took out a compact and carefully powdered her nose. "Is he rich? He must be if he can afford a cruise like this."

Mary looked at her with distaste. "I don't really know, but I don't think he has money. He's an actor."

"Probably has a rich family."

Jayne and Terry had disappeared from the railing with a final wave. Soon they'd be coming down the gangway, claiming their luggage. And mine, too, Mary thought. Poor Jayne, stuck with all my stuff. I hope customs doesn't give her too hard a time.

"Let's go over and wait for them by the gate, Patricia. It probably will take some time to get the baggage off and go through customs. We won't see them again until they've cleared."

"Okay. We have a lot of news for Jayne, haven't we? She'll be surprised about you and Michael. And wait until she hears about our apartment!"

Mary tried to change the subject. "Lord, what a crush! We're lucky Charlie insisted on sending us in a limousine. We'd never even *get* a taxi, much less load Jayne's luggage and mine and Terry's into one. See? The bags are put under the letter of your last name. I wonder what Jayne did about that. Probably put Richton tags on everything. Poor lamb, she'll have an awful lot to declare to the customs inspector. I'm afraid I bought much more than the duty-free hundred-dollar limit. I'll repay her, of course." Mary realized she was chattering like a magpie. What would Patricia think when she got a good look at Terry? Not that he was flagrantly gay. He'd toned down tremendously since that first day she and Jayne saw him in the dining room. Still, Patricia was a city girl. You didn't grow up in New York without developing the antennae that made you instantly recognize one of "the boys." Don't let her be rude to Terry, Mary prayed. No telling what the infatuated Jayne would do if her mother made some snide remark in front of him.

It seemed forever before the two young people, their mountain of luggage loaded onto a cart, pushed through the exit. Jayne threw her arms around Patricia while Terry hugged Mary. There was much laughter and introductions and excitement before Jayne said, "Where's Michael? Couldn't he come with you?"

"No," Mary said. "I'll explain later. Let's get out of here, shall we?"

Jayne seemed to understand without another word. "Sure. Let's go. Can we drop Terry? He's going to the St. Francis Hotel until . . . until he finds an apartment."

Patricia looked surprised. "Oh? You don't have an apartment here, Terry? I thought you lived in San Francisco."

"I do, Mrs. Richton. Live here, I mean. But I gave up my apartment just before the trip."

"I see. Well, I'm sure you'll find a wonderful one. The town is full of them. In fact . . ."

Mary hurriedly interrupted. "You and your mother will stay overnight with me, Jayne. Terry, will you come for dinner?"

"I'd love to, if I'm not intruding on a family reunion."

"Not a bit of it! I want to hear what's been going on this past week."

"Speaking of that," Jayne said, "did everything go all right on the flight home? How's the colonel?"

"He's doing all right, thank heavens. He's been staying with one of Gail's daughters but he leaves for Atlanta today. I spoke with him this morning. He said to be sure to give you and Terry his love. Such a rare human being, our Beau. He wants us to visit him one of these days, but I suppose we never will." Mary sounded regretful. "People lose touch when a voyage is over."

A familiar voice behind her spoke up. "I hope that won't hold true with us, Mary. You must come to Chicago!"

"Peggy!" Mary embraced the tall, fair-haired woman. "I'm so glad we got to see you. Patricia, this is Mrs. Lawrence. I'm sorry! I mean Mrs. *Robin*. She's our newlywed. She and the captain were married in Hong Kong. My sister, Patricia Richton, Peggy. Jayne's mother."

"How do you do." Peggy acknowledged the introduction. "I was hoping to meet your husband, Mary dear."

"He couldn't make it. How's Tony?"

"Fine. Busy right now, of course. We're spending the

night at the Clift. Maybe you and Michael could come by this evening for a drink?"

"Oh, I'm so sorry we can't. How long are you staying?"

"Just overnight. Tony sails tomorrow and I'm flying back to Chicago." Peggy gave a tinkling little laugh. "Such is the life of a captain's wife! Well, another time, hopefully. I won't keep you. By the way, have you heard from Christopher?"

"As a matter of fact, I had a nice note from him yesterday." Mary hoped she sounded as casual as she tried to. "He seems fine."

"Perhaps he'll come and visit you and your husband one day. Such a charming man, my dear. So devoted to you. It would be a pity if you lost touch with him, too."

Bitch! Mary thought. You've never forgiven me for not coming to your ridiculous wedding, have you? You're probably sorry Michael isn't here so you could start him asking questions. Too bad you don't know it doesn't matter anymore. She smiled sweetly. "Yes, Christopher is a darling. I'm sure I'll stay in touch with him and a couple of other *good* friends." She didn't embrace Peggy again. "We must run, I'm afraid. Give my love to Tony. I do hope we'll all sail again, one day." Suddenly Mary regretted her rudeness. Impulsively, she kissed the other woman. "I hope you'll be happy, Peggy. Let me hear from you. If you get to San Francisco again . . ."

"I'll call you. That's a promise. Good-bye, Mary. Mrs. Richton. Terry, take good care of Jayne. You're lucky to have her." She waved her hand and disappeared.

"What was *that* all about?" Patricia asked.

"Nothing," Mary said. "I'll tell you about it later."

The atmosphere was strained when the three women finally reached Mary's apartment and deposited her luggage and Jayne's in the foyer. They'd had very little to say in the car after they let Terry out at his hotel, and the uneasy silence continued as they sat down in the living room to catch their breath. Jayne kicked off her shoes and she sighed deeply.

"Well," she said, "*that's* over! The worst part about a trip is the departure and return. Especially the return.

Those customs boys are thorough, Aunt Mary. Fortunately, we didn't have anything madly expensive to declare. Did you have a problem with your jewelry when you went through customs in Hawaii?"

"No. Just paid a little duty on the jade."

Patricia perked up. "You didn't tell me you bought jade, Mary. How come you haven't shown it to me?"

"I don't know. I guess I forgot about it with all that's been going on." Another lie. The ring and heart Christopher had given her were hidden away. Patricia was all too wise about the value of things. She'd know Mary could never have afforded to buy such expensive jewelry. "There are just a couple of pieces," she said now. "I'll show them to you another time. There are a few little gifts in the luggage Jayne brought. Souvenirs, really, for all of you."

She hasn't told Mother about Christopher, Jayne realized. Well, that was no surprise. But maybe she'd told Michael. They hadn't mentioned him again, but Jayne sensed he wasn't going to be around. Everybody's hiding something, the girl thought. Aunt Mary's reluctant to talk about Michael. I'm nervous about telling Mother about Terry. And even Mother herself seems to be holding back some important piece of news.

"Maybe we'd all better talk," Jayne said in her forthright way. "You can cut the tension with a knife in here."

Mary nodded. "Michael's left," she said simply. "We've separated. The call he made to me on the ship was a packet of lies. There's no deal with Harry Carson. It was the last straw, Jaynie. I couldn't take it anymore." She looked knowingly at her niece. I didn't tell him about Christopher, the look said.

Jayne bit her lip. "I'm sorry, Aunt Mary. Will you get a divorce?"

"Not yet. He's asked me to wait and think it over. I told him I would." No need to mention Rae Spanner. Or to say she hadn't decided what to do about Christopher. Jayne would hear about Rae eventually, no doubt, and she'd understand now that Mary was in a turmoil about her lover.

281

"I have some happier news," Patricia said.

"What's that, Mother?"

"Charlie Burke's going to give you a receptionist's job at the radio station."

Jayne was amazed. "You're kidding! Aunt Mary told you I wanted to stay in San Francisco? Oh, Aunt Mary, thank you! It was wonderful of you to line up a job for me!"

"Your Aunt Mary didn't do it," Patricia said proudly. "*I* did. *I* talked to Charlie."

"*You* did? Then you don't mind that I won't be going back to New York?"

"Patricia smiled broadly. "Mind? I'm delighted!" She turned to her sister. "See, Mary? You were wrong. You were afraid I was taking too much on myself, assuming Jayne would like to live here. I know my own child. I knew she'd want to stay!"

Before Mary could answer, Patricia rushed on. "And there's more, Jayne. I'm going to stay, too! I've found us the most adorable apartment. I'll be able to take care of it and you. We'll have a wonderful time meeting new people and doing different things! I'm so excited, honey! So glad you agree!"

It took Jayne a moment to digest what her mother was saying, and then she looked stunned. "You plan to stay, too? I don't understand. What about Daddy?"

"He'll manage. I doubt he'll miss us."

"But . . . but you obviously don't know about Terry." Patricia looked at her sharply. "What about Terry?"

"I'm going to live with him. I plan to stay in San Francisco, but *Terry* and I are going to share an apartment." Jayne looked helplessly at Mary. "I thought you knew, Mother. I thought that's why you lined up the job for me. I assumed Aunt Mary must have told you."

"I thought it was your place to tell your mother," Mary said softly. "I'm sorry, Jayne. I guess I was wrong to let her go on with this idea, but I didn't know whether you and Terry might not have changed your minds this past week."

"Live with that boy?" Patricia's voice began to rise.

282

"What are you talking about, Jayne? You barely know him! No! I won't permit it! And what about me? I've made plans. I've even put a deposit on our apartment. I can't stay here unless I live with you! You tell him tonight. Tell him your mother is staying here and you're going to be with her!"

"I'm sorry, Mother. I can't. Terry and I intend to look for a place tomorrow. We've been talking about it for weeks. It's time for me to leave home anyway. I'd have done that in New York. Even if Terry hadn't come into the picture. I'd have gone out on my own. I'm sorry you're disappointed," Jayne said again, "but it is something you should have discussed with me before you went this far. Aunt Mary was right. You did take too much for granted."

Patricia turned her rage on Mary. "What kind of sister are you? You knew about this all the time! You let me take that apartment and make my plans and all the time you knew what my ungrateful daughter was up to! It must have given you quite a kick! I'm sure you had a good laugh behind my back, seeing me make such a fool of myself!"

"Patricia, I didn't! It wasn't that way at all. I tried to tell you not to make plans, but you wouldn't listen. I didn't feel I had the right to tell you what Jayne was thinking, but I did everything I could to make you wait until she returned. But you were so sure of yourself you paid no attention."

"I might have paid attention if you'd said she was sleeping with this actor from San Francisco! I might have guessed she'd figure some way to get her hooks into him!"

"Mother, stop it! Aunt Mary did all she could to stop you, I'm sure of that. But nobody can stop you when you make up your mind to do something. You never think about anybody but yourself. You don't give a damn what I do unless it inconveniences you! Well, that's just too bad!" Jayne was in a rage. "You'll just have to go home where you belong. You have no right to walk out on Daddy. He's never given you any reason to leave him. For God's sake, how could you have done this to him even if

283

I'd agreed to your idea? How could you desert a man who's so devoted to you?"

"How could your precious Aunt Mary throw out Michael?" Patricia's answer was a snarl. "She wants to be free. So do I. You don't understand. You and your damned youth! You don't understand what it's like to be trapped in a dull, pointless existence with a man you've never given a damn about. My God! I have more reason than Mary! At least Michael is one hell of a lover! I can tell you that! Your father is a bore in bed as well as out of it! I haven't even had *that* going for me!" She halted abruptly, silenced by the expression on the faces of the women opposite: shock on the part of Jayne, horror in Mary's eyes as they heard this unexpected confession. Patricia lifted her chin and tried to bluff it through. "All right. I admit it. I slept with Michael. His wife went off and left him for two months. He was lonely. So was I. Don't sit there in moral judgment, you two! Don't you see how desperate I was about my life? Don't you see why I have to stay here, Jayne? Why I have to leave your father? I don't say it was right of me to go to bed with my sister's husband, but she asked for it, leaving him alone so long. Anyway, I wasn't the only one. That Rae Spanner . . ."

"Shut up!" Mary screamed. "Shut up, Patricia! Don't use my absence as an excuse for what you did! And don't pretend you were so desperate for affection you went to bed with my husband! You're using that to justify leaving Stanley. Well, if you're so unhappy, leave him! But don't blame it on me and don't expect Jayne to feel obligated to get you out of a marriage you got into because you were as wanton and uncaring then as you are now!" Mary's eyes blazed. "Leave this child alone! Leave us both alone, Patricia, now and forever! Go home. Go tonight. I'll get you a ticket on the next flight to New York, and I never want to see or hear from you again!"

Patricia seemed to collapse. "Mary, I don't blame you for hating me. What I did was terrible. It was just an involuntary thing. Michael and I . . ."

Mary interrupted her. "I don't want to hear about

Michael and you," she said coldly. "I'm tired of your ugly games. Fed up with your selfishness. You have no heart, Patricia." She seemed suddenly exhausted. "My God, I might even have forgiven you if you'd fallen in love with my husband. But you don't love him or anyone. You played on Michael's weakness, just as you're trying to play on Jayne's. You disgust me. I can't bear to look at you."

Jayne sat mutely through the terrible exchange, unwilling to hear her mother's dreadful words. Now she looked pityingly at both women; the betrayed and the betrayer. What Patricia had done was unspeakable, but she hadn't done it alone. Michael had been just as guilty and the hurt Mary felt must be doubly crushing. Not enough the thing with Rae Spanner, whoever *she* was, but to know that your own sister . . . Jayne shuddered. "Aunt Mary's right, Mother," she said. "I think you should go back tonight. I'll call Daddy and tell him where to meet you."

Patricia looked at her imploringly. "Jayne, please don't do this to me. Let me stay with you. We'll work it out just fine. I won't be in your way. You can still see Terry as much as you like. I tried so hard, Jaynie. I even got you that job. I thought things would be wonderful for us. We'd be pals, roommates . . ."

"No, I can't do that. Mothers and daughters aren't pals. Not even under the best of circumstances. I can't live with you. Even before tonight I knew that."

Defeated, Patricia began to weep. "All right. Get the ticket. Call your father. Tell him you're sending me home to die."

"You won't die." Jayne said. There was no emotion in her voice. "You'll make the best of things, the way everybody else does." She got to her feet. "Where's your round-trip ticket?"

"I don't have one. I only bought one-way."

She never had the slightest intention of going back, Mary realized. She planned this all along. Planned to stay here with Jayne. Or maybe with Michael if she could get him. She probably knew before she arrived that she'd

285

have an affair with my husband. I wonder if she was foolish enough to think he'd leave me for her? A cynical smile crossed Mary's lips. It would have served her right. If she'd gotten Michael, who would have supported her then? It was ludicrous. Insane. She wished they'd all go away. All of them. She desperately wanted to be alone.

"Mother, I don't have enough money for your air fare. Do you have a credit card?"

"Never mind, Jayne," Mary said wearily. "Charge it to me. Just get her the hell out of here."

Chapter 23

When the long-awaited letter finally arrived, Christopher was almost afraid to open it. Let it say what I want it to, he silently prayed. Let it be a message from Mary telling me she can't live without me. Slowly, almost fearfully, he slit open the envelope and began to read. It was a long letter, and as he carefully absorbed every line, Christopher felt his heart beat faster, his spirits alternately rise and fall with each paragraph.

He frowned and shook his head sadly as Mary told him of the sudden death of Gail DeVries and her return from Hawaii with the colonel. Damn it, if only he'd been aboard to help. She shouldn't have had to go through that alone, with a broken-hearted old man to care for and comfort. It took him a minute to realize she'd been home for more than two weeks before she sat down to write to him. The idea hurt, even while he recognized his own foolishness. I'm like a lovesick schoolboy, Christopher thought, expecting Mary to think of nothing but me when she's had so much else on her mind.

He read on. So Jayne and Terry had moved in together after all.

> They've taken a room in a house on Powell Street. I won't deny that it worries me. Jayne is working at "my" radio station. Charlie Burke

was kind enough to give her a job that will support them both while Terry looks for something to do. God knows what that will be. I can't imagine there'd be much demand for actors in San Francisco, but I must say Jayne seems quite happy and carefree. Oh, for the optimism of youth, my darling Christopher! She is so sure things will work out for them. I wish I were as serene about it. Terry is a sweet young man and Jayne truly loves him. I believe he loves her, too. But I confess that I still have more than nagging doubts about this "conversion." To me, Terry seems restless and somehow tentative in this new situation. Jayne doesn't see this side of him. I hope I'm wrong, but I can't shake that awful feeling in my bones about the whole arrangement. Jayne's mother was furious about it, of course, but not for any of the reasons you might imagine. She met Terry only once, briefly, when the ship arrived, and she has no idea of his past. My sister is, to put it mildly, a selfish woman. The idea of her daughter "living in sin" did not bother her, but the failure of her own plans did. She was prepared to live with Jaynie in San Francisco and let that child support her! There was a terrible scene when she found that was not to be.

Get on with it! Christopher found himself thinking. I don't have that much interest in Jayne and Terry. It's *us* I want to know about. It was as though Mary was working up to the part of the letter that mattered to him, as though she was afraid to put down the words that were personal and precious to them both. They came at last.

Dearest, I know you must think I'm stalling, going on about everything except what is the most important thing in the world to me—my love and desire for you. Perhaps I am. Not that my longing to be with you has diminished one iota. If anything, it grows stronger each day and each night. How I long to be in your arms, my beloved Christopher. How lost I am without your tenderness and your laughter. And how fearful I am that you will not understand what keeps me from flying straight to you when I tell you that I'm free to do so.

Michael moved out more than a week ago. The break came not because of you and me. He doesn't know about us. It was simply the culmination of all the things I thought of before I took the cruise, and a few more that happened after I returned. I don't lie, even to myself, when I admit that knowing you made it even more difficult to go on with my marriage. But I'm not the kind of woman who leaves one man for another, no matter how much she adores the new-found love. I'd have stayed with Michael, sweetheart, even though I'd yearn, every waking and dreaming moment, for you. I'm of that idiotic, irrational breed of females who can't shake a sense of obligation to an innocent person. But Michael is a man I can no longer forgive as I might a naïve and naughty child. Forget the infidelities which occurred while I was away. Who am I to cast stones? No, the breaking point came not through his unfaithfulness, unspeakable as it was, but, as I suppose I always knew it would, through his lies and his sense of unreality. There was no "big deal" as he told me. There never will be. And I know, at last, that I cannot pretend, as I have for so long. I am ashamed of his shallowness—and my own. The important thing is the ability to live with myself, and to look up to the person with whom I share my life.

That comes effortlessly with you, my darling. You are my dream, my ideal, my longed-for lover. More than anything, I want to set the wheels in motion, get a divorce and be Mrs.

Christopher Andrews. If only it were that simple. But I gave Michael my word I'd wait awhile before making the final break. Why was I so silly? I can't answer that. A hangover, I suppose, from fifteen years of reluctance to knock the props out from under him. Pity for his distress. Or, perhaps, a leftover feeling of guilt which I know, logically, is absurd and which, emotionally, I am prey to.

But I did it. I gave my word that he'd have a chance to "prove himself." He won't. I know that. I'm sure he'd admit it too, if he could bear to be honest with himself. There will come a time when I can freely and gladly write finis to the episode. A time when I can belong to you, my love, in the way you need a woman to belong. Stay close to me with your letters and your support, dearest. Give me, I beg you, time to tie up the loose ends and rid myself of the real and imagined encumbrances.

I want to come to you, Christopher. I know that in my heart. And in time I will also know it in my head. I love you, darling, and I pray that when the miraculous moment comes you'll be waiting for your adoring Mary.

He read the last part of the letter again. The part about them. For a long moment, he sat staring into space. She was the most honest, the most compassionate woman he'd ever known. The least he could do would be to give her the time she pleaded for. And then his desolation changed to something near anger. No. He wouldn't wait indefinitely while she allowed that spineless husband of hers to pretend he could set things right. She owes Michael nothing. She knows that. She's afraid. There was fear between every line. But afraid of what? Afraid of entrusting her life to someone else? Of giving up her work, her independence? Fearful of moving to the other side of the world with someone she'd known such a short time? The end of her marriage had come. She was free, yet she delayed, with flimsy excuses about giving her word and feeling pity. She believed what she said. He didn't doubt that. She simply didn't understand that the break had to be swift and clean. She didn't know she was afraid, she who seemed so strong and fearless in every other way.

There's only one answer, Christopher decided. I must force her to choose between me and the invalid excuses she's making to herself. I mustn't go on being understanding and patient. Not for her sake or mine. She needs a strong hand for her own good. It was a chance, a risky move, but he saw, as the doctor had said, that subconsciously Mary was asking him to make the decision for her. And the only way he could do that would be to threaten not to wait. He might lose her by pushing her. But he'd certainly lose her if he permitted an endless period of separation. Geography and time. Too much of one, too little of the other.

Before he weakened, he took out pen and paper and answered the cry for help from the woman he loved.

* * *

Charlie Burke sat by the bedside, holding the hand of his dying wife. This gaunt woman who looks older than her years bears no resemblance to the Tracey I married, he thought. She was so beautiful then, so lively and full of fun. What happened to us? Where did our paths separate? She was unhappy for so long, unwilling or unable to follow where I was determined to lead. Perhaps I failed her, had too little patience, expected too much. All the stories he'd ever read, all the sad tales he'd ever heard of men "outgrowing their wives" came back to him. Always they blamed the woman. She didn't keep up, socially or intellectually, with an increasingly successful husband. She wanted the marriage to stay as it was in the beginning when they were young and on the same level of interest and ambition. The man changed and his wife stood still. That's the way all the sad stories went. Including his.

Charlie felt a lump in his throat, a sense of remorse for the things he should have done. If only he'd tried harder to understand, to be more tolerant of her limitations, perhaps she'd not have turned to drink for courage or forgetfulness. He'd been reasonably faithful. The phrase struck him as ridiculous. There was no such thing as "reasonably faithful." It was as impossible as being "a little bit pregnant." You either were or you weren't. And of course he hadn't been. He'd had his brief affairs over the years, but he'd never gotten himself seriously involved. Still, he sought comfort elsewhere and that, meaningful or not, was infidelity and self-indulgence. All those excuses he made to himself about the lack of love at home, the disgust he felt at living with a drunk, the anger at her unwillingness to be a partner he was proud of, all those were a cop-out. He should have been strong enough, considerate enough to work on the problems with her. Maybe if she'd felt more important to him, none of this would have happened.

He leaned over and kissed her forehead. In a drugged sleep, Tracey felt and heard nothing. The doctor said it was just a matter of days. Perhaps hours.

"I did care, Tracey," he said softly. "Please forgive me."

* * *

Wearing only a pair of brief swim trunks, Michael lay on a plastic chaise in the backyard of his mother's small house in North Hollywood. He'd arrived a week before and since then he'd spent every day baking in the hot Southern California sun.

Carrie Morgan had not been particularly surprised to get the phone call saying he'd like to come down alone for a while. She knew what that meant. She was only amazed that Mary hadn't gotten fed up years ago. Michael wasn't a bad human being, Carrie thought as she looked out the kitchen window and saw him lying motionless in her "patio." He was simply too handsome, too spoiled. Somewhere he'd developed the belief that the world owed him a living, that he never really had to work for it as other people did.

His mother sighed. Much of what he was was her fault, she supposed. She'd adored him, pampered him, supported him as best she could on the little she had. She'd been too easy on him, too quick to forgive. It was a blessing that all her attention hadn't turned him into one of those queer fellows you saw everywhere, the ones they said got that way because their mothers held on too tightly to them, were too protective and possessive.

Well, Carrie thought, there'd been no danger of his being a mama's boy. Michael had been anything but. A hell-raiser, in fact, despite his sweet nature. A lusty woman-chaser from his high school days. What he hadn't been was a man prepared to be a husband. His first wife, Linda, couldn't take it. And now Mary, though she stuck much longer, had reached the same inevitable conclusion: Michael was a spoiled child. No real woman could live with that forever. The day had to come when Mary reached the end of the rope. Carrie Morgan always knew that. That's why she wasn't surprised when he came home. He had nowhere else to go when his wife threw him out. Not, of course, that he'd ever admit that was what happened.

He'd arrived, bag and baggage, with some transparent story about there being more opportunities for him in Los Angeles than there were in San Francisco.

"Mary and I agreed I should come down here and look the situation over," he said. "In fact, it was her suggestion. We're both fed up with the North."

"I see. I must say I'm surprised, though, Michael. I thought Mary loved her job. She's done so well at it."

He'd been very casual. "Oh, she likes the job well enough, but it doesn't matter that much to her. That is, she'd prefer to live here when I get this project of mine going. Of course, she can't chuck the radio show until I do. You see, I have a great idea for a men's boutique, Mother. This is the place for it. San Francisco's much too uptight for the kind of swinging thing I have in mind. I figured down here it would be much easier to get backing and open up a shop. I'll get one of those good locations on Rodeo, probably. All I need is financing, and there's plenty of loose movie and TV money around here. It shouldn't be too tough to get started."

"And then Mary will come down?"

"Of course. What else?"

Carrie didn't answer. It was all lies, as usual. Maybe not the part about wanting to open a shop. That was typical of Michael's daydreams. Probably he'd tried it and failed in San Francisco. He'd tried so many things. He was lying when he pretended that he and Mary weren't separated; that it was just a matter of time before she joined him. Michael's marriage was over. His mother was certain of that, even if he chose to lie about it. Maybe he can't admit it even to himself, she thought, the old protectiveness returning. How often can a man try and fail?

"Well, that's fine," she said cheerfully. "It will be nice to have you around for a while, son."

He grinned. "Glad to be here, Carrie-baby. You're still the best cook in the world!"

But he'd done nothing about looking for his financing since he'd arrived. He's spent every day working on his tan. He'd made no phone calls or set up any business appointments. Probably he had no idea where to start. And there'd been no word from Mary. If Michael called his wife, Carrie wasn't aware of it. Certainly Mary hadn't tried to reach him.

Mrs. Morgan wished he'd come out with the truth, admit his marriage was over, make some sensible plans for the future. He could live with her for a while. She had room and it didn't cost that much extra to feed him, but a forty-five-year-old man couldn't just go on forever living off his mother, doing nothing but lying in the sun.

He'll talk when he's ready, Carrie told herself. There's no use pushing him. I already know the story. I've lived through it before.

*   *   *

Rae Spanner opened her morning mail and a check for twenty-three thousand dollars fell out. There was a brief note inside.

Dear Rae,

I'm returning your loan and hope you won't mind my keeping out two thousand dollars for the time being. I'm going down to L.A. to get a boutique started and I'm temporarily a little short of cash. I'll mail you the balance in a couple of weeks when the interested parties there get all the papers filled out.

Thanks very much for everything.

Michael

So that's where he was. Los Angeles. Of course. Where else would he go except home to Mother? Rae already knew the Morgans had split up. Everybody knew. The grapevine in their circle worked well. Mary's cleaning woman told a friend who told her employer who told . . . well, it went on and on. Within twenty-four hours, the news was all over town.

The only thing people didn't know was where Michael had gone. Rae made a shrewd guess that Mary herself might not be sure. She probably knows about Michael and me, Rae thought. I figured that when she didn't call. Not that she's called any of her old friends, as far as I know. The woman who works for her says she's living alone. The sister's gone back to New York. The only person she ever sees is her niece. And Charlie Burke. Maybe there's something going on there. There've always been rumors about those two, and now that Tracey Burke is dying. . . . Could be Charlie Burke was the reason for the breakup. No. As low an opinion as Rae had of her own sex, she couldn't make herself believe that Mary was already planning to step into Tracey's shoes. Some other woman, maybe, but not Mary. She was much too square for that kind of macabre planning.

What difference did it make why they'd separated. The fact was, they had, and that, Rae thought, is very good for me. In her cold, calculating way, Rae Spanner was in love with Michael. Until now, she hadn't thought of him as a husband. She'd settled for what she could get, never dreaming he'd leave Mary. Probably he hadn't wanted to.

The shoe certainly was on the other foot. But that didn't matter either. The end result was the same.

All I have to do is give him time, she decided. He'll get fed up with Los Angeles. He won't do any better there than he did here. Michael is a sweet toy to be owned and cared for. An expensive possession that gives pleasure. I'm better equipped to own him than either of his two previous wives. They probably expected him to be a provider, the head of the house. It's not a role Michael's cut out for. He wants the good things of life handed to him as a reward for his charm. I'm willing to accept that. And I'm the first one who can afford it.

She glanced at the return address on the back of the envelope. She'd wait a couple of weeks and then make a quick trip to Los Angeles. She'd take a bungalow at the Beverly Hills, arrange quiet little dinners at the Hermitage or Le Restaurant, rent a shiny Mercedes for Michael to drive.

She wouldn't rush it, but she wouldn't wait too long. Just long enough for him to get bored in his mother's house. Long enough for him to realize that nobody in Los Angeles was going to back one of his crazy schemes, but not so long that he'd have a chance to meet one of those young, blond, tanned girls who seemed to be turned out on a production line in Southern California.

I really want him, Rae said to herself. I'm not blind to his shortcomings. Or mine. I need an attractive husband who can be manipulated. I'm getting too old to cruise around. Michael suits me fine. And I'll be the best thing that could happen to him.

* * *

When the phone rang at five o'clock in the morning, Mary was startled into frightened wakefulness. A call at this hour could only be bad news. As she reached for the receiver she wondered whether something had happened to one of her parents. Or Jayne. Or Michael. But it was a controlled, sad-sounding Charlie on the line.

"I'm sorry to call you at this hour, Mary, but I had to talk to someone."

She was instantly alert. "Tracey?"

"Yes. She died three hours ago."

"Oh, Charlie, I'm so sorry! Where are you? Are you all right?"

"Yes, I'm all right. As all right as I can be. I'm in our apartment. They called me at two o'clock this morning and told me. I've been walking around ever since, thinking, remembering how she used to be. She was wonderful, Mary, long ago. You never really knew her when she was happy. She was funny, then. A pixie of a girl. You'd have liked her."

Mary swallowed hard. "I always liked her, Charlie. I always wished I could help her somehow."

"I know. You were her only friend. She liked you too." There was a little silence and then Charlie said, "I hate to ask you, but could you help me with the . . . the arrangements? I have to pick out something for her to wear, and go to the funeral home and make a lot of decisions. There's no one . . ."

"Oh course, dear. I'll be right over. I can get there within the hour."

"Thanks. I really appreciate it. It's a hell of an imposition, I know."

"Are you crazy? You're my best friend! Make some coffee and I'll be there before it's through perking."

As she hurriedly dressed, Mary felt grief for the man. God knows it hadn't been the best marriage in the world. Tracey had been a burden to Charlie and herself for so many years, a difficult, frightened, often hostile woman. But she had her appealing side, too. It wasn't hard to imagine what she'd been like as a young woman. Nor to guess the remorse Charlie now felt because, like any human being, he'd been driven nearly out of his mind by her behavior. It was sad to think Tracey had no friends closer than her husband's business associate. Mary stopped, suddenly comparing her own situation with Tracey's. I have no close women friends either, she realized again. I've lived for my work and for Michael. We had our circle of acquaintances, mostly couples, but there's no one I can go to with my troubles. There's Charlie, of course, but he's a man, with a man's point of view. And Jayne, young enough to be the daughter I never had, can't really understand the way I feel. If I died tomorrow, someone as remote as I am to Tracey would pick out my burial clothes. No. Jayne would do that. And that doesn't matter to me anyway. What I desperately need is a woman to talk to now, someone who can understand and identify. I'd hoped it would be Gail DeVries. At one time I even thought I could be close to Rae Spanner, a woman of my generation. That's a sick joke if I ever heard one. Friend? Rae is as loyal to me as Patricia is.

Since her traumatic departure, Mary had tried not to think of her sister. After her initial outburst, she'd forced herself not to let her mind dwell on Michael and Patricia's behavior. It was too ugly to visualize. Mary's work at the radio station brought her into daily contact with all kinds of sordid things. The public loved "juicy stories"—wife beaters, rapists, child molesters, incest, all the sickness of the human race covered in the news reports. She accepted these things in an objective way, but when horror struck close to home it was too loathsome to think about. It was as though a protective curtain had dropped. She could think of Michael's affair with Rae with distress, but with some understanding. She could not accept the idea of her sister in Mary's own bed with her husband. The idea made her physically ill. It was more than hate she felt for Patricia, it was revulsion.

No time to think of that now, Mary told herself firmly. My friend needs me. He's all alone over there, waiting.

When he opened the door, she saw he'd been crying. She held out her arms and embraced him soothingly. Charlie quickly wiped away his tears.

"You must think I'm a hypocrite," he said. "God knows Tracey and I weren't a devoted couple anymore. I didn't even think I'd cry when she went."

"Of course you'll cry. Death is part of life, Charlie, and we all mourn. Maybe we're crying for ourselves. That's all right, too. You can't lose someone who's been a part of your life for so long without feeling emptiness and regret."

"Yes. I regret so much. I let her down, Mary. I stopped loving her when she needed to be loved."

"She couldn't accept love," Mary said softly. "She was too full of her own insecurities to give or take it. I don't mean to speak unkindly of the dead, my dear, but you did all you could. No one could have done more. Most people wouldn't have done as much. You stuck by her. She always had someone to lean on. She knew that."

"Thanks," he said. "Thanks for coming over at this ungodly hour. Thanks for everything, Mary."

"I'm your friend," she said again. "I always will be."

The next few hours were a nightmare. Mary had never done this before. Death has never touched me in this intimate way, she thought, as she went through Tracey's closet, picking out a dress and underwear, taking them to the funeral home, telling the attendant how Tracey wore her hair and what kind of makeup she preferred. This was more real and more terrible than a few weeks ago when Gail died. These awful duties were thrust on Gail's daughters. Her heart ached for them as she thought of their going through what she and Charlie were enduring now. He'd pulled himself together. Even at the gruesome moment when an unctuous undertaker ("funeral directors" they called themselves these days) led them into a big room full of caskets, Charlie did not break down again, though she saw his eyes widen in horror. She knew her reaction was the same and she felt her knees begin to tremble.

"I'll leave you alone to make your choice," the man said. "You'll find the price on the back of every card." He discreetly withdrew, leaving Mary and Charlie surrounded by the wood and metal reminders of death.

"Let's get this over fast," Charlie said, looking around at the vast, morbid display. "God! You don't go bargain hunting for this kind of thing!"

They made a quick selection and fled from the room, back to the hushed office of the man in charge. Mary's head swam at the dozens of questions that had to be answered, the hundreds of details Charlie managed to give. Tracey's vital statistics, the information for the death notice in the papers, the arrangements for pall-bearers and limousines and cemetery plots and flowers. She recoiled, as Charlie did, from queries about "slumber rooms" and "viewing hours."

"None of that," he said. "I want to remember my wife alive. I want her friends to remember her that way, too. I want the services simple and as soon as possible. Tomorrow morning, in fact."

The director looked shocked. "But Mr. Burke, there'll only be time for a notice in the afternoon paper. And your friends . . ."

"My friends will understand."

"Of course." The man's voice dripped practiced sympathy. "At times like these, the bereaved . . ."

"Thank you very much," Charlie said. "Good-bye."

Outside, they stood for a moment on the steps of the funeral home, gratefully breathing the clean, fresh morning air, watching the city go about its business of the day.

"Life goes on," Charlie said. "Not an original thought but something to hold on to. I'm sure that man in there thinks I'm heartless."

Mary took his arm. "No one who knows you could ever think that," she said. "The others don't count."

He looked at her. "What counts in this world, Mary? Love, loyalty, friendship, work? Everything comes and goes so fast. We don't cherish what we have. We don't appreciate what we're given. We're always looking for something more. Some new person to stimulate us, some new challenge to be met, some compliment to bolster our egos. Hell, what's it all about anyway? What do *you* want in this world, my friend? What would make you happy?"

Mary was silent for a moment. "I'm not sure. Peace, I suppose. Serenity. A sense of what I'm meant to be. A contentment with what I am."

"You're too young for those kind of wishes. They're the desires of the old."

She smiled. "These days I'm feeling old, Charlie. Very old and torn apart."

"Want to talk about it? Really talk, I mean."

How kind he was. Even now, at this terrible hour of his life, he cared about her happiness. She shook her head.

"Not now, dear. Not until this is over. Maybe not for a while after that. But one thing is for sure—when the moment comes to pour out my heart, you'll be the one I'll come to."

Chapter 24

He never understood his wife, Stanley Richton had long since realized, but the woman who returned from San Francisco was even more baffling than the one who left. Since her abrupt arrival two weeks before, Patricia had been colder and more uncommunicative than ever. In answer to his questions about Jayne, Patricia simply said, "You might as well forget your precious daughter. She's moved in with some no-good actor she met on the ship. She won't be back."

Stanley stared at her. "Is that all you have to say?"

"What more is there?"

"For God's sake, Patricia, you're talking about our only child! Who is this man? Where are they living? Are they going to get married?"

"I don't know any of those answers. She didn't choose to enlighten me. She couldn't wait to get me out of town, that's all."

"You don't even have her address?" Stanley was incredulous. "You just left, like that? Not knowing anything of this man? Not having any idea whether she's going to be all right? I can't believe it! What does Mary have to say about it?"

Patricia's anger flared. "Mary? Why should Mary give a damn? She's much too wrapped up in herself to worry about her family!"

He tried to be reasonable. "That doesn't sound like Mary. She's devoted to Jayne."

"And I suppose I'm not?"

"I didn't mean that. I simply meant it doesn't fit Mary's character to let anyone she loves get involved in something so important without knowing more details than you seem to have. Mary must know this man pretty well if they were all on the ship together. Does she think he's a solid citizen? Is she in favor of this move? You must have discussed it with her. What did Mary say when Jayne decided to stay in San Francisco?"

Patricia was furious. "Mary, Mary, Mary! I'm sick to death of Mary! You think she's so marvelous. Well, let me tell you, Mary is the most selfish, egotistical, overbearing woman you'll ever have the misfortune to meet! All she cares about is *her* life, *her* job, *her* freedom! She's thrown Michael out. What do you think of that, Stanley? Chucked out her husband of fifteen years! He's not good enough for her. Not successful or famous enough. Not perfect enough for St. Mary! Don't talk to me about Mary! I think she put Jayne up to this. I think she encouraged it to keep our daughter near her. She's nothing but a damned, frustrated, barren woman who'd like to own a child without the bother of having one!"

"I think you're crazy," Stanley said slowly. "I think there's a lot you're not telling me. What happened between you and your sister? What did you do to her, Patricia?"

"What did *I* do to *her*? Why don't you ask me what *she* did to *me*?"

"All right. What did she do? What really happened out there?"

Patricia's eyes blazed. "I've already told you. She fostered this indecent relationship between Jayne and Terry What's-his-name. Then she made it clear that I wasn't welcome to stay in her apartment even for another day. What a bitch! No appreciation that I'd been there cooking and cleaning for her husband! No thanks that I even got Jayne a job so she could stay in San Francisco! She's a phony. A grade-A, first-class Judas. If you want

303

to blame someone for your daughter's behavior, I can tell you where to point the finger!"

He hardly heard the last words. "*You* got Jayne a job so she could stay in San Francisco? You mean, even before she returned you'd made plans for her to stay? I don't understand. Did she write and tell you she wanted to stay? Did you already know about this Terry person?"

"No. Of course I didn't know. Do you think Jayne ever confides in me?"

"Then, why . . .?"

"Why did I get her the job? Because I thought we'd all move out there. You and I and Jayne. I thought we could start a new life. Mary has good connections. I thought she could help you get started in a business. I love California. You would, too. I couldn't presume to get a job for *you*, but I thought at least if Jayne was working it would tide the three of us over until you got settled. I even put a deposit on a nice apartment for us. But no. Our self-centered daughter had other ideas. To hell with us, she said. And Mary went along with her. I've never been so disappointed, Stanley." Patricia forced herself to sound unutterably sad. "I'm heartbroken that Jayne is so cruel and Mary so conniving. They're alike, those two. All for themselves and the devil take the rest of us."

He was thoroughly bewildered by the elaborate story and by Patricia's sudden switch from an angry woman to a disenchanted one. He could believe his wife had made plans to change their lives without so much as consulting him. It was like her. And why not? He'd always gone along with anything she wanted to do, even consenting to the California trip when he knew it was far too long a visit with Michael. Michael, he thought suddenly. Somehow, some way, this has something to do with Michael. Patricia's bitterness toward Mary was deeper than his sister-in-law's support of Jayne, if, indeed, she had approved the girl's decision. Something more had happened between the sisters. Something irrevocable. He thought what it might be and immediately dismissed the idea. No, not that. Not even Patricia would be capable of that. He felt a terrible sadness knowing he'd lost his daughter, probably forever. He worried about her. She was still just a baby in his eyes. She'd always be his baby. She wasn't the way Patricia painted her. Jayne was a warm and loving girl. As Mary was a gentle and generous woman. What's the real story? Stanley wondered. God help me, I may never know.

The senior Farrs, when Stanley and Patricia went to have dinner with them a week later, were equally appalled by the events in San Francisco. John Farr flew into a patriarchal rage when he heard how Jayne was living, and his anger was directed at Patricia.

"You permitted that? What kind of mother are you? You allowed that young girl to announce she is going to live in sin and you just washed your hands of it and came home? I've never heard anything so monstrous! Why didn't you stop her?"

His fury had no effect on Patricia. "What should I have done, Father dear? Locked her in a room? Dragged her by the hair, screaming, onto the next airplane?"

"Yes, by God, if you had to! It was your duty to stop her!"

"My duty! What about your duty? Are you going to order Mary to reconcile with her husband? Are you going to permit her to turn out a man who's never done anything but cater to her wishes and devote his life to her? If you're feeling so moral, why don't you do something about your own child?"

Stanley intervened. "Patricia, don't be foolish. Your father is talking about a twenty-one-year-old girl, not a thirty-nine-year-old woman. I'm sure your parents are upset, but Mary and Michael are adults. It's quite a different thing."

"Oh, is it? I don't think so. They're fatuous about Jayne and they don't give that much of a damn about Mary, that's all. Whatever love was left over from my dear, dead brother was reserved for their grandchild. I don't have much use for Mary, but she was right about one thing—our parents hardly knew we were alive, they were so busy mourning their dead son. I haven't heard any screaming about the actions of their daughter! Not

305

that I care, but you'd think they'd be just as meddlesome about that as they are about Jayne! Why am *I* a bad mother, subject to all kinds of criticism because my child doesn't obey me? Why don't they try giving orders to their own?"

Camille Farr spoke for the first time. "We're heartsick about Mary's problems," she said. "There's never been a divorce in our family. Don't you think the failure of any of our children makes us wonder how much responsibility we had for it? But you know Stanley's right, Patricia. Trying to control a grown woman like Mary is unrealistic. Being firm with Jayne is something else again. I think you and Stanley should go out there and bring her back. You can't allow her to ruin her life."

Patricia snorted. "Don't be naïve, Mother. She's already done that. You don't think your wonderful granddaughter is a virgin princess, do you? I'm not going near her. Let her learn her lesson the hard way."

"Patricia!" John Farr was horrified. "You can't mean that! I'm seventy-seven years old. As old as the century. I know things have changed. I'm aware of what goes on these days, young people living together out of wedlock, having illegitimate children, all the terrible things we read about every day. Nor do I condone the attitude of a mother who won't even attempt to protect her own child!"

"So don't condone it." Patricia shrugged. "If you think you can do something about it, go out there and try. Or let Stanley go. I don't do well in the heavy-parent role. I won't degrade myself that way, begging or threatening. She's made her bed and I'm sure she's enjoying it!"

"You're an unnatural mother," John Farr said heavily.

Patricia didn't blink. "Probably," she said. "If you recall, I never wanted to be one in the first place."

* * *

Jayne saw Mary every day at work, sometimes had a quick lunch with her and, in the next couple of weeks, dined with her aunt a few times. But even when the two

306

women were alone, they did not discuss Patricia. It was as though they wanted to put out of their minds the sickening scene that had taken place in Mary's apartment. Only once did Mary obliquely refer to her sister. It was over lunch at Lehr's Greenhouse Restaurant.

"Have you been in touch with your parents?"

"I dropped them a note, giving them my address and home phone number. Daddy wrote. He's terribly upset, of course. So are the grandparents. I guess I'm really a 'fallen woman' in their eyes."

Mary understood the implication. Jayne had heard nothing from her mother, of course. She wondered what version of the whole story Patricia had given Stanley and the Farrs. Whatever it was, Patricia painted herself as the helpless victim. Camille's letter had confirmed that.

"I had a note from Mother," Mary said. "She and Dad are distressed, you're right about that. I don't know which one of us is the bigger sinner in their eyes—you for living with Terry or me for living without Michael. Mother went on and on about the sanctity of marriage and the disgrace of divorce." Mary gave a little smile. "I never mentioned divorce in my letter to them, but somebody did. Three guesses who."

"Aunt Mary, I've never really been able to tell you how terrible I feel about . . ."

"Hush. I know. You needn't say it. Let's face it, Jaynie, I wasn't faithful either."

"But you'd never have had an affair with your own . . ."

Mary interrupted again. "Let's drop it, okay?"

"Sure. But you don't mind my asking if you've heard from Christopher, do you?"

"I had a wonderful letter from him. He still feels the same."

"And you?"

"I feel the same, too."

"What are you going to do about it? You've taken the first step, leaving Michael. *Will* you divorce him and go to Australia? That's what you want, isn't it? My God, Aunt Mary, you're entitled! If you had qualms before, you certainly can't have them now."

Mary took a deep breath. "It's not that simple. I want Christopher, but that's another big step. Living on the other side of the world. Making all new friends. Giving up the work I love. You don't do these things lightly when you're my age, Jayne. You want to be sure. Very sure. I told Christopher that when I answered his letter. I asked him to be patient with me, that I'd promised Michael I wouldn't rush into a divorce. I need time, honey."

"Time for what?" Jayne had the impatience of the very young. "You know what you and Christopher felt for each other wasn't just a shipboard romance. You really love each other. You're perfect together. You're liable to blow it, Aunt Mary, if you let too much time go by. No man's going to wait forever. Especially an attractive one like that. He's been pretty damned patient, if you ask me. How long can you keep him dangling?"

Disturbed as she was, Mary was amused. It was as though the roles were reversed and she was the younger, getting advice from a more experienced woman. "Haven't you ever heard about 'absence making the heart grow fonder'?"

Jayne made a face. "Haven't you ever heard about 'out of sight out of mind'? And while we're spouting clichés, what about, 'A bird in the hand is worth two in the Australian bush'?"

Mary put up her hands in mock surrender. "All right, all right! Don't lecture me anymore! Let's talk about you, for a change. How are things?"

"Great. I love the job."

"I know that. I also know you're doing well. Everybody at the station is crazy about you. I mean how are things with you and Terry?"

"We're settling in. He's having a hard time finding something to do. There isn't all that much work for an aspiring actor in San Francisco, but he'll get there. It's just a matter of the right break."

The words made Mary uneasy. If she stayed with Terry, Jayne was heading for a replay of her aunt's life. The girl was smart. She could go places, Mary thought. And God help her, she could end up as I did: taking care of a man who was always waiting for the big break. Mary chose her words carefully. "Has Terry thought of some other kind of work? There's an awful lot of competition in the theater. Has he ever considered another field?"

Jayne seemed astonished. "Another field? No, I don't think so. Why should he? This is the one he wants."

"Wanting isn't always the same as getting, Jaynie. People have to be realistic, too. Especially when they're sharing their lives with someone else."

"We're doing all right." Jayne set her jaw stubbornly. "It's only been a couple of weeks and he's out every day, looking."

"I see. Well, fine. I'm sure the right thing will come along." Mary picked up the menu. "Shall we order? What looks good to you?"

"Cottage cheese and fruit salad, I think."

Mary frowned. "Why don't you have something more substantial? They have a nice little steak here."

"Too much in the middle of a day."

"A hamburger, then."

Jayne sounded slightly annoyed. "Aunt Mary, please don't act as though I'm living on peanut butter and spaghetti at home. Terry and I eat very well. You don't have to make sure I have a solid meal at noon."

"I'm sorry. I didn't mean to insult you."

Jayne looked apologetic. "No, I'm the one who's sorry. I shouldn't have snapped like that at nothing at all."

"I understand. I do it myself quite a lot these days. It seems to be an unsettled time for a lot of people. Charlie, for one."

"How's he doing? He seems like himself at work, but of course he would."

Mary thought for a long moment. "He's all right. He feels sad and regretful, the way people do after someone dies and you wish you'd been kinder and more tolerant. But Charlie's an honest man. He wouldn't pretend to be destroyed by Tracey's death. That would be hypocritical. His life with her was hell for a lot of years. This is a release for him, as well as Tracey, terrible as it may sound. But that's the truth. She wasn't an easy woman to live with. It wasn't all her fault, but she really didn't try to help herself. She just gave in to her weaknesses and didn't put up a fight. I don't think she wanted to, in the end."

"You're spending a lot of time with him, aren't you?"

The unsubtle question made Mary smile. "We have dinner almost every night. But he's not a part of my indecision about Christopher, if that's what you're thinking. Once upon a time, I might have fallen in love with Charlie. We're well suited. Compatible. Yes, I could have visualized a life with Charlie once, but that was 1976 B.C."

"B.C.?"

"Before Christopher. What else? Come on, let's order."

"Right. One more question before we do, though. Where is Michael?"

"Los Angeles. He sent me a card. He's staying with his mother." Mary's eyes grew sad. "And, as usual, he's very enthusiastic about a new deal."

* * *

The positive attitude Jayne assumed when she spoke about her life with Terry was, in fact, an outward show of bravado designed to fool not only Mary but herself. Inside, little claws of doubt had begun to scratch at her confidence, making her unwillingly wonder whether she'd done the right thing in choosing to live with this sensitive but unpredictable young man. Characteristically, Jayne tried to ignore them. The subtle changes in their relationship were, she told herself, only those of any two people living under the same roof and coping with the mundane details of everyday life. A room and a hot plate in San Francisco did not provide the romantic ambiance of a cruise ship. The vacation atmosphere was over, and the reality of daily living, from shopping for groceries to watching TV in the evening, was an understandable letdown from the glamour of life at sea or the excitement of exotic ports.

If Terry seems different to me, she thought, I must seem different to him, too. The young woman who went sleepily to work every morning and returned tired and disheveled from fighting her way through the supermarket every evening was a different Jayne than that carefree creature who'd seduced him aboard the *Prince of Wales*. Terry was still sweet and gentle with her, but in only a few weeks of their new arrangement, passion had dwindled. They still made love, but the wonder and exaltation he'd felt on the ship no longer were there. It was, she sometimes felt, as though he had a duty toward her, a duty he seemed almost reluctant to assume.

He was moody these days, too. Often he sat for hours, simply staring into space, not speaking. She tried to find out what was wrong, but Terry always gave the same answer, one she could not fully accept.

"I'm depressed about finding work," he said. "This isn't an actor's town. Los Angeles or New York, maybe, but not here."

She tried to kid him out of it. "Come on! What do you mean, 'not here'? Of course there's work here! There's theater all over the place!"

"Sure. Most of it road-company stuff from New York. You don't think Debbie Reynolds hired local talent to do the revival of *Annie Get Your Gun* at the Orpheum, do you? Or maybe you think I could break into Vincent Gardenia's role in *Plaza Suite* down at the Curran?"

"No, honey, but there must be other things. Local companies. Or how about television?"

"Television?"

"Listen, the best years of my life were spent watching shows with a San Francisco setting! How about *Ironsides*? Or *The Streets of San Francisco*?"

He smiled patiently. "Jayne, dear, those shows are off the air now. Besides, they might have filmed them here but they didn't cast them here, except for extras, I suppose. No, I ought to do what I originally planned—go to New York, where at least there's opportunity."

I, she thought. Not *we*.

"Terry, are you sorry we got into this? We can get out of it in twenty minutes. We're not married. If you're unhappy living with me, please say so."

He looked genuinely alarmed. "No! You know I'm not

311

sorry! My God, Jayne, don't even mention such a thing! You changed my life! I need you!" He calmed down. "I know I'm not easy to live with. Try to remember that it's a whole new world for me. The kind I've always wanted. I just get in the dumps, thinking I'll never make it in the theater. I adore you. You know that. I'm low, but not because of you. Believe that. Please believe that."

"Of course I believe it," she said soothingly. "So stop worrying, will you? It's only been a few weeks. Nobody falls into a job that fast. Not," she laughed, "unless they have pushy relatives like mine."

"I've done terrible things to you," Terry said soberly. "I've alienated you from your family. I've put the financial burden on you. Maybe you're the one who's unhappy, Jayne. If you are, tell me. I can take it. God knows I don't want to make you miserable."

"Do I look miserable? Sweetie, things are going to be fine. It's just an adjustment period we're going through. After all, neither one of us ever lived with . . ." She stopped, embarrassed. "I mean, not like this."

He knew she was thinking of his time with Paul. Does she sense that's what's really wrong? Terry wondered. Does she guess that I can't get him out of my mind—that I miss Paul and can't stop wanting to see him again? Not that I'm going to. That's over and done with. Ancient history. I have this wonderful girl and I'm going to be a man for her sake.

"Hey," Terry said, "what are we being so gloomy about? Tell you what. Let's go out for dinner tonight. What would you like? Chinese? Japanese? Italian? Russian? How about Indonesian? We could pretend we're back in Bali! San Francisco may not be heaven for actors but it's paradise for eaters. Come on, luv, what do you say?"

She got into the spirit of adventure. It was so good to hear Terry sounding enthusiastic and excited again.

"I choose Mexican," she said. "I'd kill for a good paella!"

"You've got it. How about Casa de Cristal on Post

Street? They're famous for paella. The atmosphere is madly south of the border. And the price is right."

They had a wonderful evening and when they came home they made love almost as they had on the ship. Jayne was happy. I'm really in love with him, she thought. I'm as committed as though I were his wife. These moods of his will pass as soon as he's working and feeling like an equal partner. We did the right thing. It was meant to be. I'm making a vow to stop feeling so uncertain. I'm going to give my doubts a swift kick in the pants. We're young. We have our whole lives ahead of us. Yes, it's going to be fine once we get over the rough spots. Maybe we'll even decide to get married and have babies. She snuggled closer to a half-asleep Terry.

"I'm crazy for you," she said.

He reached for her hand. "You're an angel to put up with me."

Jayne smiled. "Naturally. Who else would bother with such a charming son of satan?"

But the vague sense of impending disaster sometimes came back to haunt her even while she pretended everything was perfect, as she did over lunch with Mary. Her love for Terry made her determined to succeed with him. Her pride would not allow her to fail. We'll show them, Jayne thought. We'll show Aunt Mary we knew what we were doing. We'll show my folks we're mature, modern people. Someday we'll even prove to Paul, whoever he is, that Terry never needed him at all. She didn't want to think of Russell King and his young bride. Her ex-lover had nothing to do with this. She hoped he was happy with his damned rich Pamela. As happy as she was with her decent, wonderful young man.

Chapter 25

On the eleventh of May, Mary's phone rang as she was preparing for bed.

"Happy three-month anniversary," the voice said.

She couldn't believe it. "Christopher? Is it really you?"

The familiar laugh sounded as though it came from around the corner. "Who else are you having a three-month anniversary with? On February tenth, 1977, we had our first dinner. I think that rates a celebration phone call, don't you?"

She was so flabbergasted she said, inanely, "But it's May *eleventh*."

"Not in Australia."

"You're in *Australia?*"

"Sweetheart, if I were in San Francisco, I'd be pounding on your door. How are you, my love?"

"I . . . I'm fine. Stunned but fine. Oh, Christopher, it's wonderful to hear you! I miss you so much!"

"Me, too." He became very serious. "I had your letter a week ago, Mary. I've written five answers and torn them up. Words on paper won't do. At least, not for me. That's really why I'm calling." He paused. "I can't accept the future on your terms, darling."

"Can't accept . . ." Her heart sank. "You mean you've changed your mind about us?"

"No. Only about the indefinite time limit. I've practically memorized that letter. You say you love me, you want to be with me. Yet you beg me to wait, God knows how long, until you fulfill that pitiful promise to your husband. You say you hope I'll understand. I do understand, dearest. I understand you're frightened of making another mistake, that you still can't bear to hurt Michael, that you're trying to come to terms with the kind of selfishness you have trouble accepting. I understand all that, Mary, but I won't take it for an answer. I'm not going to wait. To hell with those doubts and promises you're clinging to. I've tried to be patient, but I've been wrong. If we love each other, we belong together. And soon. We're not children, sweetheart. I don't have years to hang around, waiting for the moment that suits everybody else. Not even the one that suits you."

She took a deep breath. "I know. I know you're right, but . . ."

"No 'buts.' I've gone along with you as far as I can. You're strong, dearest, but I'm stronger. You need that, Mary, if you're ever going to be the happy woman you should be."

She began to cry softly, half with joy, half with doubt. She tried to answer, but no words came. Christopher's voice became more gentle.

"Let's set the date," he said. "Mary? Are you listening?"

She swallowed hard. "Of course I am. Oh, Christopher, don't you think I want to know the very hour, the very minute I'll be with you? If only I could!"

"Why can't you? Is there anything in your life that can't be settled three months from now? I don't know where you Americans go for those quick divorces, but I'm sure you can find out. You can give your old friend Charlie plenty of notice, get rid of your apartment, do whatever you have to do. I don't give a bloody damn what plans you have to change or what promises you have to break. You belong to me and I'm coming to get you. We'll be married in San Francisco on August tenth. Six months from the day we met." He chuckled lovingly. "See what a romantic I am?" Then his tone became firm again.

"I'm serious about this, Mary. Completely serious. I love you and I don't want to live without you, but somebody's got to make this decision and make it stick. It's no good going on this way. We'll lose each other if we do. If that has to happen, better now than a year or two years from now. I know I'm taking a desperate chance. Frankly, it scares hell out of me, but I have to do it. Shall I come for you on August tenth, my love, or shall we pretend it was all a wonderful dream and end it now?"

She was silent for a moment, gripping the receiver so tightly she felt her palm grow wet. He was right. It was unfair to ask him to wait for some unknown, far-off date. And unthinkable that she might lose him.

"Come for me," she said, gently. "I'll be waiting."

She heard his sigh of relief. "Thank God. You'll never regret it, dearest. I swear to you, we're going to be the most indecently happy people on this earth."

"Yes. We will. I feel happy already. Relieved. Free. Like a weight's been lifted. Oh, darling, if only you were here, holding me. You don't know how I've wanted you! Every single night since . . ."

"Stop it or I won't be able to wait until August!" He sounded boyishly eager. "Good God, woman, you drive me crazy even over the telephone!"

Mary laughed. "Wait until I get my hands on you! Make the days go fast, Christopher. Make them race by!"

"I'll give orders to the clock. Sweetheart, if I could only tell you . . ."

It was her turn to interrupt. "You don't have to. I know. And we have the rest of our lives to say it over and over—I love you, I love you, I love you."

After she hung up, Mary went to her jewelry case and took out the ring Christopher had bought for her in Hong Kong. She hadn't worn it since she left the ship. Now, for the first time in fifteen years, she took off her gold wedding band. Making a little vow to herself, she slipped the jade and diamond ring on the third finger of her left hand. She couldn't wear it in public yet. But three months from now . . . Smiling, she went to bed and fell asleep holding Christopher's ring next to her heart.

When she woke the next morning she thought for an instant that it had been a dream: Christopher's call and her promise to marry him in August. But his ring on her finger told her it was true. She had agreed to get her life in order and be ready to start a new one in three months. The thought overwhelmed her. The romantic in her felt nothing but soaring joy at the prospect; the practical side of her nature chilled her with the realization of the people she'd have to abandon, the utter upheaval she'd create. Was any love strong enough to weather such drastic change? Yes, Mary told herself as she slipped Michael's wedding band back on her finger. Ours is. The next few weeks would be agony, but they'd pass. She was frightened by the thought of burning all her bridges. Christopher knew that. But she'd do it. It was her life and she wasn't going to waste it through timidity. She felt strong and sure of herself. Thank you, God, she said silently. If Christopher had written, she might not have been convinced. But the sound of his voice, the reminder of all the strong and wonderful things he was, brought her to full awareness of what she would not, could not let go.

Methodically, she mentally listed what she must do: tell Michael she wanted an immediate divorce and that she planned to remarry; tell Charlie she was leaving to move to Australia with a man she'd never mentioned to him; tell her parents all those things. Involuntarily, she shuddered. They'd be so shocked. None of them knew of Christopher's existence. Only Jayne knew. Jayne. In a strange way, she worried more about leaving her niece than any of the others. That was silly. The girl was young and self-sufficient. She'd chosen her life and she'd handle it. For that matter, they'd all handle things. She wasn't indispensable to any of them. They wouldn't die without her. The knowledge, so long denied, came as a relief. It was true, as she'd told Christopher, that she felt she'd shed a terrible weight. There'd be adventure and excitement ahead. And most of all, the kind of emotional security she'd never known in thirty-nine uneasy years.

* * *

Terry knew it was only a matter of time until it happened. Every day for a week, he'd had lunch in the little coffee shop where he used to regularly meet Paul for a hamburger. Every day he waited, hoping Paul would come in from his nearby office and there'd be an "accidental" meeting with his former lover. Terry loathed himself for it, but his desire to see the man was an obsession. He told himself that he only wanted to know, once and for all, that he was over his attraction. If he saw Paul again, heard about his marriage, made himself accept the fact that both their lives had changed, he'd be all right. Then he could give Jayne his wholehearted devotion. He could settle down and be content. Jayne deserved that. She didn't deserve this half-man he was, pretending to be happy with her and always thinking of the one person for whom he felt such longing.

He couldn't bring himself to call Paul. The sense of rejection was still there, as was the hurt and disappointment that had caused him to leave on the cruise without telling anyone where he was going. I ran, Terry thought. I was too cowardly to stay around and hear about his marriage. But I can take it now. I can face him and congratulate him and put him out of my mind forever. Until I do that, no matter how much I care for Jayne, I can't belong to her or anyone. Maybe, he thought hopefully, when I see him again it won't even bother me. Maybe I'll feel nothing, or even wonder why I was so bound to this selfish, conniving, ambitious man. I want it to be that way. I want to see him once more so I'll know what a fool I was, and how lucky I am to have something so much stronger and better.

But on the day Paul finally appeared, Terry knew instantly that his feelings had not changed. The sight of the tall, handsome figure coming in the door plunged him into despair, even as his pulse quickened. I wish we were still together, Terry thought. I wish he was coming to meet me.

For an instant, Terry thought of hiding behind the menu, sneaking out, if possible, unrecognized. Instead, he half rose from his seat in the booth where he was toying with a cup of coffee and gestured toward the man who was looking for a place to sit. The amazed, delighted look on Paul's face as he hurried toward him set Terry's heart racing.

"Terry! For God's sake, where have you been? I've been trying to find you for months!" Paul slid into the seat opposite him. "You look great! Jesus, I can't tell you how glad I am to see you!"

Terry tried to sound calm. "I've been away. Took a long cruise to the South Pacific. How are you, Paul? How's the marriage going?"

"It isn't going. In fact, it never went. I didn't do it, Terry. I couldn't."

"You didn't do it? Why not? I thought it was so important to you, to your career. What made you change your mind?"

"You." And then as though he'd said the most matter-of-fact thing in the world, he said, "Have you ordered? Shall we get that out of the way before we talk? You want the usual?"

Terry nodded and sat silently as Paul gave their order to the waitress. He was in a state of shock, incapable of speech. Paul lit a cigarette and leaned back, looking at him intently.

"You," he repeated as though there'd been no interruption. "Selfishly, I wanted to go through with the marriage. It made sense. She's a nice woman. She understood why I was marrying her. She even offered, finally, to have you share the apartment with us, if that would make me happy. A *ménage à trois,* I think it's called. But I knew you wouldn't do that. Hell, I wouldn't do it either. Two weeks after you and I split up, I told her I couldn't marry her. I said you were the only person I wanted to be with. I looked for you to tell you, Terry, but you'd vanished from the face of the earth."

Terry still said nothing. Paul changed his plans because of me, he thought. He really couldn't let me go. He felt an overpowering wave of happiness. Paul cares more for me than for his ambitions. And I care more for him than anything in the world.

319

"Hello, there." Paul was smiling. "You look like you've seen a ghost."

Terry managed to return the smile. "I think I have. You were dead to me, Paul. It's as though you've returned from the grave."

"I'm very much alive, thank you. More so now than I've been for months. Can you forgive me for what I almost did, Terry? Can you understand how a person can almost rationalize himself into anything?"

"Yes." The thought of Jayne came into his head. "I can understand."

Paul sounded humbled. "Then we can forget all this ever happened? We can take up where we left off? I'm still in my apartment. *Our* apartment. It's all there waiting for you." He stopped, troubled by something in Terry's face. "Unless you don't want to come back. Maybe you've changed your mind about us. Maybe there's someone else."

Terry looked tortured. "There is and there isn't. I have something to tell you, Paul."

At the end of the recital, Paul said gravely, "She sounds like a nice girl."

"She is. A wonderful girl."

"Does she want you to marry her?"

"No. That is, we haven't discussed that. It's been on a live-together basis. But she loves me, Paul."

"And you?"

"I love her too." Terry pushed his untouched lunch aside. "Who am I kidding? I'm fond of her. Devoted to her. Grateful to her. But that isn't love. I've used her, Paul. I thought she could make me forget you. I wanted desperately to forget you, but I couldn't. My God, why do you think I've been haunting this place for a week, hoping you'd come in? I couldn't bring myself to call you. I prayed I'd know, when I saw you, that I was through with you and that whole part of my life." He gave a mirthless laugh. "But I knew what I'd always feel where you're concerned. I just had to confirm it, that's all."

"And now?"

Terry looked miserable. "I've got to tell her, of course.

She'll pretend it's all right. She'll be casual about it. She puts on a very civilized façade, very liberal and liberated, but inside she's going to hurt. She'll feel rejected, Paul, and that's a lousy feeling. Take it from one who knows."

"I deserved that."

"I didn't say it to punish you. You did what you thought was best, just as I did. It's a damned shame we hurt two decent women in the process."

"You've grown up a lot in a few months, Terry."

"Yes. And I have Jayne to thank for it."

Paul frowned. "Maybe if I met her . . ."

"No. I don't want you to fight my battles for me. I'll tell her in my own way, in my own time."

The earlier roles were reversed. Now it was Terry who was the stronger and more decisive.

"How much time?" Paul asked.

"I don't know. A few days, a few weeks. I can't hit her between the eyes with this. I have to lead up to it, prepare her. Not that she isn't half prepared as it is. She's bright. She knows I'm restless and different than I was on the ship. I've pretended it was because of the no-job situation, but I don't think I'm fooling her. Life in a one-room, hot-plate pad is quite a change from a cruise ship. A big change for both of us. Jayne accepts it a lot more easily than I do, and I'm sure she thinks my surroundings are part of my depression."

"Where are you living?"

Terry told him.

"My God, Terry, that's a dump!"

"I'm damned lucky to have any place, especially when I'm living on her salary." His face took on that stricken look again. "God, I hate to hurt her this way! She's been mother, mistress, friend, and now . . ."

"You won't do her a favor by prolonging it, Terry."

"I know. But I won't rush home today and pack. I want to be sure she's going to be okay before I walk out."

"But we can see each other in the meantime?"

Terry hesitated. "I'd like to say no, but I can't. Yes, we'll see each other."

321

"And you'll come back to stay as soon as you can?"

Terry nodded. "Yes. It's where I belong."

* * *

Michael came onto the patio where his mother was sitting and threw himself onto his favorite chaise. He looked troubled.

"Who was on the phone?" Carrie asked.

"It was Mary."

"Oh? How is she?"

"I don't know. She just said she had to talk to me and that she'd fly down day after tomorrow for the day. I offered to go up there but she said no, it made more sense for her to come here."

"I see. She didn't say what she wanted to talk about?"

He shook his head. "No, but I can guess. I'm sure she wants a divorce."

Carrie looked surprised. "So soon? It's only been a month since you left. You told me last week it was a trial separation."

"I thought it was, but something in her voice tells me Mary doesn't want to go on this way. Oh, she was sweet. Almost too sweet. She sounded the way people do when they're talking to somebody who's terminally ill."

"Michael! What a dreadful thing to say!"

"All the same it's true, Mother. She wouldn't come flying down here unless it was terribly important. Something she had to tell me to my face. And what could it be except that she wants to end our marriage?"

"Perhaps not, dear. It could have something to do with her job. Maybe they want to transfer her somewhere. Or perhaps it's about the apartment. When is your lease up?"

Michael smiled. "Nice try, Mom, but you know damned well if it was something like that we could discuss it on the phone. This is the first word I've had from her in a month. And probably the last."

Carrie's heart went out to her son. She shared his instinct about this sudden visit from Mary. But why? Couldn't she wait, as she said she would? What was the rush? It was true that Michael had made no progress at all since he'd been in Los Angeles. Carrie had been meaning to speak to him about that. She'd planned to tell him he should go back to San Francisco and get a job, any job, to prove to his wife that he was really trying to be self-reliant. If only he'd be honest with her and with himself, Mary might well take him back. It was this dissembling, this bluffing that drove a woman crazy. She could accept a man as he was if he was manly enough to face facts, admit his shortcomings and say, I'm never going to be a world-beater, but I love you and I hope you can love me as I am.

But Michael had not been able to do that. He thought it mattered so much to Mary whether he was successful. He was incapable of understanding that it was not achievement that counted but mature recognition of one's abilities and limitations, and, above all, a willingness to face facts. Women are so much better at that, Carrie thought. They can overlook so many things if a man has enough genuine bigness to admit that he's merely average. But Michael couldn't bear to think of himself as average. He lived on dreams, saw a tycoon in the mirror when he shaved, lied to himself and everyone. He'd done it all his life. He was doing it still, pretending he was setting up meetings in Los Angeles with important bankers, talking flamboyantly about his plans and his future.

He's so dear, Carrie thought. So genuinely affectionate and kind. But there is this flaw. I've always known it. So have his wives. And none of us has been able to make Michael realize that we could love him for what he is if only he'd stop trying to make fools of us.

"If it's true," Carrie said gently, "if it's true that Mary's coming to discuss a divorce, what will you say to her, Michael?"

For the first time, he put up no defense. "What can I say, Mother? Oh, I'll try to talk her out of it. God knows I don't want it, but if she really wants to be free I won't stand in her way. She's been patient longer than most women would be. She's believed all my dreams, or at least pretended to. She's been loyal and uncomplaining. But

323

she knows nothing will ever change. She's going on forty and if she ever has a chance to start over, this is it. I don't blame her. I blame myself for being a spoiled, selfish, blind bastard who never carried his share. Mary's too good for that. She deserves someone who'll look after her, make her feel like a wife instead of a caretaker." He paused. "Maybe she's already found him. Charlie Burke's wife died, you know. He's always been in love with Mary. Maybe now . . . I don't know."

Carrie wanted to cry. She'd never heard him sound so defeated. His unhappiness was her own. He was her child and it was painful to hear him admit failure. How miserable he was under that confident exterior. She longed to put her arms around him and soothe him as she had when he was a little boy, tell him things would be all right, that this was only temporary trouble which would pass. But it wasn't. She knew that. Mary was too self-sufficient for him. Her protectiveness had been the worst thing for Michael. She'd asked nothing of him. Consequently it became easier and easier for him to think nothing was required. Not that Mary didn't mean well. She'd loved her husband once, believed in him, was willing to give him time to find himself. But time had run out. Forty is the age of evaluation, Carrie thought. One suddenly realizes that half, or more than half, of one's life is gone. It's a frightening time when one takes stock and grows frantic about the future.

"Maybe you're jumping to conclusions, Michael." She tried to sound optimistic. "You don't really know why Mary's coming to see you."

"I know. You do, too, dear. Don't hate her for it, Mother. She has a right to a better life. She's paid her dues."

"Don't say that! You've been a wonderful husband in so many ways. You've adored her, been proud of her. You haven't envied her success as so many men would have. You haven't given her material things, perhaps, but you've been more than generous in other ways. You've been as loyal and uncomplaining as Mary has. It can't have been easy for you, either."

324

He smiled. "Bless your heart. The mother tiger to the end, aren't you? Your baby is never to blame. But I *am* to blame. I took the easy way. Loved her? Yes, I still do. Proud? Not really. Subconsciously, I've always been jealous of her, I suppose. I liked the comforts her success brought but I hated the fact that I didn't supply them. I didn't know how. I still don't."

"But you could, Michael! If you'd set your sights a little lower, ask Mary to let you take over the responsibility for both your lives, show her you can be depended on. You can start over, both of you. Maybe more modestly than the scale on which you live now, but you could make it. You could move here, the two of you. You'd get a job and . . ."

"Don't," he said. "Don't grasp at straws. You know it wouldn't work. People can't go backwards. The thirty-year-old man Mary married is no different than the forty-five-year-old one she now wants to leave. I was notoriously unsuccessful then and I haven't done one damned thing to change it since. I never will, Mother. I'm not fooling myself. I'd hate a grubby life and Mary would hate it more. We're spoiled, both of us, and we're too old to start over like a couple of ambitious kids. Mary has her career and all the pleasant things that go with it. Even if she hasn't found someone else, you don't think she could give that up, do you? I couldn't ask her to, even if I could hold out some kind of promise of total rehabilitation, which I can't. No, it's over. I'm as sure of that as I am of my own name. I've seen this marriage disintegrating and I haven't done one damn thing to save it. I didn't want to look at it squarely because I kept hoping there were enough good times to hold it together. But I knew this would come. I knew it when Mary went away without me. I knew it in the way she kissed me good-bye. Hell, I denied it to myself. Like I deny everything I don't want to think about. But I *knew*, Mother. If I hadn't, I wouldn't have done some of the things I did while she was gone."

She didn't ask what those things were. Women, she supposed. But the problem was deeper than unfaithfulness. It was, she now saw, an ongoing cancer whose roots lay somewhere in the years behind them. Carrie sighed. "You always have a home here, Michael."

"Thanks, dear. I know that. But I can't start living off you again. You're at the age where I should think about taking care of you, not the other way around."

"I'm all right. You don't have to worry about me."

"Of course I don't. But I also don't have to burden you with a forty-five-year-old dependent."

"What will you do?"

"I'm not sure. But I won't kill myself, I promise you that."

"Such a thought never entered my mind!"

Michael smiled again. "Hasn't it? Funny. It has mine, more than once. But I'm too much of a coward."

"Stop talking like that! You're still young. Even if you lose Mary it's not the end of life. Maybe it will be the beginning. Maybe it's for the best." Carrie was terribly agitated. "Why are we speculating like this? We don't even know what's in Mary's mind."

"Right. We're crossing bridges. We'll just have to wait and see. Cheer up, old girl. The thunderbolt has not yet struck. Maybe it won't." He patted her hand. "And if it does, I'll survive. Everybody survives."

Carrie nodded. She wants to believe, Michael thought. Christ, so do I. But I don't. I don't believe in anything. He thought of the letter in his pocket. Rae Spanner was coming down to Los Angeles next week. He knew what that meant. She'd heard of the separation and she was moving in on him. Well, let her. He'd had enough of love. Love was for kids. Love was starry-eyed and romantic, looking toward the future, building and growing. Love was giving and sharing. I've been through that. Twice. With a remarkable lack of success. I'm as jaded and cynical as Rae, who's probably ready for a convenient arrangement in her declining years. Fair enough. So am I.

* * *

Mary knocked on Charlie Burke's office door and opened it. "May I come in?"

He looked up, surprised. "Sure. Got a problem?"

"I'm afraid so. Several." She took the chair opposite his desk. "Charlie I have to talk to you about something personal and professional."

"Okay. Want to go out to lunch?"

She shook her head. "No, I'd rather say this here. Maybe I can be less emotional."

Bad news. The thought flashed across his mind as though it were a news bulletin. "Shoot," he said.

"I . . . I'm giving notice, Charlie. I'd like to leave in three months. Sooner, if you can find a replacement." Mary's hands were clenched tightly in her lap. "I've been happy doing this job. I love it. I love you. I haven't been a great star, but it's been a wonderful experience and I'll miss it."

He managed to hide his surprise under the professional attitude he knew she wanted. "What's wrong? You have a better offer?"

"In a way. I'm going to be married in August. To a man I met on the ship. His name is Christopher Andrews. He lives in Australia. I'll be moving there."

This time, Charlie made no effort to conceal his amazement. "Married? Australia? Mary, what the hell are you talking about?"

"I'm flying to Los Angeles day after tomorrow to tell Michael. I wasn't sure until last night. I kept putting off the decision. It seemed so selfish. But then Christopher called. He won't wait for me forever, and he's right. He won't sit around while I try to come to terms with my conscience. It's August or never, and I can't lose him, Charlie. He's everything I've ever dreamed of. For one thing, I finally know what love is. It came late, but it came swiftly and surely and with such joy, such utter confidence. You'll like him. He's kind and gentle but he has the strength I need. I'm going to be happy with him, happy in a way I'd given up hoping I could be."

Charlie was nearly speechless. He stared at her for a moment and then he said, "Are you really sure, Mary? You hardly know the man. It's such a big step, giving up the work you like, moving so far away. I know it's over with you and Michael. I understand that. But aren't you rushing into something without enough thought? How much do you know about this Christopher? What if he isn't what you think? People get pretty dazzled by a shipboard romance, you know. Especially when they're not happy at home."

Her voice was quiet and contained. "I know. I've thought of all those things. I've thought of nothing else since he left the ship in Japan. Even when I came back, I was still hoping things could be different with Michael and me. I thought his dreams had come true, that he'd be established and I'd rediscover the feelings I'd lost. But it wasn't true, Charlie. It was more disappointment, more lies, more of everything that's made me so unhappy for years. I can't spend the rest of my life that way, not even for Michael, well-intentioned as he is. I want more than patience that was turning to condescension. I want a whole man."

"I understand that," Charlie said again. "But I don't want to see you make another mistake. Can't you spend some time with this man before you marry him? Can't you get to know him a little?"

"How? We're thousands of miles apart. Besides, I do know him. I know him better than I've ever known anyone. We're into each other's heads, Charlie, as well as into each other's hearts. We're not children. It's not just physical, it's a feeling that's hard to describe. He makes me laugh, he makes me comfortable. It's as though I've been close to him forever." She rose and began to pace the floor. "You know me, dear friend. It took something powerful to give me courage for this. I've been frightened. Scared of the future. Terrified of hurting other people. Feeling like a damned heel about Michael. But I know I can't waste more weeks and years feeling half alive. And that's all I've been, Charlie. Half alive. Until I met Christopher. And then it was as though something inside me that had been dormant suddenly sprang into full bloom. I felt . . . I *feel* like a woman. Not dependable, understanding, disciplined good old Mary. A woman. With a man to share her life and make her proud and thankful.

328

Can you understand that? Can you believe I know how right this is? Would I tear up my life and other people's lives if I weren't utterly, irrevocably certain?"

"No," Charlie said softly, "no, you wouldn't. Funny. I sensed you'd met someone on the ship. In one of your tapes, the interview with the captain, I thought you were having some kind of romance with him. I had the wrong guy but the right instinct. Love was in your voice, Mary. But it was love for somebody else." He got up and took her hand. "I'm happy for you, dear. I know what it must have taken to get to this decision. I'm going to miss you. Not only in the job but in my life." He stopped. No need to tell her what his own hopes had been. She didn't need that remorse on top of everything else. He supposed she knew he was in love with her. It didn't matter now. She'd found the one she wanted. "We'll have dinner tonight, okay?"

Mary nodded, struggling to hold back tears of relief.

"You'll tell me all about Christopher. He must be one hell of a guy."

"He is." The note of pride crept back into her voice, and with it Charlie felt his pain return. To hide it, he said, "We should start thinking about your replacement, I suppose. I know the station would like to keep the show going. Any ideas?"

"A crazy one. I thought about it this morning."

"Crazy like what?"

"Jayne. I know it sounds ridiculous, Charlie, but I could train her in three months. She's bright and ambitious and articulate. If you'd let her work with me around the clock I know I could teach her the techniques. She already has the interest in people that's so vital to this job. Would you give her a chance? You gave me one and it worked. Please. Will you?"

"I don't know, Mary. My God, she's thoroughly green! At least you'd worked around radio for a while. She's a baby. I'm not sure . . ."

"She's only a couple of years younger than I was, and a hundred years older in terms of experience and worldliness than I was at her age. I have a good feeling about

329

it. Not just because she's my niece. She has vitality and enthusiasm and so much strength it almost scares me. I see myself in her. I also see a kind of compassion that's important. She cares about others. Maybe too much. But that vulnerability and caring will help her identify with the kind of people we like to have on the show. Real people. Unknown people." Mary's eyes were shining. "Take a gamble, Charlie. You've never been afraid of a risk. And we have three months to see whether it will work."

He laughed. "You always could sell me anything. Okay, we'll give it six weeks. By that time we'll know whether Jayne can handle it. If she can't, we'll have to start looking for someone else. Unless," he said wistfully, "you change your mind in the meantime."

Mary shook her head. "I won't. It feels too right to me. And Jayne in my job feels right too. She'll be terrific."

"Let's hope, for your sake as well as hers. You and your damned tidy mind, Mary! You want to know she's earning a good living, don't you?"

"That's part of it. I admit I'd rest easier if I knew she was better off financially. But I wouldn't suggest it if I didn't think she'd be great. I swear it, Charlie. You know I have a sense of obligation to you, too."

"Fair enough. You want to tell her or should I?"

"You tell her about the job, but not until I've told her my plans. You're the first one after Christopher to know about those. I haven't spoken to Michael yet, as you know." Mary looked unhappy. "That's going to be the hardest part. I dread it. What will happen to him?"

"He'll manage, Mary. Everybody has to live with disappointment. Michael's no different than the rest of us."

Her eyes told him she knew what he meant, but all she said was, "You're the best man who ever lived, Charlie Burke."

"No," he said. "Only second best."

Chapter 26

On the short flight back from Los Angeles to San Francisco, Mary sat dry-eyed and thoughtful, remembering the scene with Michael. Amazing how calm they'd both been, almost businesslike about this momentous event in their lives. The final parting was strangely anticlimactic, as though they both knew the actual decision had been made the night Michael left the apartment and neither believed they'd ever be together again, despite the words and promises exchanged.

Michael expected this, she thought. He hardly reacted when I told him about Christopher. All he'd said was, "Oh? Somehow I thought it would be Charlie. I hope he's a good man, Mary. You deserve one."

His passive acceptance troubled Mary more than a wild outburst of rage would have. This was a different Michael. He'd never been like this. This defeated, quiet, numb person was someone she didn't know. It was as though he didn't care, as though he already felt alone and the divorce was a mere formality. I'm worried about him, she realized. I don't know what I expected. Some kind of fight, I suppose. At least a strong protest or justifiable accusations about my own unfaithfulness, which, in a sense, matched his own. I expected emotion of some kind and there was none. Only this air of having given up on everything. That was worse than the anger she'd anticipated. If he'd been furious, she'd have felt less guilty. His resignation was the worst kind of mute accusation, the way one felt when one spanked a helpless puppy or sent a naughty child to bed without his supper.

In her mind, she relived the brief hour, a drama played out against the mundane background of the little house in which Michael grew up. Carrie had greeted her with reserve and Michael had given her only a quick kiss on the cheek before they retired to the patio, where his mother left them alone. Mary felt nervous and awkward as she said, almost formally, "You're looking well, Michael."

"Thanks. I've been soaking up a lot of sun."

A small silence fell between them before Mary said, "I don't quite know how to say this. I've done a lot of thinking in the past month. I know I promised to give it time, but . . ."

He interrupted as though he wanted to spare her. "I know. It's not a temporary separation. You want a divorce, don't you?"

She couldn't look at him. "Yes. Yes, I'm afraid I do." She managed to raise her eyes. "I met someone while I was away, Michael. He wants me to marry him."

"I see." There was no change in his expression as he made the remark about Charlie, no visible emotion when she said she was leaving the country. He simply listened, nodding as he might have nodded if she'd been talking about two other people. Mary found herself protesting that Christopher really wasn't the cause of the final break. As though she sought reassurance, she said, "We haven't been happy for a long while, Michael. This would have come in any case. I'm not right for you. You need someone who'll lean on you, make you feel nine feet tall. I've never been able to do that for you. I suppose it's not in me to have faith in anyone except myself."

The minute she said those last words she realized how ridiculous they sounded. Obviously she had faith in Christopher. She stopped, confused, aware she'd been babbling like an apologetic idiot. It was, almost for the first time in fifteen years, Michael who was in charge of the situation.

"It's all right," he said. "I understand. Funny, before you came I was prepared to try to talk you out of it. Now I know I can't. I know I shouldn't. You're generous to say you're not right for me, Mary. In a way that's true. But don't spare me. I'm more wrong for you than you are for me. I'm not going to stand in your way. I love you. I wish it were all different. But it isn't different. It won't ever be. You have a lot of years ahead. I can't ask you to spend them with a cripple."

"You're not a cripple! Michael, you're wonderful! You only need the right woman to bring out the strength in you."

He shook his head. "No. But never mind. That's not your problem. Your problems are over and I'm glad, for your sake, they have a happy ending. I mean that, Mary. I really do. God knows I'm miserable at the thought of losing you. But I'm not surprised. I lost you a long time ago. I wouldn't want you back because you felt sorry for me. I couldn't live with that. I've already had a glimpse of it. Pity instead of love in your eyes. Patience instead of passion when we made love. I hated it. I pretended it would pass when one of my wild schemes came through, but it wouldn't have, not even if I'd gotten lucky. You might have stuck it out if I'd gotten on my feet, but it wouldn't have been any good. We were too far apart, Mary dear. The gap already was too wide."

She blinked hard, trying to hold back the tears. "I didn't know you realized. God, how you must hate me!"

"Never. I could never hate you."

They sat in silence for another long moment. The sun was warm on Mary's face but inside she felt ice cold. How can I do this? she wondered. How can I walk away from more than a third of my life? If only he'd be bitter, outraged, accusatory. I could take that more easily than I can handle this selfless understanding, which is the worst punishment of all.

Michael watched her as though he was drinking in every detail to remember forever. Keep up the good work, old boy, he told himself. You've burdened her too long. This is your moment of atonement. At least you can set her free with some semblance of dignity, some gesture of independence.

"If you hadn't come to me," he lied, "I'd have come to you. I want out, too. We don't like loose ends, Mary. It's better this way. Better for both of us. I gather you'd like to move on this right away. So would I. I suppose Mexico is the most convenient place."

"Yes." She was surprised how small her voice sounded. "I suppose it is. I can fly down and . . ."

"Let me do that. I have nothing but time. I'll get working on it from here. Should be easy to arrange. There are no children involved, no property. I imagine the whole thing could be done in a couple of weeks."

"You needn't. I mean, I'm the one . . ."

"I'll take care of it. Call it my last gift to you. God knows I've given you few enough." He smiled gently. "And don't offer to pay for it, please. I can afford it. I owe you much more than that."

"No, you don't! You don't owe me anything, Michael. We had some wonderful years. I only wish . . ."

"Of course you do. So do I. But we're grownups, not romantic kids." He got to his feet. "You'd better go now, dear. I'll be in touch."

She hardly remembered leaving. She wanted to kiss him good-bye but she dared not. I've already done that, she thought sadly. I kissed him good-bye the day I sailed. Instead, she took his hand in both of hers and looked up at him, seeing again how handsome he was and how basically good.

"Good-bye, Michael. Thank you for everything."

He didn't answer, but with his free hand he reached out and gently stroked her hair.

* * *

Jayne called Terry from the office late the following morning. "Mind if I desert you this evening? Aunt Mary's asked me to have dinner. Says she has some girl talk."

"No, of course not. Go right ahead."

"There's leftover meat loaf in the fridge."

"Fine, but maybe I'll go out and grab a hamburger. You going to be late?"

"I don't think so, I'm going home with her straight from work. We'll probably have an early meal. I should be home by ten at the latest."

"Have a good time. Give Mary my love."

"Thanks, darling. I love you."

Terry winced. "Me, too." He hung up the phone feeling like dirt. She loved him and trusted him and he didn't deserve either. He'd told her nothing about seeing Paul again. He couldn't bring himself to do it, couldn't stand the pain she'd try to hide. But he'd have to tell her soon. It was only a few days, but already Paul was getting impatient. Well, at least they could have a few hours together this evening. Paul left work at five and Jayne wouldn't be back before ten. If only I didn't feel as I do, Terry thought. If only I had strength to call Paul now and say I never want to see him again. Instead, he slowly dialed his friend's private office number and said, "You free for dinner tonight?"

* * *

"I'm glad we're having an evening," Jayne said. She snuggled up on Mary's couch. "We haven't had much of a chance to talk lately."

"I know. How's Terry?"

"Okay. A little down in the dumps about nothing happening. He's starting to make the rounds of the advertising agencies now, hoping he can pick up some modeling jobs. Magazine ads or television commercials. He hates not earning any money. I keep telling him not to worry, I'll give him a chance to make up for it, but it bothers him."

Mary frowned. "And it doesn't bother you?"

"No. Only that it makes him unhappy. Otherwise, what difference does it make who earns the bread?"

"Yours is a different generation," Mary said. "I wish I could have felt that way." She took a sip of her drink. "Jaynie, I went to see Michael yesterday. He's going to

335

get a Mexican divorce. And I'm going to marry Christopher in August."

There. It was out. The simple, bald facts that spanned years and could be told in an instant. Jayne raised her glass in salute.

"Well, hooray! God bless! That is good news!" She quieted as she thought of the ramifications. "How did Michael take it?"

"Almost too well. He's being wonderful. I felt like a dog."

"Don't," Jayne said. "You did your best. You both did. When things don't work, there's no point in prolonging the agony. Tell me, what finally made you do it?"

Mary told her about the call from Christopher. "I knew in that instant I couldn't lose him. He forced my hand. And I'm glad he did. But I'm sad about Michael. He seems so . . . I don't know, mechanical. As though the life has gone out of him."

"He'll be okay, Aunt Mary. It's no good being with someone who wants to be somewhere else. Michael knows that."

"I'm sure. But right now it's pretty hard on both of us."

"It's going to be hard on everybody having you way off in Australia. I'm going to miss you. And Charlie must be desolate! Have you told him?"

"Yes." Mary bit her lip. She'd love to tell Jayne what was in store for her, but it would be better if the girl heard it from Charlie. It would seem more like a recognition from her employer than a favor from her aunt. "Charlie was great. As always."

"Super guy."

"He is that. God, I'm going to miss all of you! It terrifies me, this move. It's so far away."

"Not really. You can jet back in a few hours if you get homesick, which I doubt. And you'll be with Christopher." Jayne laughed. " 'Mary Andrews.' Well, we'll just have to try to rise above that, won't we?"

Mary joined in her laughter. "Thank God Mother didn't spell it 'Merry'! Oh, Jayne you are so good for me!

You're always so *up*. It's a joy to be with you. I couldn't love you more if you were my own daughter."

"Thank you. I feel the same." She paused. "Speaking of which, have you told the New York contingent what's happening?"

"No, not yet. I don't know whether to call or write or fly back for a weekend. I should see Mother and Dad before I go. They're getting on, and I'd hate to leave the country without seeing them again."

As though by mutual consent they did not mention Patricia. Jayne fiddled with her drink, absently stirring the ice cubes. Finally she said, "I have some news for you, too. How do you fancy 'Wales' as a boy's name, as in 'Prince of Wales'? Or if it's a girl, do you think 'Singapore' is too outrageous?"

Mary stared at her. "Are you saying what I think you are?"

"Yep. Pregnant. Found out yesterday. About two months along. Which pinpoints it to the first time Terry and I slept together in Singapore. Wouldn't you know I'd pick that fertile moment to be caught off guard? I quit the pills after the fling with our purser friend. Figured nothing was going to happen with Terry. Well, obviously it did."

Mary felt sick. Pregnant by this young man? By this erratic free spirit with no job and no prospects? God! She tried to pull herself together.

"Does Terry know?"

"Not yet. I'm waiting for the appropriate moment. I have a feeling it's going to come as quite a shock. Heterosexual sex was enough of a surprise for the poor darling. I don't know how he'll react to fatherhood." Jayne seemed almost blithe about it. "I expect he'll adjust. He once said he liked children. Not," she added somewhat balefully, "that we were discussing them in this context. But actually, I think he'll be pleased."

"So you'll be getting married."

"I don't know. I suppose so."

"You *suppose* so."

"Well, yes, I'm sure we will. For the sake of the baby. I don't think it's fair to the kid otherwise."

337

"How about fair to yourself? We may live in an enlightened society, Jayne, but unwed mothers are still viewed with some degree of disapproval by most people!" Mary forgot her good intentions. "Besides, it wouldn't sit well with the listeners. If you're going to take over my job, you'll be in the public eye. Pregnant's okay if you're married, but with that kind of show it would be impossible for an unmarried mother to gain acceptance from the audience. Maybe even from the station."

Jayne sat bolt upright. "If I'm going to do *what?*"

Mary sighed. "Damn! I wasn't supposed to tell you. Charlie's decided to try you out in my spot. We both think that with three months' training you could take over the show."

"You're kidding! I couldn't possibly, Aunt Mary! I'd love to, of course! Lord, what a break! But I have no experience. I don't know how to interview. I've never spoken a word on the air. It's crazy!"

"No, it isn't. You can do it. I know you can. We'd work hard together and you'd be great. You *will* be great. But, darling, you now understand why you must marry Terry. Unless . . . That is, are you sure you want to have this child? Things are unsettled with Terry. His career, I mean. And now with this new job coming up for you . . . it might be more sensible . . ."

"I want the baby, Aunt Mary. I'll have it with or without Terry, though I'm sure it will be with. God, it's all marvelous! If I make good, I'll get more money in the new job. Not as much as you, of course, but enough to live in a better place and afford a nurse for little what's-its-name. Isn't it *wild* how things work out?" She gave a whoop of delight. "I can even be grateful that it's radio and not TV! Nobody will see me bulge on the air!" She jumped up and threw her arms around Mary. "Oh, thank you, darling! Thanks for the chance. I'll try like hell to make you proud of me!"

Mary hugged her. "I'll always be proud of you, Jayne. I may think you're foolish sometimes. Headstrong, even. But I know whatever you do is honest."

Jayne backed off and looked at her affectionately. "I

338

know you have doubts about Terry. You're right to. But we're going to be okay. Especially now." She gave Mary a little smile. "One thing's for sure—this is the appropriate time to tell him the big news. Crazy, but I have a hunch that child's going to be happy to hear he's going to have a child of his own."

Child, Mary thought uneasily. Yes, Terry is a child. Another Michael with even greater handicaps. Dear Lord, I hope Jayne can handle it. Please let her be right about Terry's reaction. Let her be right about him all the way. God forgive me, I wish she wouldn't marry him. Even more, I wish she wouldn't have this baby.

"Jaynie, what if . . . That is, suppose Terry doesn't want to be married? I mean, I hope you're right about his reaction, but what if you're wrong?"

"I told you, Aunt Mary. I'll have the baby anyway."

"Darling, you can't do that. Raise a child alone? It's too much to tackle."

Jayne shook her head. "Thousands of women are doing it these days and it seems to work out fine. If Terry doesn't want to marry me, I won't force him. Remember me? I'm the product of the 'had to get married' syndrome. Do you think I'd want a child to grow up knowing what I've always known—that I was the reason two unwilling people had to live together? I said I'd marry because it was better for the baby. Well, it is, of course. Better to be legitimate and have two parents, but only if the parents want you and the marriage. Otherwise, the kid is better off with one who really loves it."

"But even so, Jayne, there's your career to consider."

"If my 'career' is shot down because I'm a mother without a husband, then we're still living in the Dark Ages, Aunt Mary. I don't really believe it would be. I don't think that audience of yours is as square as you believe it is. Or that the station is, either. But if they are, then I wouldn't know how to communicate with them anyway. I wouldn't be the right person for the job."

"You really feel strongly about this," Mary said slowly. You really want this baby that much."

"Yes, I do. I'm not anti-abortion when it's a necessary

thing, emotionally or physically. I'd have one if I hated the idea of a baby. But I'm hung up on the idea that this pregnancy was meant to be. For Terry, maybe, because I think it's important to him. But mostly for myself. I guess I'd like to give a child the kind of maternal love I never felt. I'd like it to feel safe and warm and protected. Maybe that's kinky. I know it sounds out of character for me, but it's what I feel. Just knowing I'm carrying a life is suddenly the most important thing in the world." Jayne laughed, "Good Lord, listen to me! Talk about sounding holier-than-thou! But I mean it. I really do. Look, I'm still positive Terry's going to be happy about this. The whole conversation is academic. Why are we borrowing trouble?"

She's right, Mary thought. This is a different world. To be a single parent is not the oddity or the disgrace it once was. There are even organizations made up of unmarried mothers and fathers. I've interviewed some of them and respected them. Why am I so strait-laced when the subject hits home? Still, I can't help what I feel. Even knowing how wrong it was for Patricia and Stanley to marry, I'd like Jayne's baby to have its father's name, as she did. Even if they divorced after it was born, the child deserves that much of a break.

"Okay, kiddo," she said. "You know what's right for you. And you know Terry much better than I do. Sorry to be a nag. For whatever it's worth, I'm with you."

"It's going to be fine," Jayne said again. "Not to worry. And I am thrilled about the job, even if it smacks of nepotism."

"You mustn't think that! Charlie wouldn't give you this chance if he didn't think you were up to it!"

Jayne smiled. "Come on. You and I know who suggested it. But I don't care. Hell, for years guys have been marrying the boss's daughter or inheriting the family business! Why shouldn't a woman try to step into her aunt's shoes if she's lucky enough to get the chance?"

* * *

It was after midnight when Terry fumblingly let himself into their room. He was very drunk and he hoped Jayne was asleep. He didn't want to talk to her tonight. Tomorrow, he thought. Tomorrow is Saturday. I'll tell her I can't stay any longer. Got to be free. Got to give her a break, too. Tomorrow. Time to talk. Saturday. S-Day. Separation Day. Surprise Day. Sad Day. Tears came to his eyes. Poor Jayne. Poor Terry, you lousy son of a bitch. He lurched and fell heavily against the dresser. The noise awakened Jayne, who'd fallen asleep waiting for him. By the dim light of the night-table lamp he saw her sit up and look at him.

"Hi," he said. "Sorry I weakened you." He grinned foolishly. "I mean sorry I wakened you."

"That's okay. What time is it?"

"I dunno. Ten-thirty, maybe?"

Jayne glanced at the clock. "Would you like to try for two hours later?" There was no anger in her voice. "You must have had a hell of a hamburger."

"Yeah. Ran into somebody . . . some people I used to know. Had a couple drinks. Sorry. Meant to be here. Mished . . . missed the deadline."

He's bombed out of his skull, Jayne realized. Odd. Terry almost never had more than a couple of drinks. Well, what the hell. He had a right. "No problem," she said. "You have fun?"

"Not very much. You?"

She hesitated. This was not the moment. Not when he was unable to think clearly. Tomorrow. Tomorrow they'd have all day to talk and plan.

"It was interesting," Jayne said. "Aunt Mary sends you her love."

Terry didn't answer.

Jayne turned over on her side. "Take a couple of aspirins and get some sleep, you disreputable character. I'll fix you a bloody mary in the morning."

* * *

From eleven-thirty until noon, Mary sat staring at the telephone, trying to get up enough courage to make the call. What am I? she asked herself. A baby? I'm going into my fortieth year. I've been independent for more than half my life. I've been a wife and a working woman and I've asked nothing of my parents since the day I left home. And now I'm afraid to call and tell them what's happened. Afraid of their disapproval, dreading their lack of understanding. Why do I need those things from them at this stage of my life? Why have I always needed them and felt so angry and wounded when they weren't forthcoming? My God, I can be so superior about everybody else's problems, so damned judgmental about women like Patricia and Rae Spanner. So much the curbstone analyst in seeing how poor, pathetic Tracey Burke went wrong. I can even be righteous about Jayne's brave, foolish stand. But when it comes to my own feelings I behave like a child. I sit here wishing my mother and father would reassure me, tell me they love me, that they want only my happiness.

It was crazy. She'd been nervous and unhappy when she had to face Michael, but there'd been this overwhelming sense of relief when it was over. She wouldn't be relieved when she talked to Camille and John Farr. She'd feel as she'd always felt, inadequate, a failure, someone who never measured up to their expectations. What do they want from me? Mary wondered. Nothing. Nothing from either of their girls. They want nothing and they give nothing. It's been that way forever. It will never change.

She heard a church clock strike twelve. She took a deep breath and dialed the New York number, hearing the phone ring three times before her mother said hello.

"Hi, Mother, it's Mary."

"Well! For heaven's sake! Is something wrong?"

"No. That is, I hope you won't think it's wrong." Damn. There it was. The first words out of her mouth were half apologetic, half pleading. "What I mean is," Mary said quickly, "I have some happy news and I wanted to share it right away with you and Dad."

342

There was a pause. "I hope you're going to tell us you've come to your senses and gone back to your husband."

"No. In fact, just the opposite. Michael and I are getting a divorce."

"I see. And that's supposed to be good news? That your marriage is over? You know how we feel about vows, Mary. Michael may not be the great, glamorous man you seem to dream about, but he's always been devoted to you. You've never appreciated the fact you have a loyal husband."

If only you knew, Mary thought bitterly. If only you knew that my "loyal husband" and your other daughter . . . To hell with it. "I always appreciated him, Mother, but the marriage didn't work. We're not right for each other. We don't communicate. We're not in touch."

Camille snorted. "What kind of new-fangled nonsense is that? 'Communicate.' 'In touch.' You're *married*, Mary. It's hard to think of any situation in which two people are more 'in touch,' as you put it. What's the matter with you? Do you think, at your age, you're going to find some millionaire! You've always been above yourself. Patricia told us how you interfered in Jayne's life. Your father and I are worried sick about that child. Have you seen her? Is she still with that young man? Can't you do something about it?"

God help me, I could strangle her, Mary thought. She's delivered her lecture on my ingratitude and reminded me of my age. Now she wants to talk about the only subject that interests her: her granddaughter.

"Jayne seems to be doing very well," Mary said. Wait until you hear her latest development, she thought. Then you'll really have something to worry about. "I had dinner with her last night. She's going to take over my job at the radio station."

It took a few seconds for Camille to understand. "Your job? What are you talking about now? You're leaving your *job*, too?"

"Yes. In August. I'm going to be married to a man who lives in Australia. I met him on the cruise. I'm very

343

much in love with him, Mother, and he loves me. I've told Michael. He was sweet about it. He's going to Mexico for the divorce."

"Sweet about it!" Camille's voice was almost a scream. "He just gave in to you, like that?"

"Yes. He loves me enough to understand."

"I suppose that means I don't."

"I didn't say that, Mother, but I hope you do. Both of you."

"Well, I don't, and neither will your father. You meet a man on a boat and as a result you divorce your husband and decide to marry some stranger. How could anyone understand that? You must be crazy, Mary! Australia? Do you intend to live there?"

"Of course. That's Christopher's home. That's his name, by the way, Christopher Andrews. He's an antique dealer. A widower with grown sons. You'd like him, Mother. He's substantial and mature and highly respected."

Camille seemed to hear nothing of that. "Moving to Australia? You can't do that! What about Jayne? You'd go thousands of miles away and leave that child in a strange city? What are you thinking of?"

All the instinct for survival rose in Mary. "I'm thinking that Jayne is a grown woman," she said. "And I'm remembering that I'm not her mother. Why hasn't her mother or her father come out here to 'rescue' her if that's the most important thing to you? Why is it up to me?"

"Because you encouraged this dreadful situation with that boy! Patricia told us. And you wouldn't even let your sister stay long enough to do something about it. You threw her out. She had no money to stay there and try to talk some sense into Jayne. But you're there. You started this, Mary, and now you're going to walk away from it. Selfish! Utterly selfish! You always have been, all your life! No wonder you couldn't hold a husband. No wonder your own sister is bitter about you. You took her child away from her and now when it's no longer convenient you're prepared to abdicate the responsibility!"

Mary was speechless. Finally she said, "Is that what you think of me, Mother? Is that the way you think it is?"

"Well, isn't it? What else can I think?"

"You might think of me. Just once. Just for a moment. You might want me to be happy. You might accept, even if you can't understand. I've begged all my life for your love, yours and Daddy's, but you've never given it. Even now, you don't care about me. You're only concerned about your grandchild. And you only believe the story you wish to believe . . . the lies Patricia told you. All right, if that's the way it is, I accept it. I'm sorry you're angry with me. Sorry you're disappointed. But I can't help that. If you don't choose to give me your support, there's nothing I can do about that, either. Except to say I wish it were different between us. I wish we . . ." Mary stopped. In a moment she would be in tears. How terrible it all was. How sad that there was such an impossible chasm between them. Her anger gave way to pity. She can't help it, Mary thought. She is what she is. Her standards are as rigid as her mind is narrow. She's my mother and it's impossible for me to reach her.

"I'm sure you'll be hearing from Jayne soon," Mary went on, quietly. "Try not to worry about her. She's enormously self-sufficient. She'll be all right. I know that's hard for you to believe, but it's true."

"I can't think what your father will say when he hears all this."

"You'll explain it, I'm sure. I'll be in touch before I leave. Good-bye, Mother. Kiss Dad for me."

"Tell Jayne to call us collect, will you, please?"

"Yes, Mother. I'll tell her."

She hung up and sat still for a long while. Then she put her head down on her arms and began to weep, for all that had never been, all that she'd longed for, all that would never happen. I wanted them to be proud of me and they never were, she thought. I wanted them to be standing by when I needed them. I wanted them to know I needed them, but I was afraid to say so. Afraid of being turned aside. Always hoping things would change and never daring to try to change them. I even hoped today.

Foolish, childish hopes that they'd feel joy for me. And they don't care. Insensitive, small-minded people. I shouldn't give a damn what they think. But I do. I give such a damn I'd crawl on my hands and knees if only they'd pat my head and say they love me.

She reached for a handkerchief and dried her eyes. So be it. The last tie was severed. She had no one now. No one but Christopher. A stranger, her mother had called him. Dearest stranger. He knew her better than the people who'd given her birth.

Chapter 27

The sound of the running shower forced Terry to open his eyes and then quickly close them against the bright light of morning. He hadn't had many hangovers, but this one made up for a dozen missed. He lay quietly, waiting for his head to stop pounding and his stomach to settle down to only moderate nausea. It had been a terrible night. Paul had been impossible, raging at him to make up his goddamn mind, calling him a weakling and a coward and worse things, accusing him of playing games and demanding, finally, that Terry tell Jayne it was over and that he was leaving her to return to Paul.

Terry shuddered. People were always pushing him. His mother had pushed him, molded him into the little slave she wanted. Jayne had pushed him, gently, into an experience that dazzled and confused him and led, eventually, to this unfamiliar life he was trying to lead. And now Paul, pushing him into making the move he wanted but was reluctant to confess to the young woman who believed he was happy with her.

Well, he'd promised Paul he'd do it today and he would. If only he didn't feel so lousy this morning. It was going to be bad enough without adding physical discomfort to the emotional agony. He opened his eyes and saw Jayne standing beside the bed looking down on him with affectionate, amused sympathy.

"Poor old thing," she said. "You do feel like death, don't you? I'll bet even your hair hurts."

Terry groaned. "Everything hurts." He sat up gingerly. "You're right. My hair does hurt. So do my teeth and my toenails."

Jayne laughed and handed him a glass. "Here's the bloody mary I promised you. Go on. Drink it. It will help."

He took a sip and made a face. "Yuk. It tastes like medicine."

"It *is* medicine, you dope. Drink it down, have a shower and I'll do us some breakfast."

"I couldn't eat."

"Sure you can. You'd better. You'll need your strength for some big news."

Terry looked up at her, surprised. "Big news? What kind?"

"Good kind. Come on. Up and at 'em. Into the shower while I repair to what is laughingly known as our kitchenette." She was in a marvelous mood. "By the time you've washed away last night's sins, I'll be ready to feed you."

He stood under the shower for a long while, letting the soothing hot water run down his body, finally easing the downpour to cool and then cold. He felt a little better. The drink and the shower revived him. His body felt as though it was coming back to life, but his mind was in a turmoil. Jayne had news. Good news. What could it be? Probably something about the job. He hoped so. If she'd gotten a promotion and could live better, it would ease his mind when he told her he was leaving. Not that he contributed anything to this meager life-style, but at least he'd know she wasn't stuck in this miserable room while he was living in style in Paul's posh apartment. He'd let her tell her news first. Then he'd break his to her gently.

By the time he'd dried himself and put on a robe he felt reasonably human, almost optimistic. He even managed to smile as he took his place at the tiny table where they shared their meals, but the sight of eggs and bacon brought a wave of nausea. He fought back the queasy

348

feeling and forced himself to eat. Jayne watched him like a concerned mother.

"Okay?" she asked.

"Great. I think I'll live." Terry refilled his coffee cup and hers. "All right, let's have your news."

"It comes in two parts," Jayne said. "First of all, Aunt Mary's going to marry Christopher and move to Australia. And they're going to let me try out for her job! If I make good, in three months the show will be mine. I'll be earning a lot more money and they can rent this wretched hole to some hippie who's been camping out in Union Square!"

Thank God, Terry thought. It was even better than he hoped. Not only will Jayne be able to live well but she'll have an exciting career to occupy her. She'll get over me quickly. She'll be so busy with her work, so involved with people that my defection will hardly leave a scar. In his relief, he forgot his hangover, jumped out of his chair and went over to hug her.

"Honey, that's terrific! I'm so happy for you! And there's no question about your making good. You'll be sensational! I'm glad for Mary, too. I never thought she'd do it." He went back to his seat. "So that's your two-part piece of news! I must say, they're two biggies!"

Jayne shook her head. "Uh-uh. That's only one part in two sections."

"Oh? What's the other?"

She hesitated and then said, "I was wondering whether you'd be happy in a *ménage à trois.*"

Terry stared at her. For a terrible moment he thought she'd found out about Paul and was suggesting they all live together, the way Paul's ex-fiancée had proposed to solve the problem. No. It couldn't be that. Jayne would have no part of such an arrangement.

"What are you talking about?"

Jayne looked half-frightened. "We're going to be three in December. I'm pregnant, Terry. It seems our first close encounter in Singapore hit the jackpot."

His mouth fell open. "Pregnant? You're going to have a baby?"

349

"That's what the word usually means."

"But you can't! I mean . . . what about the new job? You won't be able to work. My mother told me what a terrible time that is for a woman."

Jayne smiled. "Darling, I'm sure your mother also told you what a death-defying experience she went through giving birth to you. That's hogwash. The kind of crap women tell impressionable kids to make them feel guilty all their lives. It's no big deal having a baby. I can work right up to the first labor pain. I'm healthy as an ox. And I'll be back on the job in no time." She stopped smiling. "I have a bigger worry than that, Terry. I don't know how you feel about the news. You, yourself. Do you hate the idea?"

He didn't know what to say. It was as though everything had fallen to pieces around him. Hate the idea? He more than hated it. He was horrified by it. It changed everything. He couldn't leave her now. He couldn't even tell her he'd considered it. Oh, God, why this? What had he gotten himself into? He felt trapped, torn between his own desires and the sense of decency that had to be bigger than his selfishness. You're an actor, Terry Spalding, he told himself. You'd better make this the best performance of your life. He'd only have to tell Jayne the truth. Tell her what he'd planned to say this morning and she'd let him go. He knew she would. But he couldn't do it. The baby was part of her "good news." She wanted it, obviously. He'd not suggest she get rid of it. Women died from abortions. His mother told him that, too. Besides, he instinctively knew that with or without him, Jayne would have her child.

As the silence lengthened, Jayne grew more uneasy. Aunt Mary is right, she thought. He isn't happy about it. Why did I expect him to be? How could I have deluded myself that he could become a different person in two months? He looked so stunned she felt sorry for him.

"You don't have to marry me, you know," she said softly. "In fact, I wouldn't want you to, unless that's what you wanted. Marriage was never part of our discussion. This needn't change it."

350

He disciplined his mind as though he were learning a new role in a play. It was important to speak the right words, assume the correct expression, make the right gestures.

"The baby doesn't change it, Jayne," he said. "I want to marry you. I've felt all along we should marry. The only reason I haven't mentioned it is because I can't support you yet. It didn't seem fair to tie you down to an unemployed actor. But if you're willing to take a chance on me, I'm all for it. You've opened a new world to me, a sane one. Something with reality and security. I love you very much. And I'll love the child as well."

Unexpectedly, she began to cry with relief. "Oh, Terry, I'm so damned glad! I kept telling myself I could take it if you walked out, but I knew part of me would die if you did. God, we all pretend to be so modern! I was prepared to have the baby alone if necessary. I was all set to put on a big act and say I understood that it wasn't a responsibility you contracted for. I even thought sometimes that you . . . that you might want your old life back. I didn't want to admit it even to myself, but I was scared as hell. Darling, you're everything I knew you were. The best. The greatest. The most wonderful guy who ever was."

If you only knew, he thought. If you had the least idea of the nightmare I've been living with, and how close I came to sharing it with you. She must never know about Paul, he told himself. Never know how close I came to leaving her for him. Paul. What will Paul say when he hears? He'll tell me I'm a bloody fool. Thank God he isn't a violent man or I think he'd kill me. Mustn't think about Paul. Mustn't think of anything but the part I have to play today and in the hundreds of thousands of days to come.

With an effort, he managed to smile. "Well, Mrs. Spalding-to-be, what's the first step?"

"The first step?"

"When do you want to get married and where?"

"I don't know. I hadn't thought that far."

"Okay. Let's fly to Vegas this afternoon and do it."

"This afternoon? You're kidding! We don't have to be

351

in that big a rush. Why not here, in a week or so? We could get the license on Monday and get married next Saturday. I'm sure Aunt Mary would have the ceremony at her apartment."

"And who would we invite to this glittering event?"

"Well, Aunt Mary, of course. And Charlie Burke. And . . . maybe you have some friends you'd like to ask."

"Nobody. And I'd rather not have any fuss, if you don't mind. Look, let's hop the plane before anybody talks us out of it."

She looked at him curiously. "Who would?"

Terry groped for words. He hadn't meant to say that. He was thinking of Paul, of course. He had to do it before Paul heard his plan and skillfully maneuvered him into seeing it as a ridiculous sacrifice. "I don't know," Terry said. "Is Mary in favor of this? I mean, you told her about the baby, I imagine. What was her reaction?"

"Honest?"

"Honest."

"I think she'd like me to have an abortion. But she knows I won't. It's not that she doesn't like you, Terry. She just wasn't certain how you'd feel. And she has some old-fashioned idea about the public not accepting an unmarried mother as a home-spun radio personality. Anyway, the problems have vanished and she'll be happy things turned out right for us. *She* wouldn't talk us out of it, or even try."

"What about your family?"

"Mother will be furious, but I don't care. Dad will be warm and loving. The grandparents will sleep easier knowing I'm an honest woman." Jayne grinned mischievously. "And they'll be thrilled when they have an eight-pound, seven-month 'premature' baby for Christmas."

For a moment he felt a great surge of love for her that nearly drove the thought of Paul from his mind. She was wonderful. We'll be good together, Terry thought. In a way he was glad this had happened. It answered, once and for all, the indecision that plagued him. He had no choice now. There was nothing to do but forget the past and go forward. The old longings would vanish. He'd have to tell Paul. But by that time he'd be safely married. In time he'd even forget. Or only vaguely remember.

"Come on, lady. Get dressed for your wedding."

* * *

The telegram came on Sunday morning, relayed over the phone by a bored-sounding Western Union operator. Stanley Richton listened attentively to the message addressed to Patricia and him.

"Terry and I married yesterday in Las Vegas. Very happy. Hope you feel the same. Much love. Jayne."

"Would you like us to mail a copy of that to you, sir?"

"Yes, please. Thank you."

He hung up slowly and went to find his wife. Patricia was engrossed in the voluminous Sunday New York *Times*, her attention focused on ads for clothes that were either too young or too expensive for her.

"Dear, that phone call was a telegram from Jayne. She and Terry were married yesterday in Las Vegas."

Patricia didn't look up.

"Pat, did you hear me? I said Jayne's married!"

"So? What do you want me to do about it? She didn't ask for our opinion, much less our approval. I'm surprised she bothered to inform us."

Stanley stared at her. "Is that all you have to say?"

"What else is there?"

"My God, our only child gets married and you act as though I've given you the weekend weather report!"

"The weather report has much more effect on me. Stanley, don't be such a stereotype of a father! Can't you see she's put us out of her life? I've accepted that. Why can't you?"

"Maybe because I *am* that stereotype, as you call it. Maybe because no matter what she does, she's my child. Yours, too, Patricia. No matter how tough you try to seem, I know you care about her. She's hurt you and you're trying to pretend she doesn't matter anymore, but that's impossible for me to accept. I know you love her, and I know she loves you."

353

Patricia shrugged and went back to her newspaper without answering. Stanley watched her for a moment and then left the room. He stood in the hall for a few seconds and then abruptly returned to continue the conversation. But he never did. What could you say to a woman who was sitting and staring at the wall, tears streaming down her cheeks?

*　*　*

Mary's housephone rang at eight o'clock Monday morning and the doorman said, "Your niece is downstairs, Mrs. Morgan. Can I send her up?"

"Certainly, Jerry. Thanks."

She stood at the open door, waiting for the elevator to bring Jayne up. When the young woman stepped out, she looked pretty and exceptionally happy.

"Well! What brings you here so early?"

"I thought I'd ride to work with you, Aunt Mary. We tried to phone you Saturday night and last night, but you weren't in, and I couldn't wait another minute to tell you."

Mary led the way into the living room. "Charlie and I were out both nights. Fact is, he was consoling me with expensive food and wine."

"Consoling you?"

"I had rather a nasty talk with your grandmother Saturday afternoon. It really put me into a blue funk. I'm over it now." She gave a little wave of her hand. "Anyway, I don't want to talk about it. I'm much more interested in what you can't wait to tell me."

"Okay. Terry and I got married Saturday in Las Vegas."

"You're kidding!"

"No way. Saturday morning I told him he was going to be a father. I must say he was staggered for a moment, but then he went into action like you wouldn't believe! I was all for a small wedding here next week, inconspicuous, of course, for obvious reasons, but he wouldn't hear of it. Next thing I knew I was on a flight to Nevada and a few

354

hours later I was being legalized by the tackiest little justice of the peace you ever saw. We spent the night there and flew back yesterday afternoon."

Mary groped for words. She was glad Terry had come through as Jayne believed he would, but it was typical of him to act on impulse. They could have waited a week. She'd love to have given Jayne some kind of wedding, even the smallest, simplest one. Stop being so damned selfish! she told herself. You had the same kind of unattended ceremony. Maybe that's why you wanted something a little nicer, a little warmer, for Jayne. You're still playing mother, she thought. Quit it. Hadn't she just told her own that she wasn't responsible for Jayne?

"Well?" Jayne was waiting for her response. "Are you going to offer congratulations or condolences?"

"Darling, you just took my breath away! Congratulations, of course! That is, I know you congratulate the groom and wish the bride happiness, but whatever, you know I'm delighted for you both! Terry's really happy?"

"Delirious. In fact, he's starting out this morning to get any kind of job he can. He's going to sign up with one of the talent agencies here and hope they can find him work doing commercials. If not, he says he'll take whatever comes along, even if it's selling ties in Macy's. Oh, Aunt Mary, you'd be so pleased if you saw him now! It's as though I'd done something wonderful for him. He's stopped being the brooding, troubled guy I've seen these past weeks. He's acting as though he's shed troubles instead of taking on new ones! I thought he'd be okay, but I honestly never expected him to be so light-hearted about it."

"That's wonderful!" Mary hugged her. "I couldn't be more delighted. Did you tell him about our job plans?"

"Sure. He was tickled to death. But I think it's all the more reason why he wants to be able to support us. It's a matter of pride, I suppose. Men are all alike, aren't they? The provider instinct is always there." Jayne stopped. "I'm sorry. That was tactless, wasn't it?"

"Not really. Michael had the instinct. He simply wasn't able to be realistic about it I hope Terry will be. Force

355

him to be, Jaynie. Don't make a child of him. No matter how successful you are, always make him think you depend on him, that you couldn't make it without him."

"Yes. I will."

"You're right, you know," Mary said as though she were thinking aloud. "It doesn't really matter who makes the money. What matters is the feeling of confidence a woman gives a man. How she handles herself. Whether she realizes where the values are. There are priorities that have nothing to do with dollars and cents. You have to know the difference between ants and elephants. Everything isn't of equal importance."

"I know. I'll remember that, Aunt Mary."

"Of course you will. You're a bright girl. Much brighter than I ever was." She became her brisk, cheerful self. "Come on, kiddo, let's get to the office. Charlie will want to discuss your future with you."

"Should I mention . . . ?"

"No. Not now. The marriage will come as enough of a surprise."

* * *

Camille Farr's voice rose an octave. "Married? Jayne is married? To that young man she met on the ship?"

"Who else, Mother?" Patricia tried not to sound impatient over the telephone. "We got a wire yesterday. They were married in Las Vegas Saturday."

"How could she? You said he's an actor. Is he working?"

"I have no idea. I doubt it."

"Where are they going to live, Patricia? What are their plans? Will they be coming to New York? Your father and I want to meet him. I don't even know his last name!"

Patricia almost laughed as she realized she had to stop and think before she said, "Spalding. Terry Spalding. Wonderful," she said bitterly. "For a minute I couldn't remember it myself."

Camille sighed heavily. "It's terrible. Terrible. A young

girl like that wasting her life. I don't understand this generation. No consideration for their families. Rushing into marriage this way."

"You weren't so happy when she was living with that boy. I thought you'd be relieved."

"No need to be nasty, Patricia. I've had almost more than I can bear. And heaven knows what this will do to your father. First Mary calling to say she was divorcing and remarrying and now . . ."

"What? What did you say about Mary?"

Camille repeated what she knew.

"Why on earth didn't you call and tell me, Mother? For God's sake, you didn't even let us know she'd phoned!"

Camille turned huffy. "After our recent conversations, I wasn't sure you'd be interested."

"Well, hell, she is my sister!"

"Don't swear, Patricia. It's becoming a terrible habit with you. In any case, I gave Mary a piece of my mind. I told her you'd told us what she did, encouraging this dreadful affair of Jayne's, throwing you out of her apartment before you could stop it. Believe me, I let her know exactly how selfishly she's behaved! For all I know, she may have been behind this marriage. She seems to have a great influence on your daughter's thinking. It's quite a coincidence that they're both marrying strangers they met on that boat. I wouldn't be surprised if Jayne was imitating Mary, now that Mary's taken this decision."

"Don't be crazy, Mother. That doesn't make sense."

"Then perhaps you'll tell me what does make sense about my grandchild rushing into marriage with a man she scarcely knows."

"She knows him." Patricia turned nasty. "She knows him intimately. For all I know, that may be why they got married. Jayne could be pregnant and stupid enough to go through with it."

"Patricia! You're talking about your own daughter!"

"Yes. It should sound familiar to you. History repeating itself."

There was a long silence on the other end of the line.

"I think you should go out there," Camille said. "You and Stanley both. That child may need you." She sounded suddenly old and sad.

Patricia quieted down, too. "No, Mother, we won't go. I'm sure Mary's taking care of everything."

"But Mary's moving away. To Australia. Jayne will have no one! What if this man can't support her? What if he leaves her? Patricia, I'll never have a moment's peace until you have a heart-to-heart talk with Jayne!"

"I'm sorry. I can't do that. I don't ever want to see Mary again. As for Jayne, she knows where we are. Let her come to us."

* * *

At his little cluttered office, Stanley Richton chewed the end of his pen and tried to think of the right words to say to his daughter. Patricia flatly refused to call or write and was insistent that he not communicate either. If Jayne didn't have the decency to tell them her intentions, if she was so inconsiderate of them she simply sent a wire announcing her marriage, then she deserved nothing from them, Patricia said. Stanley did not agree. He didn't even believe Patricia meant what she said. He'd seen her crying. He knew she felt wounded by all that had happened, miserable inside. This estrangement had never been clear in his mind. Whatever happened in San Francisco when Jayne and Mary returned remained a mystery. All he knew was that Patricia had drawn her pride around her and that it would not allow her to reach out to her sister or her daughter.

It troubled him terribly, all of it. His child's sudden marriage, the new way of life she'd created without a word to her parents. And now that Mary was going away, he was even more disturbed. The thought of Jayne with no one but a stranger to turn to made him sick with anxiety. Be sensible, he told himself. Stop thinking of Terry Spalding as a stranger. He's your daughter's husband. Your son-in-law. She's his now. His to protect and care for. He must be a great guy. Jayne wouldn't pick out any other kind. He found his hand shaking slightly as he began to write.

My dearest Jayne,

Your mother and I were surprised, of course, to receive your telegram, but I hasten to tell you that we are as delighted as you hoped we'd be. Anything that makes you happy guarantees our feelings, because you are the center of our lives and the object of all our love and faith and pride.

Sometimes, my dear, people have trouble expressing their devotion. In these past few years, as you've become a young woman, I've wished I could treat you as I used to when you were a little girl. Remember the walks we used to take? Remember how I'd buy you hot dogs and ice cream in the park and you'd get sick to your stomach and your mother would give us both hell when we got home? She raised the roof because she loved us, because she didn't want you to ever feel physically sick or me to feel emotionally upset because I'd foolishly indulged you. So she read us both out. That was her way, Jaynie. She pretends to be hard sometimes, but it's only to cover how she really feels. She's afraid of weakness, in herself even more than in others. I admire her strength and I see it in you, in a very good way. I also see in you the sentimentality that is your father's heritage. It's not a bad combination, dear. Steel can be soft and candy can be hard, if you know what I mean. Your old man has never been very good with words, and that's as close as I can come to saying that in all good human beings there is both vulnerability and false pride, and sometimes we forget that every man and woman has a second person inside.

I didn't really mean this letter to go this way, dear heart. But I know you'll wonder why your mother hasn't been in touch, and I want you to know that she'd like to be. I said in the beginning that we are happy for anything that makes you happy. Your mother doesn't admit to that happiness right now, but it's there. I know her. She's angry and she feels rejected and it's hard for her to accept what's happened because she was not a part of it. But she loves you, Jayne. She's less happy about it than I, but she loves you as much. More than anyone or anything in the world.

I know your Terry must be all the things I wish for you. All we both wish for you. You are incapable of loving someone who is not sensitive and honest and deeply caring. For those are your qualities, sweetheart, and your father believes that you would instinctively seek them in the man you marry.

Give him love from his new mother and father. Tell him we are proud to have a son. And remember always that you are my little girl, and that I am rejoicing with you and adoring you always.

Dad

P.S. We don't know what you'd like for a wedding gift, but this little check will, we hope, be useful. Buy something as beautiful as you are.

He wrote a check for a thousand dollars and then reread the letter. It was a terrible letter, he thought unhappily. He hadn't said any of the things he wanted to. He'd like to have told her his secret dream of one day walking down a big church aisle with her, all in white, on his arm. He wanted to say that she was the greatest accomplishment of his life, the thing that made all the dreariness and drudgery and day-by-day frustrations worthwhile. He wanted to beg her to come back with her husband, to live near him and her mother, to produce beautiful grandchildren who would be the joy of their later years.

But he couldn't say those things. He didn't know how to say some of them. Others he dared not say lest she feel some unnecessary guilt for being so far away. He'd liked to have said, Live and love, darling Jayne. Consume every hour of life with enjoyment. Be free and unafraid. And know that I am here if ever you need me.

He was tempted to tear the letter up and simply send the check and a short, warm note. It was unfair to apologize for Patricia. She'd be furious if she knew he was trying to explain her to her daughter. But Jayne would understand. They'd always understood each other, he and his child. They'd been conspirators, allies and friends. They'd shared more than forbidden treats in the park. They'd shared confidence and love. More closeness than she'd felt with Patricia. More closeness, in a way, than he'd felt with the woman who was his wife.

Poor Patricia. She's missed so much while she's nursed her anger, fed on her frustration, hidden all her gentle instincts under a layer of vanity and discontent. Stanley sighed as he sealed the envelope. No need to tell Jayne these things. She already knew them, too.

Chapter 28

Christopher frowned as he read Mary's latest letter. Its tone was adoring. She spoke, as she did every week, of her love for him and her confidence in their future. But between the lines he sensed waves of anxiety, not so much for them as for others, Jayne in particular. He'd been totally amazed when she wrote of Jayne's marriage to Terry Spalding. Despite his worldliness, Christopher found it hard to accept homosexuals and unable to believe they could change as completely as Terry seemed to have. I'm old-fashioned, he thought. I'd want to kill one of my boys if he'd gone that way. And if I had a daughter who'd chosen to marry a "convert," I'd do everything in my power to stop it. His heart ached for Mary. Though she totally denied it, he knew she was deeply troubled by the step Jayne had taken and the reason that precipitated it. Pregnant, for God's sake! No wonder Mary's agitation came through. It was a terrible time to leave this young woman who was like a daughter to her. Arranging the job thing was lucky, but that took care of only part of Jayne's problems. When Mary left, she'd be alone in San Francisco, emotionally dependent on a young man who'd never known such responsibility, one who might, at any moment, revert to his old ways and leave her alone with a baby to care for.

Damn young fools, both of them. Jayne shouldn't be

having this child. Shouldn't be married to its father. Mary would be worried about her from August, when she left, until December when the baby was born. And even after that, he supposed. Bloody selfish kids. They never gave a thought to how they might mess up other people's lives.

An alarming thought struck him. What if Mary decided not to marry him until after Jayne had her baby? She hadn't mentioned such a possibility, but he realized that was what was really troubling him in all this. He reread that part of the letter. Since her marriage, Jayne had heard nothing from her parents. They'd probably disowned her, he thought. Not knowing that Patricia and Stanley were unaware of Terry's background or Jayne's condition, he could imagine their revulsion and grief, which would make Mary's feeling of responsiblity all the greater. Yes, it was quite possible Mary was toying with the idea of postponing her own plans, to stay and give support and comfort to this heedless child. Well, he wouldn't permit it. Jayne was an adult and accountable for her actions. Mary would not be allowed to change the date they'd agreed on.

Not that she'd indicated any such thing. He'd been delighted to learn of her arrangements with her husband, relieved that Michael had not been difficult. She wrote positively of August and of his arrival and tried to pretend she felt nothing but happiness. He knew better. Blast the miles between us, he thought. If only I were there to reassure her.

Well, why not? Why did he have to wait until August to go to the States? He could go now, in June. See for himself what was happening. At times like this, a woman needed a man to take charge, to reinforce the rightness of her actions. He consulted his calendar. The next two weeks were impossible. But after that, there was no reason why he couldn't make a quick trip to San Francisco. He smiled, thinking how thrilled she would be. Hell, how thrilled *he* would be! The anticipation of being with her physically excited him, and even that fact amused him. She makes me feel young, he thought. Even thinking about her makes my heart race. Thank God the doctors tell me I'm in the pink. I can make Mary happy for years to come.

* * *

"How's everything going?" Charlie looked at his companion across the luncheon table.

Mary smiled at him. "In what direction?"

"Well, let's start with Jayne. Professionally."

"Swimmingly. She takes to this business like a natural. In the past three weeks I've had her with me at every taping. She absorbs like a sponge. Even makes constructive suggestions. Remember that interview with the Good Samaritan's widow? It was Jayne's idea to set up a fund for her and those four little children, and we've already gotten twenty-seven thousand dollars in donations from private citizens and business firms. It's terrific for that poor woman and not bad public relations for the station, either. Jayne's going to be fine, Charlie. She's blossoming in this field."

"And in others, I suspect."

For an instant, Mary's face darkened. "You've noticed. Yes, she's beginning to show a little. But only your eagle eye would spot it. It doesn't matter, does it? I mean, it won't spoil her chances for the job."

"I don't see why. Nobody knows about her private life, how long she's been married, any of that. She does have a husband. I can't see why anybody would object to her having a baby. When's she due?"

"Just before Christmas."

"She can tape in advance, the way you did when you went on the cruise. No problem."

"Right," Mary said. "No problem."

"You don't sound very convincing."

"Oh, Charlie, I'm crazy, that's all. It worries me to death that I'll be gone in August and she'll have to go through those last four months alone. And have the baby alone."

"Alone? What do you mean, 'alone'? She has Terry.

364

And I'd be amazed if Patricia didn't come out for the event."

"She hasn't had a word from Patricia. A lovely letter from Stanley, but nothing from her mother. Not surprising, I suppose, knowing my sister. Still, you'd think if your child got married, you'd managed to forget your own disappointment long enough to be supportive of her."

"Don't they know she's pregnant?"

Mary shook her head. "Jayne won't tell them. Not yet. She says they'd only act like outraged Victorian parents. Personally, I think she's afraid they'll think less of her. Stanley, anyway. She adores her father."

"Not very realistic, is it? They can add."

"Of course. Jayne knows that, too. She's just postponing an unpleasant scene. I can't hate her for that, Charlie. None of us likes an ugly confrontation."

"No, I suppose not. Speaking of confrontations, what do you hear from Michael?"

"Nothing. That bothers me, too. I thought by now he'd let me know his plans."

"I assume you've gotten yourself a lawyer."

She looked surprised. "A lawyer? No. Do I need one. I thought since Michael was getting the divorce, he'd arrange things with someone in Mexico. Isn't that how it's usually done?"

"I can't be sure, not having gone through it, but things can get sticky, even in the most amiable of partings. You'd better find out about things like community property as well as the decree itself."

"Community property? We don't own anything, Charlie. The apartment's a rental and the furniture isn't valuable enough to ship to Australia, especially to the home of an antique dealer. I thought I'd give it to Jayne, as a matter of fact."

"No bank accounts? Savings? That kind of thing?"

"I'm ashamed to say we haven't been able to save much. We have a joint checking account with too much in it. I've been meaning to switch some over to a savings, but all this happened and I kind of forgot that I'd built it

365

up so Michael could use it while I was away. But he hasn't asked for anything, and I assume he won't."

"What's the bank balance, if you don't mind my asking?"

Mary looked embarrassed. "I hate to admit that I don't know. About fifteen thousand, I think. The May statement came from the bank but I didn't even open it. There's been so much else on my mind. I'll check it tonight."

"Good idea." He shook his head. "I'm surprised Michael's so co-operative. It just doesn't ring true."

"He's a nice man, Charlie."

"Sure he is. But he's also a man who doesn't want to be divorced. A man who asked you to wait. A man who, to my surprise, didn't turn a hair when you told him there was someone else. Nice is one thing. Saintly is something else. Unless . . ."

"Unless what?"

Charlie hesitated. "He had a thing with Rae Spanner while you were away. Did you know?"

"Yes. I knew. I also know what you're thinking. You're thinking maybe Michael's being agreeable about the divorce because she's in the background."

"Could be. She's rich. And persistent. I hear she flew to Los Angeles last week." He reached for her hand. "I don't want to hurt you, but Michael's the sort who'll look for the next person to take care of him. He's not a bad guy, Mary, just a dependent one. If Rae has offered to set him up in style, it would be understandable that he might consider it. I have a hunch you'll be hearing from him soon. Since Rae's visit he might not feel the need to hang on to you after all."

She felt sick. "You make him sound horrible. Like an adventurer. There's more to Michael than that. There's a sweet, generous side as well."

"Of course there is, my dear. But he likes comfort and he knows he can't get it through what he can earn. It's a flaw, Mary. A weakness like alcoholism or drug addiction. He can't help it. He'll always need a strong woman. He always has, hasn't he?"

"Yes," she said reluctantly, "but I hoped he'd find someone who needed *him*. Someone who'd force him to take responsibility. A woman who'd restore his pride. Not Rae Spanner, for God's sake! She'd be the worst thing that could happen to Michael!"

"From your point of view, yes," Charlie said gently. "But from Michael's? I'm not sure. I think he's given up on himself a lot faster than you've given up on him. I think he knows Michael Morgan better than you do after fifteen years of living with him."

She thought back to the conversation in Carrie Morgan's backyard. Charlie was right. She never stopped trying to put her standards into Michael's head. Even now, when she'd left him, she was still trying to make him what she wanted him to be, not, probably, what he wanted to be himself. Was she doing that for him or for herself? Why do I have this compulsive thing about everybody else's future? she wondered. Does it lessen my own guilt? Reinforce my own ego? Why can't I let them all work out their lives for themselves? Michael. Jayne and Terry, too. I impose my ideas, my yardsticks of success and happiness on others. Wrong. I should leave them the hell alone.

She squeezed the hand that lay on hers. "You're right. I should butt out of everybody else's business and take care of my own. Thanks for the good advice. About everything. You're the big brother I always wanted."

He smiled his thanks. Terrific, he thought. Just what every man needs to hear from the woman he loves.

* * *

When she got home later that afternoon, Mary went through the pile of mail left untouched on her desk and found the bank statement showing her checking account balance as of the end of May. Incredulously, she looked at the figure. Three thousand dollars! it was impossible! The damned computers had made a mistake. Swiftly, she sorted through the canceled checks, noting the rent payments and utilities. She'd done her taxes before she left on the cruise and paid them in February. Even subtracting

367

the money Michael used while she was away, there should have been thirteen thousand or so left. It took only a minute to see that the bank was not wrong. There was a check made out to "cash," signed and endorsed by her husband on their joint account, in the amount of ten thousand dollars. She stared at it, disbelieving. It was dated April 15, the day after Michael moved out.

Her first reaction was terrible disappointment that he'd done such an underhanded thing. And then sorrow turned to rage. How dare he? How dare he steal her money, the money she'd worked so hard for, the money that didn't belong to him in anything but the legal sense? The more she thought of it, the more furious she became. No wonder he hadn't mentioned community property. He knew he already had more than his share. He'd made a fool of her again. Deliberately, this time. Actually flaunting his dishonesty. He had to know that sooner or later she'd discover what he'd done. What did he think she'd do then—forgive him, as she always did? Consider it a small price for her freedom? Had it been his revenge for her "desertion" of him? Was this the way he repaid fifteen years of easy living at her expense?

She reached for the phone to call him in Los Angeles and confront him with her knowledge. But halfway through dialing his mother's number, she replaced the receiver. Charlie was right. Even in an "amiable parting" things could get sticky, he'd said. Well, this was sticky all right. It wasn't simply the money. It was an insult to her intelligence, a denial of her ability to judge people. In her wildest dreams, she'd never have believed Michael capable of cheating her. Lying to her, yes. Even being unfaithful. But this deliberately arrogant gesture showed her a side of him she didn't know existed. That was far more painful than the ten thousand dollars he'd appropriated out of who-knew-what emotion. Money had never been that important to her. It always amazed her to see what greed could do to people, how families fought over estates and husbands and wives over property settlements. She'd have given Michael the money if he'd asked. Even that night when she was weary of everything about him and their marriage, she'd have made him a gift of it. But he hadn't asked. He'd simply taken, thumbing his nose at her in one last I'll-show-you gesture. The root of all evil, she thought. Love of money, the ultimate weapon of modern man.

She felt drained, the anger subsiding, an awful sense of futility taking its place. Let him have the money. She didn't care. But let him get out of her life once and for all, this stranger with a false face.

* * *

Hard as he tried, Paul couldn't keep his mind on his work. It had been more than two weeks since he'd seen or heard from Terry. Not since that last evening when he'd laid down the law and demanded Terry stop his nonsense and tell that woman exactly where things stood. Terry had agreed, promised he'd speak to her the next day. The kid had been drunk, but not so drunk he'd forget that promise. Paul had expected to hear from him that Saturday, but days passed without a word. He kept expecting the phone to ring, left word with his secretary that if Mr. Spalding called he was to be interrupted even if he was in a meeting. He stayed home at night, waiting to hear. He even went daily to the coffee shop where Terry had waited to find him. Nothing. Several times he thought of calling that dreary little studio apartment, but he held back. For the first time in their relationship, Terry had the upper hand. It was not an arrangement Paul liked and he certainly wasn't going to compound it by making an anxious overture. Damn him, he thought. Why doesn't he let me know what's happening? Maybe he's sick. Paul was suddenly alarmed. Worse, maybe he never made it home that night after he left my apartment. What if he'd been mugged or even killed? Terry was so drunk when he left, anything could have happened. He was a fool not to find out. What difference did it make if he humbled himself once more and called? He'd already confessed he couldn't live without him. What was one more admission of need? Anything was better than this uncertainty.

369

He dialed information, wondering as he did whether the phone Terry told him they'd had installed was under the name of Spalding or under her name. He couldn't remember it. Jayne something. Roberts? Rickman? No, Richton. That was it. Stupid of him not to have gotten Terry's number from him, but he hadn't thought he'd ever want to call there.

"We have a new listing for a Terrence Spalding," the operator said. "On Powell Street. Would that be the one, sir?"

"Yes." He jotted down the number. "Thank you."

Paul glanced at the expensive watch on his wrist. "Nine-thirty. She'd have gone to work. He heard the phone ring three times and then Terry answered.

"Where the hell have you been?" Paul asked without preamble. "Christ, I thought something had happened to you! Why haven't you called? I've been crazy with worry!"

"I'm sorry."

"Sorry! Is that all you can say? What's going on? Not a word out of you in two weeks. And you're still living with her. What game are you playing now, Terry?"

"No game, Paul. Everything's very serious."

He felt his stomach lurch. "She made trouble when you told her?"

There was a pause. "I didn't tell her. I didn't have a chance. Look, I know I should have been in touch with you, but I knew how angry you'd be."

"Damn right I'm angry! I'm angry that you haven't had enough guts to tell her how things are. Just when do you plan to do that?"

"I . . . I don't think it's something we can discuss on the phone. Could I meet you someplace later today?"

"All right. Lunch? The usual place at twelve-thirty?"

"Yes. I'll be there." Terry's voice sounded strange.

"You sure you're all right? You sound funny."

"I'm all right, Paul. See you in a little while."

Paul sat for a moment after he hung up, digesting the conversation. Something was terribly wrong. He could hear it in Terry's almost frightened tone. That bitch!

Somehow she's hanging on to him. Probably sniveling and saying she needs him. Playing on his soft-heartedness. The kid didn't know how to be tough. Well, I do. If he can't cut himself loose, I'll do it for him.

* * *

As he approached the coffee shop, Terry wondered how he'd get through it. So much had changed since the last time he was there. Then he was praying for a glimpse of Paul. Now he dreaded this last encounter, feeling as nauseous as he had when he was sure Paul was married. In spite of his nervousness, the irony of it struck him. A couple of weeks ago he'd cringed at the thought of meeting Paul the married man. Now the tables were turned. Thank God we're meeting in a public place, he thought. I'd be afraid to be alone with him when he hears what's happened.

Paul was waiting when he entered. Terry was struck again by the elegance of him. His clothes were so beautifully tailored, his jewelry expensive and discreet, even his thick hair carefully cut in a not-too-short, not-too-long style that suited the successful broker image he projected. By comparison, Terry thought, I look like what I am: an out-of-work actor. For a moment he wondered what attracted Paul to him. What is it, he thought, that makes a handsome man like this want to share his life with me? For that matter, what makes a beautiful, intelligent girl like Jayne love me and want to have my child? I have so little to offer either of them. Only adoration. I adore them, and they know it.

He slid into the seat opposite Paul and tried to compose his expression into a pleasant, noncommittal one. His companion obviously was making an effort to do the same.

"You're looking well, Terry. I had a vision of you lying battered and bruised in some hospital. You were pretty smashed last time I saw you."

Terry managed to smile. "I had the worst hangover of my life the next day."

"Oh? So bad you couldn't tell your friend what you promised? I can understand that. But I'm a little puzzled about a headache that's lasted two weeks."

The waitress appeared.

"Just coffee, please," Terry said.

"That's all you want?" Paul asked. "No lunch?"

Terry shook his head. "I'm not hungry."

"In that case, neither am I. We'll just have two coffees."

The waitress sniffed. "I'll have to charge you the minimum. It's our busy time, you know. You might as well . . ."

Paul cut her off. "I don't give a damn if you charge fifty dollars! Just bring the coffee!" He settled back and looked at Terry. "Okay. Let's have it. What's wrong?"

No way to avoid it. Better to get it over fast. Terry took a deep breath. "I'm married, Paul. The day after I saw you, Jayne and I flew to Vegas and got married."

The other man said nothing. He simply sat there, waiting for an explanation.

"She . . . Jayne's pregnant. Going on three months. She wants the baby." Terry was sweating. "What else could I do? I couldn't abandon her, not when she's carrying my child. She didn't make demands, Paul. She said I didn't have to marry her, that we hadn't discussed marriage when we made the arrangement to live together. I could have walked out, but it would have been wrong. I couldn't leave her to have my baby alone."

Paul put a cigarette into a Dunhill holder and calmly lit it. "You seem very sure this is your baby," he said.

"Of course it's mine! Whose else would it be?"

"I don't know. Maybe she was pregnant when you met her."

"No! She wasn't. Jayne wouldn't do such a thing. She's the most honest woman I've ever known."

"She wouldn't have to go much, would she? How many women have you known?"

"Don't do this, Paul." Terry's voice was pleading. "Don't be clever and try to put doubts in my head about Jayne. Be angry. Be furious. I wouldn't blame you. You gave up a marriage because of me. I promised to come back to you. I wanted to. I would have. But now I can't." He suddenly spoke more strongly. "I'm not even sure I want to anymore. I can't hope you'll understand, but I'm happy, except for what I've done to you. Jayne and this child have given me a reason for being something more than I'd ever be if I had you to look after me. Maybe I needed that. Maybe I needed to grow up. If you're my friend, if you care about me, you'll try to understand that." He waited, expecting an outpouring of abuse, but Paul answered in a quiet, almost sympathetic way.

"Terry, I can't say I'm not thrown by this. Damned near desperate, I'm so disappointed. But in a funny way, I'm almost proud of you. The reason I care so much about you, I guess, is just because you are what you are, and you can't do anything but what you think is right. I could kill that woman for coming into your life, but she's here and she needs you. I suppose you need her, too, though I don't like to admit that." He stubbed out his cigarette. "We can't always have what we want in this life. I'm old enough to know that. Sometimes we have to settle for what we can get. What I'm saying is, I'd like to be friends with you and Jayne, if the two of you will let me. If you say no, I'll understand. Hell, I didn't even offer you that much a few months ago when I was going to walk out. But I hope you'll let me be on the fringes of your life. I promise you I won't cause trouble."

Terry could hardly believe what he was hearing. Paul being understanding, almost humble? It was the direct opposite of what he'd expected and relief flowed over him like a soothing breeze.

"I . . . I don't know what to say. Jesus, Paul, you're terrific! I wish I could have behaved as well when it was the other way around."

"Give me credit for a little maturity, Terry. I may be selfish but I'm realistic. I'd rather see you under any circumstances than not see you at all."

"But you do know . . ."

"I know it's over between us. The way it was, I mean. But we can be friends, can't we? You must trust me

373

enough to know I wouldn't lie about anything so important. I want your friendship, Terry, if that's all I can have."

"Of course you can have it! Jayne's, too. You'll like each other. I'm so grateful, Paul. It's like having the best of both worlds."

The older man smiled. "I don't find it quite the best, frankly. The best would have been your coming back to me. But I know you won't. Don't worry, Terry. I'll find other companionship. But I don't have to lose touch with you, even if it's on a different basis."

Terry's face glowed. It was going to be all right. He'd explain it to Jayne frankly. The most understanding of women, she'd accept the reality of this sophisticated, civilized solution. Why couldn't they be friends? Ex-lovers often were. Even divorced people. Jayne and Paul were intelligent creatures. They'd be congenial. They might even grow fond of each other. "Say, you know what? Suddenly I'm hungry. What about you?"

"Let's order lunch," Paul said. "My appetite's come back too."

As he studied the menu, Paul secretly watched Terry's relaxed face. Incredible! He'd really swallowed all that bull about understanding and friendship. He was such a child, so completely without guile himself that he couldn't see how preposterously out of character Paul's proposal was. How could Terry possibly think he'd sit back and accept this gracefully, pretending to respect the young man for his decision? Terry might be able to convince Jayne that such an unlikely platonic friendship was possible, but if she believed that she was as big a fool as her husband. Be cool, Paul told himself. The only way to break up this marriage is to pretend to condone it. Ingratiate yourself. Subtly make Terry see what a mistake he's made. The kid couldn't be bullied into doing something against his damned conscience, but he could be seduced into the kind of discontent that would end this ridiculous alliance he'd made. Time. Time would take care of it. It was only a matter of handling things right.

Chapter 29

Since she'd been living alone, Mary had developed the habit of waking at an ungodly hour each morning. Sometimes it was as early as five o'clock, the world still dark outside her window, quiet and peaceful as only a big city can be before it springs into action. She didn't mind this early return to reality. Sometimes she had terrible nightmares from which she was glad to escape. It was an actual relief to recognize the familiar surroundings, the feel of her own big bed, the sight of her dressing table on which a picture of herself and Michael remained, an enlarged snapshot taken of them on a happier day, years ago, at Fisherman's Wharf. She wondered why she kept the picture there, now that she was an unmarried woman. More habit than sentiment, she guessed. It was part of this room, as Michael's "valet," the wooden stand that used to hold his jacket and trousers, still was. She'd changed nothing, feeling it was all temporary. In less than two months she'd be on her way to a new house and a new bedroom to be shared with a new husband.

She liked this period of quiet contemplation, an hour or more of lying undisturbed by voices. The world was much too noisy the rest of the day. People talked too much, as though silence were dangerous. It was one of the good things about Christopher. He could sit silently beside her, holding her hand, communicating his thoughts without the need for words. Not so with Michael, who'd been a compulsive conversationalist. She wondered, idly, why that had been so. Perhaps it was to cover his insecurity, to reassure her and himself that his mind was always active, always planning a future, articulating schemes he tried to believe were real. She wondered if he'd continue to be that way. If he married Rae Spanner—and that triumphant woman was letting half of San Francisco know this was the plan now that Michael was free—would he try to convince her, too, that his success was just a step away? Probably not. Rae had no illusions as a young Mary had. She'd be bored with Michael's dreams, indifferent to his goals. Rae was buying companionship, social and sexual convenience. She was no starry-eyed girl believing in a future with a man who'd make her proud.

Funny, Mary thought. I feel no bitterness toward her or Michael. They're unhappy people, both of them, and well suited. Since the day she discovered Michael had virtually cleaned out their joint account, she'd had no contact with him. Charlie was outraged when she told him, but once the shock passed, she was almost indifferent.

"Let him keep the money," she said. "If he was that desperate, he must need it badly. I don't care."

Charlie thought she was mad to let herself be cheated, but she'd just shaken her head and told him to forget it. She wasn't quite sure, herself, why she felt that way. She'd felt so angry at first. So betrayed. But later it didn't seem to matter. It was ridiculous to think that perhaps, subconsciously, she felt the need to pay for her freedom. But it was possible. Charlie, Jayne, everyone told her the guilt was not hers, but somewhere inside she irrationally felt she'd failed. Perhaps it eased that sense of failure to know he'd behaved so badly about the money. His thirty pieces of silver, she thought whimsically. Strange it hurt more than the knowledge of his unfaithfulness with Rae and Patricia. Or maybe not strange. She'd cheated, too, but not in material things.

She lay back and watched the sky lighten. Fifteen years and nothing to show for it except memories, some good, some frightful. Memories and a sheaf of papers from a

Mexican court severing the marriage of Mary and Michael Morgan. There were regrets. Things she wished she'd done differently. But there was this serenity, as well. Sometimes her peacefulness disturbed her. She didn't mind living alone. It was blissfully selfish. So much so that at times it worried her. Perhaps I shouldn't marry again, she thought anxiously. Maybe marriage is an un-natural state that deprives people of that most precious commodity: privacy. Instantly, she denied the idea. She loved Christopher. She wanted to live with him. It was the damned time and distance again. She hadn't seen him since the fourth of April. It was now almost the middle of June. There were moments of panic when she could hardly remember his face, when she wondered how she dare link her life with someone she'd known such a short time, when she felt frightened of a foreign country and of people and customs strange to her. At those times she reread his letters, gathering strength from them, knowing she'd be safe in his care. Her happiness would return then, and her certainty, and she wished again that August would come quickly.

There were days when she even wondered why she had to wait almost another two months. Jayne was catching on so quickly to the job she could step into it tomorrow. Mary had come to realize what an ambitious girl her niece really was, much more ambitious than Mary had ever been. I worked to make a living, her aunt thought, but Jayne really wants a big career. She's much more dedicated to power and success than I ever was. Much less frightened of failure. Jayne could handle failure if it came, God forbid. She'd pick herself up and start over, knowing she had brains and beauty and the kind of drive that young, liberated women had these days. But she wouldn't fail, not at this job or any in the future. She'd go onward and upward. Probably to local television. Maybe to national. Who knew where Jayne would be in fifteen years? A celebrity, most likely. One of the most admirable women who managed a big job, a household, children and husband, neglecting none of them, being admired and ap-preciated by all.

And where would Terry be when that day came? The thought of him brought a frown of anxiety. It was such a strange marriage. Terry seemed to have grown up in the past few weeks. He'd even gotten a job not much of one for a man of twenty-six, to be sure, but a real job nonetheless. He was working in a brokerage house, learning the business, starting at the bottom, and Mary gave him full marks for abandoning his hopeless love of the theater and settling down to something substantial. What troubled her was the way he'd gotten that job. When Jayne told her what he was doing, Mary had been more than a little surprised.

"Terry in stocks and bonds? I didn't know he had a head for finance."

Jayne laughed. "Neither did I. Neither did he. It was his friend Paul's suggestion. Paul got him the job in the firm where he's something of a big shot. And, I must say, it looks as though it might work."

"Paul? Who's Paul?"

"Paul Le Compte. Terry's former lover. The one he ran away from when he took the cruise." Jayne said it as casually as if she'd disclosed that Paul was a second cousin. "He's quite an interesting man, Aunt Mary. Very smooth. Terry and I have been seeing a lot of him lately. He has a really posh apartment near the Marina, with a view from his terrace that's to die from! Even a Japanese manservant who dishes up yummy dinners. We're together at least a couple of times a week. It's become quite a threesome."

Mary was shocked. "Jayne! You can't be serious! You're seeing the man Terry used to . . . to be attached to? The three of you are spending time together? It's the sickest thing I ever heard of! It's unnatural! How can you possibly be around a man you knew was your husband's . . ."

Jayne was unruffled. "Darling, it isn't a revival of Noël Coward. Everything's up-front these days. We don't play cute little sophisticated games. I know Paul still has a yen for Terry. Gullible, trusting Terry. He's such a child he really believes Paul is willing to settle for friendship. He's absolutely delighted that his old friend and I get on so well together. We both pretend to Terry that we're best buddies, but of course we know damned well all we're doing is keeping an eye on each other. Paul knows I know what he's up to. He also knows I have no intention of letting him win."

It was unreal. Mary stared at her helplessly. "Jayne, you don't know what you're doing. Letting Terry work with that man. The two of you spending evenings with him. It's insane! Don't you know how devious a man like that can be? Do you want to lose Terry?"

"Not at all. On the contrary, this is the way to keep him. If he felt he couldn't see Paul, he'd only be more anxious to. Forbidden fruit, that kind of thing. No, this way Terry's happy. I come off like the relaxed wife he wants me to be, a marvelous contrast to that all-consuming mother who turned him off women in the first place. And sooner or later, Paul will lose his cool. He'll make a mistake and Terry will sweep him out of his life. Our lives. But *Terry* has to do it. As long as there's the least idea that I'd keep him and Paul apart, he'll hang on to his old memories. When he sees that this new 'friendship' is just a trick, he'll be done with it once and forever."

Mary shook her head. "I don't understand. I think you're playing with fire."

"Come and see for yourself. Paul's been wanting to meet you. Why don't you have dinner with us Saturday night? I'm sure it will be fine with Paul, and you haven't seen Terry for weeks."

"I don't know. I'm not sure I have the stomach for that kind of thing. I'd probably feel ill at ease."

"Don't be silly. Why should you? I mean, we're not playing musical beds. It's rather fascinating, as a matter of fact. I must admit to you, Aunt Mary, that I'm amused seeing Paul grow more and more frustrated. He knows he's fighting a losing battle. I'm nasty enough to take some satisfaction from that. It's like a tug of war and my side is getting stronger with every pull."

Mary was still distressed " 'A tug of war,' " she repeated. "With Terry in the middle. You're not being fair to him, Jayne."

The girl's eyes flashed. "I'm being more than fair. I'm protecting him from himself. I love Terry, but he's an innocent. I won't let him go back into that life with Paul. He's going to have a wife and a baby and a chance to grow into a self-respecting man instead of a dominated toy. Paul's kept him a child. He took up where Terry's mother left off. Terry's a late starter, but he'll make it. I'll see to that. There's good material in him. He just needs self-confidence and he's getting that with the first real job he ever had, and a pregnant wife who needs him." Jayne smiled reassuringly. "I know what you're thinking. That I'm directing his life. That I'll only make him weaker in the long run because I'm so much stronger. I know how to handle my strength, Aunt Mary. Terry will never feel threatened by me."

She believes that, Mary thought. I wish I could believe it, too. "I have to trust your judgment, Jayne. I remember my mistakes."

"I'm not you, Aunt Mary. And Terry isn't Michael. I don't mean that unkindly, but it's true. This is another time and another situation."

Yes, it is, Mary thought now as she slowly rose from her bed and went toward the kitchen. Jayne will never be torn as I was by some outmoded ideas of a woman's role in marriage. Or a man's. She's taken on a big job in her personal life, but she knows it's a challenge. I never did. I wasn't prepared, as she is, to cope.

I'm not looking forward to this dinner tonight. I don't really want to meet the man who was so important to Terry. Who still is, for that matter. I can't be as pulled together as Jayne is about this whole thing. I hate it. It repels me. More than that, it frightens me half to death.

* * *

Christopher snapped the lock on his suitcase and double-checked his ticket. On Sunday morning, San Francisco time, he'd be knocking on Mary's door. He supposed he was acting like an adolescent, not telling her he was arriving, but he wanted to surprise her. He could imagine the look on her face when he called. She'd think he was phoning from Sydney, and he could almost hear her gasp when she realized he was as close as the Fairmont Hotel. Darling, darling Mary. God, he'd missed her so much! Maybe he could talk her into an earlier date than August. She was free now and she said Jayne was going to be great in her job. If he could convince her that Jayne was also going to be perfectly okay, physically and emotionally, Mary could leave with an easy mind, every doubt overcome. Jayne will help me, he thought. She's always been on my side.

His son James drove him to the airport. "Be sure to give Mary our love," he said.

Christopher nodded. "I'm glad all of you like her. It's important to me, and it will make things easier for her."

"We think she's a knockout, Dad. Especially because she makes you so happy. I wish she'd come back with you now."

"I wish so, too. If I can talk her into it, she will. But we'll have to see. She's so conscientious about that job of hers, for one thing. Won't leave until she's sure things are under control."

"Do you think she'll miss working? It's going to be a big change for her."

"I don't know," Christopher said. "If she finds herself with too much time on her hands, I'm sure she'll dig up something to do. Very enterprising, these American ladies." He grinned at his son. "But I'm hoping she'll be busy looking after me. I'm a demanding old codger, you know."

James affectionately agreed. "Sure. You're a bloody martinet, you are, guv'ner. Give us all a pack of trouble, you do." He patted his father's shoulder as they pulled up to the airport. "Good luck," he said.

Christopher waved as he drove away. Nice boy, he thought. I have two nice boys. He thought briefly of Terry. Poor bugger. If he'd had the family love my kids did maybe he'd be a different young man. He hoped

Jayne was really straightening him out. Hoped it for his own sake and Mary's, as well as for that unlikely young couple.

He wondered what Mary was doing at this moment. He tried to picture her in San Francisco and couldn't. But I know what she'll be doing this time tomorrow, by God! His own eagerness amused him, and anticipation made him look boyishly handsome. An attractive woman in the waiting area stared at him with unconcealed interest. Christopher smiled politely and buried himself in his newspaper. Since the day he met Mary, he didn't know any other woman existed. He'd waited most of his life for her, and thankfully the waiting soon would end.

* * *

Jayne and Terry picked her up in a taxi a little before seven on that Saturday evening.

"You look marvelous, Mary," Terry said. "Paul will be bowled over. He's a big admirer of yours anyway."

"Really? I'm surprised he ever has a chance to hear the program."

"It's only recently that he has," Jayne said meaningfully. "Now that I'm getting involved in it, he's gotten a little radio in his office and listens to every show. He's extremely bright and his comments are very helpful. I think you'll be interested in hearing some of them."

"I'm sure I will." It's starting already, Mary thought. We've begun the little cat-and-mouse game. Is Terry totally ignorant of what's going on? The young man in the seat between them seemed tense, almost desperate, holding Jayne's hand. He knows what's happening. Mary realized with alarm. He's not stupid. I thought he didn't see what he had no wish to, that he chose to be blind about the struggle that's taking place over him. But that's not so. He's in quiet agony over the way things are going between his wife and his friend. Why can't Jayne recognize an impossible situation and put an end to this farce?

Suddenly, Mary felt terribly anxious. Everything seemed unnatural, evil. She told herself she was being overly dramatic, imagining things, but she dreaded the evening with an agitated Terry, a falsely gay Jayne and the still unknown third member of the triangle. She hoped she could escape early without seeming rude.

Jayne chattered all the way to their destination while Terry said nothing. He had a troubled, faraway look. How changed he is, Mary thought. He's become a young man without hope. For a moment, she was ashamed of Jayne. She was as bad as Paul, maneuvering this boy's life. I hope she knows what she's doing, Mary prayed. I hope the end she believes in justifies the means.

Paul's high-floor, terraced apartment overlooking the Bay was as posh as Jayne promised. And Paul himself was as advertised: smooth and interesting. It wasn't difficult to see why anyone, male or female, could be attracted to him. He had an elegance about him that was more European than American. He even kissed Mary's hand when they were introduced, managing it gracefully and naturally, as most men did not.

"This is a long overdue pleasure," he said. "I've been looking forward to meeting you, Mrs. Morgan." He smiled. "Especially since I'm one of your great admirers."

Mary was determined to hide her feelings. She, too, smiled and said, "Please call me Mary. I'm delighted to be here, Jayne's told me how kind you've been to her and Terry."

He dismissed that with a deprecating gesture. "Terry and I are old friends. I was only too happy to find him interested in the boring world of brokers. As for Jayne, she's a delight. You're fortunate to have such a bright and beautiful niece."

"I quite agree. I'm terribly proud of her." Mary looked around as they entered the living room. "What a lovely place! Jayne said it was beautiful but she didn't do it justice. Your taste runs toward the oriental, I see. So does mine. I find Chinese and Japanese furnishings the most beautiful of all, and you have so many magnificent examples."

"I've been a collector for many years," Paul said. "Afraid I have an overacquisitive nature. I can't resist

383

anything I fall in love with, even if it's sometimes wildly overpriced."

What a stilted, mannered exchange we're having, Mary thought. Like two fighters, sparring before the main event. What main event? This is not my battle. It's Jayne's and Paul's. I don't have to know what makes this man tick. It's not my problem, so why am I reading double meanings into everything he says? Why do I feel when he's talking about overpriced things he loves and must acquire that he really means Terry, not these inanimate objects? She accepted a glass of champagne and lifted it in the direction of the two young people, who'd been silent since their arrival.

"To Jayne and Terry," she said. "A long and happy life."

Paul raised his glass. "And to friendship."

"I'll drink to that," Terry said. "All my best friends together at last." He swallowed his wine in a gulp and refilled his glass from the bottle in the cooler beside the cocktail table.

Jayne said nothing, but Mary saw her exchange a cynical smile with Paul. How can they do it? Mary wondered again. How can they play this waiting game, subtly edging each other toward some fatal error in calculation? Perhaps she was over-reacting, but there *was* something sinister about this outwardly perfect evening. All through dinner, though the conversation seemed easy and harmless, she had the feeling that every word from Jayne and Paul was fraught with terrible significance. I'm not alone, she realized. All four of us are on edge, Terry most of all. He was drinking too much. He'd had almost a whole bottle of champagne before and during dinner and was now starting on stingers when they returned to the living room for coffee. He was too keyed up, too obviously nervous. Can't Jayne see it? Mary thought. Can't she make him slow down? He's getting blind drunk. She's probably afraid to say anything to him. She'd sound like a nagging wife, and nothing would please Paul more. God! Is Terry worth all this? Can Jayne really care that much or does she just want to prove a point?

384

Mary was surprised to see the butler come in with a plate of brownies and put them on the low table in front of the sofa. Brownies? How totally out of character after a dinner of caviar mousse and sole amandine! Terry reached for one and only then did Jayne put out a restraining hand.

"Hey," she said lightly, "I don't think you need those after all the booze. You know Paul's brownies. That recipe's straight from Alice B. Toklas."

"One won't hurt," Terry said. "I've had them often."

"Not after a gallon of champagne and two stingers, silly. We'll have to call the rescue squad!"

"He can handle it, Jayne," Paul said calmly. "He's a big boy."

Jayne flushed. "You're supposed to be his friend, Paul. You should know better."

Mary was totally confused. What was all this about brownies? She watched Terry eat one of the little chocolate cakes, saw the distress in Jayne's eyes and the satisfaction in Paul's.

"Would you like one, Mary?" Paul held the plate toward her.

"No!" Jayne's voice was sharp. "She wouldn't like one. Paul, that's a terrible thing to do! I don't think Aunt Mary knows what they are."

"Oh, come, Jayne." His voice was condescending. "Your aunt is a worldly woman. Of course she knows."

Mary gave a little laugh. "I'm afraid I'm totally lost in all this. I honestly don't know what you're all talking about."

"Alice B. Toklas brownies aren't as innocent as they look," Jayne said. "They're full of marijuana. Maybe a little hashish, for all I know. Depends on how creative Paul's feeling when he makes them."

Mary's eyebrow lifted, but she tried not to seem shocked. "I see. Now that you mention it, I have heard of them, but I've not come in contact with them before. No thanks, Paul. I think I'll pass."

"Of course. As you like. Jayne doesn't care for them either."

"She doesn't know what she's missing." Terry took a second one before he could be stopped. "Dee-licious!"

Jayne looked half angry, half afraid. "Terry, stop! You know you can't handle that stuff." She bit her lip, knowing she was playing right into Paul's hands, acting like a prude. "No one can," she said. "It's dynamite, especially after you've been drinking. Paul will agree with me, honey. We don't want you to get sick."

"Never felt better." Terry got to his feet. "Who wants to dance?"

"Nobody," Jayne said. "Come on, darling. Sit down and relax."

Terry paid no attention. "Want to dance. Dance with me, Mary?"

She shook her head. "I don't think I could keep up with you." She glanced at her watch. "Besides, I really should be getting along. It's past eleven. Can I drop you and Jayne on my way?"

It was as though Terry didn't hear her. He was totally out of control, weaving his way around the room, humming to himself. The other three watched, the women anxiously, Paul with a permissive half-smile on his face.

"Don't worry about him, Jayne," Paul said. "He's high as a kite, but he's having fun. You don't want to be a downer, do you? Don't go yet, Mary. Please. It's early. And tomorrow's Sunday."

"It's been a lovely evening, Paul, but I really must . . ." She stopped. Terry had suddenly disappeared. "Where did Terry go?"

They'd taken their eyes off him for only a minute, but he'd vanished. Jayne stood up. "He's probably in the bathroom being sick. I'd better go get him and take him home."

"I'll go," Paul said. They were all standing now. "I'm sorry, Jayne. He used to be able to handle that stuff. I guess he doesn't have the tolerance for it anymore."

"There are a lot of things he can't tolerate anymore," Jayne said. "Including . . ."

Mary let out a small cry, interrupting her. "He's out there! Out on the terrace! My God what is he doing?"

They rushed to the open door and stood frozen. Terry was balancing himself like a tightrope walker on top of the ledge that surrounded the terrace. Arms outstretched, dipping and weaving like an aerialist, he was picking his way along the high, precariously narrow concrete barrier. Sensing their presence, he glanced toward them and laughed.

"Look at me! Should have been in the circus!"

Jayne started toward him but her aunt held her back.

"Don't frighten him," she said quietly. "One misstep . . ." Her voice was barely louder than normal as she called out to Terry. "That's terrific, Terry. You're marvelous! But come on in, will you? It's too damned cold out there."

"It's nice." Terry's voice was happy. "Makes you feel like a bird. I can see a hundred miles, I bet. It's so pretty I can see the Golden Gate Bridge, Jayne. Remember when we sailed under it?"

"Of course I do, darling. But we really have to go home now."

"Out there is Alcatraz." Terry was swaying on the edge. He giggled. "No more prisoners. Just tourists. That's nice. I used to be a prisoner, didn't I, Paul? I was your prisoner. No more. Got a wife now. Gonna have a baby." He began to sing. "Oh, if I had the wings of an angel . . ."

Paul's face was pale with fright. "Terry, for Christ's sake, get down from there! It's twelve stories, you fool!"

Terry kept smiling idiotically. "What's everybody so upset about? Come on, join me! Such a great view. Free. You feel free out here." He lurched dangerously and Paul raced toward him, heedless of Mary's warnings.

"Terry! No! Wait!"

The sudden, loud voice made the man on the ledge turn quickly. For a moment he looked puzzled as he realized he'd lost his balance. Terry seemed to fight for a split second and then, almost as though he was pleased, he raised his arms above his head and was gone.

Jayne's horrified screams split the silence of the night. Instinctively, Mary grabbed her, fearful the girl might try

387

to follow. Paul stood as though rooted, not more than two feet from the wall, paralyzed with horror. None of them dared look over. They knew too well what they'd see lying on the street far below. For a few interminable seconds they were like a tableau, punctuated by Jayne's shrieks of anguish, which went on and on until they became part of the sirens that announced the arrival of the police.

Only two, maybe three minutes passed before the patrol car came. Mary remembered thinking, inanely, that it must have been close by. She stood holding Jayne in her arms, not knowing how to still her cries, not believing, quite yet, what had happened. She was aware that Paul did not move, and in one of those crazy flashes of clarity she wondered whether she was holding on to the wrong person. Paul looked as though he might be the one who'd insanely go after Terry. But when he heard the police sirens he turned and faced the two women. Over Jayne's hysterical screams, Mary heard him say, "I killed him. I killed Terry." He brushed past them and disappeared into his bedroom. An awful premonition overtook Mary. Quickly she guided Jayne inside and turned to the Japanese butler, who stood, equally stunned, in the living room.

"Go see if Mr. Le Compte is all right."

The man nodded and approached the bedroom door as Mary forced Jayne to lie down on the couch. She sat beside her, holding her hand, patting her, relieved to hear the yelling begin to turn to sobs and moans.

"Door locked," the butler said over his shoulder.

"Can you force it? Try. It's important."

The man threw his shoulder hard against the door, but it didn't budge. "Door no open," he said.

"Go get help," Mary ordered. "Quickly!"

But beore he could do so, the doorbell rang urgently. Paul's manservant opened it. A policeman and another man, apparently the building superintendent, stood in the entrance.

"Where's Mr. Le Compte?" the officer asked. "The super says the man on the street must have fallen from his apartment. He recognized him."

Mary pointed toward the bedroom. "In there, but it's locked. I think you'd better get in quickly, Officer. I'm afraid . . ."

"I have a master key," the superintendent offered.

The two men went in and came out quickly. The policeman's face was gray as he looked at Mary.

"I don't think you'd better go in there, ma'am. It's not a pretty sight."

Mary glanced at Jayne. The girl seemed only semiconscious, understanding nothing.

"Did he . . . ?"

"Yes, ma'am. A straight razor."

"Oh, my God!"

"Ambulance is on the way. Too late for either of them, I'm afraid, but maybe the doctor should look at the young lady."

"Yes," Mary said. "Yes, of course. She's my niece. That's her husband who . . . who fell. She's pregnant. This shock. I don't know."

"The doc'll be here in a few minutes." The policeman was kind, gentle. "Don't worry. She'll be all right." He seemed almost embarrassed. "Could you answer a few questions, please? Tell me what happened here?"

No, Mary thought, I can never tell you what happened. I don't know what happened. Terry was an actor. Was he really as out of control as he wanted us to believe or was he playing his final role? Was it an accident, or was this his way out of a situation he couldn't tolerate? She shuddered. What would happen now? Jayne might lose her baby. She was ashamed to realize she almost hoped that would be the case. Terry gone in this terrible way. Paul taking his own life. How responsible would Jayne feel for what happened? How much would she want a child to remind her every day of so many unanswered questions?

"Ma'am? Do you feel up to giving me a few facts?"

"Yes. The man . . . the man who fell is Terry Spalding. It was an accident. A silly game where he was pretending to be a tightrope walker." Her voice broke. "A silly, senseless game."

"I see. Sorry to ask, but had he been drinking? Or were there drugs?"

Mary wanted to deny both things. She already envisioned the publicity that would be so hard on Jayne. God knows what the papers would dig up about Terry and Paul. The butler knew. So did the super. He'd led them right to the apartment Terry once occupied. But there was no use lying about the liquor or the drugs. There would be an autopsy. They'd find out anyway.

"We had some champagne," she said. "And I believe there was some marijuana in a brownie Mr. Spalding ate."

The officer shook his head. Dumb bastard. Stoned out of his mind. Drugs. Car crashes. Homicides with Saturday Night Specials. Young guys like the one down there in the blanket. Girls, too, sometimes. And all the grief-stricken people they left behind.

"About Mr."—the policeman consulted his notebook—"Le Compte. Paul Le Compte. That right?"

Mary nodded.

"Clear case of suicide, of course. But could you give me any idea of why he did it? Had there been an argument of some kind?"

"No. No argument. We were all friends. It was just to be a quiet little dinner." Mary looked at the young officer helplessly. "I have no idea why Mr. Le Compte did what he did. I suppose he felt responsible for . . . for the other things, the champagne and the brownies." Suddenly she was exhausted. She wished the doctor would come and look after Jayne. The girl lay still now, eyes closed. She seemed to be barely breathing. "Where is that ambulance?" Mary said angrily. "Can't you see my niece needs care?"

"Just a minute, Mrs. . . . sorry, I'm afraid I don't know your name."

"Morgan. Mary Farr Morgan."

He wrote it down carefully before he recognized it. "The lady on radio?"

"Yes."

"My wife listens to you every week!" He looked impressed for a few seconds before he became the professional again. "I guess I'll have to ask you to identify your nephew, Mrs. Morgan. Sorry, but I'm sure his wife isn't up to it."

"Can't that wait? I want to be sure she's all right."

"Sure. No rush. The morning will be okay." He seemed ill at ease. What the hell was a woman like Mary Farr Morgan doing mixed up in this kind of thing? A suicide. An accident, if it was. For all he knew, the guy in the bedroom might have pushed the other one over the side. Booze and drugs. Jesus! You never knew. When his wife talked about Mary Farr Morgan he always imagined some nice little old grandmotherly type. Not this good-looking dame who couldn't be more than forty. He was relieved when the ambulance guys arrived. The intern quickly examined the young woman and suggested she stay in the hospital overnight.

"It's nothing to worry about," the doctor said. "Everything seems okay, but she's in shock. In her condition, it pays to be careful. If you give me the name of her doctor, we'll notify him she's being admitted."

From somewhere in the back of her mind, Mary dredged up the name of the obstetrician Jayne had once mentioned.

"May I go with her in the ambulance?"

"Sure."

"What about . . . the others?"

"We'll take care of it," the doctor said. He looked at the policeman. "Identification?"

"Got it all. Mrs. Morgan will make it official tomorrow."

It's not happening, Mary told herself as she followed Jayne's now quiet form on the stretcher. None of it. Not the ambulances and the police cars. Not the morbidly curious crowds and the newspaper reporters and television crews who kept trying to ask her questions as she came out of the building. How did they get here so fast? she wondered. Time seemed to have stood still, but glancing at her watch she saw it was more than half an hour since

Terry had stood on the ledge. She brushed the press aside.

"Not now," she said. "Please. I have to go to the hospital with my niece."

"Did he fall or did someone push him?"

"Maybe he jumped?"

"Why did Le Compte slash his throat?"

"Is it true that Spalding and Le Compte . . . ?"

Mary turned on them angrily. "Have you no decency? Can't you see there are more important things right now than your questions?"

A man she recognized from one of the TV stations caught her arm. "Hell, Mary, you, of all people, know this is just our job! You understand!"

She stared straight at him. "I don't care about your job. And I'm tired of understanding. You can quote me on that!"

"Some attitude from one of us," the another reporter said nastily.

Mary didn't answer. I'm not one of you, she thought as she climbed silently into the ambulance. I'm not a radio commentator now. I'm a woman who's just seen two lives destroyed and another one jolted beyond endurance. What do you want from me, for God's sake? Headlines? Good quotes? You don't need me for that. You'll find plenty to write about, plenty of grist for the gossip mills. Say anything you want. I don't give a damn.

Chapter 30

Michael quietly opened the front door of Rae Spanner's apartment and picked up the Sunday paper. He tucked it under his arm and sneaked back to his own bed. Thank God, Rae didn't insist on sleeping in the same room with him. He could make love to her, but he didn't want to wake up next to this woman who'd so quickly come to take him for granted. She kept mentioning marriage, but Michael had side-stepped the issue since he moved in with her ten days ago. Who needs marriage? he thought. Marriage is for kids hellbent on overpopulating the world. I've tried it twice. So has Rae. Why should either of us risk being three-time losers at our age? And it wasn't as though either of them was hung up on "appearances." They were both free, and who cared if they lived together? Correction, he thought. Who cares if I live with Rae?

He'd drifted into the arrangement easily, almost fatalistically, after the divorce. He had little choice. No job. No prospects. And he couldn't stay forever at his mother's little house, it was driving him wild. Rae had come down and made another businesslike offer, this one involving his total time. He accepted indifferently. What did it matter? Besides, he was almost broke. The ten thousand he'd drawn out of his and Mary's checking account had dwindled alarmingly. It went fast when you bought clothes, rented a car, flew first-class to Mexico and back and paid the expenses of the divorce. He'd spent quite a lot on Rae when she was in Los Angeles, too. Good restaurants were expensive. A dinner for two could run more than a hundred dollars with wine, and he'd bought a number for her before his divorce. Not to mention all the entertaining he'd done before that, when he was trying to make contact with some of the Southern California big shots.

He felt bad about the money. Mary must know by now. Probably she hated him for it. Okay. Better she should hate him than feel sorry for him. He knew it was wrong to take it, but it was only a little more than he could have asked for under the community property laws anyhow. Half of fifteen thousand was what he was entitled to, if he'd cared to make a fuss. Not to mention the furnishings and other things. So it wasn't so terrible, after all.

He sighed, thinking of Mary. He wondered if she'd heard he'd moved in with Rae. Of course she had by now. The grapevine was fast and reliable. He dreaded the day he'd bump into her. Not that it wasn't finished. She had her Australian. But Michael still loved her. So much that he didn't want to see her again. Thank God she'd be moving away. The memory of her would slowly fade. She'd be somebody else's wife. He allowed himself a cynical smile. And I'll be Mr. Rae Spanner, he thought. No amount of logic was going to keep that dominating woman from having her way. Rae wanted to be married. It was only a question of time before he'd either agree or get out. He knew he'd agree. He wasn't likely to get a better offer.

He picked up the front section of the paper and sat bolt upright. A two-column headline at the bottom of the first page stunned him.

MARY FARR MORGAN'S NEPHEW
DIES IN PLUNGE FROM BALCONY
Second Man Suicide in Same Apartment

Shortly before midnight Saturday, Terrence Spalding a nephew by marriage of radio commentator Mary Farr Morgan, fell or jumped to his death from the twelfth-story balcony of 1628 Marina Avenue, home of a mutual friend, Paul Le Compte. Minutes after the tragedy, Mr. Le Compte was found in the bedroom of the apartment, an apparent suicide from razor wounds.

According to police, Spalding, aged 26, was walking on the ledge of the wall-enclosed terrace when he lost his balance. Tashi Yoko, Le Compte's houseman, told reporters that there'd been a dinner party given by his employer and attended by Mr. Spalding and his wife, Jayne Richton Spalding, and her aunt, Ms. Morgan. Shortly after eleven, Mr. Yoko heard excited voices from the living room and came out to see Mr. Spalding balancing himself on the terrace railing while the others tried to coax him down.

"Mr. Terry was laughing," Mr. Yoko said. "He thought it was a joke. Then he fell. And Mr. Le Compte locked himself in his room and took a razor to his throat."

Police tentatively confirmed the account. Rumors of drugs and alcohol could not be confirmed, they said, pending autopsies of the two bodies. It was reliably learned, however, that for several years before Mr. Spalding's marriage, he and Mr. Le Compte, a broker aged 33, shared the luxury apartment.

Ms. Spalding was hospitalized for extreme shock and Ms. Morgan could not be reached for comment. At the hospital early this morning, Charles Burke, a family friend and Ms. Morgan's employer, would say only that it had been a tragic accident and details would be released later.

Michael dropped the paper. Good Christ! Mary hadn't even mentioned Jayne being married when they talked in Los Angeles. For all he knew, she was living in San Francisco with her mother, the way Patricia planned it before the girl returned. He read the article again. The implications were horrendous. I should call Mary, he thought. She must be out of her mind. No. She'd be all right. She rose to occasions like this. Besides, Charlie Burke was very much in evidence. And there was no surprise to that.

* * *

Pan American Flight 816, nonstop from Sydney, arrived in San Francisco at 11:20 A.M. Christopher deplaned, feeling weary despite his anticipation. The damned time change was a nuisance. They'd picked up a whole day on this trip, so he'd left Australia at three o'clock Sunday afternoon, *his* time, and reached the States on Sunday morning *their* time. No matter what the clock or the calendar said, it was a long and tiring trip, and he'd be glad to get to the hotel and have a bath and a change of clothes before he saw Mary. Once again, he felt buoyed by the surprise in store for her. He'd call the minute he got to his room. They'd have lunch together. Or brunch, as the Americans called it. Maybe she'll pull something together for us at home, he thought hopefully. I want to be alone with her, to hold her in my arms. It seemed an eternity.

* * *

Mary lay across her bed, fully dressed as she'd been at the fateful dinner party. She couldn't sleep, though she'd been there for hours. All through the night, she'd been at Jayne's side at the hospital. She'd called Charlie soon after they arrived, and he'd come over and kept the vigil with her, though Jayne didn't know they were there. They'd heavily sedated the young woman, a blessing, no matter a temporary one.

The doctors and nurses had urged Mary to go home
396

and get some rest. "Your niece won't be awake for hours," they said. "It's pointless for you to stay here. You've had a terrible shock, too, Mrs. Morgan."

She'd refused to leave until Jayne woke and Mary could see for herself that the girl was all right. That had been at seven o'clock this morning. She'd opened her eyes, looked confused for a few seconds before memory returned. Mary took her hand and held on tightly, not knowing what to say.

"Terry's dead." Jayne's voice was leaden.

"Yes, darling. It was a tragic accident. A ghastly one."

"*Was* it an accident?"

"Of course! You remember the condition he was in. He was just playing a prank, trying to frighten us. I'm so sorry, Jaynie. So terribly, terribly sorry."

The slender figure in the bed shuddered. "The baby. Is the baby all right?"

"It's fine," Mary said gently. "No problem."

"Thank God for that. At least I'll have his child. Paul can't take that away from me."

Mary drew on all her strength. Jayne didn't know Paul was dead, too. No reason to tell her at this moment. One horror at a time.

"Paul could never take anything away from you, sweetheart," she said. "He couldn't take Terry and he'll never be able to take Terry's child."

Jayne's eyelids were drooping. "I'm so tired. It's hard to remember. . . . Everything is a blur." Tears slid slowly down her cheeks. "I just know he's gone. I loved him, Aunt Mary. We were happy."

"I know, darling. You made him very happy. That's what you must remember."

"Don't want to sleep. Can't help it . . ." Jayne's voice drifted off.

"Sleep," Mary said. "It's your best medicine. I'll be right here."

Only then did she go to the morgue to identify, with horror, what remained of Terry. After, Charlie took her home. Hours ago. There were so many things to be done and she didn't have the energy to do them. Thank God for Charlie. He was seeing to the funeral arrangements, as he'd done all too recently for Tracey. But this time Mary was incapable of helping him. Neither of them knew what to do with Paul. If he had family, they were unaware of it. We'll have to find out, Mary thought. His office will know. Nothing can be done today, in any case. Nothing until after the autopsies. The thought made her cringe. She hated the idea of violating a body even after death, but that was the law in cases such as this.

She couldn't grieve for Paul, of course. She couldn't even sincerely mourn Terry's passing, except for the effect it would have on Jayne. She'd have given anything to undo the events of the past few months for Jayne's sake. If only I hadn't take her on the cruise, Mary thought once more, none of this would have happened. That was stupid thinking, she realized, but she couldn't help it. But if she was irrationally blaming herself for Jayne's problems, God knows Patricia would blame her even more now.

Patricia! Mary suddenly sat up. She hadn't called Patricia and Stanley! They'd have to be told right away. Undoubtedly they'd want to come out, to be near Jayne, even though Stanley had never met Terry and Patricia had seen him only once, briefly, the day the ship returned. Still, he was their son-in-law. Their daughter's husband. Jayne would want them informed. Reluctantly, she reached for the phone. Half-past eleven. She hoped they'd be home at half-past two on a Sunday afternoon in New York.

* * *

"I think we're the only people left in New York on a weekend in June," Patricia said petulantly. "Other people have country houses, or at least get invited away for the weekend." She fanned herself. "It's so damned hot in here! Are you sure the air conditioner is working?"

"It's working," Stanley answered. "Feels perfectly comfortable to me."

"Well, I'm dying of the heat!"

"Maybe you're having a hot flash."

She knew he meant it as a joke, but it wasn't funny. "I'm having no such thing! What kind of a crack is that? I'm years away from those symptoms!"

"Okay, okay," Stanley said placatingly. "I didn't mean it, hon. I'm sorry you're uncomfortable. Maybe I can turn the air conditioner up higher."

"Turn to 'frantic.' Then it and I will be even."

The phone rang and Patricia impatiently went to the bedroom to answer it. Probably her mother complaining about something. Her "hello" was tinged with irritation.

"Patricia? It's Mary."

"Mary?" Her voice dripped sarcasm. "Mary *who*?"

She ignored the sarcasm. "Patricia, I have some terrible news." As quickly and briefly as possible, Mary described what had happened the night before. "Jayne's all right," she said. "She'll probably be released from the hospital today. I'm going to bring her here to stay with me for a while."

Patricia listened incredulously. It was a dreadful story. Even so, she sensed that Mary was leaving out some details.

"This Le Compte man. Who was he?"

"A friend of Jayne and Terry's. He and Terry shared the apartment before, and he'd gotten Terry a job in the firm where he worked."

"Was he gay? Was Terry gay?"

Mary tried to suppress her annoyance and failed. "I don't know," she lied. "What difference does it make? They're dead, both of them."

"It all sounds very fishy to me."

"Patricia!" Mary was at the end of her rope. "This isn't the time for gossip! For God's sake, your daughter has just lost her husband! She's in shock! It's damned lucky this didn't bring on a miscarriage. I'd think you would . . ."

"Miscarriage? You mean Jayne's pregnant?"

Mary could have kicked herself. She should have known Jayne hadn't told her parents anything yet and probably didn't plan to until she was further along. Well, it didn't matter now. They'd have to know eventually, but it would have been better if they'd heard it from their daughter.

"Yes. She's going to have a baby in December." She could almost see Patricia ticking off seven months on her fingers. "That's right," Mary said boldly, "she was pregnant when they got married. You and Stanley would be the last people in the world to condemn her for that." Instantly she regretted her nasty crack. "I'm sorry. . . . That was uncalled for. I just meant . . ."

"I know what you meant. You never miss a chance to rub it in, do you? Well, at least my daughter and I know how to give of ourselves, which is more than anybody can say for you!"

Mary was too done in to fight. Patricia was hopeless. She was the guilty one, the amoral creature who'd slept with her own sister's husband, and she was behaving as though it was Mary, not she, who should be on the defensive. It was all too ugly, too absurd. *Give of herself.* Patricia didn't have an unselfish bone in her body. She thought of nothing but her own desires. Even now she probably was figuring out how she could make this tragedy work to her own advantage. Her next words confirmed that suspicion.

"I'll get a flight out there this afternoon. I presume you'll be willing to put me up, too, under these circumstances?"

Mary hesitated. She never wanted to lay eyes on Patricia again, but she was Jayne's mother. She had a right to be at the funeral of her daughter's husband. But that wasn't why she was coming. With Terry out of the way Patricia probably hoped to expedite her original plan of sharing an apartment with Jayne. And now that the girl was pregnant, there would be an even stronger reason for Patricia to move in on her daughter and pretend to take care of her and the grandchild when it arrived. Jayne won't want that, Mary thought. She'll never live with her mother. She doesn't even like her.

"I could put you up for a few days," Mary said reluctantly, "but if you're planning a longer stay . . ."

"I'll make my plans when I get there, thank you."

400

"I'm sure you will." Mary tried to sound unconcerned. "What about Stanley? Won't he want to come, too?"

"I don't know. I really don't see how he can. We can't afford the trip for both of us. It would mean hotel expenses, too."

"If he wants to come, we'll manage." As she said it, Mary wondered how they would. Maybe Stanley could stay with Charlie. Or she could get a folding cot and put it in the living room. Or maybe both Patricia and Stanley could stay in the little place Jayne and Terry had shared. If it came to the worst, she'd pay for a hotel room for them. That would be best in any case. She couldn't face having Patricia under her roof. Why on earth had she said she would? "Now that I think of it," Mary said, "why don't I just arrange for you to stay in a hotel? It would be more comfortable for everybody and then Stanley can come too."

"I told you, Mary, we can't afford that expense."

"You can be my guest."

"We don't want your charity. No. Stanley had better stay home."

"For God's sake, Patricia, what difference whether you're here or in a hotel? You're a guest either way."

"I won't be beholden to you. Not after the things you've done."

In spite of herself, Mary began to laugh. Her sister was perfectly willing to move into the apartment, drink the liquor and eat the food, but letting Mary pay for a hotel was "charity." And always this reproachful thing, as though Patricia was the injured party in their broken relationship. To hell with it. I don't care where she stays, Mary thought. This is no time for family feuds. We seem to be forgetting that we have a grief-stricken young woman on our hands, and an ill-fated young man to lay to rest. Why are we squabbling over these petty details?

"Do whatever you like," Mary said. "I really don't care."

"I'll be there tonight. Please tell Jayne I'm coming."

Mary had hardly hung up when the phone rang. For a

moment, when she heard Christopher's voice, she thought he must somehow have heard about the tragedy in Australia. But he sounded much too ebullient or that.

"Hello, sweetheart, what are you doing for lunch?"

"Christopher? Where are you?"

"Only a few blocks away, at the Fairmont."

"The Fairmont! Here? How? When?"

"Got in this morning. How are you, darling? When can I come over?"

She began to laugh hysterically, uncontrollably. Christopher was alarmed.

"Mary! What is it? What's wrong?"

Gasping, she finally managed to calm down. "Nothing. I mean, dear God, what next?"

He felt terribly let down. This was not the reaction he'd expected.

"You sound as though you're sorry I'm here," he said stiffly. "I suppose I should have let you know I was coming. I rather thought it would be a happy surprise."

She realized how her laughter and her first words must have sounded to him. He knew nothing of the past eighteen hours of her life.

"Oh, sweetheart, it is a happy surprise! The most wonderful thing that could have happened at this very moment. You're like a gift from heaven. It was just too much, suddenly, on top of everything else. I . . . I've dreamed for months of the moment when you'd arrive. I planned the things we'd do before we left together, the time we'd spend here as Mr. and Mrs. Andrews. I wanted our reunion to be full of laughter. Real, happy laughter, not hysteria. Christopher, the world's gone mad and you arrive in the middle of it . . . I mean, I'm happy, but it wasn't the way I planned it . . . that is . . ." She stopped, aware she was rambling.

"Calm down." His voice was firm, reassuring. "Tell me what's been going on here. Take it one step at a time."

"Yes." Again, she repeated the hideous story of Saturday night. "And now I'm bringing Jayne to stay in the apartment," she concluded, "and Patricia's flying in

402

tonight, and we'll be surrounded by people and grief, and there'll be no privacy for us and no joy the way I imagined it. It's not fair!" She sounded like a disappointed child. "You're here and I want to spend every minute alone with you. Oh, God, that sounds so terribly selfish! I know I shouldn't be thinking of myself at a time like this. It's just that I didn't expect you until August, and to have you come when things are so dreadful and I'll be pulled apart by so many obligations and I haven't slept and I'm such a wreck and this isn't the way . . ."

"Be quiet!" There was love in the command. "Mary, darling, we're not children. What difference if this isn't the reunion we both imagined? I'm here at the time you need me most. It's a miracle. As though something told me to come. Dear heart, I don't care who's around. We don't need storybook settings, for God's sake! We have years to be alone together in any romantic spot you care to name. I'm not concerned about that now; I'm concerned about you. You're all that matters to me." He paused and said gently, "I'm coming right over. We'll get through this together."

"Yes," she said. "Please. Come right away, Christopher. I need you to hold me and never let me go."

"I never will. Never again."

*　*　*

Jayne woke for the second time and lay staring at the ceiling of the hospital room. She remembered it all vividly, now, in every unbearable detail. It's my fault, she thought in despair. My fault for trying to play God. I tampered with another person's life, so certain I knew what was best for him. I refused to beleve Terry couldn't be happy in the kind of life I wanted. I was so arrogant about my ability to outwit Paul. I was wrong. Paul won in the end. And Terry? Terry knew what he was doing last night. He couldn't pretend any longer. A dry sob escaped her throat. I killed them both and I'll be punished for it. I deserve to be punished.

Why can't I cry? If only I could weep for Terry and the baby who'll never know him. Even for Paul, who cared in a way I'd never be capable of. For myself and my blind determination to have things my way.

And what now? Where am I headed with this baby inside me? Perhaps I should abort. It's not too late. Yes it is, she answered herself. Too late to release Terry. He's already done that for himself. Wrong to snuff out another life on top of those I've already taken. Not to have this child would make it all meaningless and futile. It's Terry's only chance at immortality. I'll love his son or daughter in the unselfish way I didn't love him.

"Jayne?"

She turned her head and saw Charlie in the doorway.

"How are you feeling, honey?"

She tried to smile. "Okay. What are you doing here? Why aren't you home getting some rest? I know you and Aunt Mary were here all night."

"Don't worry about us. I took Mary home a few hours ago. I don't think she slept, but she did lie down. Your mother's on the way."

"Oh, no!" It was an involuntary reaction she quickly tried to cover. "I mean, there's no need for her to make the trip."

"She wants to, I'm sure. In any case, Mary had to call her. I think in her own way your mother loves you very much, Jayne."

Jayne thought of her father's letter. I suppose she does love me. And in *my* crazy way, I guess I love her, too. She's done some terrible things to people, but who am I to condemn her now?

"Is my father coming, too?"

"I don't know. There seemed to be some confusion about that." Charlie seemed nervous. "There's something else Mary just told me. Christopher Andrews has arrived in town."

"Christopher? How did he know?"

"He didn't. It was a weird coincidence." Charlie sat down next to the bed. "I know this isn't the moment to

404

discuss it, but I have a hunch he'll want to take Mary back with him, and I wondered how you'd feel about taking over the show within the next few weeks, instead of waiting until August. You see, I don't think Mary will go unless you reassure her that you can handle things alone. Not just the job, but your whole life. I'm afraid she feels totally responsible for you, now that Terry's gone. She may give up the whole idea of Christopher because of some silly notion that none of this would have happened if she hadn't taken you on the cruise. We talked about that again last night, before we knew Christopher was arriving. I told her what nonsense it was to feel that way, but I'm not sure she believes me. You'll have to make her believe it, Jayne. You're the only one who can make her stop feeling guilty about any part of this."

"She wouldn't! She wouldn't give up the best thing in her life to stay here and look after me."

"Wouldn't she? She adores you. You're the child she never had. I even tried to be practical about it. Told her to remember that if she didn't leave, you couldn't step into her job. She said she'd thought of that. She said she was sure she could get a job at another station. She would, too. The way she's feeling right now, she'd resign and go to work someplace else, rather than deprive you."

Jayne was stunned. "That's insane, Charlie! What are we going to do?"

He shook his head. "I don't think there's anything I can do. Whether it's now, August or never, I'm afraid Mary's departure depends on how convincing you can be. I'm sorry to burden you with this, my dear, but Christopher's appearance puts a new light on things. We can't let Mary throw away the thing she wants most, out of some exaggerated sense of guilt or duty."

For a moment, Jayne forgot herself and Mary. This dear man. He loved Mary so much he was willing to drive her away. Not many other people would be so selfless. Wasn't it a temptation for him to agree with Mary, to say that she should, indeed, stay here and look after her niece and the unborn child? It would have been so easy for him

405

to play on those very guilts he mentioned. Mary trusted his judgment, and rightly. He had only to encourage her and she'd break it off with Christopher, stay in San Francisco, get another job and, probably, one day marry Charlie. But he cared too much to do that. Jayne looked tenderly at his troubled face.

"You really love her a lot, don't you?"

Charlie smiled. "She's the most idiotic, pig-headed, insecure, vulnerable, strong and necessary woman in the whole damned world. And yes, I love her a lot."

"I know how to fix it," Jayne said.

Charlie nodded soberly. He guessed what was in her mind. He rose heavily and put his hand on Jayne's.

"You love her, too."

"Very much. Enough to hurt her if it will help."

* * *

It was impossible, Mary thought, that with all the grief and worry on her mind she could still respond like a schoolgirl when Christopher arrived and put his arms around her. She clung to him, trembling. He kissed her deeply and then held her at arm's length.

"You're more beautiful than ever."

Despite herself, she laughed. "Beautiful? With no sleep and all that's happened since last night? Christopher, my darling, love really is blind."

"I never saw you more clearly than I do at this moment. Never wanted you more."

"Nor I, you."

He forgot his weariness as Mary forgot her troubles. He pulled her close to him, feeling the soft, familiar shape of her body.

"Talking can come later," he said. "God, how I've missed you!"

Mary closed her eyes, feeling the wonderful weakening in her legs, the sense of floating on some all-enveloping cloud of desire that blotted out everything except this moment and this man. It was wrong, she thought briefly, to be so happy when others were so sad. No, not wrong. This feeling of delight was something apart. Rejecting it would not diminish Jayne's sorrow or bring Terry back to life.

Gladly, gratefully, she drew Christopher even closer toward her. For a little while, at least, the reunion would be all they imagined.

Chapter 31

Outwardly, she appeared calm, a well-dressed, still-beautiful middle-aged woman in the window seat of economy class on the late-afternoon flight to San Francisco. But inside, Patricia was a mass of rage and frustration. She glanced to her left at Stanley's impassive face. He stared ahead, saying nothing to her, aware of her anger and unmoved by it. For once, he'd been more determined than she. This afternoon, when she reported Mary's bad news, Stanley had taken matters into his own hands.

"Start packing," he said. "We're going out there right away. That poor child must be going through hell!"

"I've already told Mary I'll be there tonight, dear. I knew you'd want me to go."

"Not *you*," Stanley said. "*Us*. You don't think I'm going to sit home at a time like this, do you? That's not just your child out there, Patricia. She's mine too."

She'd tried to placate him. "Of course she's ours. I know how you feel, but this is a mother's job, Stanley. Jayne will understand. Men just aren't good around grief. You know how you hate funerals."

"I love my daughter more than I hate funerals. I don't wish to discuss it. We're going together."

She began to be exasperated. "That's foolish! If you go, it will cost a fortune. Two plane fares. And we'll have to stay in a hotel. Jayne's going to be at Mary's and

408

there'll be room for me, but not for you *and* me. For heaven's sake, be practical for once in your life! You can't do anything for Jayne!"

He stared at her coldly. "I beg to differ. Maybe I can do more for her than you can."

"Such as?"

Stanley took a deep breath. Hurting people was foreign to him and he hated it, but she left him no alternative. "Such as giving her the feeling of being loved and understood."

It was Patricia's turn to stare. "Are you saying *I* don't love and understand her?"

"No. I think you love her. Understand her? I'm not sure. We've always had a special closeness, Jayne and I. Maybe fathers and daughters manage that better than mothers and daughters. I don't know. I do know we've shared a bond of trust. Her hand has always been in mine. She's never felt threatened by me or competitive with me, and she knows I'm always on her side. Do you think she feels that way about you?"

"What you're saying is that you've always spoiled her rotten!" Patricia was furious. " 'Bond of trust,' indeed! She was always able to twist you around her little finger. I was the one who tried to keep her feet on the ground while you filled her head full of ideas about how wonderful she was! I was the heavy. Understand her? You bet I understand her. She's been selfish since the day she was born, thanks to you. Look what she's done, staying in California, marrying that simpering little actor, getting pregnant by him. And now I suppose she'll expect us to take care of her and her baby until she can find another man. My God, do you think I've liked being the disciplinarian? Don't you think I'd rather take your easy route, giving her everything, never criticizing her, always buying her love? But I couldn't do that. She had to learn that the world is cruel and people are rotten and everything doesn't come up smelling like roses, the way Daddy would like her to believe!"

Stanley shook his head. "And this is what you think a mother's job is? This is the comfort and solace you're going to offer her? No, Patricia. I'm not going to let you go out there alone and tell Jayne what a fool she's been. I'm not going to give you a chance to rub her nose in her mistakes. You'd like that. Just as you'd like to make Mary's life miserable. You're jealous of both of them. No," he said again, "you're not going to stir everybody up the way you did before. God knows what you did then. But this time I'll be watching you. You and I will go as loving parents to be with our widowed daughter. We'll be there to lend our support, not to make accusations or cause her more grief than she already has. I don't know what we're going to find when we get there. All I know is that the past is history and we have to see where Jayne wants to go from here."

She'd never heard him sound so confident and unmovable. Once again, Patricia tried to appeal to reason. "Stanley, you don't believe I'll be anything but sympathetic. Surely you can trust me to be understanding *now*, even if you don't think I've been in the past. And there *is* the money. Probably Jayne will want to come back to New York. There'll be the cost of that as well as Lord knows what other bills she may have. We can't afford double travel expense for no reason."

"There's every reason," he said quietly. "She needs both of us. As for the expense, how better could we spend our money? But if you're really worried about that, Patricia, why can't we stay in Jayne's apartment instead of a hotel? She'll be at Mary's. I'd think you'd prefer not to stay with your sister anyway, after the things you've said about her."

He had her. There was no way she could keep him from going. Damn him, Patricia thought now, as the plane flew swiftly westward, he's going to mess up everything. I was sure, in her vulnerable state, Jayne would leap at the idea I had before: that we could share an apartment. And Michael's free now. I could get back together with him. But no, Stanley has to tag along to ruin my life as he always has.

* * *

410

Mary lay in the crook of Christopher's arm, savoring the feel of him beside her.

"How long can you stay?"

"In San Francisco? As long as you need me, darling."

She gave a sad little smile. "That would be forever. I mean *really* how long?"

He gently disengaged his arm and sat up. "I'd planned ten days or so. A couple of weeks maybe. I thought perhaps I could talk you into winding up your affairs by then and going back with me, instead of waiting until August."

She raised herself to his eye level. "I can't, Christopher. Not now. Maybe if this thing hadn't happened to Jayne . . . But I can't leave her now. I was worried even before. I didn't have that much faith in Terry, but I'd convinced myself that at least she had a husband. Now she has no one. I'm sure she won't want to go back to New York. She couldn't live with her parents again, Patricia especially. And she's coming into a good job here that will mean she can support herself and her child. No, she'll want to stay, and she'll need me, darling."

"So do I."

"I know. But in a different way. You're not helpless and frightened, my love. You're not bereaved and alone and terribly young. We forget how young she is, Christopher."

He didn't answer for a minute. Then he said, "Answer me something honestly. If this hadn't happened, this thing with Jayne, and if I'd arrived this morning, would you have gone back with me? Would you even have come in August, knowing Jayne was pregnant and Terry was undependable? Or would you have asked me to wait longer? Until the baby was born, perhaps? Or until Jayne was safely remarried to someone you approved of? Would you have gone on and on, Mary, setting our life aside because you felt indispensable?"

"I . . . I can't answer those questions, darling. Nobody knows what he'll do in a terrible situation until he's faced with it. You know I love you. I love you more than anything in the world, but . . ."

"No," Christopher said, "you don't love me more than

411

anything in the world. You love your conscience more. Forgive me for saying it, dearest, but you also love more the feeling of being needed. And you can't comprehend that my needs and your own are as important as Jayne's."

"That's not true! I'm not indispensable to her. I know that."

"Do you, Mary? Do you really?"

"Yes, of course."

"Then have some faith in her. She'll look after herself. She's strong. And unselfish. The *last* thing she'd want is to feel obligated to you, knowing you're giving up your life for hers."

"But I'm not giving it up. It's just a matter of . . ."

"Time?" he finished for her. "How much time? We lost a lot of our lives before we found each other. There aren't that many years to squander. I can't wait forever," he said quietly. "I can't live on dreams and promises and sacrifice. Perhaps I'm not as generous as you. I want to live with the woman I love and enjoy whatever time is left. I won't sit around for months and years, darling, while you fret over a lovely child who isn't even your own. She has parents for that, if there's worrying to be done. It's not your job, Mary. *I'm* your job. At least you led me to believe I was."

She sat with eyes closed. "I don't know. What you're saying is right. The logical part of me accepts it, but the emotional side . . . Please don't push me right now, Christopher. It's been such a hard time. Everything is so sad and frightening. Let me think. Just a few days, that's all I ask."

He kissed her gently. "Of course, my love. Don't think this is easy for me, either. But it has to be done, and *now*. So that if, God forbid, you feel held here, we can try to accept that and go our own ways."

"Yes. You're right. It's not fair to prolong the agony. Or, the ecstasy." She managed to smile. "I'm blessed to have you. You're my comfort and my job."

He glanced at the bedside clock. "And your friendly reminder, as well," he said lightly. "Didn't you tell me you were going to pick up Jayne at four? It's three now. Hadn't we better move?"

"Will you go with me?"

"Naturally. I love that young woman. She fancies herself as invincible as her aunt."

Mary got up reluctantly. "I'm ashamed of myself, being so happy these past couple of hours while Jayne is so miserable. I'd like to wish it all away, Christopher. More for my sake than anyone else's. I'd like to wish away last night and the next few days. I dread tonight when Patricia arrives. I hate the thought of seeing her. My own sister. I can't stand the thought of the act she'll put on at Terry's funeral, as though she gave a damn about a boy she scarcely knew. I don't want to see Jayne's suffering now and in time to come. I'm a terrible person. A heartless beast."

He stood beside her, gathering her again in his arms. "No, you're not a terrible person. You're human, my love. You're admitting what most people would feel in your situation and not be honest enough to admit. There's nothing wrong with that, darling." He hugged her hard. "In fact," Christopher said, "it's the first hopeful sign of imperfection I've seen in you. And I like it. I like it very much indeed."

Charlie was in the room when they arrived to collect Jayne. The girl, fully dressed, seemed composed, but her face was white and drawn and there were deep, dark circles under her eyes. The full impact of the tragedy struck Christopher when he saw her. Mary was right. She was so young to be widowed and friendless and with six months of pregnancy facing her. It was cruel of him to try to separate her and her aunt, but there was no choice. Mary would leave soon or she'd not leave at all.

Jayne managed a little smile of greeting when she saw him. "You must have a sixth sense, Christopher. How did you know to turn up at the right time?"

"I'm a witch. Or, rather, a warlock. Didn't you know? How are you, Jayne?"

"So-so."

"Of course." He felt ill at ease. What was he expected to say? He could manage nothing more than a trite, "I'm sorry, dear. I liked Terry." He expected her to burst into tears, but she merely looked at him with her big eyes and nodded.

"I know. He liked you, too. So much has happened in the four months since we met, hasn't it? All our lives have changed. Yours and Aunt Mary's and mine. Even Charlie's."

The mention of his name made Mary realize she hadn't introduced him to Christopher. For that matter, she hadn't uttered a word since she arrived. The sight of Jayne looking so small and helpless had brought back all the horror she'd almost forgotten in the past few precious hours, and she was speechless with sympathy. She rallied now and said, "I'm sorry. I forgot you two hadn't met. Charlie Burke, Christopher Andrews."

The men shook hands, quickly appraising each other. So this is the man Mary loves, Charlie thought. No wonder. There's power in him, not only in his grip but in the directness of his gaze. I like him, damn it.

"Glad to know you," Charlie said. "I guess congratulations are in order."

"Thank you. I know you hate to lose Mary, but I hear you have an excellent replacement." Christopher in turn was sizing up Mary's boss and best friend. Nice chap, he decided. A damned attractive man, this recent widower. No wonder Mary was so fond of him. For a split second, he entertained the crazy idea that Charlie might have something to do with Mary's reluctance to leave. No. Mary wasn't in love with Burke. She loved him. That was different.

"I'm shot with luck," Charlie said in answer to Christopher's compliment. "Jayne's going to be terrific in the job. She's had a good teacher."

There was an awkward silence before Mary said, "Well, young lady, are you ready to leave? You're all checked out. We stopped at the desk on the way up. I thought it best if you came home with me for a while, okay?"

414

"Fine." Jayne sounded as though it didn't matter where she went. "I hear Mother's on the way."

"Yes. She should be in some time this evening. I . . . I told her she could stay in the apartment, too."

"Really? *That* surprises me."

Mary felt the blood rush to her face. There was a slight edge to Jayne's voice. Or was she only imagining it?

"Our differences don't matter, Jayne. You're the only one we're thinking about."

Jayne seemed to accept that. "What time is she arriving?"

"I don't know, exactly."

"You mean nobody's going to meet her?"

Again, Mary was taken aback. What was this sudden concern for Patricia? Jayne knew the awful thing her mother had done. She'd been part of it. And she hadn't even been in touch with her since the night she put Patricia on the plane back to New York, the night of the ugly disclosures.

"I think somebody should go to the airport," Jayne continued. "I'll do it, if nobody else wants to. We can't let her get on a bus late at night, all alone."

"Darling, you can't! You're in no condition. Besides, we don't even know what flight she's on."

"Can't we call Daddy and find out?"

"I don't know," Mary said helplessly. "He might have decided to come with her."

"Then Grandma and Grandpa would know."

"We'll check it out," Christopher said. "I'll be glad to go and pick her up."

"You don't even know her!" The words burst, involuntarily, from Mary's lips and they sounded outraged. Hearing them, she stopped abruptly. What was the matter with her? Was she afraid Patricia would seduce Christopher as she had Michael? She must be going mad. It wasn't the ridiculous fear that her sister would be attractive to Christopher that frightened her. It was Jayne's concern that surprised and, yes, annoyed Mary. Jayne was acting as though she was actually eager to see her mother, as though all that had gone before was forgotten and she couldn't wait to rush into Patricia's arms. Mary felt a bleak, indefinable sense of loss, made stronger by Jayne's next words.

"I'm glad she's coming. I knew she would. I need her. She doesn't even know she's going to be a grandmother."

"Yes, she does," Mary said in a small voice. "I told her on the phone."

"You told her?" Jayne sounded reproachful. " I wish you hadn't, Aunt Mary. I was looking forward to doing that myself."

"I'm sorry. It just slipped out while we were talking."

"Talking? Or fighting?"

Christopher began to feel uneasy. Something was terribly wrong here. It was as though Jayne was deliberately trying to hurt her aunt.

"Look, my friends," he said, "why don't you continue this discussion at Mary's? We're anxious to get you out of here, Jayne, and I'm sure you're more than ready to leave."

"Right," Charlie agreed. "My car's nearby. I'll bring it around to the front door."

"Why don't you go with him, Christopher?" Mary said.

He started to protest and then sensed she wanted to be alone with her niece for a few minutes.

"Good enough. We'll be downstairs."

When the men left, Mary looked sharply at Jayne. "What's this all about, honey?"

"What's *what* all about?"

"Jayne, don't put on an act. You seem so cold toward me. And you sound as though you can't wait to see your mother."

"Is that so unnatural?"

"Under ordinary circumstances, no. But in view of your last meeting . . . and the fact that she's never so much as acknowledged your marriage . . ."

"You don't understand Mother, Aunt Mary. She just can't express the love she feels for both of us."

Mary was stunned. "Love for us? What are you saying? She tried to rearrange your life to suit herself. She didn't care whether she was destroying my marriage! She's acted

416

as though neither of us exists ever since she left here! That's love? I don't want you to be alienated from your mother, but I don't understand this hundred-and-eighty-degree turn you're doing, being so anxious to see her, saying how much you need her, trying to convince me she cares but can't find the words to say so!"

Jayne hesitated for a split second before she said, "Are you jealous, Aunt Mary? I don't love you any the less. I'm grateful for all you've done for me. You're a terrific lady. But *she's* my mother."

"I see." God, it was funny. You never really knew people. She'd have bet her life that if it came to a choice, Jayne's loyalties would have been much more with her than with Patricia. Not so. In her hours of sorrow, the girl acted on instinct, reaching out for the one who gave her life. How clearly is she thinking? Mary wondered. Is she still in shock? Is grief overwhelming her usually rational view of things? And why do I feel so wounded by this rejection? Perhaps I am jealous. I'd begun to think of her as my own, more of a mother to her than the one who really is. Wishful thinking seems to be my specialty.

But sensible as she tried to be, Mary felt bitter. Where had Patricia been when Jayne was trying to handle her strange marriage? She hadn't cared what was happening to her daughter. Only Stanley and I cared. Or so it seemed. I'm not big enough to think that Patricia simply can't express love. I don't believe she knows that emotion. She's destructive and opportunistic. Jayne saw that once. She may remember it when she sees her mother again. Right now she's like a little girl, afraid and unhappy and clinging to "Mommy." Damn you, Patricia. You'd be all she wants to believe you are. If you're not, I'll kill you.

"Aunt Mary?"

"Yes, dear?"

"Don't you think we'd better leave? They'll be waiting downstairs. And there's . . . there's a lot to do. Charlie's been wonderful, arranging things for Terry, but I still have to make some decisions. Like the service. I want Terry cremated, but there should be a service of some kind, and someone to say a few words about him." For

417

the first time, Jayne's eyes filled with tears. "There's nobody, is there? His only friend is dead, too."

Mary forgot her feeling of having been betrayed. She went to Jayne and put her arms around her.

"Don't worry. We'll find a minister."

"No. I'd like it to be more personal. Terry wasn't religious. Do you think Christopher would do it? There won't be many people there. Just the family, I'm sure. And maybe some of the people from his office, or the radio station. But I'd like some kind of simple acknowledgment that he lived and did the best he could."

"Darling, I don't know. Christopher really didn't know him that well."

Jayne looked heartbreakingly sad. "None of us did," she said. "That was the trouble. None of us really knew him at all."

* * *

As long as she lived, Mary would not forget the sinking feeling she had when Patricia and Stanley walked into the apartment and Jayne rushed headlong into her mother's arms. She would not forget the petty sense of envy she felt as Patricia held her daughter, nor the look of triumph in her sister's eyes as she gazed over Jayne's head as though to say, See? Blood's thicker than water. I'm the one she needs.

Jayne turned from her mother, finally, to be embraced by Stanley.

"Oh, Daddy, I'm so glad you're both here! We called and Grandmother told us you were coming."

He soothed her as he had when she was a little girl who'd fallen and skinned her knee. "It's all right, baby. We're with you. We'll take care of you. There's nothing to worry about."

Mary stood silently, a little apart. Christopher and Charlie had left a little while before, reluctant to intrude on this intimate moment. Mary, herself, felt like an intruder. She wasn't part of this family. Not really. It was

418

mother, father, child, joined in a closeness not even their nearest relatives could touch.

Gently, Stanley released his daughter. Jayne gave Mary a fleeting glance and then went over to sit close to Patricia, holding her hand, almost as though she was flaunting her dependence on her mother.

"Mary, how are you?" Stanley kissed her cheek. "This is all so terrible. Thank God you were around. I don't know what Jayne would have done without you."

"She's very brave, Stanley. I don't know where she gets her strength." Mary stopped, embarrassed, realizing how that must sound to him.

He smiled, understanding. "She comes from a long line of strong women," he said. "It's the Farr in her, I suppose."

"I didn't mean . . ."

"Don't be silly. It's not important where we get our strength. Only that we have it to draw on." They were speaking in low tones. "Have all the arrangements been made?" Stanley asked. "Is there anything I should do?"

"No. Charlie Burke has done everything. I . . . I identified the body this morning. It was ghastly." She shuddered and went on. "We've set the services for Tuesday morning. The casket will be closed, of course, but Jayne's asked Christopher to say a few words and he's agreed."

"Christopher? Who's Christopher?"

"Didn't Mother tell you? Jayne and I met him on the cruise. He's here at the moment." She didn't want to discuss the muddled state of her own affairs. "He knew Terry and liked him and, frankly, there's no one else. No friends. No family. Jayne told me that Terry once mentioned his father, but he hadn't seen him in years. We don't know how to get hold of him, or whether he's even alive."

"I see. And the other young man?"

Mary sighed. "Still at the morgue. We won't know until tomorrow when his office opens whether he has family or not."

Stanley glanced over at Jayne, who seemed deep in conversation with her mother. "Patricia seems to think

419

there was something, well abnormal about him and Terry. It doesn't matter now, if there was, unless it affects Jayne in any way."

"It doesn't affect her. It was part of Terry's past, but all that changed when he met Jayne." It was a lie, but a good lie, a "percentage lie," Christopher would have called it. "He was utterly faithful to Jayne and divinely happy with her, as she was with him. Whatever you may hear or read in the papers, don't believe there was anything unnatural about the relationship, or about that last evening. I was there. I know. They were all friends. Terry's death was an accident, brought on, I'm sorry to say, by drugs and alcohol. Paul's remorse was so great he couldn't live with it. Simple. Tragically simple."

Stanley sighed heavily. "She's going to have a baby?"

"Yes. She's happy about that. It's like keeping part of her husband."

"Do you think, after all this is over, we can persuade her to go back with us?"

Mary looked toward the young woman who meant so much to her. Jayne seemed to be absorbed in whatever Patricia was saying, her head nodding in solemn agreement with her mother's words. She seemed oblivious to her aunt.

"I don't know," Mary said heavily. "I can't predict her reactions anymore."

Chapter 32

It had seemed an eminently sensible idea last night, but this morning Mary told herself she was an idiot to have given the Richtons and Jayne her apartment while she took the miserable little room Terry and Jayne had shared for a few, brief, troubled weeks.

It was a terrible place. Depressing at any time and more so on this Monday morning with its reminders of Terry: his clothes crammed beside Jayne's in the small closet; his shaving things in the windowless bathroom; his copies of *Variety* and *The Hollywood Reporter* flung untidly on the floor beside the comfortable chair. Poor, lost Terry. Even now, though she vividly remembered his last moments and, even more horribly, the broken shape of him she identified later, she could hardly believe he was dead. Jayne couldn't believe it, either. She was a different girl, a sleepwalker, going through the motions she thought were expected of her. And she seemed to have turned away from Mary. Her cruelty hurt.

Like last night.

When Mary suggested perhaps it would be more comfortable for them to use her place and she'd sleep in this one, she'd honestly expected Jayne to veto the idea. It had been only a polite offer, something one did automatically, but Patricia, predictably, had leapt at it.

"That makes sense," her sister said. "Stanley can take the couch in the office and Jayne and I will share your room. There are three of us and one of you, so it really would work out better, as long as you don't mind."

Mary looked at Jayne, but the girl was silent. She knows I'd planned on her staying here with me, Mary thought. Why doesn't she offer her apartment to her parents? That would work just as well. Instead, it was Stanley who protested.

"We can't do that, Patricia," he said. "No need to inconvenience Mary. We already talked about staying at Jayne's."

His wife gave him an angry look. "I'd like to be near my daughter tonight. It would seem to me you would, too."

"Well, of course, but . . ."

"It's all right," Mary said. "I don't mind if Jayne doesn't."

"Jayne would prefer it, wouldn't you, darling?" Patricia purred.

"Yes, I would."

So a surprised and wounded Mary had taken Jayne's key and come to this dreary "studio apartment." She called Christopher the moment she arrived and told him where she was. "It's frightful," she said. "God knows how those children stood it!"

"I don't want *you* to stand it. It's ridiculous for you to be there. I'll come and get you and bring you to the hotel. I have plenty of room. Besides, love, I want to be with you."

She'd been tempted. A clean, spacious suite at the Fairmont was appealing. So was the idea of being held and comforted by Christopher. But she was too upset, too confused to inflict herself on him.

"Not tonight," she said. "Tomorrow maybe I'll be able to change the arrangements. It was stupid of me to mention it. To be honest, I thought Jayne wouldn't want it. She knew I was just making a gesture. But something's happened to her, Christopher. Something beyond her grief, I mean. It's as though she's pulling away from me. As though she's almost trying to make me dislike her. I don't understand."

I do, he thought. She's setting you free, but you haven't come to that realization. Perhaps I wouldn't have either, if I hadn't had a drink with Charlie and heard about his discussion with Jayne in the hospital. This is her way of bringing us together. She has more heart and more sense than any of us. And more willingness to sacrifice. She'll give up your love if she has to, to make sure you have the happiness she wants for you.

But he couldn't say this to Mary. In time, it would dawn on her what Jayne had done, but before then she'd feel hurt and rejected, as bewildered as a woman whose devoted child had suddenly, inexplicably turned on her.

"I don't think Jayne's thinking straight right now," he said soothingly. "There's nothing in her but emptiness, Mary. It's understandable, an all-consuming absorption with her own loss. Don't judge Jayne these next few days. She won't be herself."

"Perhaps not. You make such sense, Christopher. I shouldn't be offended by the things she says and does. I forget the shock she's been through." Mary felt a little better. "You do understand if I don't come there tonight, don't you? It's not that I don't want you. There are just times when it's better to be alone."

"However you want it, dearest."

"Besides, they might need to reach me for something, and I can't very well tell them I'm staying at the hotel with you."

He couldn't resist laughing. "Mary, Mary, you are so bloody proper! What difference would it make if they did know you were here? We're free and a good bit over twenty-one."

She sounded slightly shocked. "But how would it look? Not twenty-four hours after this tragedy and me enjoying myself with you."

He didn't remind her that she'd "enjoyed herself" a little more than twelve hours after the tragedy. Her mind wasn't on him at this moment. She was physically and emotionally exhausted. He wouldn't add to the jumbled feelings Jayne deliberately had provoked.

"All right, darling. Try to get some sleep. Call me when you wake."

This morning she wished she'd accepted his offer. She'd slept hardly at all, though she couldn't remember ever being so tired. All night she'd lain awake in the lumpy bed, puzzled over the new, distant Jayne. She'd lied when she told Christopher he made sense about Jayne's attitude. It didn't make sense. She and her niece were closer than Patricia was to her daughter. Jayne knew the kind of woman her mother was. How could she turn to her this way, shutting me out? Mary wondered. Has she always secretly been on Patricia's side, perhaps even forgiving her the affair with Michael, possibly rationalizing that Mary had been no angel, either? No, that couldn't be. She simply responded unthinkingly to the ties that exist between mother and child, ties that remained intact, strained as they might be by all kinds of outward disappointments.

Me and my damned, frustrated maternal instincts! Mary thumped the thin pillow and tried to go to sleep. The love I felt I should have had from my own mother was what I tried to give first to Michael and then to Jayne. I smothered them with it, thinking I was doing the right thing. And ultimately they were both relieved to be free.

Never again, her mind said. Never again love more than you are loved in return.

* * *

In the bed beside her mother, Jayne also lay sleepless that Sunday night. She would not let herself think of Terry. He'd wanted to die. She knew that. He couldn't face the conflict within him, the tearing apart that never would be resolved no matter how hard he tried to make himself believe it could. He's gone. It's better for him. He never was of this world, somehow. Even with all he lived

424

through, he didn't understand the games grownups play.

She mourned for him but accepted the inevitable as she now saw it. Almost as hard to bear was what she was doing to Mary. It wasn't easy, saying cold things to her aunt, pretending she preferred to be with Patricia. I hate my mother, she thought. I suppose I should be appalled by that idea, but it's true. Hate her pettiness, her insensitivity. Hate the triumph she feels because she believes I've come running back to her.

Just let me get through the next few days, Jayne silently prayed. Let me see Mary off to her new life with Christopher, convinced I don't need her. Even let her despise me, if that will take away the responsibility she feels. Then I'll tell Mother and Dad to go home where they belong. I'll lose myself in my new job, have my baby, take care of it myself. I'm not a girl, I'm a woman alone. And I can function as one, even if no one seems to believe that.

She felt sick, remembering the things Patricia said after Mary left. Once she was gone, Jayne let down her guard in front of her parents.

"We shouldn't have let her do that. It's an awful place. Aunt Mary's so generous, but there was no need to drive her out of her own house."

"I quite agree," Stanley said. "Your mother and I should be sleeping there."

Patricia looked disgusted. "You two are so naïve! You don't think that's where she's gone, do you? Really! If you're so concerned about her, why don't you call her boy friend's hotel room and ask to speak to her?"

"No, Mother. She wouldn't do that. Not tonight. To her, it would seem disrespectful."

"Disrespectful!" Patricia laughed. "You must be kidding! You don't seriously believe she's going to miss a chance to be with her lover! Grow up, Jayne. You, of all people, talking about respect! Where was her respect when she was sleeping with that man all over the South Pacific and poor Michael was here all alone, trying to prove himself to her? You think she's so high and mighty.

425

So damned decent. Well, she certainly encouraged you to get yourself into a dirty mess! Marrying that fag! Approving of your affair with him before! Disrespectful!" Patricia said again. "She has the morals of a bitch in heat! I feel sorry for Michael, discarded now that she has something better. You can bet she'd have hung on to him forever if she hadn't found a rich one!"

"Patricia, stop it!" Stanley's words were a command. "I don't want to hear that kind of terrible talk about your sister. Mary's a fine woman. She gave Michael everything she could, probably more than he deserved. As for Jayne, Mary didn't push her into anything. She did what her heart told her. And I hardly think this is the time to speak ill of Terry, even if you have so little concern for your daughter's feelings!"

"Oh, shut up, Stanley. You don't know what you're talking about, so don't give us your opinions. I knew Michael. You didn't."

Jayne bit her lips. She knew him all right, she thought. You're two of a kind, parasites both of you. How dare Patricia stand there and moralize after all she'd done? How dare she criticize Mary and me? She felt revulsion for this envious woman. You've fed off Daddy most of your life, but you won't feed off me. He's stuck with you, but I'm not. Jayne gave her mother a long, level look.

"We all see things through the eyes of our own experience, Mother," she said meaningfully. "That doesn't mean we see them as they are."

Patricia stared back at her. My daughter loathes me, she realized. She really despises me. Would she be spiteful enough to tell Stanley about Michael and me? Never. Silly, sentimental Jayne wouldn't hurt her father that way. But why has she been playing this game since we arrived, pretending to be so glad to see me, almost ignoring her beloved Aunt Mary? What was she up to, this strong, defiant young woman who suddenly pretended to be so helpless? No matter. She and Mary thwarted my plans once before, but they won't do it again. I'm here. And here I mean to stay.

* * *

By the time Tuesday came, Mary thought she would drop with fatigue. She and Christopher had spent most of their time with Jayne and her parents and it was the most trying experience of a lifetime. Patricia was so "in charge," Stanley so clearly troubled and Jayne seemingly indifferent to her aunt.

Stubbornly, not understanding, herself, why she did it, Mary continued to sleep in the little apartment. Christopher said nothing more about the hotel. Nor, even in the few minutes they managed alone, did he discuss their future. He was waiting. He'd said all he could. It was up to Mary to decide the course of her life. She knew what his restraint meant. He was not a man to change his mind. Either she left with him or he left alone for all time.

Jayne's coolness toward her had culminated in a dreadful confrontation. Mary found her alone Monday afternoon and reported that Paul's office had contacted his sister in Des Moines. She was flying to San Francisco to take the body back for burial there.

"Des Moines? What an odd place for Paul to come from," Jayne said. "I'm sure he'll hate to go back. Not nearly chic enough for him."

Mary was disturbed. "Darling, I know how you must feel about Paul. You have every right, but it doesn't become you to be so cynical."

"Oh? What *does* become me, Aunt Mary?"

"The way you've always been. Those are the things that become you—the warmth, the generosity, the understanding. I know you're in a terrible state of mind right now, Jaynie, but you frighten me. I don't feel I know you, and that's crazy! I thought I knew you better than anyone did. And since Sunday night you've been, well, a stranger."

"My husband just killed himself. What do you want me to be, the life of the party?"

Mary recoiled. "No, of course not. I understand your grief. But Terry didn't do that, Jayne. You saw it. He was clowning around. It was an accident."

427

"Have it your way."

Mary tried once more. "Why can't I reach you? Why are you closing doors between us?"

The girl turned on her angrily. "Because I want you and everyone else to stop peeking through keyholes! Stop masterminding everything, for God's sake! I've had it up to *here* with your sacrifice and your eternally knowing what's best for everybody! Leave me alone, Aunt Mary. You have no idea what I've been through, long before Saturday night. You think everything can be solved as long as you're standing by, ready to pick up the pieces. Well, everything can't! Sometimes the pieces are too complex to fit into this patchwork quilt you seem to think life is. We don't fall into neat little squares and circles and triangles you can stitch together. Some of us have funny, warped shapes. I don't fit into any pattern, so can't you please leave me the hell alone?"

Mary felt as though she'd been physically attacked. Jayne was making no sense. That's not the way I am, Mary thought. I don't consider myself omnipotent, not by any stretch of the imagination. She stopped. Or do I? Everything seems to point that way. At least it does to Jayne.

When she spoke, her voice was a quiet contrast to the near hysteria of the younger woman. "I didn't know you felt that way, Jayne. I'm sorry. I didn't realize you felt so . . . so supervised."

"I do. By you. By my parents. Even by Charlie and Christopher. I feel everyone watching me, waiting to see what mistake I'll make next, just itching to get in and tell me how to run my life. Well, I want all of you out of it! You're driving me mad with this wait-and-see attitude. I'll manage. I don't need advice and help and jobs made for me and mothers ready to move in on me and people acting as though I can't . . . can't . . ." She stopped, trembling, and then abruptly burst into tears and fled the room.

In a few minutes she heard the front door close and knew Mary had left the apartment. She took a deep breath and then dried her eyes. That finally did it, she thought. She'll go with Christopher now.

* * *

Such a pathetically sparse gathering. They occupied less than three pews in the funeral chapel. "The family" sat in the first one, and a smattering of unfamiliar men and women were dotted haphazardly on the benches in the rear. Mary recognized none of them as she entered. Probably people from Terry's office she supposed, though he'd hardly been there long enough to make friends. Here and there she saw young men unmistakably from the community of Terry and Paul's past, come for what reason? To pay their respects or to satisfy a morbid curiosity about the kind of woman Terry married? It made no difference. There were no blood relatives to wonder about Terry's odd friends, though she regretted Terry's father was not present. No amount of searching through the dead man's papers had produced a clue about the long-gone Maurice Spalding. Perhaps he was dead, too. As far as his son was concerned, he'd been dead for years.

Patricia and Stanley flanked Jayne, and Mary sat beside her brother-in-law, Charlie next to her and Christopher at the end of the row where he would soon rise and speak of the one they'd come to bid good-bye. It was an imposition to have asked Christopher to do this, but there'd been no choice. Of the people Jayne knew, Christopher was the only one who'd spent any time with her husband. Except me, Mary thought. And God knows I couldn't do it. It was sad to think this marriage had been so devoid of mutual friendships. Paul had been their only shared acquaintance, an ironic commentary on the state of this ill-fated union.

Since Jayne's tirade the day before, Mary had barely exchanged a dozen words with her, though she and Christopher continued to have meals with the Richtons, to stand by, as it were, until this final gesture had been made. Then no more, Mary thought sadly. Let them make their

429

own plans from here on in. I'm making mine. As quickly as I can, I'll leave with Christopher. If Jayne wants to be on her own, let her. The thought came without bitterness, with only a kind of aching disappointment that Jayne did not care about her as Mary once believed she did.

* * *

As the soft organ music played and they waited for the signal for Christopher to speak, Patricia glanced over her shoulder toward the back of the chapel and was surprised to see Michael come in and sit alone in one of the back rows. She felt a little jolt of pleasure and surprise. He looked well, tanned and prosperous. She wondered what he was doing now that he was divorced. Every unattached woman in San Francisco must be after him, but she'd be in the race, too, once she'd sent Stanley back to New York and moved into an apartment with Jayne. Patricia gave him a little smile and a nod of recognition, but he seemed not to see her. He was staring straight at the back of Mary's head, as though he willed her, not her sister, to turn around and acknowledge him.

Don't get your hopes up, Michael, Patricia sent him a silent message. She's not coming back to you. In a minute you'll be listening to your replacement.

* * *

Charlie Burke's mind went back to another time, not long ago, when he'd been part of the ceremony of death. Tracey had been gone such a short time, but it seemed forever. He'd had none of the "trappings," not even as much as these small gestures. He hadn't wanted a fuss. His wife wouldn't have wanted it either. Oh, hundreds of people would have turned out, but because of *him*, not for her. Tracey had no friends either, he thought. Like Terry, she never "fit in." And like him, she probably welcomed the finality of release from a world she'd spent years trying to escape. Rest in peace, both of you, Charlie thought.

You are the true victims of our age, not strong enough to survive and not weak enough to admit it.

* * *

Stanley felt a great knot of anxiety as he sat holding Jayne's hand. It was frightening to see her so calm, so utterly still and dry-eyed. Only twenty-one and pregnant with a child who'd never know its father. Widowed when she should have been still carefree and sought after, or safely married to a dependable young man who'd care for her. He wondered what had drawn her to Terry Spalding. From what he gleaned, Jayne's husband had been, at best, bisexual, weak and futureless. Yet there must have been something in him that Jayne saw and wanted. He wished he could have known Terry. Somewhere in his character was the key to Jayne's outlook on life. Somehow he filled a need, and Stanley didn't know what that need was. She's not like either of us, he thought. She's not hard like Patricia or passive as I am. What goes on inside my little girl's head? And will she ever permit any of us to know?

* * *

At a signal Christopher rose slowly and took his place behind the podium. He looked over the small audience and allowed his gaze to come to rest on Jayne's unnaturally calm face. I know you, he thought, better than I knew Terry. I think when you asked me to do this you wanted me to talk to you, perhaps to help you understand yourself, even more than to eulogize your husband. He began to speak slowly, his eyes never leaving Jayne's.

"Never doubt love," Chrisopher said. "Never question it when it comes onstage, but be happy for its entrance. And do not weep when it makes its exit, for it leaves behind it the sweet aroma of caring, a fragrance to linger the rest of your life.

"Terry was an actor whose role was the very essence of love. He did not give off the powerful emanation of arrogance or the acrid smell of greed. His was not a nature

431

that returned cruelty with hatred or selfishness with villainy. Nor was he a competitive man, consumed with ambition and enslaved by the material things of life. He worshiped beauty and was the consummate artist in the theater of life. In his mind and heart, all creatures were heroes and heroines. And every drama had a happy ending. Even his own.

"He was very young, but he had the wisdom of age even while he never lost the trusting qualities of childhood. His was an endless searching for truth in its finest form—a truth he found in the woman he married. In her he discovered the tenderness and compassion he worshiped. In her he found a friend who understood and appreciated the Terry all too few of us were privileged enough to know, or wise enough to recognize. He loved her in a way he never loved before. In a way that made up in depth what it was not fated to have in duration.

"I knew Terry only a few short weeks, and in an atmosphere in which few things are real. But he discovered reality and found it good. I saw him change and bloom and develop in that time, saw him give of himself and receive, in abundance, the devotion he deserved. He left too soon, too tragically, but he lived a lifetime in twenty-six swift-flowing years. He left us with grace, and with memories that will sweeten forever the air we breathe.

"He played his part well, right up to the final curtain. And we applaud him."

There was not a sound when Christopher took his seat. I did a rotten job, he thought. I had ugly thoughts about Terry once, thanking God my own sons did not have his "affliction." My hypocrisy came through in those vacant, inadequate words. I was terrible.

The little group stood silently as the casket was taken out. Only then did Jayne make her way to Christopher, reaching for his hand.

"Thank you," she said. "I know those words were meant for me, but Terry would have been glad."

"I wish I could have done better for you, Jayne."

The girl shook her head. "No one could have. I'll remember every word the rest of my life. You captured him the way he was, Christopher. I don't know anyone else who could have done that. I don't know anyone else big enough to understand."

Patricia touched her arm. "Time to leave, Jayne. We're going out the back way. I hear there's a crowd of photographers out front."

Jayne looked at Charlie Burke. "If they think we're news, we shouldn't disappoint them, isn't that right, Charlie?"

He nodded. "They'll see a lot of you from now on. You're one of them."

Overhearing the brief exchange, Mary felt a sense of shame, remembering Saturday night and the way she'd treated the press, brushing them off, angry with them when they were only trying to do the job for which they were paid. Jayne, so new to the world of reporting, was already much more the professional. Even in this moment of grief, she knows what it means to be a public figure, even a local one. She'll be much better at it than I ever was, Mary reflected. To me, the job was a way of earning a living. It will be that to Jayne, too, but much more. She senses the responsibility it bears, the obligation to her peers that takes precedence over her own need for privacy.

With a sense of dismay, Mary realized she felt envy. It had seemed the perfect solution to all their problems, this idea of Jayne stepping into her shoes. But until this moment, it had not struck her how much she was going to miss the recognition, the challenges, the exquisite feeling of satisfaction in a job well done. These would be Jayne's now, these interesting, stimulating sensations. She did not begrudge them, but she felt a terrible sense of impending loss for the life she was leaving. It was not true that her job had been only a paycheck. It had kept her vital and interested, made her feel important in her own right. Was it shallow to admit she'd miss the sense of being somebody? Not shallow, perhaps, but immature. What Christopher offered was much more important, deeper and more lasting. What had he said? "Never doubt love."

She didn't doubt it. But there were all kinds of love.

Love of work. Love of a city and its people. Love even of power, a potent aphrodisiac, modest though the power might be. I love Christopher, she thought. But I love other things, too. Other people. My co-workers. The endlessly fascinating men and women I interview. I love Charlie. And Jayne. The real Jayne, not this strange person who'd appeared disguised in her skin, with none of the endearing qualities.

Again, she felt the bewilderment of the past few days. She could not fathom Jayne's sudden cruelty. What have I done to her? Mary wondered. What has brought on this bitterness, so abrupt and incisive, as though it were coldly calculated to alienate me?

And in a moment of blinding clarity she knew. My God! How could she have been so stupid not to have seen through Jayne's inexplicable "change of heart"? It was an act, all of it. An act for my benefit, Mary realized. Jayne knew my reluctance to leave her alone. She knew I'd lose Christopher if I kept delaying, pushing his patience to the brink. This is her way of releasing me from my feeling of responsibility. She really has tried to make me hate her. She's put on a merciless, merciful performance to let me leave without guilt. She knew rejection was the only thing I'd accept. There was no other way, even if I was devastated by her "treachery."

Mary's throat tightened at the thought of such generosity. Could I have done the same? No. Being loved has always been too important to me. I've craved it, bought it at any cost, needed it to sustain and nourish me. Jayne is bigger than that, and braver. This estrangement must have been even more of a hell for her than for me.

"Sweetheart?" She felt Christopher take her arm. "Hadn't we better leave now? The others have all gone."

Mary came to with surprise. It was as though she'd been standing there for hours, fascinated by relevations about herself and her niece. She looked around halfdazed, almost unaware of where she was. She saw the concern on Christopher's face.

"Are you all right?" His voice was anxious. "Do you

want to go out the back door to avoid the photographers?"

She shook her head. "No, if Jayne can face them, I can. It's part of our job." She smiled. "For whatever it's worth, I'm still Mary Farr Morgan."

Chapter 33

The six of them returned to Mary's apartment and the inevitable letdown set it. Even Patricia was silent as, with a proprietary air, she used Mary's key to open the front door.

Jayne looked exhausted. She'd been marvelous with the press, composed and dignified, thanking them for their kindness and consideration, fending off their outrageous questions about the events leading up to these last moments, graciously smiling a sad little smile of refusal when they tried to press her about drugs and alcohol and even, incredibly, about Terry's relationship with Paul.

"My husband was all the good things Mr. Andrews said about him," Jayne answered. "There's nothing I can add."

"Is it true you're taking over your aunt's job at the station?"

Charlie stepped in. "Certain things are under discussion. If there's to be an announcement, ladies and gentlemen, this is hardly the place for it."

"Then it's true? What's Mrs. Morgan going to do?" They turned their attention to her. "There's a rumor you're leaving radio, Mary. What's the story?"

She could feel Christopher waiting for her to tell them. Felt Jayne and Charlie's eyes on her. Saw the discomfort on Stanley's face and the smug satisfaction on Patricia's as her sister waited for her to publicly abdicate her career. Not really knowing the effect of her words, she said, "My plans are still tentative. There are personal as well as professional considerations. As Mr. Burke told you, we'll have an announcement at a more suitable time."

She was hardly aware of the frustrated grumbling of the reporters, so conscious was she, suddenly, of Christopher tensing beside her, of the others looking at her with surprise. Without elaborating, she took Jayne's arm and led her to the limousine. Solicitous hands helped them all inside and not a word was spoken on the short ride home.

Inside the apartment, they stood uneasily in the foyer, the unspoken question she'd raised hanging in the air. Jayne finally broke the tension.

"I think I'd like to lie down for a while, if nobody minds," she said.

Patricia was instantly the solicitous mother. "Of course you should, darling. I'll go in and turn down the bed for you."

Mary and the three men remained standing until Charlie said, "Well, I'd better go on down to the office. In spite of everything, it's still a working day." He shook Christopher's hand. "You did a fine job. Just right. I know it wasn't easy."

"Thank you." Christopher was tense, distracted.

"I'm going to get some air," Stanley said. "Be back in a little while."

The door closed behind them and Christopher and Mary were alone. Nervously, she walked into the living room and he followed.

"Would you like a drink, darling?"

"No," Christopher said, "I'd like an explanation."

She nodded and sat down, almost primly, on a straight chair. "I . . . I don't know where to begin. I love you. I want to be with you but . . ."

"But you can't give it up," Christopher finished for her. His voice held no reproach. "You can't give up your home and your job and the security of familiar people and things. You couldn't bring yourself to say, back there,

437

that you were getting married and leaving it all. You don't want to, my dear. I realize it now. I suppose I've always known it but I wouldn't let myself face the truth. You're not meant to be an idle, dependent woman. You need something of your own, something more than being a pale reflection of me."

She looked as miserable as she felt. "What's wrong with me, Christopher? I adore you. I'd be so proud to be your wife. I've waited forever for someone like you, a strong, decisive, protective man. It's not you I doubt, or our love. It's myself. I want it all—you and our life together and my work. And I know that's not realistic. I have to choose and I don't know how."

He was very gentle. "You know how, darling. We had a lovely special moment. A love affair build on wishful thinking, a storybook thing that hoped for an impossible happy ending."

She didn't want to hear it. "No. I'm not sure that's true. If you can only give me a little more time . . ."

Christopher shook his head. "We've been over that. I'm too old to be patient. Perhaps I wouldn't be patient even if I were young; youth is headstrong and eager, too. But the sad truth is, my love, we were never meant to be. I've refused to admit it, but I know you can't do all the changing. And that's what it would take, Mary. It's too much to ask. I'm too selfish, too settled in my ways, too vain, perhaps, to give you freedom to be yourself. Passion would dwindle with proximity. It would never disappear, not between us, but it would turn from a raging fire to a slow, steady flame. And you'd be restless and empty when days became routine. Being a wife and hostess isn't enough. Vicarious living is not your style. You need to be Mary, wrestling with demands, stimulated by problems, feeling alive and curious and productive every day of your life."

She was weeping now. "It's wrong. Those things don't matter. The only thing that matters is love."

"For some women, sweetheart. For some just as fine as you, but differently oriented. You need love, Mary, but not to the exclusion of everything else. You say you want

438

it all. You can have it. You *will* have it with the right man."

She shook her head. "Never. I'm a fool. Don't let me do this, Christopher. Don't let me throw away what we feel for each other."

He put his arms around her, raising her gently from her chair. "You can't throw that away, any more than I can. What we feel is for all time, no matter what. There are all kinds of love, dearest, and we've known the best. It will live as long as we do, perhaps better in memory than in an uncertain future. We've had the blessing of knowing what great love is. We'll never forget that sweet, rare sense of having shared a dream." He held her close. "Good-bye, my darling Mary. Don't regret, not for a moment."

Before she knew what had happened, he was gone. Her heart felt as though it would, literally, break. Christopher, Christopher, her mind said, what have I done? How could I let you go? For what? Some insane unwillingness to trust my emotions? Some stupid fear that there are things I'll regret never having done? What things? What could possibly be more important than this overwhelming love I feel?

I could have changed, she thought. I could have learned to live as other, happier women do. I would have been fulfilled. Christopher's wrong. It would have been enough for me. But not for him, she realized. He saw that, even if I couldn't. He saw me in my own surroundings and recognized the difference. I'm not the clinging playmate of the cruise, the dazzled, happily obedient woman who adores him to the exclusion of all else. He knew I couldn't give him what he needs, and that he'd be miserable and guilty watching me try. He loves me too much to demand what he knows he must have in a wife, and what I'd never, wholeheartedly, be able to offer. He's putting my happiness ahead of his own, in his wisdom and his love for me.

I wish I were able to hope he finds the woman he needs. I can't. Not yet. The desolation is too terrible, the wound too open and sore. Not yet can I be that unselfish or even that certain that what we're doing is right.

A wave of nausea rose. Blindly, she stumbled toward the bathroom and was violently, wretchingly ill.

When she came out of the bathroom, Patricia was lounging in a chair by the window, sipping a drink.

"Your boy friend leave?"

Mary cringed. "Yes."

"So what are your plans? When are you getting married?"

Mary sank slowly onto the couch. No use postponing it. "We're not," she said.

Patricia sat up straight. "You're not? What the hell does that mean? You're not getting married *now?* Or not *ever?*"

"Not ever. It's over. Finished. Christopher's going home."

"What happened, for God's sake?"

Mary put her hands over her eyes. "I really don't want to talk about it." Especially to you, she added silently. Of all people, I don't want to talk about it to you. But Patricia wasn't going to let her off that easily.

"You damned well had better talk about it! I don't know how you've managed to mess it up, and I don't particularly care, but my daughter's involved in this. If you're not leaving, what does that do to Jayne's future? If you're going to stay in that job, where does that leave her? And me? We can't run a household and support a child on that lousy little receptionist's salary! She was counting on getting the program!"

"She'll get it," Mary said wearily.

"Oh, sure!" Patricia dripped sarcasm. "Sure she will. The minute Charlie Burke hears you're not going to Australia, all bets will be off for Jayne." Patricia began to pace the room. "What a lousy thing to do! You got that girl's hopes up and now you're going to kiss her off and say, 'So sorry, dearie, I've decided I want my job after all.' No wonder she detests you. You don't give a damn about anybody but yourself."

Mary looked up. "Jayne doesn't detest me, Patricia.

440

She's been pretending to so I'd leave with an easy conscience, thinking she didn't want me around. She thought she was making it easier for me to do what I wanted. It was a wonderful, unselfish act, and it took me a long time to see through it."

"Bull! She knew who to turn to when she was in trouble—her mother, not her frustrated aunt who tried to take over. You've seen how close we've been these past two days. It's me she needs. Get that through your head! And I'm going to stay with her. This time you can't drive me away."

Mary was too drained to argue. "Believe what you want, Patricia, about me or Jayne or yourself. But start believing one thing—Jayne will never let you back in her life. She's done a good job of fooling both of us since you arrived. I've caught on, but apparently you haven't."

Patricia looked at her narrowly. "What are you up to? You divorced Michael to marry this dream man of yours and now, all of a sudden, it's over. He must have dumped you, and now you think you can pick up the pieces and go on as though nothing happened. You're trying to drive a wedge between my daughter and me. Again. I see it now. You'll keep on being the great Mary Farr Morgan and you'll take care of Jayne and my grandchild. You'd like that, wouldn't you? Having her depend on you. Hell, you'll probably take Michael back now so you can run his life again, too!"

"You're wrong about everything," Mary said quietly.

"Yes, Mother, you are." The voice from the doorway startled them. Jayne stood looking at the two women. "I've been eavesdropping. Aunt Mary's telling you the truth. She didn't leave Michael for Christopher. She took that trip to decide whether she could live with an unsatisfactory marriage. Meeting Christopher was a million-to-one shot. She'd have left Michael in any case." Jayne's voice sharpened. "Particularly when she came home and found out you'd been sleeping with him."

"Don't, Jayne," Mary said. "This isn't your problem. Don't get into it."

The girl sat down, facing them. "I have to get into it. A
441

large part of it concerns me. I did try to make you feel I didn't need you, Aunt Mary. I was so sure you should go with Christopher. Not because of the job. I wanted that, I won't deny it, but I wanted the right thing for you even more."

"I know," Mary said. "I don't know why it took me so long to see what your motives were." She managed a smile. "You're a good actress. You had me believing you couldn't wait for me to leave."

"But you knew you couldn't." Jayne almost echoed Christopher's words.

"No. I didn't know it. Christopher knew it. In the end, he saw me more clearly than I saw myself."

"God, I'm so sorry!"

Mary nodded. "So am I. It makes no sense from a practical point of view. Or," she added wistfully, "a romantic one. But the facts are there, Jayne. There's some kind of restlessness in me, some kind of drive that won't let me settle into a vacuum, not even with a man I adore. I hate it. I hate myself for it. But it's there, and there's no use kidding myself that it isn't."

Patricia snorted. "I never heard such a ridiculous thing! Are you crazy, Mary? You could have a life without a worry in the world and you throw it away for some kind of stupid 'drive'? You'd rather work and struggle for another forty years than be rich and pampered and secure? I think you're out of your mind. I don't even think you're telling the truth. I think the guy walked out and you couldn't stop him, so you're handing out this great story about your 'restlessness.' Maybe you can fool a twenty-one-year-old girl, but I'm too smart to swallow that line."

"I don't give a damn what you swallow!" Mary flared. "I don't care what you think about me. What anybody thinks! All my life I've tried to please people. Mother and Father. Older Sister. Husband. None of you cared about me, but you were perfectly willing to use me. And I was dumb enough to let you. Well, that's over, Patricia. Nobody's going to use me ever again!"

Patricia looked scornful. "Use you? That's a laugh! You've had it your own way all your life. Picking the job

442

you wanted. The husband. The life-style. Used you, Mary? Not for a minute. Let me tell you who's been used—me. Knocked up and forced to marry. Stuck in a dull, dreary life with a boring man. Seen my only child estranged by the wild ideas you put in her head. And now you're going to take her away again, aren't you? You're going to make her believe that I don't love her, that she's only an escape for me."

"You said it, Patricia. Not I. You made your life. Don't blame other people for what it's become. Look at your daughter. You don't hear her blaming anyone for the unhappy situation she's in."

"It wouldn't be such an unhappy situation," Patricia snarled, "if you were out of the picture!"

"Stop it!" Jayne's voice was trembling. "Stop hurling accusations at each other! And stop using me as a pawn in all this! I can't stand it! I know what I feel for both of you. I'll make my own decisions and neither of you will make them for me." She looked from her aunt to her mother and said, more evenly, "I'm going to stay here in San Francisco and work. There's a future for me, even if it doesn't mean a top job right away. We were all dreaming, thinking I could take over Aunt Mary's. I'm not ready for it. We just wanted to believe I was. In a few years, I'll have a job like hers. Maybe a better one. But for now I'm going to wait and learn and watch for my own opportunity; not one that's handed to me on a silver platter because Charlie Burke would do anything for Aunt Mary. Don't you think I know that's what it's been? I'm twenty-one, green as grass. I'm a quick study, but there's no way I could handle this now. It's been scaring me to death, but I felt I had to take the chance. Not only for myself. For Aunt Mary. Well, I don't have to do that now. I can serve my apprenticeship and be ready when the time comes."

Patricia stared at her. "And meantime, Miss Noble, how do you propose to live and take care of a child?"

"The same way thousands of other women do, Mother. I'll stay in the same apartment. I'll find a Day-Care Center for the baby. It won't be luxury, but we'll manage. I believe in myself. I was willing to take care of Terry. I certainly am willing to take care of his child."

"No, Jayne, you're wrong," Mary said. "You *can* do my job. I want you to do it. I've made something of a name for myself in this town. It will be much easier for me to move on to the next thing. Television, maybe. I've had offers, but I couldn't bring myself to desert Charlie. Maybe this is the hand of God, pushing me forward. Telling me something. And don't believe you were picked as my successor out of sympathy or charity. You weren't. Charlie wouldn't do that. He has too much of a sense of responsibility toward his own job. You'll be ready to take over in August, as planned. And I won't starve, I promise you."

Jayne looked uncertain. "I'm not sure. I still think . . ."

"Trust me," Mary said. "I'd never lie to you."

"Very touching," Patricia said. "Very convenient. You two will work out your lives to suit yourselves. I'm sure you don't care, Jayne, but where does this leave me?"

There was pity in her daughter's eyes. "It leaves you where you should be, Mother—in your place as a wife to a man who loves you very much. You can't live with me. We'd both be miserable. You can't attach yourself to my life. It wouldn't work. I'm sorry. Sorry you're unhappy and frustrated. Maybe you *should* change your life. I don't know. I only know that if you can't live with what you have, *you'll* have to find some other way to make it different."

*   *   *

Mary and Charlie sat by the bedside, looking fondly at the radiant girl.

"This is the damndest place I ever spent Christmas Eve," Charlie said. "Not even a fireplace to hang a stocking."

Jayne laughed. "Santa Claus doesn't care. Why should *you*? He drops in at hospitals through the laundry chute, I suspect. And leaves the best presents of all in the maternity ward." She carefully opened the blanket wrapped

444

around the bundle in her arms. "Isn't she beautiful? Isn't Mary Theresa Spalding the damndest hunk of female you ever saw?"

"Sensational," Mary said. She glanced around her. "So is this the florist's shop you call your room. I never saw so many glorious bouquets. And you must have a thousand cards and letters and telegrams. Your fans love you, Jaynie. Is it permissible for me to say 'I told you so'?"

"She's made your ratings look liked chopped liver these past five months." Charlie put his arm fondly around Mary. "Not that you're doing too badly on your own, much as I hate to admit it. I don't care for competition. Thank God your TV slot isn't opposite the Jayne Spalding radio show!"

"Big deal," Mary said. "I'm still local." She smiled. "And that's the way I like it. This is my town. The rest of the world can stay out there where it belongs."

"Speaking of the world"—Charlie glanced at his watch—"you stars can stay here celebrating if you like, but I'm a working stiff. Okay if I leave you here, Mary? I have to check out the six o'clock news."

"Sure. Meet you at Ernie's at eight-thirty."

He kissed them both lightly. "Hate to leave my two favorite women," he said. "Oops. Sorry. My *three* favorite women."

"Your harem will miss you," Jayne said. "Merry Christmas, Charlie, and God bless you."

They were happily quiet for a few minutes after he left. The two-day-old Mary was surrendered to a nurse, and Jayne settled back on her pillows, comfortably regarding her aunt.

"It's okay for you to say 'I told you so.' Things have worked out, haven't they? For both of us."

Mary nodded. "Not the way we thought, but yes, they have worked out."

"Those roses are from Michael," Jayne said. "Michael and . . . Rae."

"Pretty."

"Were you upset when he got married?"

Mary looked at the young woman. It was a blunt question but there was no malice in it. If anything, there was a tiny undercurrent of sympathy. "Upset? No, not exactly. There was a little pang when I read about it. Only natural, I suppose. Like seeing him that day at the funeral. He was so much a part of my life. Anything that happens to him, even a glimpse of him, makes me remember. Nice things, mostly." She seemed thoughtful. "Marriage to Rae isn't what I'd have wanted for him, given a choice. I'd have wished him someone softer, more in need of protection. But when I look back, I realize I was always trying to put him into a slot he neither fitted nor wanted. It was what I thought he should want. I had quite a habit of doing that, it seems."

"I know. It was true with Terry and me. It doesn't work." Jayne's face clouded. "I wish he could have seen his daughter, though. For her sake, as well as his."

"It wasn't meant to be, dear. Many things aren't. We have to think that's for the best, too."

Jayne knew she was thinking of Christopher, probably still wondering whether she'd done the right thing. "Do you hear from him?"

Mary didn't pretend. "Christopher? No. A thousand times I've been tempted to call him. I've written a hundred letters and torn them up. It's getting better now, as he said it would. Sometimes I go for a week and hardly think of him. I've discovered that memories are lovely things, but they belong to the past. Happy ghosts. There's today and tomorrow to concentrate on."

"Is Charlie in your tomorrow?"

There was a long pause. "We'll see. Charlie and I have everything in common, including a love of our work. We care deeply for each other, and we both need the kind of contentment we've never known. We might find it together one day. I don't know. It's too soon for me to make another big step, even with someone I've known so long and well. One day, maybe. If it's in my future, it will come."

"I didn't know you were such a fatalist."

Mary smiled. "Don't know that I am. But I spent too

many years making things hard for myself. And for other people, too. This way seems easier."

Jayne looked troubled. "But you have no regrets, have you?"

Her aunt walked to the window and pretended to look out. Her words came over her shoulder, slowly, like slivers of pain. "Regrets? We all have regrets. Where is the perfect life, my dear? Who lives a flawless existence without doubts and tears and bad decisions? Not I, certainly. Nor you, or, for that matter, anyone who reacts from the heart." She came back to the bedside and took her seat again. "All we can do is put our mistakes behind us and try like hell not to repeat them. Learn from them, but not dwell on them or allow them to make us feel cheated. There's nothing constructive in the words 'if only.' We bury the past decently, Jayne, knowing we did the best we could, even though it wasn't perfect. We forgive ourselves, as well as others."

"Like I have, with Mother. I don't hate her anymore. I pity her."

Mary nodded. "Yes. It's what I've learned about my own parents. They give what they can. No more, no less. They're not gods to be pleased or devils to be exorcised. They're just there, and we can only hope they understand when we seem less than perfect. And try to understand, ourselves, when they're not all we'd like them to be."

"I'd like to take the baby back to New York to visit them sometime," Jayne said. "I'm never going to stay, but they should see her."

"Of course. Maybe I'll go with you when you do."

There was a little silence.

" 'I carry with me the sweet aroma of caring, a fragrance to linger the rest of my life.' Remember, Jayne?"

"Of course." The younger woman's eyes misted with tears. " 'Never doubt love,' " she repeated. " 'Never question its entrance or weep for its exit.' "

Each reached for the hand of the other. We've both lost so much, Mary thought. But we've won, too. In a way, we grew up together, through a shared and special time. Different days are ahead, but they're made all the more precious by those gone by. There's so much to be grateful for.

And so much to remember.